PRAISE FOR

Doctors and Friends

"A prescient, human, and hopeful portrait of medical experts on a pandemic's front lines."

—*People*

"The lives of three doctors—friends since medical school who meet for an annual get-together—are thrown upside down when a contagious virus begins to spread across the world in this eerily prescient and timely novel written before the COVID-19 pandemic. Martin's complex characters are infused with such raw emotion that they nearly jump off the page."

—*Newsweek*

"*Doctors and Friends* is an astounding achievement. It's both an eerily timely portrait of a world in the grip of a deadly pandemic and a poignant dive into the interior lives of the medical workers at its forefront. I was profoundly affected by these characters. I became emotionally attached to them and deeply invested in the outcome of their stories. I know they will stay with me for a long time."

—*New York Times* bestselling author Cristina Alger

"The beating heart of this fast-paced and intensely moving novel is the warm, life-sustaining friendship between a group of doctors on the front lines of a global pandemic. Martin shines a sharp, compassionate light on the lives of the women behind the masks and scrubs during a crisis that is both achingly familiar and punctuated by twists and turns you won't see coming. I couldn't put it down!"

—*USA Today* bestselling author Meg Donohue

"*Doctors and Friends* is a stunning medical drama that will resonate with readers everywhere. I was riveted. Kimmery Martin's sharp, smart writing is infused with compassion, emotion, and a belief in the healing power of friendship, love, and hope."

—*New York Times* bestselling author Jayne Ann Krentz

"Written prior to COVID, *Doctors and Friends* is an eerily foretelling and poignantly relatable tale of a devastating pandemic that upends the world. Three female doctors and friends remind the reader of the heart-wrenching tragedies and impossible choices that make such a cast not only heroic but human." —*New York Times* bestselling author Kristina McMorris

"A cast of characters rendered so poignantly in Martin's empathetic hands that their joys and sorrows become our own."

—*The Charlotte Observer*

"This is the pandemic novel I didn't know I was longing for! I loved it."

—Anne Bogel, host of the *What Should I Read Next?* podcast

"An incredibly prescient book that is both thrilling and inspiring. Martin draws upon her deep knowledge to create a story and characters that are stunningly real. At turns hilarious, heartbreaking, and intense; I flew through this book." —Kathy Wang, author of *Impostor Syndrome*

"Martin's *Doctors and Friends* is nothing shy of stunning. While delivering the depth, wit, and soul that continues to garner both readers' love and critics' acclaim, she deftly reminds us that no crisis will ever shrink our capacity for love—and when threatened—our will to fight back. Absolutely brilliant."

—P. J. Vernon, author of *Bath Haus*

"Would it be strange to say I found a pandemic novel comforting? Chapter after chapter, I looked forward to basking in the friendship, humor, and genuinely good intentions of these women doing all they could to save their loved ones, one another, and the world from a mysterious and fast-moving disease. Kimmery Martin's fictional world was just the respite I needed from our real one."

—Mary Laura Philpott, author of *I Miss You When I Blink*

"Yes, *Doctors and Friends* is timely, but it's so much more than that. It's an introspective, heartfelt story of deep friendships, impossible choices, intense twists, and a great deal of what we all crave right now: hope. Put this on your TBR immediately!"

—Liz Fenton and Lisa Steinke, authors of *How to Save a Life*

"Gripping and compelling, *Doctors and Friends* is an eerily prescient 'what if' pandemic scenario. Martin has created a powerful narrative of friendship and loss."

—Julie Clark, *New York Times* bestselling author of *The Last Flight*

"Martin's riveting latest focuses on a group of doctors during a pandemic. . . . Martin fills the hospital scenes with vivid descriptions and moving moments. This fully realized account of a fictional pandemic manages to convey the deeply personal as well as the bigger picture."

—*Publishers Weekly* (starred review)

"With echoes of Richard Preston's *The Hot Zone*, John M. Barry's *The Great Influenza*, and Anna Hope's *Expectation*, *Doctors and Friends* is precise in details but sweeping in scope and impact. With an innate understanding of emergency room medicine, the inner workings of government agencies, and the complexities of decades-long friendships, Martin's novel is compelling to its core."

—*Booklist* (starred review)

"There is beauty in Martin's gem of a story that confirms that friendship is a powerful force."

—*Library Journal* (starred review)

"A well-written apocalyptic tale about a global pandemic that is all too realistic."

—*Kirkus Reviews*

PRAISE FOR
The Antidote for Everything

"Martin's trademark witty repartee makes her characters fun to be with, and she both entertains and tackles thought-provoking questions of honor and integrity in a world where facts matter little."

—*Booklist*

"A moving story about the absolute power of friendship and the utter feebleness of intolerance."

—*New York Times* bestselling author Chris Bohjalian

"Intense and vibrant . . . A binge-worthy page-turner that'll rival your favorite prime-time medical drama."

—*Wall Street Journal* bestselling author Kerry Lonsdale

"With her signature compassion and sharp writing, Kimmery Martin delivers a poignant yet compulsively readable story examining the timely topic of medical discrimination. I loved it—and have a new must-read recommendation for book clubs everywhere."

—Colleen Oakley, *USA Today* bestselling author of *You Were There Too*

"With incredible voice and scalpel-sharp wit, Martin deftly navigates the light, the dark, and the in-between of the human soul." —P. J. Vernon

"Close on the heels of her successful debut, physician and novelist Kimmery Martin has once again crafted a tale that will thrill readers while simultaneously illuminating how the business of medicine too often fails patients and physicians alike. . . . A story of friendship, loyalty, and redemption, Martin's second novel is sure to become as beloved as her first." —Meghan MacLean Weir, author of *The Book of Essie*

PRAISE FOR
The Queen of Hearts

"Martin leverages her own background as a doctor to great effect throughout. . . . [She] is equally insightful about many aspects of long-term female friendships, especially the blind spots that they often contain by necessity."

—*The New York Times*

"A gripping and emotional novel perfect for fans of Meredith and Cristina's iconic friendship, *The Queen of Hearts* is the perfect book for fall."

—Bustle

"Martin's extraordinary sensitivity and empathy shines through during moments of crisis, which draw out the subtle, complex shades of her characters. . . . [T]he beautifully rendered characters and compelling, rhythmic storyline make *The Queen of Hearts* a thrilling read, and a fascinating look into the medical world. It's an impressive debut, full of warmth and excitement."

—*The Harvard Crimson*

"Fans of *Grey's Anatomy* are sure to enjoy this new release, a novel about friendship, success, and secrets set amid the day-to-day drama of a hospital in Charlotte, North Carolina."

—*Southern Living*

"Kimmery Martin's excellent debut novel serves up an irresistible mix of romance, ER drama, friendship, and betrayal. Martin, a physician herself, writes in a clear and lively way. . . . In her hands, dramatic hospital scenes and routine kitchen conversations are equally compelling."

—*BookPage*

"A secret from two doctors' pasts may put what they cherish most under the knife: their friendship. A book about female friendships that unapologetically wears its heart on its sleeve."

—*Kirkus Reviews*

"Martin's debut novel, about pediatric cardiologist Zadie Anson and trauma surgeon Emma Colley, is a medical drama executed with just the right balance of intensity, plot twists, tragedy, and humor. . . . A remarkably absorbing read."

—*Booklist*

TITLES BY KIMMERY MARTIN

The Queen of Hearts
The Antidote for Everything
Doctors and Friends

DOCTORS and FRIENDS

Kimmery Martin

BERKLEY
New York

BERKLEY
An imprint of Penguin Random House LLC
penguinrandomhouse.com

Copyright © 2021 by Kimmery Martin
Readers Guide copyright © 2021 by Kimmery Martin
Penguin Random House supports copyright. Copyright fuels creativity, encourages diverse voices, promotes free speech, and creates a vibrant culture. Thank you for buying an authorized edition of this book and for complying with copyright laws by not reproducing, scanning, or distributing any part of it in any form without permission. You are supporting writers and allowing Penguin Random House to continue to publish books for every reader.

BERKLEY and the BERKLEY & B colophon
are registered trademarks of Penguin Random House LLC.

ISBN: 9781984802873

The Library of Congress has catalogued the Berkley hardcover edition of this book as follows:

Names: Martin, Kimmery, author.
Title: Doctors and friends / Kimmery Martin.
Description: New York: Berkley, [2021]
Identifiers: LCCN 2021010461 (print) | LCCN 2021010462 (ebook) |
ISBN 9781984802866 (hardcover) | ISBN 9781984802880 (ebook)
Subjects: LCSH: Physicians—Fiction. | Virus diseases—Fiction.
Classification: LCC PS3613.A7822 D63 2021 (print) |
LCC PS3613.A7822 (ebook) | DDC 813/.6—dc23
LC record available at https://lccn.loc.gov/2021010461
LC ebook record available at https://lccn.loc.gov/2021010462

Berkley hardcover edition / November 2021
Berkley trade paperback edition / October 2022

Printed in the United States of America
1st Printing

Book design by Ashley Tucker

This is a work of fiction. Names, characters, places, and incidents either are the product of the author's imagination or are used fictitiously, and any resemblance to actual persons, living or dead, business establishments, events, or locales is entirely coincidental.

NOTE TO THE READER:

The writing of this novel preceded COVID-19 and therefore there is no mention of the real-life pandemic. In this fictional universe, it does not exist.

For Casey, Christina, Jill, Kelli, Kristin, and Whitney.

I love you.

To everything there is a season,
A time for every purpose under heaven:
A time to be born,
And a time to die;
A time to plant,
And a time to pluck what is planted;
A time to kill,
And a time to heal

—Ecclesiastes 3:1–3

CHARACTER SPECIALTIES

Dr. Kira Marchand
Infectious Disease
Atlanta, Georgia

Dr. Candee Compton-Winfield
Emergency Medicine
New York, New York

Dr. Hannah Geier
Obstetrics & Gynecology
San Diego, California
(also in *The Queen of Hearts*)

Dr. Georgia Brown
Urology
San Diego, California
(also in *The Antidote for Everything*
and *The Queen of Hearts*)

Dr. Vani Darshana
Internal Medicine
Berea, Kentucky

Dr. Zadie Anson
Pediatric Cardiology
Charlotte, North Carolina
(also in *The Queen of Hearts*)

Dr. Emma Colley
Trauma Surgery
Charlotte, North Carolina
(also in *The Queen of Hearts*)

ALSO FEATURING:

Dr. Jonah Tsukada
Family Medicine
San Diego, California
(also in *The Antidote for Everything*)

CONTENTS

PART FOUR: AFTER ARTIOVIRUS

DOCTORS and FRIENDS

PART ONE

AFTER ARTIOVIRUS

1 | This Thing's About to Blow

KIRA | ATLANTA, GEORGIA

ONE BALMY EVENING NEAR THE END OF A BALMY WINTER, A man sidled up to me in a corner of an Atlanta mansion.

He had a request.

Before I go into detail about the repellent nature of the man's proposal, I should temper your expectations. I know very well how my voice comes across in person, let alone in the recounting of a history. I have a sense of humor, but it's sometimes mistaken for condescension. Similarly, to my dismay, my sense of compassion during tragedy has occasionally been misinterpreted as judgment. Throughout a mass calamity in which millions of people died, we were hobbled by fear and grief and hardship and isolation, yes; but at the same time, we learned humanity is resilient beyond all reckoning. We shared a mutual hope. Women still gave birth, nurturing tiny new humans first inside and then outside their bodies. We still created art and music and literature. Our scientists continued to innovate, our doctors to heal, our educators to teach.

On a lighter note, we still extracted comedy from tragedy, finding new ways to laugh at ourselves. We swapped pandemic jokes. We watched late-night comedy routines. We captured funny snapshots, wrote pithy quips about them, and flung them into cyberspace. If a society can't meme itself out of a disaster, what hope is there?

But this is not our collective story as a society. This is my story—and also Compton's story and Hannah's story and a little bit of Georgia's story—and it represents the most difficult circumstances of our lives. For my portion, you're stuck with my voice, such as it is.

I hope you can forgive me.

FOR THE LAST fifteen minutes, I've been hovering at this party clutching my drink—a Manhattan—trying to act as if I were interested in the beads of condensation crawling down its beveled-glass surface. Earlier, I'd attempted to infiltrate the nearest knot of people but found myself largely unable to secure any purchase in the smooth waterfall of words. Every syllable I uttered ended up the same: an aborted reach, followed by a slide back down the conversational slope.

Twenty minutes before, I'd been rolling along the streets of Buckhead as they became wider and posher and leafier, navigating past Hummers and Land Rovers and various other luxury vehicles until the huge home hosting tonight's event floated into view like a glowing mother ship at the top of a hill. Ten thousand watts of incandescent bulbs burned brightly against the night sky, illuminating a pair of cream-jacketed valets trying to wave me down. I ignored them. No one drives my truck except me.

My truck! My truck is really an economy hatchback from which I've removed half of the back seat. This vehicle, which I've named Herman, has been with me for twelve years over multiple continents, so he doesn't exactly boast the latest technology. He also looks like ass, having sputtered through monsoons and deserts and, in the worst of times, literal wars. I've replaced and rotated his tires, changed his brake pads and calipers, swapped out his filters, substituted his belts and hoses and batteries, and flushed his radiator and transmission. There are more than two hundred thousand miles on this sucker, and there's no way I'm getting rid of him until the tragic day when he finally and irredeemably croaks. As always, driving him makes me happy.

In the house, though, I've lost a bit of my composure. I can't control my fidgeting; of its own accord, my body yearns toward the door. My foot taps, a relentless, skittish beat. My face too is a failure: I can feel it settling into the kind of gritted-teeth smile produced by young kids who are being forced to pose.

Part of this reaction is physical. Even though the room, a grand, high-ceilinged sweep of space, has been cleared of furniture, the air circulates poorly. Flames roar in a ten-foot-high fireplace anchoring one end of the room, its mantel heaped with drying pine boughs and berry-encrusted twigs. The beribboned garland is clearly meant to invoke a festive yuletide spirit, but in me it produces a burning desire to figure out where the fire extinguishers are stored. Whoever decorated the mantel didn't hold back elsewhere either; even without furniture, the room appears to have been fluffed by a herd of manic elves. There's red and green shit everywhere: glass stars, hunks of mistletoe, human-sized nutcrackers standing sentinel in the corners, all of it somewhat shimmery from the radiance of the fire.

But my discomfort stems not just from the ostentatious decoration, or from the oppressive warmth, or from the perfumed but acrid scent of other people surrounding me, shooting up my nose like a chemical weapons attack. It's not only the sound, the chittering and cackling of too many voices straining to make themselves heard.

It's the bodies.

Even if I close my eyes and block my ears, I can sense them. Mere feet from me, they span all directions, appropriating space, emitting sound waves and social urgency and, without a doubt, respiratory particles.

A party, it should be obvious, is not my thing. By now, you've gleaned a few more facts about me, or you think you have. *Socially awkward*, you're thinking; *oversensitive. Insecure.* Or maybe this: *too introspective.*

I feel the need to defend myself from your assumptions, even though they are logical. Despite my earlier warning, I'm actually good with people. My people, anyway. I like my people. I'm not a hermit or overwhelmed by sensory stimuli either; I can state without any exaggeration that I've endured some of the harshest conditions the planet has to offer.

I'm just not great around a lot of people. Especially now.

To my left, a blond bejeweled woman in her fifties gazes with rapt attention at an older man at her side, her fingers stroking the green circular pin at the top left of her long, floaty dress. His suit sports a corresponding pin, also on the left, at his lapel. Next to him, another couple, a beefy white man and a rail-thin, much younger woman, display their respective pins in the same spots. I reach for my pin, securely attached to the right side of my blazer. There's no mandate regarding pin placement—you can put it anywhere on your torso you like, as long as it's easily visible—but to me it's come to serve as a signal for handedness. Right-hand-dominant people tend to pin theirs on the left, and vice versa, making it easy to keep a running tally of the lefties.

I've spent little time in society over the last several months, but still, I'm amazed at the ease with which these people have adapted to the fear that first gripped the world not even two years ago. The acute sickness caused by the artiovirus is rare now, vanquished by an army of public health servants, and, ultimately, a vaccine, but our world still bears the ghostly imprints of the lost: children who live with grandparents instead of parents, schools without qualified teachers, and above all, hospitals still in crisis mode because of a lack of doctors and nurses and cleaners and techs. There are, however, still plenty of hospital administrators.

Despite our losses, merriment shines on most of the faces here. Please understand: I don't judge them, these people who are trying to return to the past. I understand the urge to repress the memories. Everyone lost someone. The particular hell of the artiovirus was its precise targeting of the otherwise young and healthy. It turned our immune systems against us, generating not a cytokine storm but a cytokine tsunami, sometimes felling people in a matter of hours. You could feel fine in the morning and be dead by evening.

But, as everyone in the country now knows, the virus harbored an even more terrible secret, one we would not suspect for months.

WHEN A HAND brushes my shoulder, I expect one of the three friends who are meeting me here tonight, or possibly somebody I know from the time when I worked at the CDC. Instead, I encounter a ferrety bald man who's made the unfortunate decision to groom his mustache into a pencil-thin line. The effect is reminiscent of a cartoon villain or, perhaps, a weasel.

"Artie Smert," he says, offering his hand in what appears to be a misguided reflex. Even before the pandemic I wasn't big on shaking hands, so I ignore his outstretched arm. Batting his eyes, the man attempts to execute a face-saving maneuver by raising the hand to smooth back his hair, which might seem a tad more natural if he weren't bald. After a brief awkward slide along his scalp, the hand drifts back down to his side.

I hadn't intended to make this guy look stupid, so I offer him an elbow to bump. Unfortunately this doesn't go any better, as he's grabbed a business card from his pocket and apparently mistakes my gesture as an invitation to deposit the card on my elbow. I retrieve it with my other hand and study it.

"You're Dr. Kira Marchand," says the man. "I've been wanting to meet you for some time."

The voice rings a bell. I read the card again. "Artie Smart?"

"It's *Smert*, actually, not *Smart*. Are you familiar with the Midwest? The Dakotas, maybe?"

I blink at the non sequitur. "I was raised in Kentucky. I bounced around the world for a while and now I live here, but I've never lived in the Midwest. Why?"

"My friend in the Dakotas pronounces *smart* as *smert*."

This line of conversation is of such confusing irrelevance I do not know how to respond. No wonder I always go mute at parties. "You left a bunch of messages with my office last year," I say finally. "You're a television producer."

"That's right!" says Smert jauntily, as if responding to even a modicum of positivity on my part. "We'd love to work with you on a show about female doctors during the pandemic. People recognize you from those press conferences where you explained what was happening . . ." Here, his eyes slide to the side. People don't like to mention the worst outcome that can occur if you survive ART, or if they do, it's usually in an undertone.

Some months into the pandemic, certain unpleasant truths about the illness began to make themselves known. By then we knew the basics: who was most likely to contract it, who was most likely to die. Like a typical virus, ART targeted the very young, the very old, and the weak. But this particular mortality curve followed an unusual shape when it came to the age distribution of the dead. Like an ongoing M, it peaked and fell and peaked and fell and peaked again; it turned out the virus had a predilection for strapping adults in the prime of their lives. Like a food snob, it cultivated its tastes precisely. It preferred men to women, eastern seaboarders over southwesterners, people with type A blood over types O or B, and so on and so on through a range of attributes. But it would—and did—devour anyone who crossed it, if the mood struck.

What we didn't know then would turn out to be far worse than the immediate deaths. ART causes a delayed but catastrophic complication in a small but significant percentage of people, brought about by an autoantibody targeting certain proteins in the brain. As of today, we cannot predict who will suffer this effect, or when, although we believe it is likeliest to occur within a year or two of recovery from the initial illness. Now that we've conquered the virus, all of humanity is united in the fervent desire to find a cure for its most infamous sequela. Barring that, they want a predictive test. Everyone wants to know who will get the complication.

Artie Smert warms to his pitch. "That press conference you did with POTUS? You're a natural-born speaker."

I offer him a glance of considerable skepticism.

"It'd be a limited-run series," he says, one finger unconsciously tracing the line of his mustache. "But not depressing. We'd allude broadly to the details of the pandemic—the deaths, the morbidity, the cratering and recovery of the financial sector—but there's no appetite out there for another exposé of those circumstances. Everyone on earth's already familiar with them. And you know, no need to go into detail about the . . . brain thing either: this isn't a horror film."

"Then what?" I ask.

"This series," he says proudly, "will focus on the personal stories of those on the front lines, especially those with an unusual story to tell. In particular, the series would focus on you."

If Smert considers this approach to be an enticement, he's mistaken. I don't watch television. While I have streamed a scientific documentary or two, I've never seen a reality show. I am ignorant of celebrity news. I barely even talk to regular people, unless I already know and like them.

Speaking of people I know and like, I spy my friends—Vani, Compton, and Hannah—perhaps twenty feet away, standing together but each speaking to people I don't recognize. None of them lives in Atlanta; they're here to support me when I give a speech later tonight. How had they managed to strike up such animated conversations with strangers?

Vani, my closest friend, catches my eye first, but then again Vani generally catches everyone's eye first. She's my age—early forties—and infinitely more alluring. Tonight, indifferent to the attention she draws, she's dressed in an electric-yellow silk concoction with an array of jeweled bracelets crawling up her arms. Even from this distance, I can read her expression, so characteristic of Vani, somehow combining an aura of peace with a ridiculous, endearing sense of humor. She's like a human embodiment of both Xanax and one of those party drugs that make people giggly.

Compton flanks her, her cap of sleek dark hair set off by an equally sleek black dress. Compton is the Ritalin to Vani's Xanax; she's beaming an intense, skeptical look to two chatty blond men who appear to be in their forties. On her other side, Hannah, pink-cheeked and fair, with her shapeless dress and messy bun, might have registered as dowdy compared to the other two were it not for the warmth in her expression, which she's aiming at an older gentleman who is apparently hard of hearing. He's got a hand cupped round his ear and I'm fairly certain the entire room can hear him shouting delightedly in her direction.

Oblivious to my distraction, Artie's still going strong. "We'd want to showcase your particular, ah, *style* in the show, of course. You were one of the first Americans to contract the illness. You were one of the few worldwide experts on this particular virus before the pandemic. People must wonder: why does a woman want to become an expert on germs?"

Why? I've considered viruses to be my mortal enemy ever since missing my own tenth birthday party after coming down with what my mother erroneously referred to as "the stomach flu." The stomach flu is not a flu at all, but everyone on earth is familiar with its symptoms.

A virus is one of the oddest entities in the universe. Neither living nor dead, it exists in a suspended netherworld, waiting to encounter a creature it can invade. Unlike normal life-forms, a virus cannot replicate itself; it is dependent on hijacking the machinery of a living cell in order to reproduce. They do this fantastically well, attaching themselves to the surface of a cell before penetrating it. Whatever vital functions the cell was carrying out are forgotten as it transforms into a kind of zombie factory to create more virus. Eventually—such as in the case of influenza—the doomed cell explodes, spewing out up to a million little viral soldiers, many of which are deformed mutants. The functional ones attack new cells, churning out even more viral swarms. They are deeply creepy little fuckers.

Still, Artie Smert hadn't asked me to describe the characteristics of a virus. He'd asked why a woman would want to study germs. This question once again strikes me mute, which is fortunate, because if I'd had the wits to answer, everyone would have witnessed language incompatible with party manners. In my case, however, I'd taken a roundabout route to my expertise. I started my career as an internal medicine doctor with an aid organization, and it wasn't until after my husband died of a sudden undiagnosed illness that I returned to the States and completed a fellowship in infectious disease, followed by special training in battling pandemics. My mentor at the CDC, a man named Waliedine Katz, turned me on to the artiovirus.

"And, yes," Mr. Smert goes on, oblivious to my mental detour, "you'd be the perfect person to explain the efforts to defeat the—" He breaks off, fluttering both hands at his temples to indicate the worst outcome of the virus.

"I can send you abstracts from some of the latest papers," I say. I catch Hannah's eye and wave, hoping she'll interpret the gesture as a distress signal. It seems to work; she nudges Compton and Vani and points in my direction. Even from a distance, I sense their protectiveness; this is the first time I've been at a public function in a very long time.

"Sure," says Smert. His beady eyes tighten, focusing on my face. "But what people would really want to hear about, I think, is your personal story during the pandemic."

I take an involuntary step back. Could Smert possibly know the real reason I left the CDC?

Having alluded to the subject he'd like to broach, Mr. Smert inexplicably stalls out. To combat my escalating pulse, I take in and blow out small, measured dollops of air, waiting for him to bring down the hammer. Finally, I do it myself.

"You want to talk about why I'm no longer at the CDC, I'm guessing."

"Certainly," he says. "I realize the pandemic was difficult for you on a personal level as well as a professional one. The, ah, situation with your children . . ."

I wait, but there is no more. He must not know—or at least he must not know for sure—the details of what I did.

By some miracle, an account of my behavior at the tail end of the pandemic, known to only a handful of people, had not filtered through the medical community in Atlanta and out to the general public. Still, for ethical reasons, I'd disclosed my action to a few people at the hospital and at the CDC, hoping some greater good would come of my transgression. To my relief, the story of what happened behind the scenes never blew up. Or, to employ a bit of irony: it never went viral.

But if this man suspects what I did, how long before some legitimate news reporter catches wind of it? The thought sends an antsy ripple crawling up my spine. Somehow, somewhere along the line, Mr. Smert must have managed to connect with someone who knows the truth.

I recall those days in fragments, long, unbroken streams of timeless waiting, my mind suspending itself in a protective haze where thoughts dissolved into nothingness before they could fully form. The blurred metallic edges of a hospital bed; the plinky little drip of IVs; slats of light cutting through parallel rows of blinds and falling in stripes across my forearms; exhaustion giving way to confusion. Sometimes this nightmarish haze sharpens into shards of distinct terror and I remember that final moment.

It haunts me still.

"I'm not interested in being on TV," I say to Smert as my friends wade through the mob to reach my side. Up close, Vani, Hannah, and Compton present dramatically different approaches to evening makeup, Vani's glossy lips and curled eyelashes and vivid yellow—yellow?—eyeshadow contrasting with Hannah's unadorned eyes and the slash of crimson outlining Compton's smirky half smile.

Smert switches tactics, pivoting to my friends. "Are you ladies coworkers of Dr. Marchand?"

Only Hannah smiles back at him. "We're old medical school friends," she says before anyone can stop her. "I'm Hannah—I'm an ob-gyn in San Diego. Vani practices internal medicine in Kentucky, and Compton's an ER doc—she was in New York City during the pandemic."

Perking up at the words *ER* and *New York City*, Smert swings his attention toward Compton, but upon encountering her total absence of expression, he swings right back to me. During our med school years, if we needed to deflate some horny clown in a bar—metaphorically or literally—we deployed Compton, who even then possessed a brittle, ball-busting sophistication. I know her well enough to state that a warm core of generosity lurks within her, but you have to excavate a layer of straight-up ferocity to reach it. We love her for it.

Before Smert can regroup, a commotion across the way catches our attention.

A crowd forms around a couple of slim men in cream-colored jackets—servers or caterers, I think—who are attempting without success to lift an enormous glass urn.

The urn is one of a pair, around eight feet tall and quite wide. It resembles more of a massive fish tank than an urn, except instead of fish it contains thousands of solid green and red decorative balls floating in water. I have to admit I'm interested; there's no way these two are going to be able to move this thing. I'm puzzled as to why they'd even want to attempt it, but then I spy the problem: a crack in the glass, running along a fault line three or four feet up, just beginning to ooze water.

"There must be a thousand gallons of water in there," someone says. "Or more." As if our heads are on a crank, everyone in the vicinity looks down at the floor, constructed of whitewashed wood and capped off by a finely knotted silk Persian rug.

The crowd surges, parting to reveal a slender woman in a floaty, frothy, long-sleeved dress—the *de rigueur* outfit for the evening, it seems—who hurries toward the beleaguered servers with pursed lips but an unwrinkled brow.

"We need to do something before this breaks," she says sharply to the jacketed men, as if this were a novel thought. Her fingers drift to the green pin on her dress collar. "Can you tip it forward and collect the water in something?"

"Ma'am, tipping it forward might break the glass," says the closest server, a red-faced blond in his twenties. He swipes at his forehead. "Plus it's too heavy."

From a man in the crowd: "Maybe we can scoot it outside."

The hostess glances down, dubious. "That would scratch the floors."

By now a sharp rivulet of water is spraying down the side of the massive container, collecting in a pool that reaches the hostess's feet. She lets out a small shriek directed at the other server. "Josh! There's water on the floor."

"Yes," says Josh, heroically managing not to roll his eyes. "I'll get a towel."

"No! I mean, yes, get a towel, but hurry."

"Maybe get lots of towels," adds the man who'd suggested pushing the urn outside. "This thing's about to blow."

The crack widens, prompting a collective intake of breath. Chatter in the room intensifies as people offer one outrageous suggestion after another: get a bunch of bedsheets set up and crack the glass with a hammer (why?); lower down a child armed with a bailing bucket (too dangerous, plus this does not seem like the kind of household that comes equipped with a child); evacuate and let nature take its course (lame); let nature take its course but film the explosion for YouTube. I have to admit, that last one does hold some appeal.

Am I the only person here who recognizes the obvious solution?

I zip through the knot of people close to the urn, picking up speed as I reach the emptier section of the room. Nobody, it seems, wants to miss the show, even if they wind up getting drenched. I mime a series of actions to my friends: running to my vehicle, extracting my tool kit, and returning. Vani's face scrunches up, confused.

Okay, maybe that was too much to try to mime.

Once I reach Herman, I rummage through the back until I find what I need. Probably I should hurry; by now there's a decent chance those nitwits back at the fancy house have decided to get it over with by hammering at the glass with their Louboutin stilettos. Picking up the pace, I charge through the foyer of the house. Back in the big room, not much has changed. A conga line of middle-aged men, their shirtsleeves rolled, are preparing to heave the urn aside. They've managed to nudge it a couple of inches from its original spot, but progress has stalled as the hostess paces in front of them, still dithering about the floors. Ignoring both the men and the hostess, I roll up alongside the urn and set down the small portable ladder I carry. From the worn canvas bag at my shoulder, I extract a long length of rubber tubing and a roll of duct tape. Working quickly, I slap the duct tape over the crack in the glass, stemming the hemorrhage, and then hop a few steps up the ladder.

It's as if I've marched in waving an Uzi: all conversation in the room ceases. The hostess in particular is dumbfounded, her mouth frozen open in the shape of whatever word she was last speaking. Taking advantage of her sudden muteness, I point to the window. "Can you open it?"

She springs to life, gamely tugging at the window sash, which doesn't budge. "Zeke! Josh!" she hollers at the servers. "Josh, the window, hurry!"

Josh comes over and also pulls on the sash of the window, but at some point, someone's painted it shut. I reach into my shoulder bag again and locate a putty knife, which I pass to Josh. Deftly, he slides it along the interior joints of the window sash, loosening the stuck paint, and manages to heave the window open. Nodding at him, I place one end of the rubber tubing inside the urn and suck for a moment on the other end—I make this quick, as people are already pointing cell phones in our direction and I don't want to wind up all over the internet in some pornographic meme—and then cap the end of the tube with my thumb before passing it to Josh. He thrusts it out the window and uncaps it, where it begins spraying water into the garden beyond.

The partygoers break into applause.

"Oh mah goodness!" says the hostess, fanning her face. "Thank you so much. You're marvelous—you saved the day! What do I owe you?"

"Nothing," I say. "Happy to help."

"Oh no, I insist. And you got here so quickly! You're truly wonderful!"

It dawns on me that the hostess thinks I'm a plumber, dispatched to handle this party emergency. I'd be irritated at the misconception, but it's hard to blame her. In contrast to all the floaty-dress women around me, I'm dressed in black pants, formerly mud-encrusted black boots that I've hosed down, and, in a nod to the occasion, a velvety blazer, which I removed a few minutes ago to deal with the urn situation. Aside from my government-issued uniforms, these are the most formal clothes I own.

"You're Dahlia, right?" Vani says to the hostess. "I'm Dr. Vani Darshana." She turns to me. "This is Kira Marchand; she's a doctor as well."

To her credit, Dahlia assimilates this information with aplomb. "A doctor!" she says, every bit as enthusiastically as she had when she thought I was a plumber. Since the ostensible purpose of the event is to raise money for medical research, the room is crawling with doctors, but you'd never know it from Dahlia's reaction. "We love the CDC around here! That's wonderful! Who are you with?"

"I've worked for everybody," I say. "NGOs in the beginning, then the CDC, in the virology branch and as a mentor for the Epidemic Intelligence Service. I'm temporarily offline right now, but I do sometimes still collaborate with the WHO. I've interfaced with the NIH—NIAID—and even USAMRIID. Depending on, you know, the situation."

Dahlia blinks, helpless against the onslaught of alphabet soup. Vani helps her out. "Kira's an infectious disease specialist," she says. "One of the world's preeminent experts on artioviruses. You might have seen her on the news."

Comprehension is dawning on Dahlia's face, polite puzzlement giving way to startled recognition, followed by an expression of singular, devouring curiosity. Sometimes this happens; people recognize me from local news clips where I've answered epidemiology questions or an interview in the *Atlanta Journal-Constitution* about virology, or they remember me from one of the national press conferences in which I assisted the president. Vani, realizing her error, trails off as Dahlia's mouth opens wider.

"You're friends with the president, right? And you're one of our speakers tonight!"

The second part of this statement is true; partly to atone for my actions a year and a half ago, I'm one of several people who'd agreed to give a short talk emphasizing the need for research dollars. Regarding POTUS: I've met her and was once drafted into a live national press conference at her behest, but describing us as friends is a stretch. That doesn't stop people from peppering me with all manner of political and nonpolitical questions about her. Atlanta is almost as bad as D.C. when it comes to power trippers.

I attempt a deflection, gesturing to my outfit. "I'm dressed wrong. I didn't know about the floaty-dress thing. I thought it was going to be a room full of CDC nerds."

"Oh, honey! That is *no* problem. You look lovely! So chic and . . . comfortable!"

The avidity on Dahlia's face clearly signals she's poised to fire off more questions, so I pivot in an attempt to escape her, forgetting who is standing to my left. Shit: out of the frying pan and into the fire.

"Great save, Dr. Marchand! See what I mean? You'd be a natural on TV."

Mr. Smert, I decide, is one of those people who respond only to bluntness. "Pardon the graphic image, Mr. Smert, but I would sooner jab a fork into my eyeball than appear on a reality television show."

Remarkably, this does not faze him. "It's not a reality show, Dr. Marchand; it's a docudrama. Starring you and a few others. You'd be famous. I mean, not like before, when you'd be quoted in the newspaper or do a press conference. I'm talking about exceptional fame."

"I don't want to be exceptionally famous. Or any level of famous."

Smert blinks, clearly unaccustomed to dealing with people who don't wish to be exceptionally famous. "Ah. If you don't want to be on-screen, we could use an actor to portray you. We'd welcome your input on the script, of course. You'd be influential in the development of your personal story line."

I try not to waste time wondering what it might mean to be "influential" in the recounting of my own history. "I don't want to share my personal story."

With an expression of triumph, he plays his trump card. "The compensation would be significant. *Very* significant."

"I don't want money, Mr. Smert."

Mr. Smert gapes, uncertain how to deal with the kind of individual who'd reject the holy trifecta of money, power, and fame. Vani seizes the opportunity to steer me past him before he can regroup. As we move toward an elegant arched doorway, I remember my manners. "Thank you, but no, thank you," I call over my shoulder. "Hope you find somebody else to make rich and famous."

2 | The Trolley Problem

KIRA | **ATLANTA, GEORGIA**

WE STUMBLE OUT INTO THE NIGHT, AN ENORMOUS RESPITE after the heat and babble and stress of the party. I inhale, welcoming the sensation of fresh air. Removing the pin from the jacket lapel, I affix it to my T-shirt, where it will be visible to anyone I encounter.

Technically, appearing in public with a pin—green, yellow, or red—is voluntary, but rewards for compliance are plentiful. It's not uncommon for people to forget their pins, but there are other ways of indicating immunity status. All cell phones in the United States have access to anonymous Bluetooth proximity technology to broadcast a signal related to the most recent IgG antibody tests of the owner, which everyone is encouraged to update at a free center. If your cell phone comes within a twenty-foot radius of the cell phone of a nonimmune person—a yellow—you'll both receive an anonymous notification. If your cell phone comes within a fifty-foot radius of a known active infection—a red—you, and everyone around you, will hear an alarm. Both yellows and reds are rare these days, of course: the virus has already burned through a sizable minority of us, and most of those who escaped it long enough have now received the vaccine.

You can go off the grid, of course, and some people do, shunning testing and pins and the vaccine. They risk losing airline privileges and certain private sector benefits, but pockets exist of disease deniers and conspiracy theorists who care little for such things. There is also a sizable contingent of fierce nonconformists who prize independence above all else. Most people comply, or try to comply, with varying degrees of success.

Compton waits until we clear hearing distance from the house before she speaks. "Well, that was . . . eventful. Good save on that glass thing."

"Thank you."

"And way to dodge poor Mr. Smert."

"Huh? Why's he poor?"

"His name." We reach a lighted stone fountain, embedded in a circular plaza of crushed white pebbles. "Art Smert? With apologies to Garfunkel, I predict zero babies named Art in the future. It's going to fall out of fashion, like other notorious 'A' names. Adolf? Attila? Who wants a name that evokes images of genocide?"

"He can't help what he's named," says Hannah.

"Smert," I muse. "I've never met anyone with that name before."

Compton consults her phone. "According to Urban Dictionary, the term *smert* refers to attempting to be smart, but failing terribly."

"Aha," I say. "The universe has spoken."

Beyond the fountain, trimmed boxwoods and yuletide camellias flank a couple of cast-iron benches; behind them, a wide expanse of lawn angles away into infinity. We sit, Vani and I on one bench, Hannah and Compton on the other. "Kira." Compton tucks an errant strand of glossy hair back into formation. "Obviously you aren't going to work with Artie Smert. But do you ever think about sharing your perspective?"

"Of course not," I say. "I see no reason to relive the most devastating thing I'll ever experience just to provide fleeting entertainment for a bunch of ghouls. I know how it works: every little facet of my life would be sensationalized and contorted to look controversial. Conflict sells. Drama sells. What doesn't sell are the anguished inner reflections of an introvert."

Even in the dim light, I can see Compton's eyes narrow.

"Maybe your inner reflections wouldn't work on television, but you know where they would?"

"Com, wherever you're going with this, I don—"

She holds out a slim-fingered hand. "Hear me out, Kiki. Other people want to capitalize on your life and, as you say, they would contort what happened to reflect their own priorities. You don't need to do it to be famous; you need to do it to control the narrative."

"No. Never. I'd hate people knowing about my circumstances, whether it came from me or someone else. Even if you set aside the consequences of my decision, I committed a serious breach of the ethics of my profession. It cost me my job."

"Not exactly," Compton points out. "You could explain. People would be sympathetic. You could write a book."

"I could write nonfiction in the field of infectious disease, sure," I say. I keep my voice light. "I *have* written nonfiction in the field of infectious disease, and somehow that failed to interest more than five people until the pandemic. But a memoir would be, by definition, my personal story."

Compton's face takes on a mulish cast I recognize as a precursor to more arguing, but before she can speak again, Hannah bails me out. "Of course you're entitled to privacy, Kiki. All of us are."

This shuts Compton up. Possibly the thought of her own experience during the pandemic—or if not hers, Hannah's—is enough to deter her; in any case, she remains quiet as Vani picks up the conversational slack.

For December, the night is mild, the air breezy and rich with the scent of mulch and pine and winter camellias. I rest my back against the bench and bob in a tide of the lulling, familiar sound of my friends' voices—Hannah's clear sweet murmur, Compton's clipped vowels, Vani's singular blend of the American South and the south of India—as they chat about the party.

I hadn't been entirely honest with Compton. In truth I have been recording my recollections, curating my memories into a semi-fictionalized narrative. I don't have literary aspirations for my journaling, once finished—it's more likely the whole thing will fester for decades in a drawer—but it's unsettling to think of my private project unearthed by an opportunist. Still, somewhere in my mind, I've been picturing how a reader might respond to what I have to say.

Unlike the addictive, empty-calorie content of reality television, a work of literature—even a journal—allows for a more meticulous and insightful interpretation of events. You can present in shades of gray; you can offer and evaluate evidence.

You can justify.

I bat away that last thought before it can take root. In about an hour, I've committed to standing up before the wealthy crowd in the house to present a short fundraising speech, geared toward extracting money from people who consider themselves philanthropists and pillars of the community, and, as such, receive nonstop requests for donations from one worthy cause or another. Kicking at a tangle of old, dead leaves clotted in a heap at the edge of the bench, I try to order my thoughts, but the public-speaking area of my brain remains stubbornly disengaged.

It doesn't seem likely I can finish writing a book if I can't even come up with a ten-minute speech on a subject I know well. I wait for a break in the conversation and direct a question to Compton.

"Hey. If you don't mind my asking, what makes you think I could write a memoir? Vani's the only one of us who can write."

"Because," she says, with the air of someone delivering the final word, "you're the most brilliant person ever."

I'm not the most brilliant person ever, but I stifle an impulse to correct her. "If I wrote a memoir that other people read, you'd all be in it. How would you feel about exposing our warts to the world?"

I expect Compton to bristle at the concept of a public display of warts, but instead she issues a tinkly laugh. "It'd be hard to portray Hannah or Vani as warty. You'll have to invent something for them." She pauses to consider her next words. "And now that I think better of it, you should probably leave my story out of it."

I've already created neat literary slots in which to file our gang of seven from medical school. Hannah's easy; she's always represented the archetypal mother figure to us. She's the organizer and the soother and the one who reins in the rest of us when we start to spiral. Hannah rarely demands attention, but she nonetheless directs the tides that pull the rest of us.

In Shakespearean terms, Vani, an internist, would be cast as the foil: studious and sensible and calm, she provides an oasis of peaceful good humor in the midst of the ruckus constantly kicked up by everyone except Hannah. She possesses that rare gift of dialing down drama without ever descending into bossiness, and something about her—her smooth, rich voice, her radiant cheer—draws you in so subtly you're hooked on her before you realize what's happened. Vani is my person; ever since we shared an apartment in med school, she's the one I call when I have a funny story or a need to vent, but she's also the person I call during those times when life seems unbearable.

Compton issues a little snort. As if she were aware of my unspoken analysis, she angles her face in my direction and cocks an eyebrow—the Compton equivalent of a smile. Birdlike and brittle, Compton's always looked as if she'd be most at home in the blue-black light of an underground speakeasy, clutching a cigarette holder and a martini, blowing a caustic stream of smoke through the rosebud of her red lips. Her elegant bitchiness masks a keen and genuine concern for others, which is an element of her personality she likes to keep submerged from view, for whatever reason. Unlike the rest of us, she's a born and bred Yankee, although she wound up at our medical school in Kentucky because her grandmother on her father's side lived in a small town outside Louisville. Suffice it to say none of the southern charm rubbed off on her during the four years we all spent together.

The other three friends from our gang aren't here tonight: Georgia, a urologist, resided in Charleston before moving to Southern California; she'd represent the feisty, funny iconoclast among us. Zadie, a pediatric cardiologist, is goofy and charming; Emma, a trauma surgeon, is introverted and introspective; they both live in Charlotte and are intertwined in our minds as the yin and yang of long-term friendship. And me?

I guess I'd cast myself as the villain. Or, no: not the villain. That's not fair. I'm not motivated by evil or even self-gain. But at the very least I'm the troubled protagonist: the character most warped from the presentation of an unsolvable dilemma. Of the seven of us, I'm the one who seems most tormented by what happened to us collectively and to me personally.

From the nearby sunporch, a woman carries on: a loud, long, grating shriek of a laugh, followed by "You didn't! You did not! Chas, tell her!" A low mumble, presumably from Chas, and more laughter.

Vani elbows me in the ribs. "What are you wearing, Kiki? Do you even own a dress?"

"Of course I own a dress." This is both true and a lie; I do have a voluminous red dress-like garment that I wore to African funerals during my WHO days, but it's nothing like whatever Vani has in mind with the word *dress*. My outfit tonight is what I like. I don't wear dresses in America, and I certainly didn't wear them when I lived in Chad. I picture showing up in my red tent to a Buckhead soiree and can't repress a grin. Vani, no stranger to the way my mind works, elbows me again. "You can't ever wear that."

"You don't even know what I'm thinking about."

"Whatever it is, it is not right. I think I overestimated your ability to assimilate here. Maybe we can get you into a cotillion class or something."

"Bah," I say, my smile widening at the image of me waltzing with a pimply Buckhead teenager, a tennis ball between our foreheads, as an officious blond lady in her fifties claps out "ONE-two-three, ONE-two-three." But my smile vanishes as the word *teenager* reverberates through my brain, and it's all I can do to repress the wild sob rising in my throat.

Vani senses the shift in my mood and reaches for my hand. Across from us, Hannah and Compton lean toward us, Hannah nearly rising off the bench. "Don't think about it, Kira."

But I'm thinking about it; there's no stopping this train. It comes at me like it always does: out of nowhere, full-throttle screaming engines, ten thousand metric tons of carnage barreling down, allowing me only an instant to process my obliteration before it happens. One second I'm adapting, I'm fine, and the next second I'm doubled over, gutted from the impact.

I lean forward, allowing my head to fall onto my crossed arms. Vani sinks too, rubbing my back, whispering stupid little nothings of encouragement until embarrassment at my neediness eclipses my distress, providing the impetus for me to rise to my feet. "I'm a nightmare," I say.

Vani is nothing if not loyal. "Yup," she agrees. "Total."

It's dumb, but it makes me laugh.

"Look," she says, switching gears. The moon has come out, and it illuminates the curve of her cheek, threading patches of glistening silver through her dark hair. "You've been through hell. It's like . . . Do you know what it's like? That famous psychological experiment, what is it called? The one with the train?"

At first I think she's somehow tapped into my internal train/shame metaphor, but then it comes to me in a flash: I know the experiment to which she's referring.

"The trolley problem," I say.

She snaps her fingers. "That's it."

The trolley problem is indeed a well-known series of theoretical moral dilemmas, which psychologists use to gauge how consistently people use logic and ethics in their decision-making. Depending on how you answer, they'll throw in enough permutations to keep it interesting. One of the better-known variants goes like this: You're the switchman of an old-school railway. A runaway trolley comes careening down the tracks toward five people who are lying, incapacitated, on the tracks. You, the railman, can pull an emergency lever that will divert the trolley to a side track in order to save the lives of the five people, but there's a catch. A single person is tied to the side track, and if you shift the trolley it will kill her instantly. Your choice must be made in an instant: do you do nothing and allow the deaths of five people—an act of omission—or pull the lever and divert the trolley to the side track, thereby directly killing one person?

Most people, when faced with this calamitous choice, do not hesitate: they opt to divert the train. Psychologists, though, are perverse bastards, so they upped the ante. This time, you are standing on a bridge above the trolley, an onlooker with no official responsibility. You observe the five people—still in mortal peril from the runaway trolley—and as you do, you see there is someone else on the bridge with you. It's a tall man, craning to peer onto the tracks below. In an instant you recognize the implication: if you nudge the man over the rail, he will land in precisely the right location to stop the train. (Please note: *I* did not invent this ridiculous scenario. Blame the ethicists.) Now your choice is even starker: do you shove one man onto the tracks in order to spare five people? The outcome, you'll note, is the same as in the previous scenario: one person dies in order to save five, but this time the results are skewed the other way. Almost no one would actively sacrifice the big man to save the others.

Hmm, okay, said the psychologists, noting these results. *Maybe this is still too easy. How could we make this a truly excruciating choice?*

Scenario number three: there is a child tied to the track. Again, you can save him by diverting the train using the switch, which will kill whoever is tied to the other track. But this time it doesn't matter because you look more closely and realize, with a sensation that defies description, that it's your child. You know—*you know*—that no matter how many people are threatened on the other side, there is no choice. This is the point where biology overwhelms logic. You'll do whatever you have to do to save your son.

Until you see who is tethered, terrified, to the other track.

Your daughter.

PART TWO

BEFORE ARTIOVIRUS

3 Antigram

KIRA

SEVILLE, SPAIN

HERE'S WHAT I DIDN'T KNOW ON THE JUNE MORNING MY children and I left the United States for a long-awaited vacation: we were only days away from the onset of the most sweeping and profound change the world would experience since World War II. Indeed, the first patients had already succumbed, their deaths a speckling of tiny data points on a soon-to-be-monstrous curve. When I think back on it now, I'm always struck by the discrepancy in scale: on the one hand, the macroscopic devastation our societies endured—economic ruin, overwhelmed hospitals, entire infrastructures that could not be sustained because of all the deaths—and on the other, a microscopic quirk of biology. The catalyst of all this chaos: a shift in nucleic acids orders of magnitude below the perception of human eyes. Somewhere, at some point before our journey, an unrecorded encounter occurred between two animals in a jungle or a forest or a desert, somewhere teeming and dripping and dense or somewhere hot and fierce and dry. Somewhere within their bodies lurked a minuscule ecosystem of doom. We'll never know exactly where this animal encounter took place, but we know what happened next: one of them passed a virus to the other. The virus, propagating and changing, traveled along a chain of creatures until finally infecting a human, resulting in a kind of subcellular roulette: a shuffling and reshuffling of the most fundamental particles of life until, out of the infinite universe of possibilities, the ball clacked down into the worst possible slot. Somewhere in the continent of Africa, death reinvented itself and targeted humanity.

The children and I were innocent of what was to come as we settled into our seats aboard the jet that would carry us to Spain. An angry rain lashed the side of the plane as it ascended into the skies over Atlanta. We should have had a spectacular view of the glittery metropolis against the twilight sky, but petulant weather gods had seen fit to blanket the region in a spitting mist of low-lying clouds. Within seconds of takeoff, the lights of the city vanished into a homogenous sheet of gray.

"Mommy?" said Beau, my six-year-old. He'd been sitting cross-legged in his seat next to me for the last ten minutes, peering at his iPad, his entire being beaming intense concentration. Tiny nose: scrunched. Huge hazel eyes: narrowed. Back straightened, almost electrified. Even his ombre curls appeared energized. He traced a line along the iPad, sounding out a few words before posing a question. "Do you media?"

"Do I what?"

"Do you do the media? Where you put your selfies?"

"Are you asking if I am on social media?" He nodded. I paused to consider this. "I have a Facebook account but only to network with other doctors. And I was on Twitter once for about five minutes, I think. It was stupid."

"What about me?"

"No, Nugget. Social media isn't for little guys."

"Ha," said Rorie, my fourteen-year-old daughter. She'd claimed the window seat and had opened the meal I'd packed, dragging her spoon through a bowl of grains with the put-upon expression of someone who'd been served her one thousandth meal of prison gruel. With a repulsed grunt, she snapped shut the reusable container. "I've been giving this some thought, Mom, and I've invented a social media specifically for you."

"Okay . . ."

"It's called Antigram."

"I don't think I like where this is going."

A sly smile. "You start out with followers—let's say you have a thousand."

"There's no way I'd have a thousand follo—"

She cut me off, an imperious hand in the air. "Your goal is to get down to zero followers, which you do by disliking people's posts. The more you dislike things, the more unfollowers you get." She thrust up a fist. "Antigram!"

"Rorie. All I meant was it's not good for your developing brain to spend too much time on a screen. That's Parenting 101. If you don't say that, I think you get arrested."

"I have to spend time on screens. Since you're always dragging me around the world, I don't have the ability to forge relationships with real human beings like the other youth."

We emerged above the clouds. Rorie's hair, impaled in a stratospheric shaft of the last of the day's sunlight, lightened from dark brown to a light brown, matching the smooth sheen of her face. She was right about the amount of disruption in her life, of course; during her short life, she'd lived in multiple cities on two continents.

"Anyone referring to themselves as 'youth' might as well have the word *facetious* tattooed on their forehead," I said, and then had to suppress a smile as I saw Beau trying to spell *facetious* on his iPad to look it up. I took pity on him: "It means flippant or deliberately unserious."

"What does *flippant* mean?"

"It means facetious," I said. Rorie groaned but Beau offered a delighted smile.

"That's wonderful," he said. "I'm going to try to be more flippant."

Rorie resumed her study of the landscape visible from the plane's window. Now that we'd departed Atlanta, the clouds had given way to clear skies, offering a view of the land below, which was, at the moment, indistinguishable from virtually any semi-urban area in the gloaming edge of night: a patchwork of headlights and glowing buildings and the road-lined edges of geometric neighborhoods. Rorie caught me looking over her shoulder and shifted to give me a better view.

"I thought you didn't like looking out plane windows," she said.

I tried to mask my surprise before Rorie could home in on it. "Why did you think that?"

"You always shut your eyes during takeoff and landing if you're sitting by a window."

I shrugged, hoping Rorie would lose interest. "Takeoff and landings aren't my favorite."

Once, years ago in Africa, I survived a plane crash. In some ways, that was the least traumatic of a series of traumas during that time in my life, but I'd never mentioned it to the children. Part of it, of course, was not wishing to unleash a flying phobia in them; but part of it stemmed from my reluctance to speak to anyone of the years I'd lived in the north-central African country of the Republic of Chad. I'd met their father there when both of us were working with an international aid organization. Daniel, a man of African heritage who'd been raised in France, had died when Rorie was seven; we'd moved back to the States shortly afterward. At the time, I'd told her a partial truth: we were leaving so I could study another kind of medicine. Beau was born after we left and had no firsthand knowledge of the continent where he was conceived.

The few people who know about the crash probably assume I'm afraid of flying. I'm not; the crash I survived had been frightening as hell, of course, but it also occurred in a tiny prop plane flown by a drunken expat American idiot. A large commercial jet, such as the one in which we now flew, bore very little resemblance to the rickety mess I'd climbed aboard that night in N'Djamena. Still, since that night, I've had to conquer a residual flare-up of nerves during every takeoff. It's a major drag, given how much I fly, and I'd had no idea Rorie had picked up on it. Kids know way more about their parents than you might believe; it's just that usually they find the knowledge boring.

Rorie plucked idly at the dog-eared edge of an airline magazine in the seat pocket in front of her. "Are we going straight to Declan's?"

"He'll be at his lab when we get there," I said, returning my attention to the interior of the plane. "We're going to meet him later near the Plaza de España."

At the words *Plaza de España* Beau sprang to attention.

He put down his iPad, rustling in his canvas carry-on until he produced his red notebook. Beau never goes anywhere without his red notebook; he'd acquired it at age four and promptly announced he would become a writer. Riffling through the pages, he settled on one and tilted his notebook to allow me a better view. It was a drawing, lopsided and off-kilter but recognizable nonetheless as one of Spain's many regional coats of arms.

"That's excellent work," I said. "Did you do that the last time we were at the plaza?"

"No," he said, smiling at his drawing. He produced a pencil and adjusted the shading. "I did it from my rememberings. I can't wait to show Declan. He says maybe one day he'll take me to the Alhambra."

I looked at Beau's drawing again; he'd made an instinctive effort at perspective, narrowing the lines at the top of the page and emphasizing those at the bottom. The word *Granada* had been underlined multiple times, with an exclamation point added for good measure. What the hell: Declan had planned this to be a surprise, but the hope in Beau's voice was too much to defer. "Well, guess where Declan is going to take you and Rorie while Mommy meets her friends?" I lifted the seat divider, pulling his compact body into the crook of my arm.

"Where? Where?"

"You're going to see the Alhambra. Then later we'll all meet up and go to Morocco."

Beau was in the process of exploding with joy when his sister interrupted. "I don't wanna go," she said coolly. "I'll stay in Seville."

I gawked at her. Why would Rorie, a fourteen-year-old, think I would ever agree to let her stay on her own? I'm big on allowing children independence, but even I wouldn't allow my young teenager that much rope.

Rorie, correctly gauging the look on my face, offered a faux-innocent glance. "I could stay with Pilar."

I tried and failed to retrieve "Pilar" from my mental contact list. Pilar was a feminine name, yes? Not the name of a . . . boy.

"Pilar Cabrera," offered Rorie. "From those soccer fields where Declan plays."

"And what," I asked, "would you be planning to do all weekend with Pilar Cabrera from the soccer fields?"

"I don't know."

"Well, that doesn't sound like a very attractive plan," I pointed out. "So you can go with Declan and Beau to Granada."

"Pilar said I could hang out with them."

"Them who?"

"Her and her friends."

So at least Pilar wasn't a fourteen-year-old boy, or, worse, a sixteen-year-old boy. Whew. Still: I couldn't leave my young teenager alone in a city with people I didn't know to participate in indeterminate activities. This was a no-brainer.

"You'll go with Declan," I said. I'd already begun to transfer my attention back to the article I was reading when a rude snort sounded at my right ear.

"No."

"No?" I couldn't remember Rorie ever defying me with such calm.

"First of all," she said, "the Alhambra sounds dumb."

"Dumb?"

Rorie batted back before I could launch into a defense. "Yes, dumb," she said, with the kind of confident scorn you find only in the very young and in people who believe vaccines are a form of government mind control. "I've seen plenty of buildings. I don't need to see more."

My mouth opened and closed, uselessly, like a cartoon fish. After a drawn-out moment I identified the unfamiliar sensation I felt twanging in my chest: a burst of pain that a child of mine could say something so moronic.

"Another thing," she said. "I don't want to hang out with Declan."

I'd been about to launch into a lecture about centuries of architecture and history, but I switched gears. The Alhambra could defend itself. "Rorie, I know how you feel about being away from your friends for a couple weeks." I held up a hand to ward off her protestations. "But I thought you liked Declan."

Declan and I have a complicated history. We'd met because we both worked on projects related to the same family of viruses—albeit on different continents—and then, propelled by what I assumed to be mutual attraction, we'd dated for several years. From my point of view, things had gone well even though I lived in Atlanta and Declan lived in Spain. I didn't need or want a man in my house all the time and I liked the excitement generated by our transcontinental meetups. I'd already been granted the one great love affair of my life and I could not fathom ever finding that again. With Declan, I was in it for the heat.

Well, not just the heat; also the companionship. I enjoyed Declan's bright mind when we discussed our similar interests. He checked all my boxes: chemistry, intellectual stimulation, geographic distance that allowed me to maintain my space.

So I was a bit stunned when he dumped me.

It turned out, as these things so often do, that our relationship suffered from a series of imbalances. First: sex. I thought we were good in the bedroom. He's too much of a gentleman to say this outright, but I gathered, later, reading between the lines, that maybe I was more attracted to him than he was to me. I'm no great beauty, but I guess I thought—if I thought about it at all—that I have the mechanics down pretty well when it comes to physicality. But this—if it's even true—was not the primary driver of Declan's decision to downgrade us to friends.

Our second imbalance: he found me cold. To my surprise, he wanted me to uproot myself and the kids to Spain, leaving behind my job at the CDC, and when I declined he felt spurned. *How could you not want us to be together more?* he argued. *If you love me, why wouldn't you want to be with me?*

I gave these questions the consideration they were due. I concluded—again, somewhat to my surprise—that as much as I was drawn to Declan, I'd be better off without another great love affair. All those metaphors people use for love: stolen breath, swelling hearts. The irony of these poetic descriptions wasn't lost on me, since in reality, a swollen heart is unable to pump efficiently and often correlates with the early demise of its owner. But, also, I got it: when I thought of my lost husband, a very real sensation of welling emotion filled my chest. When I thought of Declan, I wasn't short of breath. My heart didn't speed up. I didn't feel the same hot, anticipatory glow I used to experience with Daniel, like an old-fashioned camera flashbulb going off in pulses, so bright and vibrant I used to worry it would be visible to everyone around us. Or if I did feel those things, I didn't want to. Loving someone that way makes you vulnerable.

With Declan, I could handle fondness and respect, and yes, lust. If something more threatened to break its way through, I batted it down, averting my gaze from his when he looked at me too intently.

So why was I visiting him now? After we got over the initial awkwardness, it turned out we managed to achieve the trickiest of adult relationships: a platonic friendship with subtle but unrealized undertones of more. We still had work in common: the virus I studied at the CDC was one of the same ones his biopharmaceutical laboratory had been targeting. We attended many of the same conferences; we knew many of the same academicians and scientists. It wasn't all professional, however, our new status: we got along. We talked. I missed the physical relationship with him and he wasn't above exploiting that desire, flirting like a mad bastard every time I saw him, just to rub it in a little. The message was clear: *Here's what you could have had if only you hadn't been so insistent on your space.*

In addition to the allure of his brain and his body, Declan had another thing going for him: a genuine fondness for my kids. He'd gingerly but hopefully mentioned adoption a few times back in the days when he thought I'd move to be with him. Now he'd offered to hang with them while I spent a few days gallivanting around Spain with my girlfriends from medical school. The kids liked him too.

Or so I'd thought.

Rorie shrugged, her loose T-shirt sliding off one shoulder. "Why would Declan want to hang out with me?"

"He likes you!"

Even as the words left my mouth I recognized my miscalculation. Let's break from this scene for a moment and assume you speak not a lick of English. Even so, if you were to listen to a recording of this conversation between me, a physician in her forties, and Rorie, a cheeky teen girl, you'd be able to identify the winner right away. One of us sounded coolly dismissive and one of us sounded like a high-pitched lunatic. It's counterintuitive. The more you allow genuine emotion to permeate your voice, the less reliable you sound. Whereas a dispassionate voice, reflective of someone who presumably cares less, is more likely to win an argument.

Sensing blood in the water, Rorie pressed her advantage. "Mom, you're oblivious to *everything*. Declan doesn't care about me. Like everyone else, he only likes Beau."

A small voice: "Declan loves us both."

Rorie and I swiveled in unison. Beau drooped forward in his seat, his round face crinkled in pain.

Beau had been born unable to tolerate conflict. The slightest hint of discord; a raised voice; an angry face: they demolished him. He'd first try to smooth things over, interjecting himself into the conversation like an undersized diplomat, offering a steady stream of praise and encouragement to the combatants. If that failed and the people remained angry at one another, he'd withdraw into himself, curling up like a desiccated bug.

Even in the grip of righteous disdain, Rorie softened toward her little brother. "Of course Declan loves you," she acknowledged. "Everyone loves you, Nugget." She paused, adding, "And you're Mom's favorite too."

"I don't have favorites."

Rorie whirled in her seat. "You can't say that with a straight face. There's no contest. If there's an order to who you care about, it goes like this: Beau, your job, me." One eyebrow drifted up, a quirk that never failed to remind me of her father. "And actually, I'd add Declan in there too, only in his case, you don't care about him enough."

"That's not true," I said, stung. "You and Beau are the most important things in the world to me. More than work, and, yes, certainly more than any guy."

"Fine." Rorie's eyes shifted upward, as if insight would materialize from the heavens if she looked hard enough. "Maybe I rank above work. But I'll never compete with Beau." Her eyes snapped back to me. "You've loved him most from the moment he was born."

Beau quivered in dismay. It took everything I had not to reach for him, but I kept my gaze on Rorie. Underneath her defiance, I could see an edge of something else, the faintest shadow of fear, maybe, or bewilderment. I didn't know whether to keep issuing the same denial—I'd already said I loved them equally—or try something else. Before I could commit to a course of action, Beau bent double in his seat, literally felled by grief at the notion that he might be favored over someone else. "Don't say that, Rorie, please," he said in a tiny voice, his face smashed down on his knees. "Don't say that."

"Oh, Beau-Beau," Rorie said, reaching across me. She made a crooning noise as she rubbed his little back. "It's okay. I'm sorry."

"Mommy loves you, Roar," he said, almost inaudibly.

"I know she does. I'm really sorry."

"I don't want to be the favorite. It would make you sad."

"It would," she agreed, leveling an intense look at me above his shoulder, "but you're not the favorite. I was being an ass."

"Rorie," I said helplessly. Rorie's eyelids fluttered and suddenly her teenaged saltiness fell away, revealing the unfeigned sweetness of the little girl underneath. "I'm sorry, Mom," she mouthed.

Now, looking back, I wish I could re-create that moment and suspend it, leaving me free to pull them both onto my lap, to wrap my arms around their bodies and breathe in the scents of their skin and contain them at these ages, while they were still innocent of what was to come. And me: I was innocent as well, unaware not only of the wave poised to break over the world but also of the manner in which our collective trauma would coalesce for me into an unthinkable choice between my children. It wouldn't happen until the last days of the pandemic, many months away. But it was coming, my future outlined already by a series of immutable events. If I'd known that then, I'd have tried harder to reassure Rorie of how much I loved her.

WE REACHED DECLAN'S flat, housed in a narrow four-story building with a rooftop view of Seville's famed cathedral, and deposited our bags. In a vestibule inside the door, some cheap bicycles stood shackled to a pole, since, like me, Declan wasn't big on cars.

Sunshine doused the streets, and I found myself grinning. There was something so freeing about being able to hop on a bicycle and swoop off, birdlike, down the narrow stone streets, pumping our legs until they ached, swerving to avoid the metal chairs of the sidewalk cafés and the inevitable clots of confused tourists. The children, thrilled with the autonomy of biking on a lovely day, whooped and hollered as they approached the Plaza de España.

In the distance, a semicircle of pink colonnaded buildings curved along the edge of the Parque de María Luisa, accessible via bridges over a goldfish-filled moat. Above us, sunlight filtered through the branches of an ancient banyan tree, dappling the ground in a flickering patchwork of light and dark. I hopped off my bike and ran a finger along the spine of a fallen leaf, broad and shiny green on one side, brown and felty on the other. Beau, who liked to play on the exposed snakelike root system of the enormous banyans, knelt on all fours a few feet from me, observing with ferocious intensity some tiny crawling thing as it meandered around the tree root.

My phone buzzed: a video call.

"I bet it's Declan," said Beau, scrabbling across the tree root to reach me. "Can I say hi?"

It was indeed Declan. I passed the phone to Beau.

"Hello!" Beau stopped walking and set down his notebook so he could hold the phone straight out with two hands. Beau adores talking on the phone, treating each call as an occasion worthy of note. He'd never walk and talk, or talk and do anything else that might distract him from the person on the other end. "Hello, Declan!"

"Hello, *mo stoirín*," said Declan. Declan is Irish. Fittingly, he employs all kinds of Irish phrases and expressions, sometimes with great authenticity, and sometimes, I am convinced, to ham it up. My children find this charming.

Or at least one of them does.

"I cannot believe the great day is here at last. Are you here?"

"We are here! And guess what, Declan!" Beau said. "Guess what!"

"I don't know, Beau. Can you give a bit of direction?"

"Nope! Guess."

"Okay," said Declan. He shut his very blue eyes, showcasing a set of very black eyelashes. His eyes popped back open. "There's an asteroid inbound to earth? They discovered a superpower gene? Your mother brought home a kitten?"

"Better," said Beau.

"Better than superpowers and kittens? You've got me."

"*WearegoingtotheAlhambra!*"

"Sorry," said Declan. He assumed a faux-thoughtful expression and cupped his free hand to his ear. "What was that? I didn't quite get it. Sounded like you said we are going to the Alhambra, but that can't be it, because—"

"That's it! That's it, Declan! We are going to the Alhambra!"

"—but that can't be it, because your mother promised I could tell you."

"Hi, Declan." I wormed my way onto the screen, looming behind Beau, who was still vibrating with excitement. "Uh. I told him."

"So I gather," Declan said wryly. "I take it it went well?"

"I'm sorry," I said. Even to myself, I sounded lame. "He was begging."

"Sure, no worries, then. The wee man is a tough one to put off. And where is the lovely Aurora?"

I tried to signal to Declan with my eyes that this line of questioning was a nonstarter, but my expression must have come across wrong, because Declan's brow wrinkled. He put a hand up to the screen as if to touch my forehead. "You feeling okay?"

Hastily, I deflected. "Yeah, great, I'm great, Rorie's great, where are you? On your way?"

"I'm not going," said Rorie, swinging a leg over her bike.

"What was that?" asked Declan.

"Nothing," I said, leveling a murderous glance in the direction of

Rorie's back as she glided in circles. Beau wandered back over to his tree root. "I'm failing parenthood."

"Right, okay," said Declan, a response that clued me in to the fact that his attention to the conversation was possibly not at tip-top level. "Listen, something has come up."

"Oh?" I said. A shock of Declan's dark hair fell across one eye, and he thrust up an impatient hand to brush it back. Like Beau, he seemed to be thrumming with an undercurrent of concealed excitement. "What's going on?"

"I can't—I don't want to say yet. We're about to start the final analysis of the first *in vivo* trials of the new drug. Can you fend for yourselves for a bit longer?"

"Of course. Take whatever time you need. I don't head to Barcelona to meet the girls until tomorrow."

He touched two fingers to his lips and then moved them toward the phone camera. "I can't wait to see you guys, Kiki."

"This sounds like something good."

"It could be," he said. "It could be very good."

4 The Nerd Version of the Green Berets

KIRA | SEVILLE, SPAIN

I MOTIONED TO THE CHILDREN TO GET ON THEIR BIKES. BEAU stood, excitement shining from every pore, and brushed his hands on his pants. "Best day ever," he crowed. "I'm going to the Alhambra! And I saw an ant!"

Rorie circled up, cruising to a stop beside him. "That's cool, B," she said, her hand alighting on his small shoulder. "Was there something special about the ant?"

"It carried a leaf much bigger than it! Into a tree hole!"

I swung a leg over my bike and set off. The children followed, Beau still chattering about the heroic endeavors of the ant. We'd scarcely left the park when my phone rang again. Beau stopped his bicycle and held out his hand.

"Can I answer?"

I glanced at the screen and shook my head at Beau. The phone call came from a cell phone with an Atlanta area code, from a number I knew well.

"Kira Marchand," I said.

"Kiki!" The voice on the other end, despite whatever circumstances had prompted the call, could not repress a certain delighted undertone. I loved this voice, at once deep and suave and full of humor. It was my mentor, boss, and close friend, Dr. Waliedine Katz, calling from the CDC.

"Wally Cat," I said.

"First things first," he said. "How are you? How are the little ones?"

Like me, Wally is a graduate of the Epidemic Intelligence Service—the EIS—and also like me, he's an occasional mentor there, devoting time to training a new squad of public health warriors every two years. Because the EIS is partly staffed by the Commissioned Corps of the U.S. Public Health Service—the public health arm of America's eight uniformed services—commissioned EIS officers are sometimes required to wear one of several uniforms, which are supposed to invoke a crisp, militaristic sense of *esprit de corps*. Every time Wally dons his Service Dress Blues, Summer Whites, Service Khakis, or—my favorite—Operational Dress Uniform (ODU) Woodland Camouflage, he manages to undermine the desired impression. Even in uniform, I'd say Wally presents more of a . . . rakish vibe.

"Beau is thriving. Rorie is currently more of a parenting challenge," I answered, striding a few dozen yards away from the children so they wouldn't hear me discussing them. I don't believe in a response of "fine" to such questions, as that makes the whole exchange a pointless formality and therefore a waste of everyone's time. If you take the time to ask the question, you deserve a thoughtful answer. To be thorough, I continued: "But I believe they are well adjusted, overall."

"Uh-huh," said Wally. He sounded nonplussed at my answer. "Right. I know you're on vacation, so I won't take too much time. I wanted to talk to you about some activity in southern Spain."

"I'm in Spain right now, Wally."

"Yes, I know. That's what I just said."

"No, you said you wanted to talk about *activity* in—"

"Forgive me. I will try to be more literal. There've been some reports on Pro-EID Com coming out of northern Africa and southern Spain, and I wondered if you're aware of them."

"Wait, Wally, back up. How do you know where I am?"

"I follow Rorie on Instagram."

Wally was on Instagram? Was everyone on Instagram? Damn social media. I made a mental note to tell Rorie to stop geotagging her locations, even though in this instance it wasn't particularly creepy that Wally, a man in his fifties, was following my teenage daughter online, since Wally is Beau's godfather and, with the exception of Vani and Declan, the closest adult friend my children have.

"It may be nothing," Wally continued. "But I've heard an interesting report."

"Okay . . ."

"I don't yet know exactly what's going on," he said. "But I heard a report of some unusual deaths. Not sure if WHO is on it."

"Reports from who?"

"No, I meant I wondered if WHO was involved."

"I meant whom."

"What?"

"Reports from whom?"

"What? Who's on first?" yelled Wally. For the record, most people refer to the acronym for the World Health Organization as W-H-O, but Wally had always pronounced it as if it rhymed with *coo.*

"From where specifically are these reports?"

"Tangier," Wally said. The jocularity dropped from his tone. "And a few from Rota."

I sat down, hard, on a tree root, recognizing the first city as one of the northernmost port cities in Africa and the second city as the site of a large American military base in southern Spain. A few meters away, Beau was hopping on one foot in a figure-eight pattern; Rorie had stretched out on a root, holding her phone above her face. They both appeared to be occupied, so I returned my attention to Wally.

"What are they saying?"

"The initial reports were of undiagnosed pneumonias, possibly an unusual viral illness, as the lung consolidations did not respond to multiple antibiotics. Fever, and, in some people, pulmonary hemorrhage. Possibly some seizure-like activity. Apparently the postmortems were strange; this wasn't on Pro-EID, but I'm hearing in one case the lungs were nearly liquefied."

"Okay, but—"

"There's a wrinkle, though."

"Yeah?"

"The first death reported by Tangier officials was a doctor. A young man. He was traveling to Morocco from his village."

"Why is that wrinkly?"

Wally cleared his throat. "The doctor was from Chad," he said.

I didn't say anything. Very few people know of my history in Africa, but Wally is one of them. I'd only been boarded in internal medicine when I lived there; it wasn't until after I'd left that I'd added a fellowship in infectious disease. My husband, Daniel, had been a surgeon, and together the two of us constituted the majority of the available physicians in the remote region where we lived.

"Kira?" Wally said. "Whatever they found on Patient Zero's autopsy was concerning enough for rumors to begin circulating online, which is how Pro-EID Com picked it up." He hesitated before adding in a quieter tone, "There haven't been any direct reports to us."

I considered this. A viral illness causing bleeding into the lungs in a young man with a presumably healthy immune system . . . Wally waited me out, no doubt anticipating the track my mind would take.

It didn't take long to summon a specific and unsettling fear. Both Wally and I had granted a lot of thought to a particular specter from the past, a killer so contagious and so brutal its worldwide death toll may have eclipsed even that of the plague.

"Nineteen eighteen," I said slowly. "Another Spanish flu?"

"I'm not thinking influenza specifically," said Wally. "But the world's overdue for something catastrophic."

I acknowledged this in silence.

"There's more, though," said Wally. I could hear a faint bristly crackle, which meant he was stroking his mustache, a mannerism he sometimes performed while thinking. I suspect he believes it gives him the air of a sexy mustachioed detective, like Magnum, P.I., or maybe a cerebral one, like Hercule Poirot. In reality, it comes across as more of a Ron Burgundy thing, or even, I regret to say, a Borat thing.

"What?"

"The first death took place in an . . . unusual location."

"Where? And are you saying the Moroccan government is asking for the CDC to get involved?"

"Well," said Wally, drawing the word out in the manner of someone who knows he's about to deliver unwelcome news. "The government hasn't put out anything official because the death wasn't in Morocco. Technically, the death wasn't anywhere."

"What do you mean, Wally? How can a death not be anywhere?"

There was a pause. "I was trying to think of something clever to say about uncharted waters," he said finally. "Got a bit hung up, sorry."

I started to ask another question—it wasn't like Wally to be so cryptic—but then it hit me. "Ah!" I said. "The death occurred in international waters."

"That's right. No, wait: I'm not sure if the waters were truly international. It happened on a ship somewhere in the Strait of Gibraltar."

"I don't see the problem."

"Here's the thing," said Wally. "I'm no expert on maritime law, but I did a speedy internet search. Normally it seems once you've sailed past the area of each country's territorial waters, then you're in international waters and the jurisdiction of the closest landmass would no longer apply."

I identified the problem. "The Strait of Gibraltar isn't very wide."

"Correct. At the narrowest point, there are only about fourteen kilometers separating Europe from Africa. So I guess we're looking at the territory of whichever country the ship was closer to when the person died. But the death of the victim—the doctor—caused a big commotion on the ship, and the information from the passengers and crew is conflicting about the timing. It appears they may have been more or less midway between Spain and Morocco when he died. To make it even more complicated, apparently there's some argument about who controls the waters of the Strait of Gibraltar."

"An argument between Spain and Morocco?"

"No," said Wally. "Well, yes, but also between Spain and England. And Gibraltar itself."

This sparked a dim memory. Gibraltar—a small settlement on the tip of the Iberian Peninsula—was a self-governing British territory. So part of the waterway between this part of Europe and Africa was technically British. The Spaniards disputed the British ownership of Gibraltar, and the Gibraltarians disputed the Spanish and also possibly the English, meanwhile the Moroccans disputed several cities and islets claimed by the Spanish. In light of so much geopolitical disputing, it was easy to see why Wally might think this case could run into jurisdictional issues. And this mattered: if the WHO were to get involved, there would need to be coordination with the index country. Throughout history, the response of the first affected country has had a mighty impact on the course of the disease, for better or for worse.

"Let's back up. Who owns the ship?" I asked.

There was another brief silence; apparently this was more bad news. "It's the Tarifa ferry," he said.

I groaned.

I was familiar with the ferry, which my friends and I would be boarding in a few days for a short stay in Morocco. It ran back and forth between the Spanish city of Tarifa and the Moroccan city of Tangier, and if you set out to pick the worst possible place for someone to bite it from an infectious disease, a crowded intercontinental ferry might top your list. The last time I'd taken it, I'd noted hundreds of passengers speaking at least a dozen different languages, all crammed into a relatively small space.

Wally didn't waste time detailing the nightmare spread that could result from this scenario. "I don't mean to pile on about protocol here," he said, "but I haven't yet figured out which country owns this particular ship, so I'm not sure where to reach out."

"Hopefully, the WHO will sort it out. What do you know about the index patient?"

"Right," he said. The click of a keyboard pattered over the line. "Here we go: African male; citizen of Chad, according to his passport; born 1985. Name of Dr. Aboubakar Seidou. Traveling alone. No signs of chronic illness. No one noticed anything unusual when he boarded."

I didn't recognize the name; I hadn't known him when I lived there. "Did he board in Morocco or Spain?"

"This was on the Tangier-Tarifa run. He came to the attention of his fellow passengers while in a line to buy drinks."

"Why?"

"I guess he was thirsty."

"No, why did he come to their attention?"

"He was next to a woman with a baby and in front of an older couple from Norway, and apparently he kept coughing on them. They did not like it when he coughed on them."

"No one likes being coughed on."

"Yes, but these people *really* did not like it. The Norwegian woman left to try to find someone with the authority to ask the man to move. By the time she returned, the guy was on the ground."

"What happened?"

"According to the Norwegian couple, whose names are"—another clicking sound—"Ole and Karine Alf, the man just keeled over."

"You mean he fainted?"

"No, I mean he died. One second he was irritating the crap out of the rest of the beer line with his hacking cough, and the next second he checked out. Stone-cold dead."

"But why—"

Wally interrupted. "Poor choice of phrase, actually. He wasn't stone-cold anything. A Canadian woman attempted CPR but stopped because he was blazing hot. I don't know much more. The ME's still got the body, apparently. Haven't been able to confirm that."

"Wait, Wally. What are you not telling me?"

Wally was silent for a moment, which was unlike him. When he spoke, the bluster had left his voice. "What I'm reading about the autopsy report worries me, Kiki. Do you have any contacts on the ground in Spain? Or Morocco? Maybe you can dig a little, see if you can come up with anything that hasn't hit the net yet."

"I'm on vacation, Wally."

"Sure," he said smoothly. "Honestly, Kiki, if anyone needs a break from work, it's you."

A break from work.

Work: sad though it is, not everyone is familiar with the Epidemic Intelligence Service. For that matter, not everyone is familiar with the Public Health Service, with the Centers for Disease Control, or even with the most basic principles of what constitutes an infectious disease. Some people still believe smallpox was eradicated by hand washing, or that chill air can make you sick, or that you can catch the flu from a flu vaccine. I spend most of my time these days in an office instead of in the field with EIS teams, but fieldwork remains my first love.

The EIS consists of a rapid-reaction squad of elite professionals deployed by the CDC in the event of a catastrophic disease outbreak. They're the nerd version of the Green Berets or the Navy SEALs or Batman. During the two years of extra training the EIS provides to its enrollees, their members are prepared to dash to the four corners of the globe to investigate, combat, and constrain microscopic killers.

Although many of them are physicians, you don't have to be a medical doctor to be accepted into the EIS. Wally, for example, possesses two degrees: a Ph.D. in virology and a master's degree in epidemiology. Some attendees hail from the fields of dentistry or nursing or veterinary medicine. Once, one was even a lawyer. All of them undergo a vigorous application process, hoping to be one of seventy-some people picked for a slot out of an applicant pool of more than six hundred.

Once selected, the chosen ones commence two years of intensive training. This starts out with Epi Boot Camp, in which they smear black camouflage on their faces, slog through a nine-mile obstacle course, and then engage in near-lethal bouts of hand-to-hand combat, *Hunger Games*–style, to weed out the losers. Okay: not really. In reality, they begin by parking their butts in a lecture hall to review the fundamentals of statistical analysis. Not quite as sexy as a physical boot camp, but there's still a certain intensity at the notion of using your intellect to outwit witless genocidal superbugs. I, for one, think Hollywood could make something quite special out of our collection of alluring brainiacs.

All this didactic stuff comes to an end after weeks of hard-core schooling, when the trainees confront the terrorism portion of the course just before they start their specialized research or leave for real-life field investigations. On an average day, bioterrorism is not something to which the average citizen gives much thought. The CDC, on the other hand, gives a colossal amount of thought to bioterrorism. To prove it, they used to haul the EIS officers down to Anniston, Alabama—of all places—and proceed to scare the shit out of them in an old decommissioned army hospital now repurposed as a ghoulish mass-casualty scene. Now: this kind of thing you probably *have* seen in a movie. Think crinkly white Tyvek suits, military-grade respirator masks, elbow-length black gloves. Heaps of bodies felled by one of the Big Four weaponizable biologic agents: plague, botulism, anthrax, and—the one I fear the most—smallpox.

I really, really hate the idea of weaponized smallpox.

But even more than smallpox, I fear a new twist on an old virus. At least with smallpox, there exists the consolation of knowing it's only likely to wreak havoc if human beings will it back into being through a complex and unlikely series of actions. Even now I don't consider myself so naive or optimistic to think that this scenario could never happen. It could. But another part of me cannot allow myself to believe something so terrible could be wrought by humanity, even with all the historical evidence to the contrary. Anyone unleashing weaponized smallpox would have to be genocidal but also suicidal, since biologic weapons don't respect borders. As horrifying as the terrorist mindset might be, outside of a doomsday cult or something similar, many of them have enough capacity for rational thought that they wouldn't want to risk the destruction of their own people. You can at least argue with a human.

A virus, though. You cannot argue with a virus.

As if tacitly acknowledging this, Wally broke into my train of thought. "It may not be a novel influenza, or whatever. It might be nothing."

I waited.

"Or," he said, "it might be the next big one."

This, of course, should have been the wake-up call for which I'd been waiting, the moment my years of training and expertise would kick in to provide me with some spider sense of impending calamity. Even as Wally spoke, an insidious enemy was preparing a full-scale assault on humanity, slithering its way into the first few lungs and bloodstreams, mounting an attack on our cells with a battalion of miniature hooks and lances and morning stars. Shouldn't I have had some subconscious awareness? When I think back on the conversation, however, I cannot recall anything of the sort. Wally had been alarmed enough to contact me, but Wally has a well-known tendency to portray every minor outbreak as an impending apocalypse. He also thrives on drama, which makes us good colleagues; we level each other out.

"I'm headed to Barcelona to get together with my med school girlfriends," I said slowly. "But we were planning a day trip to Morocco with Declan and the kids. I'll see if I can reach anyone in the public health system there."

Wally snorted at the mention of Declan; he'd cooled to any mention of him ever since learning Declan had urged me to give up my job to be with him. "Good, let me know if you reach anybody. And have fun. Rorie's post said she wants to ride a camel in Morocco."

Really? A camel? What was up with all the adolescent static, then? "Dec's got the kids for a few days while I'm with my friends," I said. "I'll tell him."

"Don't do anything dumb," said Wally, the gruffness in his voice doing little to mask an underlying tenderness. "We need you to come back."

RORIE WATCHED AS I rummaged through my travel bag. Since we'd be taking a day trip to Morocco—a Muslim country—I added a pair of waterproof full-length khakis. Compared to many places, they're fairly tolerant of shorts-wearing female infidels over in Tangier, but the first thing you learn as an EIS officer is to be as respectful as possible of local customs and beliefs. It helps with cooperation and it sends the message that you're there to assist, not to assert authority over the people suffering in an epidemic. I wouldn't be traveling in any official capacity, of course, but it never hurt to be prepared.

Downstairs, the door chimed as it opened. "It's Declan," hollered Beau. He charged for the stair landing, his duffel clanging against the backs of his knees hard enough to send him sprawling forward onto the floor. He scrabbled back up. "I'm fine! I got it!"

Trying to repress a smile, I turned to Rorie. "Honey, I hate to pressure you, but you have to adjust your attitude: Go with Beau and Declan and have fun? Or go with Beau and Declan and ruin everything by acting like a sullen twit?"

A fluttering eye roll.

"Okay, I'm going to decide for you. You'll go with Beau and Declan and be miserable."

"Fine. I'll be nice."

Reverse psychology. Works every time.

"Great, throw some stuff in a bag. Make sure you have your chargers."

"I know, Mom!"

Beau loped back into the bedroom, his bag still thunking him in the backs of the legs, followed by Declan.

A word about Declan: he's sexy. In my experience most people have a defining characteristic that tends to overshadow their other features: they're prissy or they're manic or they're remarkably unflappable or whatever. Declan's thing is that he's smoking hot. It's not so much conventional attractiveness as it is pure animal magnetism, the kind some people convey in the mere flick of an eyebrow or the hint of a smile. I realize you might not consider attractiveness a character trait, but in Declan's case it undoubtedly constitutes part of his personality. It's also nondiscriminatory: you could put him in a room with an elderly schoolmarm or the pope or that chunky freakshow that runs North Korea—to name a few non-sexy types—and he'd be unable to repress a come-hither look. It seeps out of his pores, because the man is a smoldering sex bomb.

"Kiki," he said, grazing my shoulder with a light hand that then traveled along the line of my neck to my face, resting briefly on my lower lip even though that is not the way you'd normally greet a friend. He flashed me a look of pure intensity: white-flecked blue eyes, dark lashes, straight black brows. See what I mean? Trailing a finger along a jawline: sexy. Touching a lip: sexy. Eye contact: always sexy.

"Thank you," I whispered into his ear. He isn't tall, Declan: only an inch or two taller than I am, but trim and strong. "I can't tell you how much I appreciate you keeping Beau and Rorie. And I can't wait for you guys to join us in Morocco."

"Delighted to have the little man," said Declan, dropping his finger from my face and ruffling Beau's hair. Beau produced a happy chirping sound. Declan turned his attention to Rorie, who still lay sprawled on top of the quilted Indian coverlet. "You're welcome as well, Aurora."

"Can we stay here?" said Rorie.

"Ah, well . . ."

"Roar," I said. "Please don't bring this up again."

Rorie sat up, conceding defeat. I expected hostility but she surprised me with a shrug. "Okay, Mom," she said. "Maybe the Alhambra will be dazzling."

Overreacting to your victory over a teenager would be counterproductive, so I kept my cool. "Worst-case scenario, you'll have lots of gorgeous pictures that you can InstaTweet on your FaceSnap."

"Very funny."

"I am so sorry you can't come to the Alhambra, Mommy," said Beau. "Declan and I will take lots of pictures for your Antigram."

Rorie snorted in delight.

"We will," agreed Declan, before pausing to take this in. "Wait, pictures for your what?"

"And we will take lots of notes, right, Declan?"

I spoke at the same time as Beau: "I don't actually have a—it's something that—never mind, it was a joke."

Rorie slid from the bed, grinning at the success of her mockery of me. "I'm gonna repack."

"Beau, why don't you help her?" I suggested. Beau, still shouldering his overloaded duffel, obediently trotted after his sister.

I'd been rolling my scarf—a delicate, almost transparent square of fine blue cotton—but now I set it down, one edge still loose.

"What's happening at work, Dec?"

His back straightened, belying the casual note in his voice. "We're close."

"The antiviral?" Declan's lab was currently assembling the final data needed in order to request a CTA—a Clinical Trial Application—for a medication he'd spent the last few years developing. The drug was a small fragment of an antibody, called a nanobody. While not as expensive to develop and produce as monoclonal antibodies, nanobodies were still costly, meaning Declan's small outfit continually faced serious funding challenges.

"Yeah. A lot of data to sort still, but yeah. If all goes well, human trials soon."

"And you're up for taking the kids out of town anyway? Ah, Dec."

He raised his shoulders in a philosophical shrug, but I caught the faintest flicker of disappointment in his eyes before a deliberate kindness replaced it. "And miss a chance for a weekend with my favorite young ones? Besides, it might not work and then I'll have something to distract me when I get the news. Cushion the blow, yeah?"

I felt a fake smile cross my face. "Of course."

We were both lying; nothing could cushion that kind of disappointment. He'd poured everything he had into this, the longest of long shots: years of obsessive, slavish work; his reputation; all his personal financial resources. If Declan's lab could produce a successful antiviral drug—one that could cure a specific viral illness, the way antibiotics could cure a bacterial illness—the medical implications would be massive. Operating on the theory that nanobodies not only could neutralize an acute infection but could potentially be used to induce a more active long-lasting immunity, the discovery would be a world-changing event if it worked and could be administered in a cost-effective way.

But if he failed, he'd risked everything: his funding and maybe even his facilities and staff. He'd have to start over.

"I'm not worried," Declan said, giving every indication of someone who was worried. Compressing his lips into an inverted line, he redirected his gaze somewhere past me to the window. "It'll work. Or it won't. In the meantime, I get to enjoy Beau and all his cheerful curiosity, and Aurora and all her . . ." He paused in a diplomatic search for the right word. ". . . sparkly sass."

"Sparkly sass?"

"Well, but you're supposed to be hostile when you're a teenager, yeah? All those adults trying to boss you when you already know everything? But actually, Kiki, she's been only sweet whenever you're not around." At this, he managed a grin at my expense, and I couldn't help smiling back; what woman can resist someone who loves her children? "I'm not claiming to be an expert or anything," Declan went on, "but I think that kind of feistiness is a normal reaction to parenting."

Time for a change of subject. "Well, enjoy your weekend with the sass. On a different note—any chance you know anybody in the public health system in Morocco? I'm hearing about an unusual illness."

"I don't," he said. "What kind of illness? Is it safe to travel there?"

"As far as I know," I assured him. "No travel advisories. Wally's got his antennae up about something. If it's real, I'll run it up the flagpole, but it sounds vague. Maybe a viral outbreak, maybe nothing. Wally's the kind of guy who sees every death as a potential pandemic."

Declan cast a thoughtful look in my direction. "What kind of symptoms?"

"Wally said flu-like," I hedged. "At least one young guy. I don't know what the other reports were."

"Hmm," Declan said.

"It's nothing, most likely."

"In my experience," said Declan, "when someone keeps saying 'it's nothing,' that's a good indication that it is actually something."

I reached for him. "Kind of like saying 'I'm not worried,' maybe?"

Declan bent his head, touching his forehead to mine. "I'm scared shitless, actually."

We stood for a moment, silent. Offering false platitudes is not my strong suit, so I didn't tell him it would be fine, that the drug would work, that he wouldn't lose his business and all his years of effort. Like many potential treatments, it was more likely to be a bust than not, and both of us knew it. Still, he seemed to derive some comfort from my presence; his hand gripped the back of my head and his breathing slowed. "Thank you," he murmured.

"For what?"

"For not saying anything stupid."

I moved my face slightly, aware of the commingling of our breaths. We'd reached such a weird limbo in our friendship; me surreptitiously hoping we'd hook up again and him surreptitiously hoping—what? That I'd finally banish the ghost in our relationship and rekindle things with him?

I wish I could forget Daniel. Or no—not forget him; I never want to forget him. But I wish he could loosen his grip on me or that my heart could—finally—expand to make room for someone else. I wish I could banish the weary, bone-deep aching that settles into me at the thought of replacing him. I wish I could alter the clichéd dream I still have with regularity; in it I'm running along a rutted road, desperate, my breath hitching, trying to get back to Daniel before his eyes close forever and he's gone.

I never make it.

"Have a blast in Barcelona," said Declan. His hands slid around my waist; his breath, warm and spicy like cinnamon, brushed my neck. I thought he might kiss me, and I closed my eyes.

"Well," said Declan, releasing my waist after a final reassuring squeeze. "We'll miss you, but I look forward to meeting your friends in a few days. And don't worry about the kids, Kiki. It's going to be the perfect weekend."

5 A Homesteader's Guide to Going Off the Grid

COMPTON

NEW YORK CITY

JUST BEFORE SHE DEPARTED FOR SPAIN, COMPTON WINFIELD blundered into a secret her husband had been keeping from her. To her knowledge, throughout the entire history of their marriage, Ellis had been an open book; gregarious by nature, he was unable to keep anything of interest to himself. Or so she'd thought; unlike her, he could fairly be described as an oversharer. So it was even more startling to realize he'd been harboring a hidden desire to leave their lives behind.

Her last day in New York had imploded, beginning with an eight-hour ED shift that metastasized into a twelve-hour shift when her last patient of the day, a forty-eight-year-old executive, had coded and almost died right as she was completing the order to discharge him. Every component of that sentence was bad: it was bad that her last patient was so complex, especially when she was in a hurry; it was bad that he coded right as she'd been preparing to discharge him; and it was beyond bad that he, a youngish man, had coded at all.

So much badness to unpack there.

Depending on how you regarded it, Compton had been either blessed or cursed by whatever fickle genies control the fates. If the patient had arrived at the ED later, someone else would have seen him. On the other hand, if his inexplicable crash had occurred later, he'd have already departed the ER and died on the street, and her career would have been condemned to suffer a slow, agonizing death of its own. Not that she presumed to compare the loss of a career to the loss of a life, but she'd run a hundred agonized replays in her mind and still could not determine what, if anything, she'd done wrong.

The near miss enshrouded her in a veil of self-reproach as she left the hospital. It embedded itself into her pores, seeping out in a cloud that announced her as a failure to everyone in the vicinity. Could you literally off-gas shame? Apparently, you could.

She rode home on the 6, the other commuters giving her a wide berth even though the train was crowded. They could detect the shame shroud, obviously, and wanted no part of it. Compton glanced around at all the usual suspects: depleted shift workers, like her; sprawl-legged, earbudded young males; leering middle-aged weirdos; old ladies in outdated shoes; soulfully sighing couples who apparently couldn't wait ten more minutes to touch each other; and the inevitable dude picking his teeth. Ah, humanity! Normally she took some enjoyment from riding the subway. It wasn't that she availed herself of public transport in some virtue-signaling effort at keepin' it real—nothing was more real than an emergency department, after all—but that it was such a stupid waste of both time and money to take a car home. She could get home faster on the 6, assuming the trains weren't down.

In an attempt to war-game the rest of the time remaining to her before she missed her flight, Compton consulted her phone. Priority number one: get off this train and obtain a shower. The thought of an overnight flight to Europe while still emanating the stench of remorse—not to mention the usual post-shift ER funk—was too much to bear, even if it meant not finishing her half-assed attempt at packing. She could buy toiletries in Spain if she had to.

More problematic was the issue of what she'd be leaving behind. She'd failed to complete the forty-page scheduling manifesto required to keep the family functional during her absence. Even though the Winfield-Comptons employed a part-time sitter, some of the kid-related tasks and household maintenance would fall on Ellis when she left, and he sucked at everything even remotely domestic. You had to break it down for him, step by step; hence the manifesto. But now there would be no t—

Compton aborted this line of thought. It wasn't productive. The subway car doors slid open and everyone attempted to bolt out simultaneously, while at the same time some jackass carrying a cello tried to board. There was a brief skirmish, which the cello wielder won by virtue of his greater mass. Everyone else had to wait, and by the time she made it, the doors were closing. No! She could not ride to the next stop. She wrenched the doors apart and flung herself off.

Okay. She'd escaped the subway and things were looking up. She felt a little better about her patient too; after all, he had survived. Or at least he had survived long enough to be handed off to the next ED doc at shift change. He should have gone directly to the ICU, but the ICU was full, so he was boarding in the ED in the meantime, all tubed and lined and ventilated and waiting on one of the ICU docs to come down and manage all his drips. He was on a couple of pressors—IV medications to keep his blood pressure high enough to perfuse his brain and body—and that was not a good sign. He needed constant attention, which meant the oncoming ED doc was going to have a hellish start to her shift.

Dammit! She was thinking about him again. Compton stopped walking for a moment, transfixed by her recollection of the man's face as he tried and failed to suck in air. Panic welled up, like vomit, in her throat. She'd almost sent him home! What had she missed? As she replayed the scenario yet again, a perverse corner of her mind supplied a mental soundtrack: thudding, ominous drumbeats. Why? Why had this happened? Maybe if she allowed herself one more time to run through it—

maybe if she wallowed in the shame and fear and dismay caused by almost losing this man, this young man, this presumably healthy man who should have been fine, who should not have keeled over, clutching his chest, just after he'd gotten his discharge paperwork—maybe if she grieved for this man, this almost death, maybe she could get it out of her system.

Up ahead, an empty bench guarded the entrance to Riverside at 103rd. Compton staggered to it and sat, letting her head fall into her hands so her hair covered her face, rocking back and forth like a disturbed person. The man was going to die; she knew it. She must have missed something, and he was going to die. It took all her energy to suppress the urge to throw her head back and cry.

A bit of time passed; Compton wasn't certain how long. She leapt up so suddenly and aggressively a passing dog walker stumbled backward, shrieking in terror. After she apologized to the dog walker, and for good measure the dog, she burst into a full sprint in the direction of her building. She was going to run out of time.

Thus preoccupied, Compton failed to notice something was off. It didn't hit her until she'd ridden the tiny elevator to their floor and entered the apartment and tucked her plastic clogs in the shoe drawer in the small mudroom off the foyer and padded down the hall to the kitchen, still panting from her exertions.

There was no noise.

Silence wafted through the air of their space on the twenty-first floor, the absence of sound a sound all its own. Compton prided herself on not thinking in clichés, but there was no better way to express it: normally, at this hour, all hell would be breaking loose in this particular smidgen of the Upper West Side. The two older children—seven-year-old Lawrence and four-year-old Rose—would be home, expressing at top volume their many urgent concerns, while Mildred, the sitter, juggled fat Baby Walter on one hip while blundering through the kitchen trying to throw together a snack. Mildred, a widowed woman in her sixties, was perhaps not the most fastidious of childcare providers, but she adored the children. An enthusiastic crafter, she engaged them in the kind of inventive home art projects touted by Pinterest devotees, using hot glue guns and googly eyes and little manipulatives like macaroni pieces and buttons. No discarded toilet paper tube ever went unutilized around here. The downside: Mildred's talents did not extend to tidying up afterward, so the place normally resembled the aftermath of an explosion at a preschool.

The children's afternoon urge to yip infected the two Maltipoos, Edgar and Horace, who would be performing gravity-defying backflips in a bid for attention. Ellis would be sequestered in his study, simultaneously drinking a scotch, working on his manuscript, and fuming at the soon-to-open financial markets in Asia, making a brave foray into the main body of the apartment from time to time with increasingly agitated demands for everyone to please bring it down a couple of notches. In short: bedlam.

Bedlam was the appropriate word. Compton had looked it up: the term derived from an old-school English lunatic asylum called Bethlem Royal Hospital, Bedlam for short, and it referred to a place of prevalent uproar and confusion, for which the Winfield-Compton residence certainly qualified. But it was also appropriate because, aside from her, everyone else in the home possessed an early-twentieth-century English-asylum-sounding name. *Mildred, Edgar, Horace, Ellis, Lawrence, Walter, Rose.* Even the doorman was named Frederick. You almost expected Noël Coward to burst through the door in a smoking jacket, spouting something cheeky.

"Mildred?" she called. "Lawrence? Rose?"

Silence.

Mindful of the time, Compton finished loading her carry-on and then trotted to Ellis's study. Empty. A quick check of the kids' rooms revealed them to be empty as well. She returned to the study, searching for the datebook Ellis sometimes still used. Had she forgotten he had a work event?

She couldn't find the datebook, but Ellis's desktop computer blinked to life when she sort of accidentally nudged the mouse with her elbow. She opened his calendar, which listed "Mtg W CF" for this evening. Clicking on the link, she tried to remember who CF could be. Ellis worked at a mid-level job in one of the private equity subsidiaries of a behemoth financial institution, and so was more frequently in a meeting than not. But this was his personal calendar, not his work calendar.

The link connected to an email. As her eyes flicked over the first few lines, it occurred to her that this was an invasion of her husband's privacy. Neither she nor Ellis had ever explicitly declared their personal correspondence to be off-limits to one another, but Compton considered her own email account to be private and she supposed Ellis thought the same. One of the earliest lessons they'd tried to teach the children involved a variant of the Golden Rule: whenever you find yourself justifying an action you're about to take, would you be okay with everyone on the internet watching you do it?

In this case, unequivocally: no. Reading someone else's email was not cool. But on the other hand—and here came the self-justification—it was a minor infraction. Compton didn't have anything to hide in her own emails. Ellis had given her no reason to think he did either, and he'd never expressly said she couldn't read his stuff. His computer wasn't even password protected, which, come to think of it, was kind of an odd omission for a guy who dealt with sensitive financial information and hostile takeovers. Was it possible that he wanted her to read it? Maybe he was having an affair and this was his passive-aggressive way of getting out.

But no: the email had nothing to do with an affair. It represented a betrayal of an entirely different sort. Compton read through the entire email chain, and then, uncertain if she'd comprehended the implications, prepared to read it again. Before she'd made it more than a couple of words, the door to the apartment banged open and a stampede of small footsteps headed in her direction. She stood so quickly a wave of dizziness nearly felled her.

The children blew past the study, not expecting anyone to be in it. But a moment later Ellis appeared, a sleepy Walter strapped to his chest in a patterned-cloth baby carrier. He rubbed his sparsely bearded chin—he'd been experimenting with beards lately—looking perplexed at finding Compton there.

"Hub City!" Ellis found it amusing to sprinkle little Compton-the-city-in-California references into his husbandly terms of endearment, although Compton went by her maiden name, not out of any particular allegiance to Los Angeles County but because she disliked her real first name. "What are you doing?"

She flopped a limp arm in the direction of his computer. "I just—"

Outside the room, the stampeding sound kicked up again. Five seconds later, Lawrence and Rose burst into the room.

"Fact," said Lawrence, skidding to a stop on his tiptoes. He rocked back and forth, his arms outstretched for balance. "Only dum-dums think unicorns are real."

"Unicorns are for real," protested Rose, but her cheeks had gone pink with worry. Today she wore her golden hair on the very top of her head, fixed in a ponytail that had been divided into three sections and braided into stiff, vertically oriented loops so that she appeared to be wearing a crown. A few downy curls escaped, framing her small face.

Lawrence teetered violently, his arms flying all over the place. "Fact. Rhinoceroses have one horn and so do narwhals. There are no unicorns."

"Mommy?" said Rose despairingly. A single shining tear dislodged itself from one of her round blue eyes and drifted down her cheek.

"Of course there are unicorns, darling. Uh, lovely pretend ones." Compton looked at Ellis for backup, lowering her voice. "Have you been letting Lawrence watch *The Office*?"

"Fact," said Ellis. "I have not allowed our seven-year-old to watch *The Office*, because that would be inappropriate." He lowered his voice to match hers. "I might have allowed him to watch a YouTube clip of Dwight a couple times."

"Dwight K. Schrute," yelled Lawrence, his voice full of admiration. He lost his balance and tipped over, taking Rose down with him.

"Where is Mildred?" Compton asked as Ellis picked up a sniffling Rose. He situated her against his shoulder and whispered nonsense into her pearly little ear until she giggled. Baby Walter, who'd somehow gone to sleep in the midst of all this, suddenly opened one eye and spied Compton. He thrust a chubby hand in her direction and let out a surprisingly manly burp.

Now they were all laughing. Despite the seeping away of the last period of time in which she could have finished preparing, Compton flopped on the tweedy man-sofa and pulled Lawrence up to her. Her oldest child, unlike Rose and Walter, possessed not one ounce of baby fat. He was all knobby knees and sharp elbows and frenetic energy. You'd have about as much success trying to cuddle a basket of forks as you would trying to cuddle Lawrence, but Compton gave it her best shot anyway. For a blissful moment, Lawrence stopped wiggling and settled against her, his warm, skinny little-boy body curved into hers. Ellis eased himself down on her other side, one hand steadying the bulk of Baby Walter in his sling and the other securing Rose on his hip. He deposited a beardy kiss on the tip of her nose. The five of them were crushed together, breathing almost in unison.

"I hope you have a wonderful time in Spain, C-dog," said Ellis. Now he kissed her ear. "You deserve a break."

"Thank you, honey," she said. She blew out a breath. "I read your email."

"Oh?" said Ellis. He stopped kissing her ear.

"You quit your job."

For a moment: silence. Not even Baby Walter breathed. Then Ellis let out a long, slow exhalation. "Yes," he said. "I did. I quit my job."

"And Mildred?"

"I gave her the day off," he said. "But I thought, you know: now we won't need her."

"We won't be able to afford her, that's for sure," Compton said. So many thoughts rushed into her mind at once it was a wonder her head didn't explode, spewing half-formed sentences all over the room like shrapnel.

Lawrence opened his mouth to say something—probably the word *fact*—but Ellis nudged Rose gently off his lap and spoke before Lawrence could get out a word. "You guys can have a half hour of screen time," he told the kids. For an instant they sat blinking, too astounded at this unexpected largesse to move. Lawrence recovered first, racing from the room before Ellis could retract the offer, Rose a beat behind him.

"Candee," said Ellis. Uh-oh: things had to really go south before he'd break out her given name. For the thousandth time, her mind detoured down a well-worn track: what the hell had her parents been thinking, giving her a name you typically encountered only in porn stars? And if they were dead set on naming her after processed sugar, why couldn't they have spelled *Candy* correctly? They hadn't even named her Candice.

"I'm so sorry I didn't tell you first." In an abrupt movement, Ellis pushed himself off the couch, standing with his back to her as he stared out the study's one window toward the thin green-and-brown band of Riverside Park, drowsy Baby Walter still strapped to his chest. "It was a spur-of-the-moment thing. I mean, I've been thinking about it for a while—you know how I feel about the direction we've taken lately—but last week I was on a plane and it occurred to me: I am absent in my own life. I see the kids for an hour a day if I'm lucky. We never have family meals, we don't see all the beautiful little milestones in our kids' lives." He turned back toward her, wearing a gaze so beseeching and earnest

Compton had to look away. "And for what? My job doesn't make the world a better place. I don't create anything real. I don't engage in innovative thinking that advances the course of humanity. I help amass monstrous wealth for a very small segment of people, often at the expense of other people."

She stared out the window, her mind still churning too violently to collect and order her thoughts. How much stress could one person tolerate in a day? The first idea to break through with anything approaching coherence was, unexpectedly, guilt. How awful to hate your life's work! Despite the brutal schedule and occasional agony of her own job, she derived from it a deep sense of purpose and engagement. In how many other occupations could you literally save lives on a daily basis? And she didn't merely save lives; even in the most mundane encounters, she wielded the power to make another human being's life a little bit less painful. This thought, of course, led to a dangerous off-ramp: the ruinous thought loop about the man who'd almost died. Who might, even now, be dying. She sucked in a shuddering breath, which Ellis, of course, mistook for distress at his announcement. Wordlessly, he stretched a hand in her direction, guilt etched all over his thin, semi-bearded face.

She'd known, of course, of the various dissatisfactions of her husband's job: his dislike of some of the men with whom he worked, his weariness with the fourteen-hour days and the constant travel, his philosophical differences with his immediate boss. But clearly she hadn't appreciated the depth of his discontent.

Her second thought, though, was less noble. How could Ellis do this without thinking of his family's financial stability? They owned investments and savings, of course, but less than you'd think: it was fiendishly expensive to live where they lived, not to mention their combined half a million dollars in educational loans. This was not a sentiment that could be expressed aloud to anyone outside New York, especially given that their lives were the very definition of privilege. But if they burned through their savings, Compton's job as an ER doc would not sustain them in their present home. Not even close; society valued hedge fund managers and M&A directors and venture capitalists about a zillion times more than emergency physicians. They'd have to leave New York.

This led to another uncomfortable issue. Was there an implied criticism of her parenting in Ellis's comments? *We* never have family meals; *we* never see our kids' milestones. Her job required switching from days to afternoons to overnights; she worked weekends and holidays; she worked through school plays and birthdays and illnesses. She had some control over her schedule, but there was a hell of a lot of unavoidable sacrifice in a career in emergency medicine. Was Ellis suggesting she'd neglected their family?

He must have read something of this on her face, because he crossed to her and picked up her hands, squashing Baby Walter between them. "You are the most wonderful mother alive," he said. "But your job is so much more important than mine. Yes, I think one of us should be home more, and I think it should be me. I know it means changing our way of life, Compton. But think of it: We can let Mildred go and I can be there for the kids. We can move to a small town somewhere"—(what??)—"and have a backyard and clean air and a garden to grow our own vegetables." (Again: what?? She'd never grown so much as a houseplant.) She forced herself to tune back in.

"But, honey," she said gently. "We don't know how to do all that stuff."

"Aha!" said Ellis in a voice of triumph. He darted over to his desk and opened a drawer, from which he extracted a stack of hardcover books. He held up the first one, entitled *Grow Your Own Food: A Homesteader's Guide to Going Off the Grid*. At what must have been an appalled look on her face, he hastily thrust that one to the bottom of the pile and started displaying the others, which were, thankfully, much saner-sounding tomes on wholesome ways to entertain children, tips for maximizing efficiency in housework, and natural products for lawn care.

"You're serious about this," she said, her voice still soft.

"I am. I am going to learn how to do this and make things nice for you." There was no mistaking the unapologetic joy in his voice. "We'll eat better, we'll be together more, and you'll sleep more." Sleeping more was Compton's most ardent desire in life; she'd worried her years of interrupted sleep had resulted in making her stupider. All those years of depriving her neurons of rest: it couldn't be good. "And," he added, in a less ebullient but still hopeful tone, "maybe I can finally sell my novel."

For a moment Compton allowed herself an imaginary window into what small-town life with a stay-at-home Ellis could be like. They'd get a real house, not an apartment. Since this fantasy could be constructed however she liked, she threw in all the clichés: a picket fence with climbing roses, an emerald-green lawn, a playhouse. A wraparound porch, enveloping an old Victorian with scalloped shingles and curly embellishments tucked into the eaves. Ellis and the children would have breakfast on the porch on clear, temperate mornings, dining on homemade meals both healthy and enticing: yogurt-berry parfaits; oatmeal pancakes; tiny, adorable vegetable quiches. (Perhaps country children were fond of vegetables.) Ellis would get into whole foods, frequenting farmers' markets and even actual farmers for the ingredients for their meals that he could not produce himself.

Once Lawrence had been deposited at the bus stop, Ellis would drop Rose at preschool and put the baby down for his nap, and then he'd make himself a nice foamy latte with their (new) custom espresso machine and settle into the bright, airy playroom/office at his computer terminal to bang out a thousand words or so on his novel. In real life, Ellis had been working on this book for at least five years, and while there were several things you could criticize about his lack of progress in getting it published, sheer output was not among them. Despite his demanding day job, Ellis produced words the way other people produced carbon dioxide.

Even though there was an unfortunate dearth of market interest in a three-hundred-thousand-word magnum opus about a financial wizard with a magical sidekick, Ellis had never given up searching for an agent. Meanwhile the book grew ever longer. Now that he no longer had a day job, who knew what lengths the novel might reach: Five hundred thousand words? A million words? It was not inconceivable.

Once Baby Walter was up, he'd abandon the computer and jog to the preschool with the double stroller—an eight-mile round trip, let's say—and fetch Rose, and then they'd play outdoors at the park or go on cultural expeditions or do art projects. Somewhere in there he'd manage to tidy up and get the laundry done and plan the wholesome, delicious dinner he'd serve later, at which point Compton would return home from work to find a sparkling home, a fine meal, and four grateful family members, all of them eager to hear about her workday.

Yes, this could work.

6 Team Mother Saints

HANNAH — BARCELONA, SPAIN

IT HAD BEEN TWO YEARS SINCE SHE HAD SEEN MOST OF THE women in their group. Every single month of those two years for Hannah Geier had been difficult, all of them following the same well-worn groove of soaring hope and crashing disappointment, to the point where the innate sunniness of her nature had begun to darken. As she scanned the crowded alley in the El Born district of Barcelona, she wondered if her friends would sense some fundamental change in her and find it off-putting.

She also wondered if she'd be the only one to have visibly aged. For the longest time, all of them had fallen into that category of doctor who had to fend off comments about appearing dangerously young to be practicing medicine. In her case, however, those remarks had fallen off lately. She knew why, even if she couldn't quite see it herself. When she took in her own reflection in the mirror each morning, it appeared to be composed of the same constellation of circles as always: round hips and bust, widely spaced round eyes, a round forehead atop round cheeks bisected by a roundish nose, and the kind of fair, easily flushed skin that offered the impression she was wandering around in a state of perpetual agitation.

"Hannah!"

She looked up to see her friend Georgia in all her resplendent glory: feathered red hair, flared jeans, some kind of long hand-crocheted coat. She, at any rate, appeared exactly the same.

"Babe!" Georgia threw down her handbag, flung up her arms, and abandoned her wheeled suitcase as she reached Hannah. The combination of her forward momentum and the slight downward slope of the street sent the suitcase careening away from them toward a group of elderly tourists. Startled exclamations issued from its members as the runaway suitcase kneecapped an old guy from behind; he stumbled forward, arms pinwheeling at the unexpected attack.

Darting toward him, Georgia retrieved the man's fallen hat, one of those Austrian numbers with a jaunty feather. "Sorry! I came in a little hot, my dude. But it's my friend! My friend!" She lifted Hannah and spun her around, kissing her cheeks. The tour group, charmed, waved away Hannah's attempts at another apology.

Georgia set her down and gave her an affectionate punch on the shoulder. "How are things in Del Mar?" she asked. "How's Harry?"

"Harry's Harry," Hannah said. Georgia nodded, accepting this as a sufficient description; the extreme extroversion of Hannah's husband, Harry, made him memorable to everyone he'd ever met.

"Where's everybody else?"

"We're the first ones." She indicated a nondescript blue door behind them, leading to the flat they'd rented. "I thought we'd wait out here 'til the others get here."

Hannah had been hopeful of spending more time with Georgia on this trip; as the only two of their group to live on the West Coast, she figured they'd share flights and layovers, thereby lessening the tedium of such a long journey. But Georgia had broken up the trip with several overnights in Charleston, visiting her old stomping grounds before arriving in Europe.

"Was it good going back to Charleston?"

Georgia didn't answer immediately. She pursed her lips, accentuating the sharp definition of her cheekbones, and stared at the sky. "I guess," she said finally.

"Georgia! What does that mean?"

"I felt different, being back there. It was like one of those dreams where you show up back in high school and you're naked, or you're in a play and don't know the lines. It was surreal and unnerving."

Hannah tried to mask the curiosity she knew must be flooding her face. This was more than she'd ever heard Georgia say on the subject of the cross-continental move she'd abruptly taken some years back. When Georgia had departed Charleston, she'd joined a practice in La Jolla, a gleaming, ritzy town north of San Diego, only thirty minutes away from Hannah, and had announced the world's longest engagement to a man Hannah still hadn't met. It was not surprising that Hannah hadn't seen this coming; Georgia typically played things close to the vest, checking in with the rest of them at infrequent intervals while divulging little of her circumstances. The little Hannah knew had been gleaned from cryptic allusions in group texts that she'd studied as assiduously as a World War II cryptographer, piecing together the outline of her friend's life as best she could from the careless fragments Georgia tossed out. Some dark trauma had been at the heart of this remarkable evolution involving Georgia's closest friend, another doctor, who had been fired from the clinic where they'd both practiced, but the details remained murky to Hannah.

"And then on the flight here they called overhead for a doctor. I could not believe this was happening to me again."

Now, this was a story Hannah *did* know. Georgia had met her fiancé, a man named Mark, when she'd responded to a flight attendant's call for help with a sick passenger on an airplane. It was the ultimate meet-cute: not only had she saved the life of the passenger, but it turned out he was a single, attractive man with an interesting job who'd been inadvertently poisoned. Only in fiction did such events occur, unless you were Georgia. Somehow she managed to barrel through life assembling an extraordinarily intense collection of oddball relationships.

"Did you have to save this one too?"

Georgia laughed. "Nah," she said. "It wasn't like last time when a stuporous man imprinted on me and I found love. This time it was a stuporous man who'd been overserved at an airport bar prior to boarding. He barfed and felt better, and we all went back to watching bad movies."

They settled against the pockmarked stone wall of the alley, waiting for the others. Of the seven members of their group of medical school friends, only Zadie and Emma had been unable to make the trip. Their absence sent a small dart of loss across Hannah's chest; she'd been longing to see them. As if reading Hannah's mind, Georgia remarked, "I know Emma can't come because her hospital is short a couple trauma surgeons right now. I forgot why Zadie said she couldn't come."

"Her kids."

"That's right. It's hard to go anywhere when you've got five hundred kids."

"Four," Hannah said. "It's only four kids. Her oldest, Rowan, is getting a big award for raising money for the Charlotte library."

A fond expression etched itself across Georgia's face. "You are so good at remembering everyone's details, HannahBear."

Zadie had the most children, but the friends were, overall, a fertile group; only Hannah and Georgia were childless. Emma had a little son, and Kira had both a boy and a girl. Compton and Vani each had three kids. Hannah had saved all the videos her friends sent in the years following medical school. She enjoyed seeing the attributes of her girlfriends—their physical features and endearing quirks—in smaller, newer forms.

Georgia took a sudden step forward. "I think I see them."

The street containing their apartment opened at one end to a bustling intersection of traffic and on the other end to a warren of ancient cobblestone alleys. Alighting from a taxi at the edge of the road, Kira, Vani, and Compton edged into view; Kira paid the driver as Compton hoisted a couple of bags from the trunk. As the taxi sped off, their heads swiveled in unison, taking in the narrow pedestrian passageway and the hordes of people and the strings of fairy lights crisscrossing the alley above their heads. Georgia jumped up and down, waving her arms, her hair going vertical in a flaming tower above her forehead. "*¡Hola, chicas frikis!*" she yelled.

Predictably, everyone in the vicinity turned. At the sight of Kira, Vani, and Compton, a ripple of visible alarm worked its way through the tour group of old people, who'd stalled out a few feet away. "There is more of them," one wit advised everyone in German-accented English. "Take cover."

After kissing everyone hello, Hannah guided them up to their flat. None of them bothered to unpack; they flung their stuff down, the others pausing as Hannah extracted from her carry-on two battered cardboard cutouts of her missing friends' faces, which she'd affixed to sticks: Emma, with her penetrating, leached-blue eyes and angular cheeks; Zadie, curvier, wearing an expression of affable warmth. Many years ago, on the inaugural run of one of these trips, they'd made a vow: anyone who could not attend would still have representation in group photos. Outside the flat again, she lined up her friends and handed out Flat Zadie and Flat Emma. They'd all perfected the technique of holding the cutouts at the right distance to make them appear to be life-sized and three dimensional.

"Wait!" said Compton. She dug in her shoulder bag, producing five clear plastic cups and a green bottle. "I know it's morning here, but I've got a teeny bit of Cava. Let's toast."

Although she herself did not drink, Vani helped Compton distribute the cups and pour the sparkling Spanish wine, her dangly earrings reflecting a dancing patchwork of stars onto the bottle. Everything about Vani reflected light: her shining black hair, the gloss on her lips. Even the beneficence of her smile seemed to throw illumination back into the universe.

"*Salud*," she said, and they tilted their glasses.

Or most of them did. Hannah noticed it even as she downed her glass: Georgia wasn't drinking.

She must have felt the weight of the stare, because her eyes widened as she thrust her midsection forward, her hands cupping her belly. "Welp," she said. "Not even here for thirty minutes and I'm already busted."

"Busted? For what?" asked Vani. She held out her hand to collect Georgia's cup and paused for a long expressionless moment as she took in its untouched contents. "No way," she said, finally. "No way! Are you kidding me?"

A secretive smile crossed Georgia's face. She undid a large brown button on her jacket and yanked it open, revealing a yellow T-shirt with the words *Let's Boogie, Mama!* emblazoned in bubble letters. The T-shirt must have been somewhat small to begin with, but now, stretched a bit, it revealed several inches of Georgia's taut but slightly widened waist, as well as a pair of jeans held together by a rubber band affixed to the button on one end and threaded through the opening on the other. "Y'all, I'm barely knocked up, but I already need to go maternity shopping," she said.

The blood in her head took an express elevator to Hannah's feet, leaving her momentarily off-balance. She waited until the dizziness cleared, allowing a muted but still genuine sense of joy to seep in. Perhaps she herself would never have a child, but at least she could be happy for Georgia. "This is the best news," she whispered. "You'll have such a beautiful baby."

Vani heard this, somehow, over everyone's exclamations. "Beautiful, yes. And he'll be . . . lively . . . for sure."

"She," said Georgia. "She'll be lively."

"You found out?"

"Nah. I'm not a finder-outer. We want the dramatic moment in the delivery room where Mark calls it out," said Georgia, referring to her fiancé. "But I already know it's a girl. It's like I can feel her thoughts."

Kira: "Don't go all woo-woo on us." She herself was the antithesis of woo-woo; she radiated logic the way other people might display a mood. As usual, she wore no makeup and her short hair appeared to have been hacked by a psychopath. Hannah squinted at her T-shirt—a raggedy olive-green thing printed with the logo of an automobile supply shop in Kinshasa, wherever that was—and admired for the millionth time Kira's disregard of her appearance.

"I'm not," said Georgia. "I thought this would never happen for me. I'm old. And now that it has, I'm telling you: it's not a boy. I don't know how to describe it, but she's definitely got a presence of her own."

Hannah froze at the word *old.* Around her, the street rippled and blurred, voices deepened and drew out into long, distorted foghorns. This happened sometimes, these little quicksands of pain appearing in the middle of a normal moment. She knew to let it pass, and it did: after only a few seconds, she could think normally again. She twisted her head from side to side: none of her friends had noticed. Good; she didn't want anything to take away from Georgia's moment.

Forcing herself to focus on something positive, she considered Georgia's declaration that she could somehow communicate with her child. It was a question she'd contemplated many times before: what elements of understanding could pass between a mother and child in the mysterious, unknowable world of the womb? At some point, the babies heard voices, felt movements, maybe even sensed the emotions of their mothers. Could they convey something back? Georgia's face, normally suffused with an animation that bordered on belligerence, had softened into an unfamiliar tenderness as she spoke of her unborn child. Hannah had seen it many times before in expectant mothers: fierce protectiveness mingled with beatific gentleness. She left her arm draped around Georgia. "Your baby will be the brightest, loveliest thing. Just like you."

"'And all my mother came into mine eyes. And gave me up to tears,'" murmured Vani, who could be relied upon to produce a literary quotation for every occasion.

"Who's that?" asked Georgia.

"Shakespeare. *Henry V*."

Georgia considered this, scrunching up her nose and then settling a hand on her hip. "'Mothers are all slightly insane.'" She grinned. "Salinger, *Catcher in the Rye*."

Vani was pondering her retort as a van puttered up and a young woman hopped from the passenger door. She scanned the alley, a hand shielding her eyes. "Hello," she called, waving a clipboard. "I am Isa. You must be the American doctors for my tour." In her mid-twenties, she was all shining skin and glossy brown hair and incandescent teeth. She walked toward the van as she spoke, motioning for them to follow.

Hannah regarded her friends as they answered Isa's questions about their specialties and locations. "Urology, San Diego," blared Georgia, thwacking herself in the chest. Compton took the next round, batting back answers to a series of questions about her life in New York City.

"I have always wanted to visit there," Isa said, twisting around in the passenger seat to face them. They'd jumped into the van, been introduced to the driver, and now found themselves sweeping along a winding road paralleling the Port of Barcelona.

"It's fun," Compton allowed. She waved an elegant wrist encased in a thin gold watch. "But it's like anywhere else: good points and bad points."

"Your name," said Isa. "Compton. Is that a nickname?"

"Compton is my last name, but also my nickname," Compton said, adding preemptively, "No one is allowed to mention my actual first name."

At this, Isa looked as though she would very much like to inquire as to Compton's actual first name, but, gracefully, she let it drop. The scenery shifted; the road widened to allow for a faster flow of traffic, and the city fell behind as they hit a stretch of open highway. In the distance, Isa pointed out the jagged peaks of the Pyrenees mountains before twisting backward again.

"And you." She motioned to Kira, in the middle row. "What is your job?"

"I'm an infectious disease specialist." Kira ran a hand through her short, flippy hair. "I'm based in Atlanta, where the CDC is, but before that I worked with an international medical group in Central Africa."

Isa turned to Vani. "And you?"

Vani beamed at Isa, because Vani always beamed at everyone. "I grew up mostly in Atlanta, but now I practice internal medicine outside a little town in Kentucky called Berea. I went to college there and came back after medical school and residency." She gestured to Hannah, in the back row. "And this is Hannah. She's an ob-gyn in San Diego."

"I do a little bit of everything," Hannah said. "Routine gynecologic surgeries, obstetrical care and deliveries, early workups for infertility."

For a mile or so, stillness permeated the van. Then Isa spoke, gesturing to the scenery, but Hannah, lost in her thoughts, did not hear her.

Every day, every hour, she confronted failure. Not the failure of other people; her own inability. In an irony so great it could only have been an intentional cosmic prank, she spent her days and nights engaging in the one activity most tailored to highlight what she could not achieve in her own life. Every day, every night, the same thing: each delivery of another woman's baby a reminder of her own childlessness.

She loved her job. Every woman who desired a child deserved to have one.

Still, sometimes at a birth she'd be swamped by grief. Her fingers and toes would sizzle; her arms would ache; her stomach would clench as if she'd been gut-punched. At these times she was grateful for her mask; behind it she'd clamp her lips until she felt them turning white. She'd sit as straight as she could, imagine her spine as a rod of steel, and force herself to inhale and exhale until she could offer congratulations to the new mother and father. No one wanted to see their obstetrician in pain on the happiest day of their own lives.

"Now we are almost to the base of Montserrat. Everyone, look, please." Isa pointed to a series of undulating, strange silhouettes against the sky. Monserrat loomed distinct from the surrounding mountains, bubbling and rippling with bizarre rock formations at its top and sides, some resembling rabbits or elephants or even more fantastical creatures: strange hybrids of humans and wolves and bears and swans.

The van ascended a series of switchbacks carved into the mountainside until it reached the monastery near the apex. Hannah wanted to touch the Black Madonna, the wish-granting icon for which the church was most famous, so they joined a queue leading toward the building.

"As the day goes on," Isa told them, "more people must wait to enter. It's good to get here before the Russians do, because they make a very serious line."

Pleased that they'd avoided hordes of serious Russians, the group entered a beautiful limestone courtyard in front of the church, where an enormous wire sculpture of a head confronted them. Beyond the sculpture, carved in stone above the entryway to the basilica, an empty-eyed Christ stared eternally into space, surrounded by the twelve apostles. Each man cradled the weapon that had killed him: Christ and Peter a cross, Thomas a spear, James a stone, and so on. Hannah been raised Catholic in the very Catholic city of Louisville—which meant she'd seen a lot of churches in her time—but the simple rebuke of this carving brought to mind all her own flaws. She allowed her gaze to drift over each of the disciples, marveling at the strength of conviction it must have taken to die a martyr.

Vani's mind must have traveled a similar pathway. "I wonder what weapon will fell each of us when her time comes?"

"Living in twenty-first-century America," Compton contributed, ever the ER doctor, "we'll probably all be shot."

"No. It will be a microbe, most likely," said Kira. As if they'd coordinated it, everyone offered her an elbow and then dissolved in collective laughter.

"I do not understand," said Isa, smiling in the way people do on the outside of an in-joke. "What is for the elbow?"

"Kira is afraid of germs, so she doesn't shake hands," explained Georgia.

"I'm not *afraid* of germs, I'm simply exercising good judgment when it comes to avoiding the transference of pathogens," said Kira.

"So." Isa swiveled. "I think you are each suggesting that death will come in some way related to what you see in your medical practice?"

"Hope not." Georgia wrinkled her nose. "I'd hate to get taken out by a giant penis."

A black-clad woman ahead of her in the line—a serious Russian, presumably—turned around. "Shhh!" she hissed.

Georgia appeared to be trying to stifle a laugh, but Hannah, chagrined, went mute as they entered the church. At the front of the sanctuary, a monk stood facing the congregation, singing what she presumed to be a Mass. A rough, slightly atonal quality marred his voice, but the song nonetheless conveyed an eerie beauty, reverberating within the dark walls of the basilica with the lilting, swoopy cadence of a bird. As he sang, an old woman, coughing, rose from a kneeling position in the back of the congregation. For a moment she swayed until a younger woman rushed to her side and guided her toward the door. As they passed, Hannah caught a glimpse of the old woman's face, pale and mottled, almost cyanotic. She faltered; did the woman need help? She took a few steps in their direction as the monk finished his song; within seconds, people rose and flooded the aisles, blocking her view of the woman.

Vani nudged her and they passed through the sanctuary to a staircase on the right-hand side of the altar, where a bottleneck in the line backed them up again. In the distance, ahead of them, Hannah could hear a cacophony of coughing.

"This site"—Isa waved her arms to encompass the basilica—"has been of religious significance since the Romans built a temple to Venus here." She stood one step above Hannah, leaning forward and whisper-speaking loud enough for all of them to hear. "Napoléon burned this church in the eighteenth century and Franco executed its resistant Catalonian monks in the twentieth." She paused as they ascended the stairwell a few steps toward a bend, then indicated two glittery mosaics depicting female figures on either wall beside them. "These are important," said Isa. "Do you know what they are?"

Kira peered at the wall closest to her. "I'm not clear on the terminology of medieval religious garb," she said, "but those look like nun outfits."

"These," said Isa, gesturing toward the nun wall, "are the Virgin Saints. And these"—she gestured toward the opposite wall—"are the Mother Saints. You can select on which side you would like to stand, and I will take your photo."

Georgia let out a sacrilegious snort, prompting the Serious Russian ahead of her to turn and glare again. She ignored this, grinning broadly. "I'm not going to get into the whole virgin/whore dichotomy perpetuated by centuries of patriarchal hypocrisy," she said, "but allow me to stipulate: none of us are on Team Virgin Saints."

Hannah fixed her gaze on the gold-etched mothers on the wall, forever frozen in postures of feminine impassivity in this windowless stretch of stairs, hidden and dormant, indistinguishable from their virginal counterparts. It rang true: throughout much of history, women had been judged not on their accomplishments or their characters or their worth as human beings, but on the simple dichotomy of their purity or their fertility, or, sometimes, their beauty. Where did that leave her? Her eyes filled and the figures blurred; for a moment all she could do was concentrate on swallowing her tears before anyone noticed.

"Yay, Mother Saints!" said Vani. "We'll do our picture there, please."

Everyone scrambled for the Mother Saints wall. Normally during a group photo, they all fought not to be on the end, ever since one of them figured out that whichever people bookended the line in a group photo appeared bizarrely wide compared to the others. But now Hannah slid soundlessly onto one end, hoping not to draw attention to the fact that of all of them, she alone did not belong on Team Mother Saints.

7 | *Respira Profundo*

COMPTON | **BARCELONA, SPAIN**

AS SHE WOKE FOR HER FOURTH DAY IN SPAIN, COMPTON REflected that separation seemed to be helping her process the seismic shift in her reality. They'd been so busy over the last few days—first Montserrat and then a tour of a vineyard and winery, followed by a series of boozy, boisterous meals in Barcelona and various museums, cathedrals, and walking tours—that she hadn't even had a chance to return most of Ellis's texts. The time difference and their deranged schedule made a video call impossible. Ordinarily, she'd have nurtured a tender, sentimental ache at the experience of departing on a transcontinental journey and not seeing Ellis and the children for a week while at the same time rejoicing in the decadent void of separation from Ellis and the children for a week. She could not, she mused, be friends with any woman who would be judgmental about this.

Almost as soon as that thought presented itself, though, another one subsumed it: at least one woman on this trip longed for a child she would perhaps never have. Hannah hadn't shared any of her feelings on the subject with them over the last several years; instead, after an initial burst of optimism, she'd gone radio silent on all her failed efforts to have a baby. All the friends knew, however, that she and her husband had sunk an enormous amount of time and money and energy into the process. They could infer from the things Hannah didn't say that she was losing hope. A flush warmed Compton's cheeks at the thought of the casual way she sometimes bitched about her kids around Hannah.

Speaking of cheeks, she'd been staring at her own in the mirror for at least a full minute without registering a single detail of her appearance. She blinked, refocusing. Early in her forties, she'd retained her health and strength. Compton assessed her face dispassionately; she knew her features lacked the geometry necessary for objective beauty: her face too thin, her nose too sharp, her gums too prominent. But these flaws were most apparent in isolation. When viewed in combination with her green eyes and the fine angle of her jaw and the fullness of her lips, people tended to believe her attractive. Still, she battled the irritating mental urge to rearrange her features into a more alluring configuration; she knew she'd bought into the ridiculous and unfair societal objectification of the female face and yet she hadn't quite evolved to the point where she was comfortable going out without makeup. Which was crap. She picked up her signature bloodred lipstick as banging sounded on the door. With five women sharing one bathroom, she'd been lucky to stay in here for more than thirty seconds without someone barging in.

It was Georgia. "Curtail your toilette, dude! I just drank three decaf espressos."

Nudging the door open with her foot, Compton shrank against the tiny sink. "Come in. Do you want me to leave?"

"Nah," said Georgia. "As a urologist, pee does not bother me."

"I think the issue is whether or not it would bother me," Compton said, but it was too late: Georgia had already taken advantage of the facilities. She finished with the toilet and yanked off her T-shirt and underwear, reaching for a towel only to discover they'd all been used. "Somebody fetch me a towel," she bellowed as she stepped into the glass-walled shower, undisturbed by the fact that her naked ass was on display.

"Still here," Compton said, pointing to herself. "Still standing right here."

"Yes, I see that. Towel?"

Hannah appeared in the doorway, her broad forehead puckered with worry at the sound of the shower. "We're supposed to leave in ten minutes."

"Can you get her a towel?" Compton asked, as Georgia turned off the water and stuck out her dripping head.

"I'm ready."

Nervously, Hannah stated the obvious. "You are not ready. You don't have on any clothes and your hair's wet."

Georgia's grin was both wicked and charming. "I'm getting in the van buck naked unless somebody brings me a motherfucking towel."

Compton wouldn't have thought it possible, but somehow a mere fifteen minutes later the van rolled away with all of them in it, more or less dry and dressed. Next to her, Georgia's thumbs were flying over her phone in a textathon with—Compton slid her gaze to the left—her friend Jonah. Jonah, a family medicine doctor, had moved from Charleston to San Diego at the same time as Georgia, following a debacle at their clinic in which he'd been targeted by a clinic administrator for providing medical therapies for transgender patients. Compton didn't know all the details, but she'd met Jonah in person when he and Georgia had visited New York City for Christmas one year. She'd taken a few days off work and they'd done all the things—the Rockettes; ice-skating in Central Park; fighting their way through the slobbering, shoving hordes at Rockefeller Plaza to watch the light-and-sound show adorning the Fifth Avenue exterior wall of Saks. Compton had expected an irritating slog through overcrowded venues she'd seen a billion times before, but the whole experience turned out to be a hoot. Jonah and Georgia insisted on embracing their Idiotic Tourist roles, wearing red scarves and berets, snapping photos of each other's foamy mustaches while drinking hot chocolate, joining in an impromptu caroling session in Bryant Park. How had she not realized what a gorgeous, smoky voice Georgia had? It had been years since Compton had seen her adopted city through fresh eyes: she'd forgotten what it was like to experience the sensation of sheer fun.

Georgia finished her texting session and dropped her phone back into her hippie-style patchwork satchel in time to tune in to today's tour. This morning they'd gotten a new guide, an earnest stoop-shouldered man named Raoul, whose enthusiasm for his native city could not be overstated.

"Now we ascend Montjuïc," shouted Raoul, "where played the American Dream Team in the 1992 Olympics." Dutifully, Compton looked up in time to see some buildings sliding by. "Farther down on this side," said Raoul, somewhat ambiguously, "you have the castle of repressed peoples." As one of those people who employed dramatic hand gestures to punctuate the end of every sentence, Raoul produced in Compton a constant urge to duck, even though she was sitting two rows away from him. Even the driver flinched from time to time. "Also: Joan Miró, the magic fountain, and far below is the bullfighting ring, a place of much evil and sadness for the bulls. Now, on your left . . ."

She listened with half an ear as Raoul launched into a short but impassioned discourse regarding the monarchy of Spain, which he was not keen on, and then for some reason segued into a description of a hellish-sounding club tower where forty thousand people went to party every night. Compton closed one eye and leaned her face against the cool glass of the van's large backseat window. They were headed to the top of Montjuïc to take a few selfies against the backdrop of the city before embarking on a tour of a few more of the highlights of Barcelona: the Gothic Quarter, the Basílica de la Sagrada Família, and Park Güell. She stole a moment to tap out a quick text to Ellis, who last night had sent a series of rambling questions regarding the location of various basic items of the children's. By unspoken mutual consent, they had not addressed the elephant between them, but Compton deliberately constructed her texts to sound kind and supportive. Even without a major life upheaval looming on the horizon, she'd been accused of sounding terse and bossy in past texts to people, and she didn't want Ellis to think she was dismissing out of hand his idea of moving from the city. The truth was she still didn't know what she thought about it. In fact, she decided, she would not think; there'd be plenty of time to sort this out with Ellis when she returned. For once in her life, she planned to defer responsibility and duty.

Atop Montjuïc the women scrambled over a series of stone terraces and sucked in their breaths at the magnificence of Barcelona, spread out below them in a patchwork of golden red-roofed buildings stretching all the way to the hazy mountains at the horizon. A few beams of sun shot though a sky roiling with heavy, fast-moving clouds, pooling in glinting ponds on the surface of the terraces.

"'I am alive, and drunk on sunlight,'" said Vani, spinning with her arms out, tilting her face to catch one of the pockets of eerie light. Above her, a golden, bare-breasted statue of a woman reclined atop a pedestal.

"Shakespeare?"

"George R. R. Martin. *Game of Thrones* series."

Compton pulled out her phone in time to capture a picture of Vani, eyes closed, face aglow against the backdrop of storm clouds. She looked impossibly beautiful, holy even, her black hair whipping in the wind, her pink lips parted just enough to reveal the iridescent edge of her two front teeth. An unpleasant shard of envy lodged itself somewhere in Compton's chest, despite the fact that Vani'd had the worst luck of anyone she'd ever known when it came to men. If a scoundrel or jackass or con man existed within a five-hundred-mile radius of Vani, she'd drift toward him with the helplessness of a hooked fish. Yet somehow she'd retained her rosy affect and—most unfairly—her rosy, lustrous skin. Compton had one doting, adoring man in her life, and yet she felt her face shriveling and wrinkling as if it were a sped-up documentary clip of fruit decaying.

A few feet away, a family of five stood taking a similar photo. Like her own family, this one consisted of a mother and a father, two sons, and a daughter, although these children seemed a bit older. The youngest of them, a boy of perhaps three, broke from the group, chugging away from his mother's side with a mischievous snort. She pretended to race after him, waving her arms in an exaggerated arc above her head as if she couldn't keep up. The other brother, delighted, began flailing around, and the father, catching on, left his place to chase him. Hannah joined Compton in watching the family's antics, her round face dimpling in delight.

"How sweet!"

Compton swung her attention from the family to Hannah, searching for any sign of pain. She found something unexpected: Hannah's expression changed from the sappiness she always displayed when gazing at a child to confusion to something a lot like horror. Compton followed her gaze.

Only the little girl stood rooted to the family's photo spot. Probably she was upset no one was chasing her. Compton's gaze had already started to drift when something unnatural in the child's stillness hooked her eye. In a flash, she understood.

The child was struggling to breathe.

Both Compton and Hannah bounded to the little girl's side, Compton silently and Hannah with an inarticulate cry. Georgia arrived a beat or two after them, skidding to a stop. Compton reached out first, catching the little girl as she crumpled. Her face had gone dusky but she didn't make a sound. She was so silent, in fact, Compton first assumed she'd suffered an airway obstruction; perhaps she'd been eating something and had swallowed wrong, lodging a foreign object in her trachea. On autopilot, Compton performed a finger sweep and then the Heimlich, but the child was in fact moving air. Compton tilted the child's head: an examination of her mouth and throat revealed no swelling.

For whatever reason, this child was not receiving enough oxygen.

A cry in the distance: the child's family raced toward them, both the mother and father exclaiming in panicked voices. Mustering her limited Spanish, Compton told them she was a doctor and that their little one wasn't breathing well; would it be okay for her to try to help? Georgia intervened, managing to get a limited history, or lack thereof; the little girl, the mother told her, had no chronic health conditions and no recent illnesses or surgeries. Compton felt the child's forehead.

Her skin burned with fever.

By now, a herd of bystanders clustered around them, jostling each other for a better view. At least three people held cell phone cameras aimed in their direction, trying, Compton supposed, to record this event in case they could generate a viral tweet about it later. Kira stood on the edge of the crowd, speaking rapidly into her phone. Compton slashed a hand through the air, motioning for everyone to get back, attempting at the same time to control her own choppy breathing enough to project authority. *Please,* she thought, inarticulate even to herself as a terrible grinding sound issued from the child's throat. *Please.*

Hannah dropped to her knees next to them. "Does anyone have an asthma inhaler?" she called out. "Or an EpiPen?"

No one responded.

A sudden certainty struck Compton: this little girl was going to die in her arms. She didn't have any means of administering oxygen; she didn't have any way to intubate. She took in the child's face; her closed eyes, the sweet curve of her lashes casting shadows against her round cheek. Air rattled through the puckered little rosebud of her lips, followed a moment later by a harsh, convulsive cough. A trickle of blood ran from the corner of her mouth. Compton stared at it, horrified. What was happening to this child?

Someone had already called for help; now, in the distance, a European siren aired its loopy shrill. Her friends gathered in front of her and Hannah. Kira's thumbs flew over her phone. Beside her, Hannah's lips moved in prayer. Georgia had wrapped her arms around the child's mother, murmuring something to the distraught woman in Spanish; beside them, the father crouched with the other two children, all of them wide-eyed and silent, their faces so horribly blank they might have been dolls.

Moving as gently as she could, Compton flipped the child onto her side and then onto her stomach, supporting her neck and head. "*Respira profundo, niña dulce*," she whispered into her ear.

Paramedics appeared and ushered Compton away as they started an IV and applied an oxygen mask to the child, easing her tiny body onto a stretcher. The last thing Compton saw was one foot, shoeless, splayed to the side of the gurney as it receded into the distance.

8 He Died the Hard Way

KIRA

BARCELONA, SPAIN

WE WALKED BACK TO THE BUS TO MEET RAOUL, WHO'D BEEN waiting with the driver and had no idea of what had just transpired. As the bus lumbered back down Montjuïc, headed for the Sagrada Família, none of us spoke; Hannah's hands covered her face, and Compton, her jaw set, stared out the window with a gaze so unfocused she could not possibly be seeing a thing. From where I sat, I couldn't see Georgia or Vani.

That limp child; that trickle of foamy blood leaking from the corner of her mouth. Since my conversation with Wally, I'd been monitoring Pro-EID Com in a half-assed way, but now I clicked the website with a greater sense of urgency.

Right away, it was clear there had been an uptick in internet traffic describing what initially sounded like an unidentified pneumonia and was now being classified as a novel virus emerging in northern Africa and southern Spain. Scrolling through the reports, I noted a change in tone and frequency over the last two days. The first report—categorized as "machine-translated" into English—had been posted about a week ago.

Because they were partly derived from nonmedical sites, culled from the internet at large, these reports tended to employ creative grammar and evolving information. Still, even though computers synthesized them, no report made it through the human chain of moderation unless it could be confirmed by a second, independent account of a possible emerging disease.

> On the evening of 21 June, an urgent report was circulated by medical sites on the internet.
>
> According to hospital authority, some medical institutions including Tangier, Rabat, and Kenitra have discovered patients with illness of unknown cause.
>
> The unexplained cases refer to the following phenomena that cannot be diagnosed: fever; pneumonia or acute respiratory distress syndrome; reduced white blood cell count; seizures; and pulmonary hemorrhage. The condition did not improve after administration of antibiotics, speculating of viral illness.
>
> No evidence exists of human-to-human transmission, and citizens need not panic.

Next, I found the report Wally had referenced, of the physician who'd died in international waters aboard the Tangier-Tarifa ferry, which had gained very little notice at the time. Following this report were a few others, continuing in a similarly vague, poorly translated vein until I reached the date of June 24, the day before yesterday. On that date, the reporting from the region increased in length and clarity but was still sandwiched between a number of other routine infectious disease reports from across the globe: dengue, Lassa fever, norovirus, malaria, measles, various forms of encephalitis, and some horror called the tomato spotted wilt virus, which was inexplicably attacking potatoes, not tomatoes. I squinted at the screen through a glare from the van's windows, tuning out an impassioned monologue from Raoul on the unbeatable views from the balconies of the world-famous Hotel Miramar.

> Authorities have made preliminary determination of an illness caused by a potentially novel (new) virus, identified in a hospitalized patient in the Spanish city of Cádiz. Next generation gene sequencing of the virus is underway, using an isolate from a patient sputum sample.
>
> Preliminary [rapid] RT-PCR indicates an RNA virus, although circulating H1N1 or any known strain of influenza have been excluded. Subsequent testing ruled out SARS-CoV, MERS-CoV, other coronaviruses, and adenovirus.
>
> According to local authorities, some patients have presented with severe viral illness, but there is no current evidence of easy transmission between people.
>
> Further data is being collected to assess the epidemiology and the clinical characteristics of the illness. More comprehensive investigation is also required to determine the source and modes of transmission as well as to facilitate public health and safety countermeasures. Spain, Morocco, Algeria, Niger, and other reporting areas will continue to monitor and report to the WHO and will be provided with clinical and epidemiological support in response to this novel virus outbreak.
>
> All countries are encouraged to conduct disease detection and response. People demonstrating clinical signs and symptoms of illness plus travel history to affected areas should be screened at international airports and borders. However, no travel restrictions are recommended at this time.
>
> External Relations and Communication
> World Health Organization

So: the World Health Organization was now involved. No major alarm bells rang in any of these reports; they'd even specifically mentioned the lack of evidence of any person-to-person transmission. Still, as every infectious disease researcher in the world knew all too well: absence of proof was not proof of absence.

NONE OF US spoke as we meandered through the throngs of people staring upward at the Basílica de la Sagrada Família. Inside the cathedral, I gaped at its otherworldly beauty. Massive branching columns, each of unique design, soared to the lofty ceiling. The effect was that of standing in some dazzling supersized forest, alight from the stained glass of each facade. Gaudí, the architect, had structured the cathedral to utilize the sun as an active element in its artwork. Composed of warm primary colors, the west-facing facade mimicked a sunset, while the cooler blues and greens of the east-facing facade provided an illumination more representative of morning. At this hour the midday sun lit the windows equally, those on the west casting a red glow on a line of people kneeling in prayer.

In the middle of the row, a young ponytailed woman, dressed in jeans and a blue college sweatshirt, coughed with such force she bent all the way forward until her face grazed the stone floor. She heaved herself to her feet, her chin tucked into her elbow, and disappeared down a nearby staircase, the echoey sound of her coughing drifting up from the floor below.

The last person in the line, Hannah, didn't stir at the girl's departure. She clasped her hands in front of her chest, her eyes closed but face tilted downward, her fair hair turned bloodred in the streaming light.

Of all of us, Hannah is the most devout; she attends church every Sunday when not on call and belongs to a variety of committees and groups in her San Diego Catholic community. Vani is a faithful Bahá'i and Emma a secular agnostic, Compton a Christmas-and-Easter Christian, Zadie a member of a progressive Presbyterian church. Georgia, I believe, ascribes to some facet of Christianity more in tune with spirituality than doctrine. I myself hold no belief in any organized religion. We all maintain different mindsets when it comes to the question of the divine and yet I've never heard a critical word from any of us about anyone else's beliefs or lack thereof.

I waited until Hannah completed her prayer, and we walked, side by side, from the church. Outside, joined by Vani, Compton, and Georgia, we wandered to a small park across the street and snapped a photo with the cathedral in the background. Before anyone could leave, I clapped my hands.

"I have something to tell you before we go to Seville tomorrow," I said.

This, I realized as soon as the words left my mouth, was a bad opener. Immediately, a chorus of unsolicited speculation rose. I was back with Declan! I was pregnant! I was moving to Spain!

I waited until everyone settled down. "There've been some interesting reports on Pro-EID Com."

The chorus rose again, only this time it consisted of groaning.

"No, listen. This could affect us."

Compton: "What, exactly, is an EID? I thought that had something to do with bombs."

"You're thinking of IEDs. Improvised explosive devices? That's different." Before I could finish my answer, Georgia butted in.

"Let me guess. It's an advance warning system that the plague is upon us."

"Yes. No. Not exactly. It's short for the Program for Monitoring Emerging Infectious Disease Communications, one of the largest outbreak-reporting systems in the world. It started as an internet monitoring system, so it picks up all kinds of nonmedical chatter about diseases and toxins and then filters them through a group of experts who moderate the reports. There are dozens on any given day, from all over the globe.

But in the last week, there've been some concerning reports from this region."

That quieted them down.

I summarized what I knew so far: scattered across a few countries, there had been a handful of illnesses and deaths that appeared to be from an unknown virus. Symptoms varied but included pneumonia and bleeding from the lungs. At least one person—a doctor—had died in passage across the same channel we'd be traveling tomorrow, possibly from this unknown illness.

My friends listened until I finished. The first to speak was Compton, who, as an ER doctor, presumably knew more than the rest of them about infectious diseases. "Is it a *new* new virus or an antigenic shift in one we already know?"

Georgia pointed at her. "We're going full-on nerd for the first question? Surely that's not the most relevant thing."

I answered Compton's query nonetheless. "They haven't identified it yet, but it's an RNA virus. It's being genetically sequenced right now, but I'd expect to hear any time now what viral family it's in."

"Is it contagious?"

Another good question: something infectious—like food poisoning, for example—wasn't necessarily contagious from one person to another. Often with emerging illnesses, a person would come in contact with an animal and catch the disease but wouldn't transfer it to another person.

"They don't know yet. So far, there's no indication of that in the reporting. There are some indications it is not easily transmissible between people."

Compton again: "Only a handful of cases?"

"That's right."

Georgia cocked her head. "I assume you're telling us this since we're headed to Seville and Morocco next? Do you think we need to cancel?"

I hedged. "I don't want to make decisions for you, especially after what happened on Montjuïc."

"Wait." Hannah. "You think that child could have had this virus?"

"I have no idea. There's no way to know. We don't even know if there is a new virus in Barcelona, let alone whether it's circulating or whether any given person has it."

"What would we do if we didn't finish our trip?" This came from Vani, who until now had been silent. "Stay here and risk getting trapped? Get on a flight home with people who could be sick? Would that be any safer?"

"I honestly don't know, guys."

Compton's face had gone very still. "That blood. The little girl."

No one responded to this.

Vani spoke again, quiet trust in her eyes. "Kiki, of all of us, you're the most qualified to assess this. I think it should be your call."

"I don't want to decide for everyone. I'm comfortable going. I mean, I don't have a choice about going to Seville; my children are there."

"I trust you." Hannah spoke gently. "I'll do whatever you do."

"It may be nothing—just isolated but different illnesses. It could be something we already know. Or it could be a new zoonotic disease. And even if it is, a lot of these zoonotic infections aren't easily transmitted. But it's not without risk."

"Zoonotic means it jumped from an animal to a human, right?"

"Right. It's a disease from a bug that originally colonized an animal."

Georgia stood from the bench. "I'm in. I'm not canceling the trip because a couple people out of a hundred million might have SARS or something."

"SARS is caused by a coronavirus. This may not be a known pathogen."

She waved a hand. "Whatever. You'll keep checking with the other plague nerds, right?"

"Of course."

"Then I'm in. If new info comes in and we need to abort, then we'll make that call. But I'm not canceling for this."

Hannah and Vani nodded agreement.

"You're forgetting something." We all looked: Compton. "It doesn't matter what we do at this point."

"Hey, what do you mean?" asked Georgia, but I was already nodding. I knew where Compton was going with this.

"You mean if the child had it, we're already exposed."

"Yes." Compton's hand drifted to her pale throat as she swallowed. "Or I am, anyway, and probably Hannah. And possibly the rest of you as well. So it might not matter what we do now."

"Well, if we knew there was a contagious disease and we knew we were infected, it would matter to anyone we come in contact with," I pointed out. "But that's too many hypotheticals at this point. We don't know any of that. Do we cancel our entire trip on the basis of so little information?"

"Then we're agreed," said Georgia. "We go."

"MOMMY!" BEAU BURST from the building and attached himself to my waist, followed by Rorie, who slouched out behind him. I breathed in the fragrance of them: Beau's little-boy scent of fresh grass and pencils, Rorie's coconutty sunscreen. I hadn't slept well last night, waking in the unfamiliar darkness more than once to find myself replaying the scene in the park, especially the frantic, helpless face of the sick child's mother. After my own kids began to squirm in my arms, I let them go. Beau sprang to Vani, clamping his arms around her and burying his face in her midriff. "Auntie Vani! Welcome to Sevilla!"

"My Beau," said Vani, kissing the top of Beau's head as Georgia, grinning wickedly, introduced herself to Rorie with a raised elbow.

In return, she received a snort. "I see you know my mom pretty well."

"We do, yeah." Georgia winked. "I'd try to get you to like me by offering you some dirt, but your mama is damn near perfect."

Rorie snorted again but couldn't repress a little smile. She'd dressed in frayed shorts and a knockoff pair of some fashionable brand of tennis shoes, leaving bare an endless expanse of lean brown leg. Mascara coated her curly eyelashes and a pair of giant gold hoops drooped from her ears, transfiguring the contours of her face into something almost unrecognizable. A few months away from her fifteenth birthday, she was at once breathtakingly young and startlingly adult.

Hannah was introducing herself and Compton to the kids when her eyes cut to the side. I sensed Declan standing behind me before I saw him. I could smell him too, some beguiling, masculine atomization of clean sweat and sex and reading books in bed. I've always possessed a keen sense of smell, which is not always a blessing in a field where dead bodies occasionally confront me. Next to me, the body language of my friends shifted; they'd seen him too. I could read their eyes, engaged and curious but reserved, driving home the realization that they suspected we might still be hooking up. As a group, we'd had our ups and downs with men over the years; there was a rule, both spoken and unspoken, that you didn't judge another woman's man unless he did her wrong in some way, at which point you were free to unleash holy hell upon him. Many an unsuspecting dude had withered under the combined force of our solidarity though the years.

Blessedly ignorant of this, Declan did his charming thing, melting everyone with his easy humor and fetching accent, introducing himself and explaining in general terms what he did for a living as we walked to a sidewalk café near the cathedral and palace. Sunlight doused everything in gleaming gold; warm, temperate winds buffeted our bare arms and ruffled our clothes. Tourists from all corners of the globe overran this part of Seville, their happy chattering filling the air with the sound of a half dozen languages.

"What does your company work on?" Vani asked, pushing her glasses up on her nose. They were her favorite pair, cat's-eye-shaped, with a tiger print. Together with her bright red lipstick, they gave her the countenance of a Bollywood star in a 1950s flick.

"Antivirals," said Declan. Nothing changed in his face; no dimming of his gaze, no loosening of the fine muscles around his eyes or mouth. His voice was the same. But I sensed it all the same: despair. He leaned into me briefly, whispering in my ear: "It's bad news. I'm worried we won't get approval."

The misery in his voice—even in a whisper—was unmistakable.

I wish I could have consoled him! I know—now—that human trials would indeed take place, but not as anyone could have envisioned them then. Declan himself would not be involved. By the time the virus closed his lab, they'd have only a handful of doses of the newly modified drug; of the five doses in existence, four would spoil in the powerless freezer. The fifth and final dose would be divided prior to Declan's illness, half of it making its way to America with me, where it would be divided again, until at the tail end of the pandemic, I'd find myself in possession of a fraction of it, enough to—maybe, possibly—treat one person.

Still, I knew none of this then. I wanted to react to Declan's whisper, but he squeezed my hand and offered a barely perceptible shake of his head: *not in front of the others.* I squeezed his hand back, hoping he could tell from the gesture how heartbroken I was for him. For a few minutes we held hands as we walked, silent as the others chatted.

"Declan, I don't recall how you and Kira met." Compton spoke as we found chairs under a wide awning, cool appraisal in her eyes.

"I heard her speak at a virology conference maybe five years ago," said Declan.

If I hadn't known better, I'd have believed him to be in a jaunty mood; he clearly wanted to conceal his emotion so as not to impact our outing. Warmth flooded me at this small kindness; I knew what it was costing him not to react to his devastating news.

He ramped up his smile to full wattage, and Compton blinked and smiled back, dazzled. If I'd been holding on to any residual tension regarding this meeting—the collision of my worlds—it drained away at Compton's expression. She was the least dazzleable of us. Still, I sought out Vani's face and found her looking directly at me. She jerked her chin in a subtle but unmistakable nod, widening her eyes. I could read her expression perfectly: *If you don't want him, I'll take him.*

I love all my girlfriends, but for Vani, I'd open a vein. She's the one whose opinion matters. She's the only person on earth who loves me without complication or reservation. She's never criticized my decision not to move to Spain to be with Declan, but sometimes I think she wonders if I'll ever have a functional relationship with a man again. Which, again, is not to say she judges me: of all our girlfriends, she's the only one who knew my husband, Daniel. She understands.

"You know what?" Declan's eyes moved between me and Vani. "I don't believe I've ever heard the story of how you ladies got to be such good friends."

"Zadie and Emma knew each other from college," I said, happy to change the subject. "Then in med school they somehow pulled us all together. Within a month, the seven of us were inseparable."

"Kira and I met the first day of medical school," said Vani, winking at me. "It was instant love. Plus we had a . . . very interesting cadaver to dissect."

"Interesting how?" asked Declan.

Laughter rang around the table.

I still retain a clear memory of my first glimpse of Vani. The week before classes began, the school had hosted a few social events on the downtown campus for the incoming first-years to get to know one another. At one of the evening events, I drifted toward one of the tables, uncertain as to how to approach anyone. Quite a few people appeared to already know each other; in the center of the room, two Amazons held court surrounded by a bobbing, jostling sea of guys. Later that week I'd learn their names—Zadie and Emma—and realize Emma disliked big social situations as much as I did and Zadie was one of those rare people oblivious to her own charm. But in the moment, I hated them. All that laughter; all that blond hair. How had they gotten into medical school?

"Good grief," said a musical voice at my left ear. "I think these cookies are recycled from yesterday's luncheon."

I peered at the table. Grease-spotted paper plates, the same mound of yellow-frosted lard that had been foisted upon us at the last event. Wait a minute . . .

"I think these same cookies have been at every function this week, actually," I said, turning to see who was standing next to me. "Somebody must feel strongly about reusing them."

A woman: dark, smooth hair, flawless dark skin, lovely curving eyes and lips and cheeks. Was everyone here going to resemble a supermodel? At least this one wasn't a tall skinny blond.

"Kira Marchand," I said, nodding formally.

"Vani Darshana."

The next week, on our first day, the silent herd of first-years trundled to the gross anatomy lab. This room, of course, had been the subject of much nervous speculation at our pre-parties. Most of us were twenty-two-year-olds; few if any of us had ever seen a dead body, let alone dissected one. In my fevered imagination, I'd conjured images of professors hunching over corpses in dim, chiaroscuro basements, spotlighted by pools of sickly green light as onlookers lurked behind medieval death masks. Instead, we were ushered into a spacious, airy room on the top floor of the building, ringed on three sides by high transom windows offering a view of vivid blue sky and delicate, lacy clouds. The windows were too high on the wall for anyone in the adjacent sky-rises to peer in; this, our instructor told us, was a good thing, since the closest building housed an old-folks home.

A few uneasy chuckles; nobody was quite sure if this was a joke. We shuffled one at a time to the corner of the room to receive our assignments and then to our respective tables. For the remainder of the year, we'd be clustered in a group of four around our particular body, which we'd dissect slowly, one organ system at a time.

"Look down," said the instructor, a short, jovial man with wide brown eyes. "The person on the table before you is both your patient and your teacher. These are all individuals who willed their bodies to medical science, many of them because they experienced great physical suffering in their lifetimes and they wished to spare others the same fate. They believed that because of you—the next generation of physicians—the world will achieve some alleviation of the misery stemming from our most profound maladies. To this noble aim, these human beings have sacrificed their earthly bodies. Treat them with reverence and respect and gratitude." He relaxed his posture, and even from a distance, I could see a twinkle light his eye. "That being said, this is not a funeral. You are allowed to bond with your classmates and enjoy this learning experience. The practice of medicine is fraught with sorrow, yes, but also saturated with *joie de vivre*. Have some fun this year, y'all."

I met the eyes of my tablemates. To my relief, I'd been paired with Vani, and also, to my consternation, with the two lithe blondes I'd noticed at the party. The four of us silently assessed one another and then, as instructed, looked down at our table. After a few moments, we became aware that everyone in our half of the room was also looking at our table. At first I thought it was because Zadie and Emma and Vani drew so much attention—from both males and females—but it was not anyone living who'd caught the eye of our classmates.

It was the dead.

Like all the other cadavers in the room, our cadaver was covered with a sheet. In the center of the mass—not quite midway between the round bulge of the forehead and the shelflike endpoint of the feet—a cylindrical protrusion rose under the sheet, looking for all the world like a foot-high tentpole. There was no mistaking what this was.

Our patient—a man, evidently—had died with a massive erection.

Which we'd have to dissect.

At the next table over, a freckled, redheaded woman leaned toward me. "Dude," she said. "I gotta watch when you guys pull down your sheet. Respectfully, of course. That's gotta be"—she gestured toward the tentpole—"some kind of world record."

Her partner, a tiny guy with small round glasses, cleared his throat. I thought he was going to reprimand the redhead, but instead he bowed and genuflected toward our cadaver. "I am not worthy," he said. The other guys at their table—two big football-player types—crossed their arms and nodded with faux solemnity. "He died the hard way," one said.

It was respect, of a kind.

I shifted from foot to foot, trying to stem a surge of nausea. Not at the thought of the cadaver—I'm not squeamish or sentimental—but at the thought of spending a year with a roomful of people infinitely cooler than me. I'd never had a boyfriend, let alone interacted with a live penis. My first real glimpse of the male physique would be arriving in the company of an overendowed corpse and a trio of socially graceful hotties. This was not how I'd pictured med school. Maybe I'd made a mistake.

Across the room, the instructor gestured for our attention and sliced a hand through the air as if signaling a race. "You may remove your sheets," he said.

I met Vani's eyes again, trying to contain the distress in mine. I must have failed, because she reached across the table and squeezed my hand. "I'm glad you're my partner," she said. She reached her other hand for Emma, who then reached for Zadie, who then reached for me, so the four of us were linked around the giant erection as if we were about to break into some kind of ultra-bizarre maypole dance. I felt the beginnings of a grin.

"Here's to the best year ever," said Vani.

DECLAN LISTENED TO the story of our first week—gross anatomy lab and all—with the same series of expressions as most men who've heard the story: keen interest, followed by a smirk, followed by an expression of abject horror at the thought of a posthumous penis dissection by a group of young women. "Aaah," he said weakly.

"Over the years, the way we met has spawned a lot of penis jokes." Vani motioned to Georgia. "Georgia's the best at them, obviously."

"I'm a urologist," explained Georgia to Declan, "not a penis connoisseur. But yes: I know plenty of male anatomy jokes. It's actually a requirement for our board certification."

"It's not," Hannah assured Declan, even as Georgia launched into one.

She pointed at him. "Unscramble the letters P-S-N-I-E to name a part of the human body that works best when erect."

"Penis?"

"*Spine*, you pervert. Nice try."

"Aaaah," said Declan again. He sat without speaking for a moment, blinking his blue eyes before giving himself a little shake. "Right! Spine!" He motioned to the server. "Anyone up for sangria?"

As everyone chatted and drank, my phone buzzed in my bag. I ignored it, caught up in watching the faces of my friends and my children and even my ex-boyfriend. With the exception of Wally, Zadie, and Emma—and my elderly parents in Kentucky—everyone I truly loved sat at this table, on this sunny sidewalk, in this ancient city that had hosted a stream of human life for more than two thousand years. Georgia: telling a story, laughing so hard she snorted her drink through her nose. Beau, soaking it all in, consumed with pleasure at being included. Rorie, trying and failing to hide her fascination at the adult conversation. Compton's wry commentary, Hannah's radiant goodwill, Vani's beneficence.

Later, looking back, this would become the moment in time from which I'd divide my existence into two sections. Mere moments later, I'd reach for my phone and know, immediately, that for me at least, nothing would ever be the same again.

9 The Dumbest Crime in History

HANNAH | SEVILLE, SPAIN

HANNAH, SEATED NEXT TO KIRA'S SON, BEAU, AT THE SIDEwalk café, turned to him somewhat shyly. She'd only seen him in person once before, when he'd been one or two years old, and since that time, obviously, he'd changed. He didn't look much like Kira. She had a wiry build and wispy brown hair, which she kept cut short; he was little but sturdy, with wild curls, dark brown at the roots, lightening to a sun-kissed bronze at the ends of the springy coils. Hannah tried to recall the appearance of Kira's husband, Daniel, but she'd seen him only in photographs.

Sensing her interest, Beau smiled at her, revealing a dimpled cheek. "Which friend are you?" he asked politely.

"I'm Hannah," she said. "I live in California and I'm an ob-gyn." Oops. Would a little boy have the faintest glimmer of the field of obstetrics and gynecology? Probably not. "That means I'm a doctor for ladies and I deliver their babies," she added.

"Did you always know you would be a doctor?"

For an instant, she considered a rote answer, but something about his solemn posture and candid little face convinced her not to soften the truth. "No," she said. "My father died when I was about your age. It was hard, the worst thing I could have imagined. But there was a man, a brain surgeon at the hospital, who spent quite a lot of time talking to me and my brother about what was happening. He was a big, funny guy—the opposite of me—but he had a way of looking right into our eyes and calming us down. He gave us comfort and understanding when we were terrified and confused. He used his expertise—his special skills—to try to save my dad. He couldn't do it, in the end, but I was aware he was one of the only people who could have even tried. And I loved the idea that there were people whose job was to save other people, or console them, or take away their pain. So from then on I knew that I wanted to do that too."

"Did you try to be a brain doctor?"

Hannah smiled. "No. That wasn't for me. I love children. I love bringing them into the world and taking care of their mommies."

Beau nodded. "That sounds wonderful. I bet you love it."

"I do," she said, relieved he wasn't grossed out. "It's usually a very happy job." She hurried on before he could ask what she meant by *usually*. "Do you like babies?"

Beau appeared to be giving his answer consideration before he spoke. Despite the dimples and the round cheeks and the glorious springy hair, he gave off the serious aura of one who pays careful attention to his environment and the impact of his own actions; he was the antithesis of impulsive. Now, that *would* be like his mom. Kira was famously intolerant of superstition and intuition, she noted minutiae that seemed to slide by most people, and she had zero tolerance for people who asserted opinion as fact. Along with Emma, their friend in Charlotte, she was the most logical person Hannah had ever known.

But if Beau possessed his mother's inclination toward literality, he tempered it with kindness. "I think I would love babies very much," he said. "I would like to know how they understand things, since they don't have words."

"There's a whole field of science studying that," Hannah told him, delighted. "It's called developmental psychology. The researchers have to come up with clever ways to assess the babies, since they can't use language."

Beau listened, his little head tilted and his big round eyes locked on hers as she told him about famous experiments in child psychology: the visual cliff, the broccoli-goldfish challenge, the emergence of empathetic crying. Around them, the others were talking about work as the server delivered plates of small appetizers to their table. She scooted her chair closer to Beau.

"You're saying babies care about what happens to other people before they can even talk," said Beau, his eyes shining. "This is a wonderful kind of science."

"Is *wonderful* your favorite word?" asked Hannah. She couldn't suppress her own smile. What a precious child.

"Yes. My other favorite word is *facetious*."

Before Hannah could inquire as to the provenance of that last term, something in the adult conversation caught her ear. Compton, on her other side, leaned across the table to direct a question to Declan.

"How'd you get interested in developing antiviral therapies?"

"Guilt, mainly," said Declan. He leaned against the wall of the entryway. "I got arrested in grad school and had to make amends."

Georgia perked up. "Now, *that* sounds interesting."

He smiled, splaying the fingers on both hands in an *I'm guilty* gesture. "I was getting my graduate degree in pharmaceutical chemistry and I messed up a lab experiment."

Georgia stared. "What happened, did you accidentally clone Hitler?"

A contrite expression crossed Declan's face. "There's more to it. It wasn't my lab work. It wasn't even a grad school thing—I, uh, broke into the lab where my buddy was a teaching assistant for one of those college bio course experiments where you grow bacteria from your own cheek swab. I thought it would be funny to switch it up so it looked like his sample had grown some sexually transmitted monster. He'd identify it for the students, expecting to see lactobacilli or whatever, and instead it would be gonorrhea. Hilarious, right?"

Now Kira interrupted. "The first time I heard this story," she said, "my initial reaction was not dismay at Declan's misdeed—which it should have been—but a burning question."

Hannah had no idea what Kira meant, but next to her, Compton snickered. She cocked a finger at Declan. "Yep. Where exactly did you come by a sample of gonorrhea?"

"Nailed it," said Kira. "And he gave me some innocuous answer, but I couldn't quite banish a flicker of suspicion, right? No matter how much he claims a policy of honesty, no man on earth is going to fess up to committing a lab crime while also admitting he's been infected with an STD. There are some things one does not share."

"It's a toss-up," said Declan, still wearing an easy grin. "Which is worse: getting gonorrhea—it wasn't mine, on my honor—or getting arrested?"

"Arrested?" Hannah asked. Her voice came out squeaky. "For that? Did you infect the whole biology department?"

"No. Worse. It was late and I was drunk and knackered and it was a stupid, stupid idea to begin with, but I'd already told the other guys I was doing it, and for some reason I felt I had to see it through."

Compton's face displayed dawning comprehension. "You messed up someone's research."

He nodded. "Yeah. Not just research but an entire room."

"But how is that even possible? Surely screwing up a petri dish or two wouldn't tank an entire lab."

"It wouldn't, no, but I made the very unfortunate decision to have a smoke while I was in there. I was a chimney back then, couldn't make it two hours without a cigarette, plus I was nervous. I lit a burner and caught my hair in it when I leaned down." He waved a hand at his hair, longer in front, clipped short in back. "Had long hair then. Managed to get my head put out but the sprinklers activated. It was possibly the dumbest crime in history."

"The university pressed charges?"

"They did, yes."

"Did you go to jail?"

Declan waited a moment and then said: "I didn't go to jail, except for the night I spent there after my arrest. By then I was wrecked, absolutely demolished with shame. One of the faculty, a virologist named Ian Murray, called me into his office a few days later and offered me a position in a new lab he was starting in Spain."

Hannah tried to work this out. "Unpaid? As penance?"

Declan shook his head. "He paid me. Not well, of course. But Murray said he didn't believe in people working for free. He'd been planning to leave the university anyway to run his own private biotech lab where he didn't have the same funding and oversight constraints, and he needed an assistant. He said with my test scores and research proposals he thought I'd be a good candidate when I finished my degree, but even more, he thought my guilt would make me loyal. And he was right."

He went on to recap his career since then: before Murray died some ten years later, the fledging lab he'd founded had attracted the interest of a group of California venture capitalists intrigued by the research the company had been conducting. With a combination of loans and increased funding, Declan had advanced the work Murray had started.

"What kind of antivirals?" asked Compton.

"Nanobodies," said Declan, for the first time sounding toneless. He gazed off across the wide sidewalk, where another little curbside café teemed with people sipping sangrias under striped awnings. "They're fragments of antibodies. We sequence them after challenging animals with proteins from an RNA virus."

Compton pressed her point. "RNA viruses like influenza?"

"Yes," Declan conceded, "but we've been looking specifically at a different virus. The same one Kira studies."

Remembering Beau—who was turning his head back and forth between the adults with unmistakable interest in this conversation—Hannah was about to ask him what was in the notebook he held when a sudden stillness captured her attention. At the end of the table, Kira was reading something from her phone.

"They've sequenced it," she said. And then: "Oh my God."

"Sequenced what? The virus?"

"Yes. They just announced it." She leaned back from the phone, squinting, as she read aloud. "'*As of 9:19 p.m. the day prior to this reporting, an academician of the SNS*'—that's the Sistema Nacional de Salud, the Spanish National Health Service—'*an academician of the SNS reports complete genomic sequencing has been carried out regarding the pathogen of these cases of unexplained viral pneumonia. The cause has been determined to be a new type of artiovirus.*'" She looked up, intensity etched across her face, and locked eyes with Declan. He too was wide-eyed, his fork arrested halfway to his mouth. "An artiovirus. I'll be damned."

"An artiovirus?" asked Hannah. She set down her fork. "They cause colds, right? I barely remember that one."

"Yes. It's named after the animal group in which it was first discovered, the artiodactyls."

Silence. Then, from Georgia: "The what? There's a virus named after dinosaurs?"

"No, no. Not dinosaurs. How could we isolate a virus from dinosaurs? Artiodactyls are large cloven-hoofed mammals, like goats and giraffes and cows and pigs. Artioviruses are not severely pathogenic in humans. I've never . . ." Kira paused, then resumed in a quieter voice. "They can cause mild disease, like colds. They're like rhinoviruses or coronaviruses." Again, she met Declan's eyes.

"Kiki! You work on this virus?"

"I do, yes. It's one of my official job titles: I'm the SME—the subject matter expert—for artioviruses at the Viral Infections Branch of the CDC. It's been an obscure job, to say the least. I need to check in at work, guys, my team is probably waking up to this."

Several people spoke at once. "Why didn't you ever tell us that?" "This is the same virus Declan's drug targets?"

Kira and Declan shot each other a look Hannah couldn't quite interpret. "We were trying to find a cure for common upper respiratory infections," said Declan. "Not this strain of the virus. But yes. Something similar."

Compton appeared puzzled. "You said pigs . . . I thought diseases come from pigs all the time. Aren't they supposed to be genetically similar to us?"

"Sure we can get diseases from pigs, and yes, they are genetically similar. I'm not saying this is from a pig, however. Antigenic shifts in viruses can come from a whole bunch of animals—pigs and bats and birds quite a lot of the time. But those have been other viruses. Artioviruses haven't been much on the radar for serious human disease, although they can cause significant pathology in animals. There are twenty or thirty types, and of those, six of them can affect us, but aside from cold symptoms, it's only been weird lesions in sheepherders, that kind of thing. Nothing major."

Vani said, "That's a quick turnaround, isn't it? For genetic sequencing of an entire virus?"

"Well, not really. An RNA virus is extremely simple compared to a human genome. But also: we've gotten a lot faster. It took scientists almost six months to determine the cause of the SARS epidemic in 2003; by 2013, when the H7N9 avian influenza epidemic hit, it took about one month to sequence the virus. Now with next-gen sequencing, it can be only hours, even for a complex genome."

Declan had closed his eyes. He sat without moving, his back extremely straight, directing his question to Kira. "Do the reports say anything else about the human cases?"

Kira bent her head back to her phone. "There's a ton of stuff here . . . let's see. There are more case reports in Spain—a handful—but I'm not seeing as much for Morocco, just a couple. They're still saying there's no evidence for human-to-human transmission, but of course caution is urged. No cases reported in medical personnel who've been treating the patients. So that's good."

"So," said Georgia. "We go?"

They were scheduled to spend the day in Seville, touring the palace and the cathedral, and then tomorrow they'd rent a van for the drive to Tarifa, where all of them, including the children, would catch the ferry to Morocco.

"Yes, I think so," said Kira. "But I may need to fly home after that." She stood, her cell phone already to her ear, and waved at Declan to follow her. "Excuse us, we're going to step away for a moment."

Hannah's eyes followed Kira until she and Declan stopped at a point down the street, speaking to one another with some intensity. Just past the two of them jutted the border of the resplendent grounds of Real Alcázar, the palace constructed for the Christian king Peter of Castile. The stones of this building, steeped in thousands of years of historical significance, must have borne mute witness to a staggering amount of disease and death. Whatever was happening now, with this new virus, would not be new to them.

Georgia must have been thinking about the palace as well, because she squinted and gestured in its direction. "I'm gonna go ahead and admit something shallow," she said. "That place is supposed to be Instagram heaven."

"George!"

"Hold up. Before anyone lectures me, I am aware we're gazing upon eleven glorious—and inglorious—centuries of European and Moorish history." She grinned, showing all her teeth. "But are *you* aware inside those gates is the exact spot where Prince Doran Martell was murdered by Ellaria Sand?"

Kira returned to the table. "Who? I never heard of them."

"The Kingdom of Dorne? *Game of Thrones*? Ring any bells?"

"Why does everyone like television so much?" Everyone laughed, but Kira didn't appear to notice; her gaze drifted past them to some indeterminate spot in the distance. "I'm sorry," she said. "I need to work for a while. You all go ahead."

Shaking off her unease of a moment ago, Hannah ushered her friends together for a photo before Kira left for the afternoon. Later, she would gaze upon this picture, of the five of them standing in the buttery sunshine in front of the grounds of the Alcázar of Seville with their arms linked and their hair blowing, as a kind of talisman of an easy happiness the world would never know again.

10 | The Subcellular War

KIRA | THE STRAIT OF GIBRALTAR

OUR RENTED VAN COASTED THROUGH THE GRAYSCALE darkness of the predawn, hills and orchards and the occasional small town taking on form and color as the sky lightened. I drove; in the passenger seat next to me, Declan typed at a blistering pace into his laptop. Everyone else slept.

I used the quiet time to organize my thoughts. Since yesterday, the scattered handful of reports on the new illness had mushroomed into dozens and dozens of bulletins, press releases, and emails. It constituted big news in this region, with the coverage spilling over from the scientific/medical community into the mainstream media, but had caused barely a blip in American news coverage, which was saturated with a political battle between the president of the United States and a coalition of congresspeople who were trying to deregulate banks.

Over the last twenty-four hours, I'd been in contact with my team, who were awaiting samples of the virus to confirm the genetic sequencing performed by public health officials in Rabat and Madrid. In the meantime, they'd reached out to the WHO and the people at the CDC who interfaced with public policy setters in the United States, just in case this thing blew up, and they'd put together a go-team from the EIS if needed. But so far, the public messaging coming from the WHO continued to emphasize that no evidence of easy human-to-human transmission existed.

Another wrinkle: the clinical symptoms exhibited by the patients in the handful of hospitalized cases were quite variable, as best the team could tell from the scattershot reporting. Some patients had pneumonia, but others suffered from predominately neurological symptoms, mainly seizures. Some experienced blood clots. Since no rapid test existed for this virus—something we'd begin work on immediately—some of these people were probably afflicted not with the virus but with something else, confounding the issue.

An hour later, the sun had risen and so had the backseat occupants of the van: Vani, Compton, and Georgia in the middle row, all of them pecking at their phones, and Hannah, flanked by the two children, in the back. After a brief but heated discussion between me and Rorie, a compromise had been reached on the road-trip music: I'd get half an hour of my stuff—a few obscure French artists and a bluegrass rap band called Gangstagrass I like because the banjos remind me of Kentucky, where I was raised—and Rorie would get no time whatsoever of the appalling misogyny that passes for popular music today. I'd made that mistake on our last car trip: I'd pulled up one of Rorie's playlists and song after song turned out to be nothing but dudes rhyming about their deep disdain for the hot but expendable hos with whom they were cavorting . . . *cavorting* being a really nice way of putting it.

"This is not a compromise, Mom. We're only listening to what you want."

"Well, now you say that, I'd have to agree this is not a compromise. This is a dictatorship. What message are you getting from this stuff?"

"It's good."

I experienced a moment of uncertainty: was it good? Maybe the problem was me. After all, I'm familiar with the cliché that you've turned into an old fart when you start griping about the musical taste of the younger generation. Would I soon be demanding Lawrence Welk while thwacking people with my cane, my wattled old ears unable to process current sound? Perhaps I was wrong about Rorie's musical taste.

But no: screw that. I mentally replayed a few choice lyrics and felt myself growing heated: What gave these narcissists the idea that banging and discarding your bitch was something to gloat about? And why did they consider these women to be brainless sexual commodities in the first place? What deep-rooted societal poison had infiltrated the national psyche to the point where—

From the middle row: "Kira? How about playing some Lizzo, then? And wasn't that our turn?"

"Shit!"

Ten minutes later I'd battled my way back to the correct road and all was well. The day, which had started out sunny and glorious in Seville, had progressed to being sunny and glorious in Jerez de la Frontera, a charming old town where we stopped for gas. The countryside around the city consisted of rolling tan hills topped with the occasional enormous silhouette of a black bull, remnants of a 1950s advertising campaign for brandy.

Ninety minutes later, as we approached the southernmost point of continental Europe, the skies over the sea filled with swooping, brightly colored objects: on the right, the brisk winds funneling through the Strait of Gibraltar had attracted hundreds of kitesurfers, the bright crescents of their sails scything against the blue horizon. I glanced in the rearview mirror to see that Beau appeared to have fallen back asleep, slumped sideways onto Hannah's shoulder, his little mouth ajar enough to show the gap where his front teeth had been. On Hannah's other side, Rorie pressed her hands to her window, enthralled. "Mommy," she said in a tone full of wonder. "Can we . . . ?"

You had to marvel at this age; one second they were huffily insisting they could stay by themselves in a foreign city, and the next they were calling you Mommy and begging to watch kites. Rorie was little still. She might wear pink lip gloss and listen to obscene music and shut the door to her bedroom every time I came near, but she also liked to crawl onto the couch with me and Beau on weekend nights to watch movies, curling into us with the unselfconsciousness of a child. Sometimes she'd even fall asleep tucked into my embrace, the warm, clean scent of her skin lulling me into an endorphin-fueled trance. I'd leave her there until my arm went numb.

"We'll stop on the way back if we can," I promised, watching her trace a finger in curlicue designs against the glass. "Beau would love to watch this."

I drove a little faster than I should have the remainder of the distance to Tarifa; making the next ferry was going to be tight. Beau awoke, blinking against the golden light. I found a spot to park and we flew through the lot to the terminal building, grabbing our tickets from a booth before joining the end of a long security queue.

On board the ship, we found ourselves in another long line for passport control. It occurred to me this could well be the same ship where the young doctor had died; Wally hadn't said anything about one of them being taken out of rotation. The idea was unsettling, given that no one knew how contagious his illness might be. Most viruses and bacteria become inactive outside a living body within a short period of time—minutes to hours, usually—but a few can hang out much longer, still capable of wreaking havoc if they find their way into a susceptible human. Smallpox, the greatest scourge of humanity, was one such monster: under the right conditions, it could survive for months—and perhaps longer—without a host.

We inched forward in the line. Since the day was warm, you could wander out onto the deck if you liked; plenty of people who'd already cleared the line had done just that, angling their bodies against the rails in the direction of the Moroccan shoreline, thinking of their irritating boss or their cheating spouse or how gross the guy standing next to them smelled or basically anything other than the subcellular wars their bodies constantly waged to fend off microscopic invaders. For the hundredth time, I checked my email: no significant updates.

Meanwhile, the ship was the perfect place to harbor a disease vector. As I'd imagined it had been on the day of the man's death, people of many nationalities crowded the interior; English and Spanish filled the air, but also German and Arabic and Chinese and French and a language that might be Farsi, along with several at which I could only guess. Sitting in a theater-style row of chairs across from the passport line, an old woman in a sari stared straight ahead, unblinking; next to her, a blond mother with a baby strapped to her chest leapt out of her seat to corral chubby twin toddlers waddling at surprising speed toward the doors to the deck; on her other side, a couple of young backpackers dozed hand in hand, their mouths open. Behind my group in the line stood a group of young Japanese men who appeared to be part of a tour; alongside them a balding Spanish man read aloud from some kind of guidebook.

Oblivious to the UN-style composition of the boat's passengers, Rorie stared at her phone, her thumbs flying over it at near-incomprehensible speed. Periodically she held the phone in front of her, made a wide-eyed kissy-mouthed face, and then sent the photo into Snapchat. She caught me looking at her and shifted a shoulder to hide the phone.

"What? I'm working on my streaks."

Ignoring the insinuation that I should know what a "streak" was, I nodded toward the deck. For a moment Rorie stared blankly, then suddenly she let out a shriek.

"There it is, Mom!"

Across the flat expanse of the sea, the white-walled city of Tangier slid into view. If you've never had the privilege of seeing the African continent, your first glimpse of it from the Strait of Gibraltar is possibly not what you'd expect. "Africa" to many people conjures up the wide expanse of a savanna; the golden grass plains of the Serengeti, maybe, dotted with baobabs, the land trembling under an earthquake of zebra hooves. Or perhaps you picture the misty jungles of Kilimanjaro, hooting with animal cries, or the cattle-centric villages of the Maasai. The breadth and depth of biodiversity in the world's second-largest continent is truly remarkable, making it difficult to summarize in any kind of homogenous image.

To me, though, two things come to mind when I think of Africa. One, of course, is my own experience living in Chad: my work there and my friends, and, especially, meeting and marrying and losing Daniel.

But when I'm able to extricate myself from my personal memories, the other thing that comes to mind when I consider Africa is the density of its cities. The most terrifying outcome of the next big pandemic will occur—and yes, *will* is the correct word—when it reaches one of the world's megacities. True calamity, most of us believe, will most likely arise in Asia, where cities of more than ten million people are most concentrated.

But a pandemic could originate anywhere. Like Asia, Africa is a natural laboratory in which many species intermingle with humans, making it an ideal place to breed a new virus. The epicenter of the world's next pandemic could very well happen here, transforming the cradle of humanity into its coffin. More than fifty cities exist in Africa with populations of more than one million people. Lagos, in Nigeria, is home to more than twenty-one million people, as is Cairo; there are millions more in Kinshasa, Luanda, Nairobi, Addis Ababa, Dar es Salaam, Accra, Johannesburg, and so many others, including the luminous city before us.

My group reached the front of the line, interrupting my musings. Without speaking, a man behind a counter stamped our passports, leaving us free to explore the ship.

"It's so beautiful," Hannah breathed, shading her eyes against the light shimmering on the water as she stared at Tangier in the distance. "It's like a fairy-tale city."

It did resemble a fairy-tale city. White buildings of various heights clung to the deep hills, their upper floors and roofs catching the sunlight in such a manner that they appeared to be glowing gold. It looked at once both modern and ancient, and, from this vantage, almost antiseptically clean.

"How about this?" I suggested. "You guys all go outside and take some pictures. I'll get in the café line and grab us some drinks."

This suggestion was met with considerable enthusiasm; I'd no sooner finished speaking than the children were barreling toward the open glass doors leading to the deck, dragging Declan in their wake. My friends followed, already wielding cell phone cameras toward the shore.

In truth, I wanted a glimpse of the area where the young doctor had died, assuming this was the same ship, or a similar space, if it wasn't. The line for refreshments was long. Everyone, it seemed, had proceeded from the passport line into this one, forming a queue that wound from the bar through rows of seating to a separate lounge area running the length of the ship's stern. I found myself behind a young group of male tourists I recognized from the passport line. Now that they'd cleared customs, they were smiling and snapping selfies.

A few moments later the smiles disappeared, and, belatedly, I registered that something had changed. At first it was subtle, almost subliminal, a fractious bubble rising amid the convivial atmosphere of the ship. The tone of the conversations around me shifted into something troubling; sharper voices, an undercurrent of anger.

It didn't take long to spy the source of the indignation. In front of me, a couple of young men stood scowling, one of them clasping his cheekbone as he bent forward. My first thought was that someone had punched him; I scanned his face for obvious injury but noted only a frothy slosh of pinkish liquid oozing down one cheek. Before I could analyze it further, the man straightened, swiping his forearm across his face with enough force to redden the skin.

It took a moment, but I got it: someone had spit on him.

The young man's friends vibrated with collective outrage. Coalescing around their affronted colleague, they bristled in the direction of a slight figure standing a few feet from them.

This, presumably, was the spitter: a young woman, dressed in a white button-down, the top few buttons undone under a tight, synthetic navy vest. I recognized the uniform; she was employed by the ferry. I gauged her age to be somewhere in her mid-twenties. In contrast to the cheek-clutching man, who seemed uninjured, this woman looked terrible. Sweat shone at her hairline; her gaze was dim and unfocused, directed somewhere into the ether as though she had no awareness of her surroundings. She hunched forward, away from the men, her hands on her knees. Even from a distance of ten feet away, I could hear the ragged scrape of her breathing.

She was sick.

I ticked off the signs of a person starved for oxygen. Flaring nostrils. Tripod posture. Fast respiratory rate. She also exhibited a physical finding doctors refer to as *paradoxical breathing*, which relates to the uncoupled coordination of the chest wall and the abdominal muscles. Normally, both move inward and outward together as you inhale and exhale: pay attention to your torso during your next breath. See what I mean? In cases of extreme respiratory distress, however, the chest and abdomen reverse direction from one another as the body attempts to obtain more air; because she was so slender and her vest so tight, the concave curve of this woman's abdomen was visible as her chest wall expanded. The spaces above her sternum and clavicles sucked inward as she breathed, creating hollows deep enough to hold water; these are phenomena known as suprasternal retractions and supraclavicular retractions, respectively. I didn't note any cyanosis—the bluish discoloration of insufficient oxygenation—but I was willing to bet that if I had a pulse oximeter, it would reveal an oxygen level far below normal.

I took a step in her direction but halted as the woman coughed, a hacking sound that went on so long it attracted the notice of everyone standing around her. The man who'd been hit by her sputum bomb hooked an elbow over his mouth and backed away, as did his friends. The sick woman brought up another glob of sputum, spraying it out into the air with such force it flew a good five feet away from her, landing at the feet of an older woman. Instead of reacting with disgust, the white-haired lady fumbled in her handbag and extracted a square of white cloth, which she proffered in the direction of the coughing woman. "For you," she said in a high, thin voice.

The young woman did not respond. By now she was no longer attempting to draw in breath; ominously, the coughing had stopped, subsumed by a gush of blood-flecked foam pouring from her mouth, the white froth becoming darker and darker until it transformed to a red tide. She clawed at her throat, fingers curled so tightly it seemed her knucklebones would burst from her skin. Her knees buckled.

She hit the floor hard, face-first. From beneath her flowed a red pool of blood, expanding in a large concentric circle that further drove back the horrified onlookers. Her body flopped, back arching, pushing her scapulae toward one another. The dull sound of her face drumming against the floor punctuated the screaming from the other passengers.

Even now, I look back and can still see the dense little knot of her hair, gathered into a bun at the nape of her neck, vibrating as the seizure gripped her. I see her slight shoulders, smashed against the ground, and her tiny belted waist and the rough navy nylon of her uniform pants, her hands splayed at her sides, fingers curled. Who was she, this young woman, drowning in her own blood a few feet away from me? Someone's daughter, someone's wife, someone's friend, someone's mother? A girl who loved reading, a young woman who danced every weekend with her friends, a conscientious daughter sending part of her salary to her aging parents? I've tried to envision her life and of course I cannot, not really. I tried, later, to find some record of her—anything, her name, even—and I failed. In the clarity of hindsight, I'm able to freeze that instant and dissect it, turning it this way and that to examine all the facets and implications and potential consequences of my subsequent actions, but in the moment, I experienced no such reflection. A few feet away from me a young woman lay alone in a pool of blood, seconds away from death unless someone tried to help her.

I didn't think; I sprang forward.

"Everybody stand back," I called, raising my arms for emphasis. This was perhaps the most pointless order ever issued, as everyone within my line of sight was already in the process of stampeding to the far corners of the room. As they retreated, I redirected my attention to the woman.

There was nothing I could do to stop the seizure. She'd have almost certainly have inhaled into her lungs some of the copious fluid spewing from her mouth. She was likely doomed, but I had to try something. I moved to her side and knelt, my shoes squelching in a sticky pool of blood. I reached a hand toward her as someone grabbed my arm and snatched it back.

"Don't touch her."

I looked up: Compton. A flush colored her cheeks; she looked as though she'd been running. Like the woman on the floor, Compton's skin sucked in above her clavicles, but in her case it was from a combination of exertion and her brittle thinness. She jerked a thumb backward, over her shoulder.

"Move, Kira," she said. "Get out of here."

"No, I—"

Compton cut me off. "If this is the same virus, I've likely been exposed. You might not be. Get back and check on your kids."

Slowly, I rose and backed away about ten feet, keeping my eyes on Compton. Carefully, she rolled the young woman onto her side to check her airway, exposing as she did a large bleeding gash at her hairline. It was clear the woman had also bitten her tongue; blood from the tongue laceration mixed with the frothier substance bubbling up from her airway, trailing down onto her uniform and staining the white collar of her shirt in a large red blotch fading to pink at its margins. Ignoring the urge to flee as the others had, Compton inspected it more closely. "Pulmonary hemorrhage," she said quietly.

The seizure had stopped. Compton pressed two fingers at the woman's neck. "Febrile," she said, more quietly. "She's blazing."

"Does she have a pulse?"

After a moment, Compton nodded: she located a weak pulse just as a rattling gasp issued from her patient's throat; her body had not quite given up. I marveled at this, as I have many times before: how, in the face of catastrophe, human beings are still programmed to grasp at life, to fight, to summon every resource they possess into the effort to defeat whatever is killing them. The human body is complex and miraculous beyond comprehension. It begins, somehow, from the mysterious and unknowable void of the subatomic world. From there it is constructed of atoms assembling into molecules, molecules assembling into cells, cells assembling into tissues, tissues assembling into organs, organs assembling into systems, all of it somehow alchemizing together into the miracle of sentient life. We burn with the desire to exist. At the end, a person throws everything they have into a white-hot supernova of resistance; one final subcellular blaze before they're gone. I've always loved the famous line from the poet Dylan Thomas, which expresses the biologic reluctance to die more beautifully than I ever could: "Rage, rage against the dying of the light."

This woman raged. Her young body, unwilling to concede defeat, still struggled for air. Each breath sounded like a last stand, a desperate, futile howl against extinction. Gently, Compton positioned her to allow for optimal drainage from her nose and mouth, noticing as she did something interesting on the woman's hand. She held it up.

A steel wedding band graced her finger: somewhere soon, someone was going to receive some devastating news. My gaze slid down the woman's finger as Compton squeezed her small hand. Her nailbeds were bright blue.

Suddenly her back arched again. I thought it was the onset of another seizure, but instead it was a death rattle; one final breath sucked in. She was gone.

Compton locked her elbows and started chest compressions. With every thrust of her arms, more bubbly fluid gushed from the woman's nose and mouth, sizzling onto her cooling skin, running down her slight body to the floor. Not for the first time, fear pierced me at the thought of what that fluid might contain, but Compton had crossed that particular Rubicon the instant she first responded.

Time passed; I couldn't gauge how much. The screaming around us abated, replaced by an unnatural absence of voices and, eventually, a dozen hushed conversations. From somewhere out of my line of sight sounded the staccato hack of a prolonged cough. Somewhere else on the boat, somewhere far away—the bow, maybe—a thin, high scream rent the air, followed by a hubbub of panicked voices and then shouting.

Compton continued her dogged compressions. She was now drenched, covered in her own sweat, blood from the floor, and flecks of frothy, bloody sputum. I switched off my thoughts, the rote drumbeat of the chest compressions filling the void in my mind so I wouldn't have to contemplate what I'd risked, for myself and my children and my friends, by not canceling this journey.

"Mommy?"

My head snapped to the side. Beau walked toward me, one hand reaching toward mine from about fifteen feet away. "No," I whispered. "Back away."

Beau blinked at the dead woman, who was only a little bigger than Rorie. A small sound escaped him. A few feet behind him, Declan appeared, and then Rorie and Hannah.

"Back away," I begged. "Please, honey." I caught Declan's eye, wordlessly beseeching him to help. He seemed frozen, one foot in front of the other, his mouth open. Hannah swooped from behind him and dragged Beau and Rorie out of sight, murmuring something to them as she did.

"Declan," I called. My voice sounded foreign to me, like someone else was speaking. "Keep them outside. Don't let them touch anything."

With a jolt, Declan reactivated. He nodded, turning in the direction Hannah and the children had gone before whirling back to face me again. He didn't speak, but he didn't have to: he flashed me a look so heavy with anguish I could read his thoughts as clearly as a chyron on a television news show. *Please, please, please don't get sick; be careful; I love you.*

I love you.

Almost as soon as I registered the meaning of his look, it vanished. I had no time to process this; in front of me, Compton pushed, almost angrily, one final time on the woman's chest and then slumped back onto her heels. "I'm calling it," she said, her voice hoarse. "She's gone."

PART THREE

DURING ARTIOVIRUS

11 | You Go to War with the Army You Have

COMPTON | **NEW YORK CITY**
Sixty Days After Patient Zero

"DR. C! FIVE MORE INCOMING!"

Much like hell, the emergency department in which Compton worked was laid out in the shape of a circle within a circle within a circle. Low-acuity rooms lined the outer perimeter, all of which were currently occupied by high-acuity patients in the throes of agony. The second ring—for the worst emergencies—contained the trauma bays and critical care equipment, and it too was filled to overflowing with high-acuity patients in the throes of agony. "Overflowing" was not an exaggeration; they'd run out of patient rooms, so rows and rows of yet more high-acuity patients in the throes of agony lined every hallway, parked on gurneys and yelling their heads off. The ones who could yell were yelling, anyway. Quite a few of them could not.

The final inner circle consisted of the administrative area. A wall of plexiglass encircled a long, curved work desk at which the physicians sat and did their charting or looked up labs or entered orders. No one had time to sit and do anything now, obviously, so all the chairs were empty, save for one occupied by a bewildered-looking unit secretary wearing an enormous antique gas mask. In theory, she was there to page people and answer the phone, but no one could hear her through the gas mask, so her entire ineffectual presence was one more horrible fucked-up thing in a horrible fucked-up charade of horrible fucked-up care. The doctors, meanwhile, looked up labs and entered orders on tablets while running from room to room trying to put out fires. As for coherent charting, forget about it.

Compton had arrived one minute earlier. This would be her seventh straight night shift, but since so many ER and critical care docs were out sick, there would be no respite; as one of the few people who had survived an infection and was therefore thought to have earned immunity to the virus, she couldn't be spared. The second she entered, people screamed for her.

She grabbed her tablet, swiped it with an antiseptic wipe, and set off into the depths of hell. A patient had just been whisked through the segregated ART entrance by a pair of EMTs. Both of them wore head-to-toe industrial-looking PPE of some off brand they'd probably scrounged on the black market, along with face shields and respirator masks. They didn't bother with the usual concise reporting they'd have delivered in the pre-ART period. Instead, one of them ran alongside the gurney, squeezing a purple Ambu bag attached to an oxygen mask, as the other gestured to the prone form on the stretcher and grunted. "Bad," he said.

Compton looked. Yes, bad. The patient was dead. She motioned to the nurse, a large man in his fifties named Jerry, to start chest compressions as the paramedics parked the stretcher.

"Downtime?" she asked, moving to the head of the bed.

"Coded en route, Doc," wheezed the smaller of the EMTs. Judging by the voice, it was a woman. "A minute, maybe. We wouldn't have brought her in at all if she'd coded sooner."

"CPR?"

"Yeah, and epi times one. Shocked twice." The EMT stared at her shoe. "You want to call it?"

Compton looked again. The patient's eyes were closed, luckily. She hated when their eyes were open. The patient was young; in her thirties, most likely, with gorgeous red hair and ugly blue skin. Compton shuddered; she also hated blue skin. Perhaps more than anything on earth, she'd grown to hate blue skin.

"She's only been down a couple minutes," she said. "Let's tube her."

The larger EMT shrugged at the idea of inserting a breathing tube for this patient. "Your funeral, Doc," he said. He and his partner eased out.

Jerry continued chest compressions, but his eyebrows rose. Like Compton, he'd also survived an early bout with artiovirus and consequently found himself one of the most sought-after nurses in this particular circle of hell. Needless to say, running a code with two people was not how this was supposed to go down. In the good old days of a month or so ago, you might have ten or fifteen people in a code room, each of them a cog in a well-oiled machine. Now there weren't enough people to comprise a code team. Instead, each doctor paired with one nurse, and, if they were really lucky, a tech. Every now and then a respiratory therapist might materialize too, but since half the hospital's population consisted of ventilated patients, they couldn't make it down to the ED much anymore. If the doctor was unlucky: no nurse and no tech, so she'd have to figure out a way to perform chest compressions and administer medications by herself, all while simultaneously inserting tubes into the trachea, the jugular, the antecubital vein, and the bladder. Plus, all of this would have to be documented somehow, to prevent conspiracy theorists from later asserting that Grandma had been surreptitiously strangled by a corrupt doctor on the take from Big Pharma.

"You don't think we should tube her, Jerry?"

Jerry shook his head, his expression terse. "I'd tube the one next door," he said. "Better chance."

Compton wasn't about to argue with one of the best nurses in the ED. She stuck her head out of the cubicle and hollered, "Body!"

A young woman trotted over and threw Compton a salute. Like Compton and Jerry, she had a green sticker affixed to her badge, indicating she'd survived an infection and presumably enjoyed some degree of immunity to the virus, although no one knew for certain. Short and busty, she wore round black glasses and a surprisingly serene expression. Her job—her newly created job—consisted of identification and disposition: she would transfer the body to the new, larger, makeshift morgue in the hospital basement as quickly as possible so the patient room in the ED could be blasted with a hoseful of some kind of disinfectant by the beleaguered environmental services people. Meanwhile, she'd also be in charge of rooting around on the body to try to find ID, and, failing that, she'd have to contact the EMTs to get whatever information on pickup location they could provide. She'd also press the dead person's index finger to a biometric reader, in case they'd been a patient of the hospital system's at some point in the past, and thus were identifiable. Then, with a volunteer chaplain as backup, she'd have the unenviable task of calling the newly departed's loved ones to break the news. Whatever happened after that was not Compton's problem.

It had not started out this way. In the beginning, after her isolation ended and she returned to the country, and then, eventually, to work, she'd been the one to inform the bereaved of their new status. As in all hospital emergency departments, a special room existed for this purpose. It had flowers and soft chairs and copious amounts of tissues, as if that could possibly make any difference. Compton had spent many an agonized moment in that room, but nothing compared to the nonstop devastation taking place in there now. Most of the time, in pre-ART days, The Death Speech had been delivered to family members of the elderly, or in the case of chronic illness and drug overdoses, the families of the not-entirely-unexpectedly dead. But after the artiovirus struck, the recipients of the speech consisted of wave after wave of young spouses, young engaged people, parents of college students, parents of tiny children, the bosses and friends and neighbors and families of people who'd been fine that morning and dead that evening. They weren't allowed in person, so the conversation took place on a screen in the room dedicated for this purpose. The ED also used that screen for conversations with the loved ones of the desperately ill, which was in certain ways worse, as those people tended to fire off more unanswerable questions.

The volume of sick people now rendered this level of civility unsustainable. No longer did doctors have the time to patiently and respectfully break the news of someone's untimely demise. That task was left for people like—Compton squinted to make out the name printed on the round-eyeglasses woman's badge—Shawna. Judging from her demeanor, she was probably pretty good at it.

Compton had been isolated in Spain for three weeks after contracting the virus herself, and therefore there had been no soothing Shawna to console her when her husband, Ellis, had died. She'd received the news alone in the utilitarian hotel room the Spanish government had commandeered and assigned to foreign victims of the illness, answering her phone to find one of her own colleagues on the other end—a tall, broad-shouldered blonde named Samantha Ziemniak, who possessed an optimistic nature so irrepressible that Compton had never seen her frown, let alone cry. Whatever had happened with Ellis had broken the dam; Samantha would not stop crying throughout the call, to the point where Compton, in a state of stunned disbelief, had found herself unable to ask more than a handful of questions.

She couldn't think of Ellis right now, not if she was going to get through this shift. She and Jerry bolted for the next bay. As usual, Jerry was right: this patient was not yet dead, although describing him as alive was something of an overstatement. He appeared to be in his mid-thirties or early forties, but that was about as far as it was possible to get in assessing his appearance, because right as Compton bent to inspect him, he turned in her direction and projectile vomited at least a full liter of dark, clotted blood. It splattered all over the stretcher, the floor, Compton, and the wall some five feet behind her.

"Fuck!" she yelped, tearing off her useless face shield. "I've been hit."

From a cabinet behind them, Jerry grabbed a stack of blue OR cloths and used one of them to dab at her eyes. "GI bleed?"

"Looks like it," said Compton, snatching another towel from Jerry and swiping at a quivering, gelatinous clump of blood stuck to her neck, just above her protective gown. "Smells like it too," she added. She turned back to the patient, giving him a quick once-over. Airway: full of blood. Breathing: ragged, fast, shallow. Circulation: he had a weak carotid, but a bluish tinge discolored his face—fucking cyanosis—and his fingers and toes had all turned a hideous eggplanty purple.

Jerry noticed it too. "He's throwing clots."

"DIC," said Compton. This stood for disseminated intravascular coagulation and referred to a god-awful condition in which the body bled and clotted at the same time. "Have we been seeing much GI bleeding? That's a new one to me."

"Yes, here and there," said Jerry, trying to start an IV in the man's arm. He gritted his teeth. "Veins are collapsed."

"I'll do a femoral," said Compton, "as soon as I get him intubated."

Jerry reached for her hand. He shook his head.

"What?" said Compton. She affixed the blade of a Macintosh laryngoscope to its handle and snapped it open, then snapped it shut again. "Where're all the videoscopes? There's going to be too much blood to see to the cords."

Jerry held out his cell phone—encased in a biohazard bag—near her face so she could read the message it displayed. Then she read it again, and her hand holding the Mac drifted down to the gurney. "We're out of vents," she said dully.

Jerry nodded, wordless.

"Then we'll tube him and bag him," said Compton, a wild tone creeping into her voice. "He's treatable! But we have to protect his airway."

"Dr. C," said Jerry. His face, though distorted behind his face shield, reflected such unbearable pity that Compton wanted to throw her laryngoscope at him. "We cannot stand here and manually bag this guy for hours. They can't spare either one of us for that."

"Then we'll tube him and get one of the volunteers to bag him."

"No one can spare a volunteer 24-7 to stand there and push air in and out of someone's lungs. Not to mention how exhausting and ineffective that would be."

"I don't care, I'm not going to stand here and let this man die, I—"

Her voice broke off as something sticky encircled her wrist. She looked down: the patient's purple hand had snaked out from beneath the sheet covering him and clenched around her arm.

"Anna," he croaked.

"I'm Dr. Compton," said Compton, forcing a calm professionalism into her voice. "We are going to take good care of you, sir. What's your name?"

"Anna," said the man again, more urgently. He tried to say more and coughed up a foul clump of coagulated blood. "She. Is all." Another bout of coughing. His face grew duskier. "By. Herself."

"Okay. It's okay; we are going to help," said Compton. "Who is Anna?"

"Anna," he whispered. "My." His eyes bulged and grew glassy. His mouth stayed open.

"He's not breathing," said Compton. She snatched a bag valve mask hanging from a hook on the wall behind her. "Jerry! Chest compressions."

Jerry just looked at her, grief somehow etched into every visible wrinkle on his forehead.

"No," said Compton. "We can't just . . . we can't . . ." She set down the bag valve mask. Another glob of something wet slithered down her cheek; she realized, dimly, it must be a tear. "I sure hope Anna is a cat," she said. Her voice came out so thick Jerry probably couldn't understand her, but he took her hand and squeezed it, and then, together, they ran to the next room.

LATER, SHE WOULD come to identify that night as the apex. Or not the apex; that sounded too achievement oriented. What was the opposite of an apex? An abyss?

Whatever you wanted to call it, that night etched a permanent scar into her brain, earning the dubious distinction of being the worst thing she'd ever experienced. It seemed the city had reached some critical mass of infectivity: the upswing on the proverbial exponential curve, vastly increasing the numbers of infected people streaming through their doors. She and Jerry crashed their way from patient to patient, focusing on the ones who could breathe on their own, for what seemed like weeks. Everything blurred together: the too-bright lights, the sounds of people moaning and other people crying, and the smells, including the damp, rotted stench from her own traitorous armpits. Weren't you supposed to lose awareness of your own stink? Her hair became matted, thick and spiky with blood and sweat; she didn't even have to push it back out of her eyes because it stood straight up on its own, as if it had been treated with some kind of salon product promising a perfect hold.

After those first two patients, the rest of them fused together in her mind, forming one long chimera of sickness: teeth clenched in seizures, red-rimmed eyes disgorging bloody tears, pink foamy sputum leaking from noses, and everywhere, everywhere, everywhere blue skin. Compton didn't eat or go to the bathroom or sit down. She and Jerry worked until her hands shook too hard to start a line.

"Dr. C," he said finally, after she'd tried three times to get a femoral IV in a semi-alert college student who shrieked like a toddler every time he caught a glimpse of Compton coming at his leg with a twenty-gauge needle. "Go on. You go on home now."

"No, I . . ." she said weakly, and then stopped. She had to blink hard to clear her vision, which had gone oozy. She stared at Jerry as he swam back into focus.

One of those burly but milk-skinned blond men who grow red beards, Jerry looked like he'd be more at home on a Viking longship than in a hospital emergency department. Like Compton, he radiated exhaustion in the set of his shoulders and the grimy creases on his face, but his voice still came out firm. "I'll stay a little more," he said.

"Then I'll stay with you."

"No, you aren't doing anyone any good right now. You go. I'll work with her." He nodded in the direction of a terrified-looking child wearing scrubs. Compton peered at her, homing in on the badge attached to her lanyard.

"That's a second-year medical student, Jerry."

He shrugged. "You go to war with the army you have, Doc. We'll be fine. See you back tonight, okay?"

"Okay, yes," she said, certain she was lying. After tonight she would never set foot in this place again, not if she had anything to say about it. Lots of people would die if she didn't come back to work, though. Also: lots of people died when she was at work. That last thought wasn't what she'd meant to think. What had she been trying to think? Compton clutched her head in confusion.

She stumbled to the doctors' lounge to pee and discard her scrubs, which were now doused in most of the major bodily fluids. After gulping an enormous amount of water straight from a fresh bottle, she removed her scrubs and showered. Afterward, feeling marginally better, she opened the door to the cabinet containing fresh scrubs and found it empty. No towels either. Of course. The heroic environmental services people couldn't wash scrubs and towels in addition to all their other decontamination duties. And who knew whether the laundry service the hospital employed was still functional?

But she'd rather pop out her own eyeball with a spoon than re-dress in the scrubs she'd just discarded. Or would she? Which one would people on the subway find more offensive: a reeking, bloody, vomitous, literally shitty doctor or a buck-naked one?

Something gleaming and bright on the door caught Compton's eye. She drifted over to it, wondering if it was a mirage. She reached out a trembling hand. It was real. Still encased in yellowed plastic from the dry cleaner's, someone's white coat hung on a hook on the door. *Please,* prayed Compton, *please, for the love of God, don't let this be a short medical student coat.*

It wasn't. It was a full-length doctor coat, owned by somebody named M. Trey Garnett III, M.D., in the Department of Colorectal Surgery. Sending out a big mental thank-you to M. Trey, she donned it, pulling her arms through sleeves so big they seemed like angel wings. M. Trey must be fucking enormous, which was excellent news, because it made the coat even longer.

Another stroke of luck: no missing buttons, which meant she wouldn't have to rewear her disgusting, sodden underwear. Still, even though it was too big, the coat didn't close past Compton's upper thighs. She'd have to sit with her legs pressed together on the subway and avoid those gusty drafts on the platforms when other trains zipped by. But she wouldn't have to ride home soiled or nude, and that was the main thing.

Compton sleepwalked to the hospital exit and waited for the mechanical doors to whoosh open. She stepped forward and blinked a few times, her eyes recoiling from the flashbulb brightness of the day but also unable to process what she saw.

Overhead, rays from a brilliant August sun streamed down at a westerly angle, cutting through the skyscrapers on the east-west-aligned streets. She'd walked out expecting it to be still dark, or perhaps a muted pink predawn. Dazed, she reached for her phone, which she usually kept clipped to the waistband of her scrubs. Her hand brushed against her naked thigh, startling her, before she remembered she was wearing M. Trey's coat and had placed her phone in the pocket.

She pulled it out and tapped it. The time came up . . . 3:58 p.m.—3:58 p.m.? That couldn't be right. She'd arrived at 7:00 p.m. last night, and usually she left the hospital by 5:00 a.m., or 7:00 a.m. on a bad shift. Had she really worked twenty-one straight hours? Or had she gone home and come back and forgotten about it? This thought, somehow, was more frightening than every other terror hammering at her consciousness. She must be losing her mind.

But the other thing that struck her, besides the unfathomable passage of hours, was the near emptiness of the street. Compton's hospital was located in lower Manhattan, and at four o'clock on a typical afternoon, the streets would be thronged with guys in suits and women in navy skirts and tourist families pushing strollers and people shuffling along talking to themselves and other people striding along yelling in Noo Yawk accents into their Bluetooths. Where were all the people? Even in these early pandemic days, the streets of New York had still hummed and bustled. Had everyone in the city died while she worked through the night? At most, there were a half dozen people in eyesight.

A gust of wind caught the edge of her makeshift dress and she shivered. Underneath her feet she could feel the faint vibration of the subway. Good; the subway was running, so someone down there must be alive. Or maybe it ran on some sort of automated schedule independent of people? She didn't know. Very much against her will, more tears crept from the corners of her eyes and plinked down onto the stolen coat of M. Trey Garnett III.

Still moving forward, she consulted her phone again. This time, she noticed all the messages crammed together in overlapping oblong shapes on the home screen. Mildred must be worried about her. Of course Mildred was worried about her! She'd expected Compton to be home half a day ago, and it had never occurred to Compton, in the midst of all the carnage, to stop and call her sitter.

Hurriedly, she opened up the phone app and punched the button for Mildred. It rang and rang and rang, and just as Compton was about to hang up, Mildred answered.

"Hello? Compton? Is that you?"

"Yes," Compton shouted, although there was no longer a need to shout. She made a conscious effort to modulate her voice back to normal levels. "Mildred, I am so sorry. I'll be home as soon as I can."

"Compton." Mildred sounded strange. Maybe she was mad? *For the love of all that's holy, don't let her be angry enough to quit.* With Ellis gone, Mildred, who was single and lived in their building, had agreed to stay on in her job, and if she left, Compton had no one else to watch the children. "Have you seen the news?"

"No, I haven't seen anything. I'm leaving work now, I . . ." Compton trailed off. "What happened?"

"They called in the National Guard. They're closing the subways soon. No one is allowed to leave."

"What?" Compton stared around, wild-eyed. "How will people eat?"

"They're going to allow food banks in every borough. Multiple locations, one every couple blocks, I think. You can go out to one of those. And people in certain jobs can go out. Your job is one of them. There's a list. But that's it."

"Oh my God." Compton stopped walking, standing still in the middle of Broadway. It didn't matter; there was only one visible vehicle for two blocks in either direction, a gray sedan. "So many people are going to die."

"They're saying the hospitals can't take anyone else. Is that true?"

Compton's weary mind flashed backward a few hours. "Yes," she said simply.

She could hardly hear Mildred's next question. "Is this the end of New York?"

Was this the end of New York? No, it couldn't possibly be. Some people infected with the virus didn't even get sick. Look at her and her friends: after the Tarifa ferry, almost one month ago, they'd been sent back to Spain and isolated. Compton herself, who'd presumably been exposed to the highest viral load, had barely become ill. She'd been fatigued and achy, with a bit of a raspy cough, and that was it. Kira, who'd also had some contact with a sick person, had been moderately sick, with high fevers, headaches, and mild shortness of breath, and Hannah, who'd also had contact with a sick person, had never gotten sick at all. Neither had Kira's boyfriend or her children. Georgia hadn't seemed to be affected much either, other than a headache. But Vani had been hospitalized; she'd had pneumonia and a seizure and had barely escaped being placed on a ventilator. By some miracle, none of them had died.

Compton tore herself away from thoughts of her friends, none of whom she'd spoken to in weeks. "How are the children?" she asked.

Mildred's voice took on a tinge of wariness, probably because in ordinary times, Compton forbade the watching of screens during the day. Since Ellis's death, however, their routines had shattered. Compton was too frightened for them to leave the house, even to visit the park, so they spent their days in stunned solitude, resisting Mildred's exhortations to try a puzzle or an art project or a board game.

"They're okay," she said. "They didn't want to do anything, so we spent the day on the couch looking at the TV. Baby Walter played a little bit in his bouncy thing, but Rose and Lawrence, they just wanted to cuddle up to me."

A burning ache rose in Compton's throat. Her poor babies. No father, and now barely any mother. She wanted nothing more than to quit her job and be the one to nuzzle her bewildered, traumatized children on the couch all day, but if she did that, even more people would die, and then some other children somewhere in the city would find themselves without a daddy too. “That’s fine, Mildred,” she heard herself say gently. “Of course, that’s fine. Thank you so much for being there for them. Kiss them and tell them I’ll be home soon, all right?”

“I will,” said Mildred, her voice thickening. “You be safe coming home.”

12 The Shortest President in American History

HANNAH

SAN DIEGO
Eighty-One Days After Patient Zero

HANNAH STRAIGHTENED HER POSTURE AND GRIPPED THE steering wheel, focusing on driving. It wasn't a bad commute: the journey from her hillside home in Del Mar to the hospital where she practiced clocked in at under fifteen minutes if traffic cooperated.

Today, traffic didn't cooperate. Hannah didn't mind a slowdown, though. She loved the serene oasis of her car, which she kept meticulously tidy. Her cup holder always held a shiny stainless mug of herbal tea; her stereo always played soothing instrumental music; her dashboard was always dustless and gleaming. But even if she'd been driving a rusty old heap like Kira's car, she'd have found a way to enjoy the downtime of the drive. Impatience rarely bothered Hannah.

At the moment, her calm nature was a blessing. For one thing, Harry sat in the passenger seat. Harry's was not a soothing presence: he twittered and hummed and jerked around in his seat as if he were being jolted with a cattle prod. She didn't blame him: he had plenty of reason to be on edge. The internal dial controlling Hannah's outward movements slid down at moments like these, while Harry's lurched upward in spasmodic fits and starts until it broke and spun in useless circles. By the time they got to the hospital, she'd probably have petrified and he'd have spontaneously combusted.

Harry reached for the car's stereo, changing the music to a news broadcast. Fleetingly, Hannah hoped for a cutesy nonstory: the unlikely friendship between two different species of zoo animals or the triumphant struggle of a Paralympian—or anything, really—but of course only one subject interested the public right now. You could not escape it, the saga of what was happening in New York; it dominated every social media page, every newspaper headline, every website, every television news report.

The rest of the country had watched in horror the images of National Guard tanks rolling through the obscenely empty streets of Manhattan, blocking entrances to bridges and tunnels, looking like a staged scene from a B-list disaster flick. But even that paled in comparison to the descriptions pouring out online from shattered healthcare workers in New York's hospitals. Reading these tales of bodies piling up, she'd tried over and over and over again to reach Compton, but: nothing. Since the awful news that Compton's husband had been one of the city's earliest victims of the virus—which Hannah had learned not from Compton when they'd been isolated in Spain but from a later Facebook post from their old med school class president—she'd called, emailed, texted, DMed, and written multiple snail-mail letters. Compton herself wasn't dead, she knew, because she occasionally tweeted terse missives about the number of dead and incapacitated people at her hospital. Her forty-seven Twitter followers had ballooned; now she had more than a thousand.

From Compton's tweets, Hannah gathered she'd gone back to work a couple of weeks after returning to New York. Hannah could not imagine how she was handling this. Or rather, she could: by throwing herself into work. In ordinary times, Hannah would have wanted to be on the first plane to the city to help her friend, but the governor of New York, working in tandem with the president, had closed the airports there only a couple of days after they'd returned from Europe. Not only that, but Compton didn't answer her messages. Hannah had worried herself sick about it, fretting at the futility imposed upon her when she longed to comfort her friend. It must be terrible for her, torn between her children and her conscience, grieving her husband, watching the ravaged city crumble around her.

New York had been hit first and harder than any other city. For a while, the illness had raged there but almost nowhere else: the early, coordinated efforts of the state and federal governments to quarantine the city had been fairly effective. Anyone with symptoms, anywhere in the country, had been asked to isolate for twenty-one days. But nonetheless the virus had seeped out, carried like a spore on the wind from wayward travelers, popping up in small but fast-moving clusters in cities with big airports: Philadelphia, Boston, Charlotte, Atlanta, Miami, Dallas. Now, in late August, air, train, and bus travel had long been suspended, and most cities had checkpoints at their major roadways to screen for symptomatic travelers, which had the effect of cutting way back on intercity travel. The West Coast was not unaffected; both Los Angeles and Seattle were reporting upticks. But none of these places had hit a big upswing yet, and the entire center of the country, far from the coasts, had seen almost no cases. Life carried on, albeit with some unease.

". . . learned what to do—and what not to do—from prior pandemics," someone on the radio droned in an officious voice. "The Corbett administration increased funding for infectious disease research and boosted supplies of protective equipment, as well as vaccine reagents and manufacturing equipment. They're mobilizing the delivery of ventilators to affected areas, and they've registered a literal army of contact tracers, who facilitate quarantine for anyone exposed. They've distributed masks and made them mandatory nationwide. This virus is a bad actor—there's no question of that—but we are more prepared than we've been in the past. And in most cities, that's working."

"Can we change the station?" Hannah murmured. Harry's eyes flicked in her direction, but without comment, he returned the audio to her music.

They parked in the patient lot, Hannah having given her physician parking badge to one of the administrative assistants who suffered from gout. If Harry noticed they'd parked about a mile from the office building attached to the hospital, he didn't say anything. He came around to where she stood beside the driver's side of the car and took her hand. They both pulled up their masks. "Here we go," he said.

"Yes."

"I have a good feeling, honey. I have a really, really good feeling."

"So do I," she murmured, and really, she did. Even with all the terrible things happening in Africa and Europe and now New York, a calm positivity engulfed her at the thought of this, her last chance to be pregnant. Good things could still happen in this tumultuous world. Over the years, they'd been through all the things: an endless, tantalizing, unfulfilled wait on an adoption list on the one hand; on the other, pelvic exams, ultrasounds, labs, invasive tests to assess whether Hannah's fallopian tubes were blocked, and even a scraping of her uterine lining to assess the expression of various growth factors. Harry had gotten off easy, but he'd had to contend with at least one humiliating test of his own. The end result of all that evaluation had been exactly nothing. No one could explain why Hannah could not conceive.

Next had come the interventions. "The REI said we could have IUI or IVF," Hannah'd told Harry one evening at dinner after the initial workup had yielded nothing but frustration and a horrific credit card bill.

"IUIRIVF?" inquired Harry. "Are we aiming to give birth to a government agency?" He slid his reading glasses back up his nose and offered her a wry look at the utilization of yet more medical acronyms. If you threw around enough gross terminology, he'd complained, no one would ever get pregnant, because hideous images of menstrual cycle diagrams and gonads would insert themselves into one's consciousness at precisely the worst moment and the entire process would screech to a halt. No man could be expected to complete the act necessary for creating a baby after being subjected to a bunch of talk about gonads.

This, of course, was not a novel complaint; anyone who'd ever been through the process of an infertility ordeal knew the whole experience was about as sexy as a genital wart. But you had to admit: the use of an acronym was preferable to trying to pronounce the word *hysterosalpingogram*, even for a doctor. "You're one to talk, Harry," Hannah pointed out in a reasonable tone. "The military might be the only entity using more acronyms than the medical field."

"Ours are funny, though. And they're not as gross."

She thought she had him on this one. "Really? Name one funny military acronym. I mean a real one, not one you guys invented."

"MANPADS," said Harry promptly. "PMS."

"Which are?"

"Man-portable air-defense system and professor of military science. We've also got FARPs. Forward area refueling points. FARPs are funny. And those are just some official ones; you're right about the ones the guys invent—they're hilarious and clever and a perfect example of American dominance. Nobody makes up funnier shit than American military personnel."

"We have made-up funny acronyms too," said Hannah, "but sometimes they're a bit unkind to the patients, so I don't use them."

"No," agreed Harry with a fond smile. He leaned across the table to kiss her. "I guess you wouldn't."

They'd tried everything Hannah's reproductive endocrinologist and infertility specialist (REI) had recommended. As a physician, Hannah had known what to expect, but even so, this had been demoralizing beyond anything she could have imagined. For whatever reason, none of her embryo transfers had taken. None of them: they'd had not so much as a single heartbeat to celebrate. They'd agreed: the most recent implantation attempt—performed more than a month ago now—would be their last. Labs so far had been promising, but Hannah wasn't going to allow herself to hope until she saw a heartbeat on a screen.

Today she'd know, one way or the other.

As they made their way through the parking lot and then the lobby of the doctors' office building and then the elevator and the back entrance to Hannah's own practice—a multidisciplinary group with different ob-gyn specialists—Harry never let go of her hand. Her fingers had started to ache, but she didn't try to pull away. It wasn't until they were settled in the exam room of Nia Epps, Hannah's partner and REI specialist, that Harry finally seemed aware his paw-like hand was crushing Hannah's fingers.

"Oh shit," he boomed, causing someone passing by in the adjacent hallway to speed up. "You need these hands to operate!"

"I'm fine," she assured him, although secretly she had to stifle the urge to rub her damp, macerated fingers.

"I don't know if you can tell this or not," he said, in the sort of faux-confiding tone one used when trying to be funny but also speaking the truth. Above his mask, his eyes crinkled but didn't quite meet hers. "But I'm a wee bit nervous."

"Me too."

"What are we going to do after this? Blow off work?"

She smiled up at him. "I'm going to stay here and see patients, and you're going to drive the car down to the base and go to meetings, and then you're going to come back and pick me up." Harry, who was ex-military, worked for the Naval Base San Diego as a contractor. "No matter what happens, we're going to carry on with our regular day, okay? We can celebrate tonight." *Or mourn*, added some contrary voice in her mind, even though she did not believe that would be necessary. This time, she'd be pregnant.

"Either way, I might have to have a beer after this."

"Harry. You will not."

Before he could work this little tease into a whole routine, the door swung wider and Nia swished in. Nia stood at least five foot ten but invariably wore killer stilettos, so next to Hannah's sweetly rounded five-two, she resembled an alien species. Hannah found herself at times intimidated by Nia's unceasing accumulation of accomplishments: she'd graduated from one of the finest fellowships in the country, she played the cello at a near-virtuoso level, and her memoir about her mother's experience as an immigrant had just been picked up by the country's largest publisher.

She also had two children and a strong sarcastic streak. Hannah adored her.

Nia must have checked her sarcasm at the door today. She didn't wait for the ultrasound tech but instead swooped over toward Hannah like some elegant but predatory stork. "I'm going to do the ultrasound myself," she said, enunciating behind her mask so they could understand her. That was one thing Hannah already missed, both as a doctor and as a patient: the ability to hear people clearly and see their faces as they spoke. You lost nuance without full facial expressions. Hannah tried as best she could to convey empathy and concern and kindness with just her eyes, but it was difficult when you were shouting at people.

"Bloodwork still looking good, my friend," said Nia. "Let's do this."

Hannah closed her eyes. At the touch of the ultrasound probe, her earlier confidence deserted her, replaced with a wash of sadness. How had it come down to this moment? There had never been a time in her life when she hadn't been obsessed with the idea of becoming a mother. She'd been the sort of little girl who carried her dolls everywhere, naming them, fixing their hair, feeding them, creating elaborate backstories for them—they'd been rescued from orphanages or saved from cruel parents or discovered abandoned in forests, and she'd loved and tended and nurtured them until their soulless plasticized bodies glowed with an almost sentient appreciation. Oh, how she'd loved those dolls! Her favorite, inexplicably named Feenie, had been bizarre-looking, with coarse blond hair and a petulant face and a lumpy, misshapen cloth body, out of which protruded sticklike plastic limbs of a malignant peachy yellow. Because of her ugliness, Hannah had loved her most. Even as a little child, she'd recognized and recoiled from the cruelty the world hurls at a less-than-beautiful female.

She wanted to experience the process she'd spent her entire adult life shepherding in others. All the years of thinking about it, all the effort and time and money and prayer and *longing*—all of it came down to this one final moment. She was in her forties. She'd likely never have another chance.

"Hannah," said Nia, and this time her voice was so quiet Hannah had to strain to hear it. For a bleak moment, she understood Nia must be preparing to console her, but as she opened her eyes, Nia's fist shot straight up, pumping at the air eight or ten times in an explosion of pure joy. It was clear from her exuberance that if her other hand hadn't been clutching the ultrasound probe, she'd have been jumping up and down like a ten-year-old.

"Congratulations, Mama," she said, swiveling the monitor. Hannah looked at the screen, and there it was amid a grainy, undulating background: the quivering little blip of a heartbeat. Her own heart froze.

Harry reacted first, leaping to his feet after a brief moment of stunned silence. "Yeah!" he shouted, both fists hammering at the air. "Yeah! Yeah! Yeah!" He turned to Hannah, snatching her hands and raising them so high she worried he'd yank her off the exam table and send her crashing through the plaster of the ceiling. She looked at him and was startled to see tears streaming down his face. "Hannah," he said. "Hannah."

Nia allowed them another long look at their child—still a formless, minute blob, but nonetheless breathtaking—and removed the ultrasound probe. She stepped back, giving Harry a wide berth. Despite his military bearing, Harry'd never been one to espouse a faux masculinity: he was plenty emotional. Love bubbled out of him with all the ardor of a teenage girl. He controlled his anger well, but when he found something amusing, he let go into full-on, head-tipped-back, openmouthed howling. His laughter could shake a concrete foundation.

But Hannah had never before seen him cry.

"Hannah," he said again, his elation spent. The years of failure escaped him in one fell swoop. At the foreign sound of him crying, she couldn't help it; she couldn't hold it in either. She sat up and scooted over to him, tilting her face up as he tilted his down, their cheeks colliding. She strained upward to press her face into his, savoring the rough rasp of his skin above his mask even as she tried to dry his face with her free hand. He grasped the back of her head, his shoulders shaking. It took every ounce of self-control she possessed not to wail aloud with joy and a weird, terrified, brand-new kind of grief. Now they had so much more to lose.

All she could do was close her eyes, trying to bring her breath under control.

Harry stroked her hair, his face still pressed to hers. "We're going to have a baby, my love," he whispered.

EVENTUALLY THEY CALMED down enough to talk. No pregnancy was without risk, of course, especially now, with a pandemic raging toward them with all the subtlety of a forest fire. Hannah watched Nia's face as she spoke but could not force herself to focus on the words. Harry didn't appear to be faring any better in the concentration department. He swiped at his eyes and fluttered his hands toward his face like somebody's old grandma, every now and then pausing to blow out a long, shuddery breath.

Nia finished up and he offered her a handshake. “You’re the greatest, Nia.”

“I’m so pleased, Harry. This is a blessed moment.”

Harry’s eyes crinkled up as he grinned. “I bawled like a little kid.”

“You’re entitled to cry all you want,” said Nia. Her eyelashes batted, dislodging a suspicious wetness of their own. “Plus, we love happy tears around here.”

After Harry left, Hannah sat for another moment in Nia’s office, stuck in that stage of suspended animation you feel after receiving life-altering news. The fact of her pregnancy was so new it felt unreal. Every time the thought crossed her mind, a burst of delight followed it, jolting her anew, followed immediately by fear. After years of trying, she’d managed to get pregnant in the midst of the worst pandemic of the century.

“Well, babe,” said Nia, “he took that well.”

“You have no idea how grateful we are.”

“I think I have *some* idea,” said Nia. Her eyes were smiling. She toyed with a silver pen, her nails clicking against it, before dropping the smile. “Listen, Hannah, I didn’t want to bring this up in front of Harry, but I think you need to consider quitting work.”

Hannah blinked. “What?”

“I know, I know,” said Nia. She set her pen down. “You’re early in the pregnancy, so it’d be a long time to be off, plus I assume you’d want a maternity leave. I’ll be honest: I don’t know how the other partners would react to carrying the slack that long, especially now. But we don’t know what would be safe.”

“The virus.”

“The virus,” agreed Nia. “We don’t have a clue what the virus does to an unborn child, or whether pregnant women are more susceptible to its effects. It’s difficult to shield yourself from inhaling viral particles during a delivery or a surgery.”

“It’s not bad here now,” protested Hannah, despite a shudder of fear blowing through her. A few of her patients flashed through her mind, including one with whom she'd commiserated for years over their shared struggles with infertility. "I've already been exposed to it, at least. I was in Spain during the original outbreak and I didn't get sick."

"Maybe so, but that doesn't mean you're immune. We need to get you antibody-tested, whenever they get that figured out. But until then, I'd lie low. And yes: I know it's not bad here, but it's coming. Look at New York."

"Have there been any new reports from the White House?"

Nia's eyes flicked toward her computer. "There's supposed to be an announcement right now."

Hannah scooted her chair around to Nia's side of the desk as Nia opened her browser. Every news outlet carried the president's daily briefings, which typically occurred in the evenings. This one must be different.

They watched as the White House press secretary, a distinguished-looking silver-haired man, finished some remarks. He left and the president stepped to the podium in front of the traditional blue backdrop, behind a wall of what appeared to be clear plexiglass. Her mask had a clear panel in front so the press corps and television viewers could see her face. She adjusted the microphone—at five feet two inches, Madam President Callista Corbett held the distinction of being the shortest president in American history—and in a clear, strong voice thanked doctors and nurses and first responders, before moving on to specifics about the plan of attack.

"It's been a long time since this country suffered a pandemic," she said, "and in that time we've made a lot of adjustments in our preparedness, because we knew not only that one day another pandemic would occur but that we're overdue for one with high lethality. When word of an emerging disease abroad reached the White House, the first thing we did was turn to our experts to coordinate a three-pronged federal plan: first, to prevent spread as much as possible; second, to initiate the best possible medical care; and third, to take steps to mitigate the unavoidable economic effects. The federal government gets a bad rap for a lot of things—deservedly, I might add—but my pledge to you is that we will use every bit of the mighty power of the U.S. government to overcome this plague."

A rustling from the press corps; the camera cut to them.

"We are going to mass-produce masks with embedded brand-new antiviral technology that may disable a virus before you inhale it," said the president. "We have an army of testers and contact tracers, and we have the reagents and supplies we need to perform mass testing, which will be essential to keeping our economy going as much as possible. We will communicate constantly with our state leaders about what resources are needed and how to get them there. And once a vaccine is available, we have the capability to produce, distribute, and administer it quickly."

She paused, a bright glint in her eyes. As the first Black female president, Callista Corbett had been attacked for any number of things, but you could not accuse her of a lack of intensity. She was small but sharp, known to read so voraciously she often landed several steps ahead of her own expert advisers.

"I cannot promise you a lack of pain," she said finally. "We are facing suffering on a scale few of us have seen in our lifetimes. But I can promise you this: we will utilize every bit of this country's remarkable ingenuity to protect you, and we will do it equally for all of us. Our plan will not leave out those of you who are most economically and medically vulnerable. If you are a frontline worker of any kind, we will do everything in our power to protect you. If your livelihood is threatened, we have a detailed plan to help you. To ensure transparency, those plans will be posted on whitehouse dot gov."

She paused again, as if thinking, and offered a wry half smile. "I'll keep the politics to a minimum. But I want you to know this: I take responsibility for whatever happens. I know all too well we are not—and I am not—infallible. When mistakes occur, we will acknowledge them and we will address them.

"It's important to understand our scientific understanding of the virus is evolving, which means we *will* get things wrong, especially at first. Despite some successes, we got off to a rocky start in New York City," she continued, leaning forward, "and the reason for that was the one thing we didn't have: much knowledge about this particular virus. Or at least most of us didn't have much knowledge of this particular virus. I'm going to introduce you to one of the few people who know a lot about artioviruses and who has been instrumental in helping us formulate our collective response. With me today is Dr. Kira Marchand, from the Centers for Disease Control and Prevention, and she'll be speaking and answering questions."

Hannah gasped.

"Are you okay?" Solicitous, Nia turned to her.

"I'm fine. That's one of my closest friends—the doctor from the CDC. I've texted her a thousand times since we got back."

The president—the president!—ran though the details of Kira's biography. After finishing, she exited the stage. Around ten slow seconds went by—the president now out of sight—and then Kira appeared, dressed in a mask with a clear panel in the front and a militaristic-looking uniform resembling those of the navy.

Hannah could not control two simultaneous and augmentative emotions blooming within her: first, sympathetic terror on behalf of Kira, who was about to speak in front of the entire United States; and second, a burning curiosity about how she'd be received. Hannah loved Kira, but even with her friends, Kira had a tendency to talk over people's heads. She didn't have a wholesome telegenic look either: her short hair veered toward the punkish side, and, apparently, at some point in her life, she'd made the decision not to bother with braces. Hannah found her serious, angular face to be compelling in its intensity, but what would other people think?

Kira started talking, and if she shared Hannah's fear of public speaking, she hid it well, sounding calm and composed and knowledgeable—all qualities you'd want in a public health official running through the more technical points of a deadly plague. She looked straight into the camera and didn't bobble her head around or say *um* a lot. A welling admiration lapped at Hannah's heart at this unexpected talent of Kira's. Since the friends had scattered around the country after medical school, none of them had ever seen each other in action at their jobs. This led to something of a regression in their personalities whenever they got together; to each other, to some extent, they were still mired in the mindsets of their twenty-six-year-old selves. Whenever they saw one another—once or twice a year—they'd inevitably spend the evenings drinking and reminiscing about the stupid yet exciting escapades of their medical school days and the unbreakable bond of their decades of friendship. Together they'd lived through hijinks and bad romances and scholastic challenges and intercontinental relocations and husbands and babies and teenagers and infertility and divorce and terrible illnesses and the loss of loved ones and the literal life-and-death intensity of their careers, and through all of it, it took only a phone call to summon instant, unconditional support from people who loved you. All this, and yet Hannah had never perceived her friends to be the experts they were in their respective fields.

". . . those are two ends of a continuum," Kira was saying. Uh-oh. What had Hannah missed? "When a virus is transmitted via respiratory droplets, that means the microorganisms are contained within tiny fluid pockets emitted by an infected person when they sneeze or cough or talk. These droplets are heavy compared to the organism itself, and they fall and settle on surfaces. So we recommend wearing masks to help protect you—and even more, the people around you—and we recommend hand washing to cleanse yourself of any droplets you might have touched.

"But airborne transmission is a more efficient means of causing an infection. If a virus is truly airborne, it is contained in a microscopic particle that can remain suspended in the air for a long period of time."

The camera switched views. Behind a second framed wall of some clear material sat a couple dozen reporters, all of them wearing odd-looking masks mounted on pairs of filter cartridges, different than those of Kira and the president. One of them waved his hand and Kira nodded at him. The masks must have been outfitted with some sort of microphone or Bluetooth connection, because when the man spoke, his voice came across loud and clear.

"Jackson MacDonald, NBC News. Can you give us an example of an airborne virus? And explain what you mean by 'more efficient means of causing an infection'?"

"To answer that second question, it refers to an epidemiological term called R_0, or the basic reproductive number," Kira said, pronouncing the term "R-naught." "It's a measure of how many other people a sick person infects. If you get an infection and pass it on to two people, that's an R_0 of 2. But it's not a biological constant; contagiousness is affected by all sorts of factors, so even the best R_0s are estimates, especially early in an outbreak.

"If the R_0 is below 1, we expect an outbreak to end, and if it is above 1, we expect an outbreak to continue. To give you the example of a droplet-transmission-type virus like influenza, the R_0 can vary a bit. It depends on the strain, how many people have been vaccinated, et cetera. But for the H1N1 strain of flu, we'd estimate it to be between 1.4 and 1.6."

Okay, Hannah was with her so far. The flu, most of the time, was contagious enough to keep itself going but not contagious enough to infect an entire population.

"Now, contrast that to the influenza pandemic of 1918, where the death toll from a novel strain of flu was estimated to be between fifty and a hundred million people," said Kira. "We think the R_0 there averaged along the lines of 1.8 to 2.8, depending on which wave and which location you're talking about. You can appreciate how a new strain of the virus and a small increase in the R_0 corresponded to a big jump in morbidity and mortality."

She stopped, surveying her audience. "Now to the first question. One of the best-known examples of an airborne infection is measles. It's an incredibly contagious virus that used to maim and kill children with regularity."

A different reporter, a middle-aged man with a pompous voice and a smooth helmet of hair, raised his hand. "So what's the R_0 of measles?"

"The R_0 of measles," said Kira, "is between 12 and 20."

There were a few audible gasps. The camera cut to the press pool, where you could practically read little cartoonish thought bubbles floating above their heads. A bunch of hands sprang up and waved.

"I think I know what you want to ask," said Kira. "I'm going to get to the R_0 of the ART virus in a moment. But it gets complicated, so I ask you to bear with me." She paused. "By the way, there's an element in the media referring to this virus as NARS-Ar-V—the North African Artiovirus—or sometimes as the Morocco Virus, and I'd like to encourage you not to do that. This virus likely did not originate in Morocco, and even if it had, the scientific community has moved away from the older practice of naming illnesses after their initial locations."

"Why?" asked someone.

"Because it leads to a big geopolitical squabble. You get people using the origin terms because they want to harm or embarrass the people or the governments in those regions, and that's counterproductive from a disease-control standpoint. So we're calling this one CARS-ArV. The 'CA' stands for 'camel-associated' since we believe the virus transferred to humans from artiodactyls like camels."

A heated babble broke out. One man raised his voice above the rest. "CAR ART? You're calling this thing CAR ART?"

"No, I'm not calling it CAR ART, because that sounds silly and this is not a silly situation," said Kira. Her voice had taken on a slight edge of impatience. "You can call it the CAR ART virus if you don't want to be taken seriously. But I'd refer to it as the artiovirus, or by its scientific name: CARS-ArV."

Light laughter in the room as the CAR ART guy took his seat. "If it came from camels, is it related to MERS?" asked the next questioner, a woman from NPR.

Kira looked relieved. "That's a good question. MERS was also associated with camels, though a different kind of camel and a different kind of virus. But it does bring up an interesting dilemma."

The press waited.

"One of the tools we use to try to eradicate a virus is to extinguish its animal reservoir. We've done that before in China with palm civets and in America with chickens and in Britain with cows. But it would be very difficult to do with camels."

"Why?"

"Well, it's one thing to take out a bunch of palm civets or ferret badgers or even chickens. They're not exactly beloved pet-like creatures. But camels are a prized animal. They're vital in a whole bunch of different areas of commerce and culture. Plus, would you want to be the one to slaughter millions and millions of camels? That would create a lot of supersized corpses, which would be difficult and dangerous to dispose of. Have you ever seen a camel up close? They're huge and they're very fetching animals."

The press calmed down. Some of them were even smiling.

"So," said Kira, "we're going to try a different approach. We're going to try to vaccinate the camels. Now"—she held up a hand—"before you ask, we don't have a vaccine yet, for either camels or humans. But that's one of the things we are working on to halt future spread of this virus. And, as you know, viruses mutate."

The babble sprang up again. Kira talked over it until it quieted. "To go back to your earlier questions, I mentioned measles. Measles is one of the most contagious viruses we have: it can hover in the air hours after the infected person has left the room, so another person can come in and contract it without ever having had person-to-person contact. There have been cases of people catching measles from colleagues who worked on different floors in the same building. As I said, we believe the R_0 of measles to be between 12 and 20." She paused, her eyes downcast. "We believe the R_0 of the ART virus to be between 14 and 24."

There was a stunned silence, and then an uproar broke out, every reporter in the room on his or her feet. Kira waved them down. "I said earlier it's complicated, and here's why. During the initial outbreaks, both in Europe and in Africa, it did not appear ART was very contagious. People were getting quite sick, but they weren't spreading it to other people unless they had prolonged, direct contact. That made it relatively easy to control. But now we are looking at a different scenario, where it is obvious that in some locations the virus is spreading more quickly, especially on the East Coast of the United States. Why? Well, we now know there are at least two different circulating variants of the ART virus of clinical significance. One of them has an R_0 of somewhere around 1.2 and the other has an R_0 of around 20. The virus mutated, or another strain emerged independently." She paused, looking into the camera. "And we believe the second variant is fully airborne."

13 Every Armchair Virologist in America

KIRA

ATLANTA, GEORGIA
137 Days After Patient Zero

MY BRANCH AT THE CDC HEADQUARTERS IN ATLANTA BY DAY looked much the same as it did by night. Which is to say: more than four months since the death of Patient Zero, a reduced number of people worked in the building, but the ones who showed up toiled around the clock. Many of the faces I'd seen every day for years were absent, most having been deemed able to work from home. In their places, a new but smaller crop of faces appeared.

Like many complex organizations, the Centers for Disease Control and Prevention consists of a structured hierarchy. A lot of people don't realize it, but the first letter of the acronym CDC stands for the word *Centers*, not *Center*. My center, the National Center for Immunization and Respiratory Diseases (NCIRD), further breaks down into divisions and then into branches. Then, within the branch, you have specific teams, and within those teams, you have leaders and, finally, various job titles.

All that to say: people who don't work at the CDC have a tendency to assume everyone there knows one another, not realizing perhaps that employees of the CDC number more than ten thousand. Meanwhile, people who work here might not know anyone outside their branch, let alone someone from a different center. Not to mention the fact that recognizing someone only from the nose up is harder than you might think.

It wasn't surprising, therefore, that I had no idea of the identity of the person who'd just offered me a salute as we crossed paths in the hallway. "Keep the faith, Dr. M," he yelled from behind his mask, not breaking stride.

That was . . . a lot of energy for so early in the morning. Still, I was grateful for the support. My new visibility had resulted in quite a bit of downside. Now that I'd appeared several times on television, every armchair virologist in America felt as if they not only knew me but were qualified to weigh in with their opinion on my opinions. Given that most of their opinions seemed to have hatched from the bowels of some antigovernment sociopath on Twitter, this had become unpleasant.

Early on, Wally and I had been summoned to a virtual task force meeting with the CDC Washington director, the chief strategy officer/COO, and the deputy director of the whole shebang, along with a slew of other luminaries, in which we'd been informed that the federal government was arranging for us to have a security detail. Immediately, we'd both protested. Wally, especially, seemed to find this proposal emasculating.

"I'm grateful, of course," he said, his face reflecting anything but gratitude. "But . . ." I glanced at him, waiting for the other shoe to drop. This conference was chock-full of M.D.s, Ph.D.s, M.P.H.s, and people with obscure military titles; they constituted some of the most powerful people in Washington and Atlanta. None of them looked as if they possessed a sense of humor. Wally, on the other hand, was renowned for his practical jokes. Once, on an EIS investigation of a mysterious sickness at the Republican National Convention (nonlethal; non-terrorism), he'd sent the team a box that turned out to contain three tiny mechanical elephants that marched around trumpeting to the tune of a popular country music song until, suddenly, they fell over and died with their legs sticking straight up. This was in poor taste, but it paled in comparison to some of his other pranks. How Wally had survived the quasi-militaristic bureaucracy of the EIS followed by the bureaucratic bureaucracy of the CDC without getting himself sacked, or at the very least reprimanded, was a mystery for the ages.

"But I won't be needing security," he finished, more or less harmlessly. I breathed a sigh of relief as he twirled the Molestache. "I am not the kind of person who can function with an entourage."

"You will both have a security detail," said the COO, with no inflection in her voice whatsoever. That concluded the discussion on this topic; the conversation moved on to something else, leaving Wally sitting there with his mouth open.

Now, in October, the promised escort had never quite materialized. The powers that be eventually agreed we were not at particular risk within the confines of the CDC itself. When Wally and I were at work, we could roam free. Whenever we set foot outside the building, however, we were supposed to gain a shadow, but after a few weeks of promises, the expense had become too burdensome or the horde of potential anti-vaccine assassins had never materialized or, most likely, someone in the government had realized neither of us was particularly recognizable or even interesting to the public, and the idea of a security detail had melted away.

Next to mine, a door shut. Wally, his arms full of reams and reams of paper, stepped into the hall. "Hey there, tree killer," I said.

Wally looked up, startled. In contrast to the buoyant young man who'd passed by a second ago, all of Wally's features had taken on a droopy cast. His shoulders slumped. His eyelids were fixed at half-mast. Even his mustache had shed its Tom Selleck vibe and now ran more along the lines of what you'd expect on a very sad walrus. He held his breath, lodged his cache of papers under an armpit to free up a hand, and yanked up his mask to cover his mouth.

"I don't like reading on screens," said Wally, mournfully but loudly.

"Oh, Wally," I said, alarmed. "You look terrible."

"I'm fine," yelled Wally.

"How about you turn on your microphone so you don't have to scream?"

"I'm not one of the stricken, if that's what you're thinking," said Wally in an irritable tone, flicking a switch embedded into the strap of his mask. "I'm fifty-eight damn years old and I'm working twenty damn hours a day, so consequently, I look offensive."

"Go home and rest, Wally, please. Sleep until you wake up. The country is not going to crumble if you take one day off."

"That's exactly what would happen. And you know it, or you wouldn't be here yourself"—he directed a pointed look at his watch—"at five thirty in the morning."

I acknowledged this with a nod. I couldn't remember the last time I'd had a full night's sleep or a decent meal or sufficient time with the children. The days had blurred into a stream of indistinguishable videoconferences and report generating and media interfacing and lab supervising and task force coordinating and data analysis, measured only in retrospect by milestones both good and bad. These kept rolling in, at a pace difficult to absorb: Europe and India were ablaze. East Asia, which had a population cooperative with public health measures, was faring relatively well, as were a few areas in Western Africa that had put their experience with prior pandemics—especially Ebola—to good use. Other countries, starved of even basic resources, faced a humanitarian crisis beyond comprehension. New Zealand, Australia, and Hawaii—all islands—had been among the earliest to fully close their borders while instituting a robust quarantine and, as a consequence, had almost no circulating disease. South America was as yet fairly calm.

The United States varied by region. New York's title as the most-affected city per capita had been taken over by Houston, which in turn had been replaced by, of all places, Des Moines, Iowa. Most other cities were less affected. Researchers announced they were edging closer to vaccine trials. Other researchers admitted the failure of every antiviral drug they'd tried so far. A handful of very famous people had died: the governor of Florida, Leonardo DiCaprio, half the bench of the L.A. Lakers. An experimental drug developed to work against paramyxoviruses had been showing some promise until researchers realized it made you deaf.

In my pocket, my phone buzzed. I eased it into view and held a finger to Wally to indicate I'd be a moment. He nodded and leaned against the wall as I slipped back into my office to answer an incoming call from Declan.

I'd begun to worry about him. The last time we'd spoken—more than three weeks ago—I'd expected the same collective dejection present in everyone's voices these days, but his tone had surprised me.

"It's going super well," he'd said. This had been a phone call at the end of September, not a video chat; Declan said his bandwidth was overwhelmed, what with everyone streaming all day. A tinny strain of music chimed from somewhere behind him, along with the sound of someone repeatedly but cheerfully swearing under their breath.

"Are you in the lab?" I asked.

"Yeah," he said, the same upbeat note present in his voice. "We've all been going in to test Humpy against the new strain." Declan's researchers affectionately referred to the newly modified nanobody as Humpy, since camelids were utilized by the specialized company they employed to challenge the animals. "Humpy" as a name for a potential medical breakthrough may have lacked dignity, but at least their first attempt at a nickname—Camel Toe—hadn't stuck. I knew he couldn't have results yet—it took ninety days to get the animals boosted and then another intricate process to isolate the RNA, sequence it, clone it, and encode it into a vector. Why was he so happy?

His next statement answered that question. "We haven't formalized it yet," he said, "but we're in with the university."

Declan had long desired an academic partnership. There were some disadvantages, but also improved resources, chief among them that they'd have access to a biosafety level 3 lab.

"Do they already have samples?"

"Not yet," he said. "We're still waiting to get more. You've still got the original I gave you, yeah?"

"I do."

"Hang on to it," he said. "It could save someone's life someday."

"You're being careful," I said, offering this as a statement.

"'Course," he said, and then, to someone else, "Not there, that one's full, you dense eejit." Back into the phone: "Of course we are. We're going to hand over the fun stuff to the BSL-3 guys in a week or so, but we've got plenty keeping us busy now. Except for Sam here; he's truly hopeless." In the background, roars of laughter; there were at least several people with him, then. "But you can appreciate it: we've got to keep working."

"Dec," I said, suspicious, "did you take your mask off to talk to me?"

He'd shifted the subject then, still dodgy a moment later when I attempted to pin down the specifics of what he was working on. He asked about the kids and offered to be on the next plane to Atlanta if we needed anything—as soon as the world normalized again—and told me in his most seductive voice that he missed me—ah, Declan!—and then: nothing. Total radio silence. The days ticked by without hearing from him. He didn't answer messages. This was so unlike him that even at work the anxiety over his well-being rubbed at the margins of my thoughts, eroding my equilibrium to the point where I questioned my ability to do my job. Surely—surely he hadn't died, right? Wouldn't someone from his lab have told me? But maybe not: who thinks to notify an ex-girlfriend in an emergency, no matter how closely they've stayed in touch?

"Dec," I said now, answering his call. "Where the hell have you been?"

There was a silence. Then, a woman's voice: "I'm sorry, is this Kira Marchand?"

Something vicious launched itself at my chest. It bored into me, stealing my breath.

"Hello?" said the woman. An Irish voice. I felt my eyes fill.

"This is Kira," I managed.

"I'm Sarah MacGuire, Declan's sister." She must have heard my intake of breath, and she spoke quickly, before I could ask. "He's alive."

A beat, to give me time to absorb this. Then: "He's been sick, though. Went straight to the ICU in hospital, and I'm awfully sorry we weren't able to call you right away. His lab closed down when a number of the researchers got sick, and they've still not reopened."

"Is he okay?"

"He's still on the ventilator, as of today. But the doctors say"—she took a deep breath—"they say he's young and healthy and he's got a decent shot of making it. And of course we can't even see him. We can't get into Spain, or out of Ireland for that matter, not that I'd let Mam go anywhere at a time like this."

"But you've got his phone," I said.

"Yes." A rustling in the background and then a tiny voice: a child. Sarah must have muted herself, because all the noise vanished momentarily. Then she came back: "Sorry. Yes, well, not his phone. I've got his tablet. Declan asked one of the nurses to send it to us, just before they intubated him. He put a list on it—contacting lab mates with instructions and so forth—but unfortunately, he failed to send us the lock code. I've only just figured it out." She took a breath. "There's a message to you."

I waited.

"It says"—the plinky little tick of an iPad's keyboard—"it says . . ." She paused. "Uh, I don't— Maybe I shouldn't have— Is it okay if I send this to you instead?"

"Of course," I said. Perhaps Declan had proposed again. Perhaps the last thing he'd wanted me to know was that he still loved me.

A minute later, it was there, in my phone; blazing-hot black type on a white screen, maybe the last words I'd ever hear from Declan MacGuire. I read them and read them again, and then I clicked the email closed, but not before they'd burned their way into my brain. I could see them when I closed my eyes.

Kiki. About the gonorrhea: It was Sean, my other mate, we got it from. Hand to my heart.

Out of nowhere, I burst out crying.

WALLY DIDN'T APPEAR to notice my distraction as I joined him in the hall. Or maybe he did but attributed my blotchy face to one of the random grief attacks afflicting pretty much everybody at one time or another these days. He pointed down the hall, in the direction of the new videoconference suite. "Come," he said. "I was about to dive into the team reports."

We worked for a few hours, reading data aggregates from various sources. Wally, who refused to read on a screen, trundled back and forth from the conference room to the printer in his office. In short order, he'd accumulated a monstrous stack of stapled articles, one of which he flicked down the table in my direction. "You seen this?"

I glanced at it and, instead of picking it up, opened it in my browser to read. Ah. Back to my old friend, Pro-EID Com. *Influx of Patients Suffering New-Onset Cognitive Deficits in Madrid*, read the headline. I scanned the article and then read it again, more slowly. When I finished, I looked in Wally's direction and found him staring at me, waiting for my reaction. I kept my voice neutral. "Have we been hearing reports of anything like this here?"

He shook his head. "Haven't seen any. PubMed isn't showing anything here; neither is Pro-EID."

I allowed my gaze to drift, unfocused, beyond Wally as I tried to pin down something hovering at the edge of my consciousness. It flickered in and out of view, tantalizing me. I'd seen something similar to this before, but where? With a cry of victory, I redirected my attention to the computer. "I think I know where to look."

Wally started toward me but I waved him back. "Sit. I'll show you from here."

He aimed a questioning look in my direction but obeyed, shuffling back to his seat at the other end of the vast table. I brought up the Bluetooth menu on my laptop and tapped into the conference room's AV system. Once the giant screen at the other end of the room displayed my computer's home screen, I clicked on the menu tab and opened Facebook. "Here we go."

"Ah," said Wally, his voice tinny through the amplification system of his mask. "The Scientific Institute of Facebook. Is this data going to be prospective, double-blinded, and peer-reviewed?"

Ignoring him, I entered a private group consisting only of physicians. This one included doctors from all over the world, mainly in the fields of emergency medicine, critical care, and infectious disease. Wally studied the posts. "Why are half these people calling themselves BAFERDs?"

"It stands for 'bad-ass fucking emergency room doctor.' Before you ask, I don't think ID docs have our own bad-ass acronym. Somebody needs to get on that."

"B-A-I-D-D," said Wally. "Bay-ad. Bad. It works."

I navigated to the search bar within the group. Hesitating for a moment, I typed in "cognitive impairment," then erased it and started over. That was too vague; there were tens of thousands, if not hundreds of thousands, of posts in this group, covering every conceivable range of topic with even the slightest relevance to the practice of medicine as a whole.

Wally caught on. "Try 'convalescent ART patient,'" he suggested.

This brought up a slew of posts, one after another detailing patients who'd recovered from ART only to present months later with confusion, odd behavior, and seizures. I scrolled through them, clicking and opening a few that seemed the most pertinent. After fifteen minutes of intense reading, I slumped back and stared at Wally.

"We need to start collating these," he said quietly.

I nodded. "Can we get a couple of the EIS officers on it? We need somebody to contact every single one of the posters in this group to get more detail. If this is real . . ."

I didn't need to finish the sentence; Wally was already punching something into his phone. Within a few minutes two people appeared, a prematurely balding man in his thirties and a similar-aged woman with prematurely gray hair. It was unfortunate, I thought, that they'd been partnered, since together they gave the impression that enrollment in the Epidemic Intelligence Service sucked the life out of you. Or perhaps that was an accurate impression; these two were already overburdened to the point of exhaustion. Nonetheless, they attended to Wally's instructions with rapt attention, both of them taking notes.

"So . . . we're looking for ART survivors who return to an emergency department—what, months later?" the woman—Erica Ogino—asked.

I nodded. "Yes. At least three or four months out from recovery—we think these are all people who got sick early on, in the very first wave, and came back months later with sudden neurological symptoms. Start a database and get every shred of detail you can about them—the time course, gender, age, presenting symptoms, progression, outcome, location, treatment, confounding factors, general health, what treatment they received during ART; everything. Maybe these posts are a case of true-true-and-unrelated, but we need to look for patterns."

A look of intrigue lit the balding guy's face. "What could cause symptoms that late? Is this some kind of reinfection?"

"We don't have any—" I began, but Erica interrupted me, tapping a finger against her chin. "The herpes virus."

"What, you think these people have herpes?"

"No, I don't think they have herpes. But that virus family is known for establishing a dormant presence in nerve cells. It hangs out in your neurons until something reactivates it, right? That's why people who've had chicken pox are at risk for shingles later on. Or think about herpes simplex: years and years later it can cause encephalitis. These patients present with dramatic onset of fever, seizures, and altered mental status, and nobody has any idea why at first because the original infection was often so long ago. Maybe this virus can do the same thing. Maybe it causes some form of cerebral inflammation when it reemerges."

If Wally's expression was anything to judge by, he found this idea as unsettling as I did. Over the centuries, viruses have evolved different mechanisms of survival. Some, like influenza or Ebola, replicate in an explosion—possibly killing their hosts in the process but relying on the afflicted person to first pass them on to others by way of coughing or sneezing or bleeding or diarrhea. But some, as Erica had correctly stated, have engineered an even more ingenious means of survival. They bide their time by setting up long-term residency in the cells of their hosts, waiting for some stressor to jolt them back into action. Close to one hundred percent of the world's adult population harbor at least one of the eight members of the Herpesviridae family in their bodies, for example, putting them at risk of recurrent mononucleosis or herpes or shingles. Occasionally, such a virus could affect the brain, either directly or by causing the body's immune system to inflict its own form of terrible collateral damage.

Given that I myself had contracted this virus, the idea was unsettling.

After they left, I started to speak, but Wally cut me off.

"Let's not jump to any conclusions, okay? Don't bring this up in the task force meeting yet; we'll either sound like fools or we'll scare the shit out of everybody." He paused, presumably to consider the consequences of scaring the shit out of the members of the task force; some of these people were tiptoeing along a mighty fine trip wire these days. "Or both. Give Erica and Hai time to investigate and then we'll bump it up the chain. If we need to."

We settled back in, Wally returning to whatever he'd been doing before and me typing notes about the Facebook posts. At eight o'clock, I excused myself to walk back to my office so I could hammer out a quick call to the kids in private before our task force meeting.

Pre-pandemic, I'd had an arrangement with an older neighbor, Mrs. Biskup, to come in on the mornings when I had to leave early. Naturally, the children referred to her as Mrs. Biscuit and adored both her and the literal biscuits she baked for them. When the virus hit the nation, Atlanta had barely been affected compared to the hardest-hit cities, but Mrs. Biskup, whose mother had died in the influenza pandemic of 1968, professed herself too terrified to leave her apartment, even with one of the new antiviral masks. This was both understandable and prudent but left me with no childcare during the busiest professional time in my life.

It was less than ideal, but Rorie was now in charge of getting herself and Beau up and dressed. Their school had gone virtual for the duration, but I still insisted they rise before eight, eat, brush their teeth, and get semi-dressed every school morning.

"Hello, Ray of Sunshine," I said to a scowling Rorie. "What time is your first class?"

"Eight thirty," said Rorie. She fluttered her eyelashes dramatically. Good; Beau's first-grade class also went online at that time. They'd be occupied until I could arrive home near noon to check on them.

Speaking of Beau . . . "Where's Beau?"

Rorie yawned and stood, then padded toward the hallway. "I don't know."

"Well, did you wake him up?"

Rorie's eyes fluttered again. "I don't know."

"You don't know if you woke him up?"

"Beau!" bellowed Rorie, so loudly I flinched. "Wake up, Mom's on the phone."

"Rorie? Are you just now getting out of bed? Don't you have a test today?"

Rorie turned her head, revealing a diagonal sleep line running across her flushed cheek. She'd definitely just woken up. "Mom, you need to chill. It's homeschool."

I could hear the ticking of our grandfather clock in the living room, followed by a pattering of feet, growing louder by the second. Rorie's phone jerked and Beau's face appeared, framed by wild, luscious curls. "Hi, Mommy!"

"Hi, Beau."

"Guess what! I know what I want to be when I grow up!"

"What's that, sweetheart?" In addition to wanting to be an author, Beau's secondary career ambitions changed on a daily and sometimes hourly basis, depending on what books or podcasts he'd most recently listened to.

"A beachist!"

"A . . . beeshist? I'm not familiar with those."

"Beach-ist, Mom. You know, like a shelleographer?" Beau held the phone one inch from his face, providing a spectacular view of his nose and teeth. "They are people who study the sand and the sea."

"Oh, that's . . . well, that sounds intriguing, Beau. Like marine biology, maybe. Is Mrs. Hartell-Lydon doing a unit on the oceans?"

"Yes!" said Beau. He was in his default mood, which was chipper. "If we didn't have to do virtual learning, we were going to make as many *papier-mâché* sea creatures as the actual ocean, but Mrs. Hartell-Lydon says we can go ahead and do them at home if we are careful not to glue our hands to anything."

"Well . . . good . . . I'm not sure we have supplies for that, though."

"Do not worry about a thing. I got it figured out," said Beau, somewhat mysteriously. Before I could inquire further as to how he planned to make an ocean's worth of papier-mâché creatures from whatever crappy art supplies we had at home, Rorie reappeared.

"I need my phone, Mom. I have, like, five hundred quizzes today. Can you bring me some sparkling water to my room?"

"What, right now?"

"Like, soon."

Honestly. Teenagers were more narcissistic than toddlers. "I'm at work, Roar. I have a meeting with the president in a few minutes."

An eye roll. Staying hydrated for a ninth-grade Spanish quiz trumped task force meetings with POTUS, apparently. Rorie tilted the phone, providing a view of her torso and hips as she slouched into the kitchen to poke around in the fridge. She'd turned fifteen a few weeks ago, and her childish figure had stretched into a new vertical dimension but also solidified into the mass of an adult. She stood an inch taller than me but possessed all the dewy beauty of a little girl, a combination posing all sorts of dangers.

Along with the physical changes had come a corresponding increase in sauciness. And boys: they now flocked to her like a swarm of ants to sugar. She'd taken to switching off her phone whenever I came into the room, issuing an affronted yelp if I tried to peek over her shoulder at the screen. This phenomenon deserved more attention than I could muster, what with working eighteen-hour days and the medical/economic collapse of the country and all. I made a feeble effort to impose some parental order before we hung up: "Reminder, Rorie: no video calls with Gnash or whatever his name is—"

"Crash, Mom! And it's a nickname. His real name is Christopher."

"Well, let's call him Christopher, then. Crash is a terrible name. It makes me think of disasters. Anyway, no video calls with him, or anyone, until your schoolwork is done."

In a tone of pure outrage: "What?"

"No video calls until—"

"I *heard* you!"

"You asked what did I—"

"Mom! You are the worst! *Everyone* video calls or Snapchats all day because we do our work together. I have to get help, Mom, because do you want me to fail? *God.* Plus, this is the only way I have to see anyone, since *you* shut down the whole country."

I'd gotten stuck on the part about everyone doing the work together. Was that a bad thing? Maybe they were honing collaborative skills that would serve them well in the future. If, on the other hand, they were crowdsourcing a couple of nerds to do all the heavy lifting while the Gnashes and Crashes coasted around doing who knows what . . . drinking virtual beer while virtually propositioning innocent fifteen-year-olds . . . I considered how to best approach this. "Rorie," I said brightly, "what if we—"

Oh. Rorie had hung up.

AT EIGHT FORTY-FIVE, the room started to fill with people from various divisions, all of them wearing antiviral respirator masks fitted with microphones. These special microphone masks were distributed to medical professionals, government organizations, certain media outlets, and essential businesspeople but had also become a hot commodity on the black market, further propagating the centuries-old American tradition of silencing the poor. In addition to the microphones, they boasted an impregnated layer of graphene foam and zinc oxide nanoparticles that in theory trapped and deactivated the protein envelope of the virus. They cost about eight hundred dollars each.

Once everyone got their personal mike turned on, or silenced—depending on whether or not they had speaking privileges—the meeting commenced. We began by checking in with various field offices. First: Des Moines. Everyone signed in to the chat room in time to see Ashok Tamboli, one of the medical epidemiologists from my team, walking toward us inside a field hospital. He wore a full Tyvek suit and a respirator and appeared to be holding a fistful of blood tubes, which he shifted to the side of his hand in order to give us a wave. One of the bigwigs requested a virtual tour of the tent hospital, so another of the med epis, a woman named Christiane Blackwell, was suited up and carrying a camera around.

The tented room in which she stood spanned acres. Constructed of durable polyethylene stretched over stainless steel beams, the interior had been laid out in a neat grid. Color-coded military-issue cots lined the rows, stretching so far into the distance you couldn't see the most remote ones. Every cot had a thin half wall behind it, from which protruded oxygen and IV tubing.

Early in the pandemic, plans had been implemented to protect health-care workers, hospitals, and society in general. Local governments made available a massive rapid-testing program and provided quarantine information for the walking well. In the most afflicted cities, once ICUs were overrun, care shifted to these negative-pressure portable tent hospitals. Any citizen who became ill was given a set of instructions: first and foremost to stay home if at all possible, for a minimum of twenty-one days. Anyone moderately sick received a home medical kit through their local health department, along with regular video follow-up. If they couldn't stay home—because of seizures or an inability to breathe or excessive bleeding or complications from blood clots or any number of other appalling symptoms that had cropped up—then they were to be transported to the tent hospital. The tent hospital did provide treatment, mainly in the form of supplemental fluids and oxygen, although there were certain medications available to battle the virus and ease the symptoms. Ventilators, if they were available, were set up in a separate section.

The primary function of the tent, however, was quarantining the sick and disposing of the bodies of those who didn't make it. They got the oxygen and the IVs and the medicines, and then they either survived or they didn't.

"How are we doing on contact tracing in Sioux City?" someone asked.

"Very well," said Christiane. She swiveled so a view of clean, white tent wall replaced the image of all the writhing people on cots. "The horse has left the barn here in Des Moines. Obviously." She regurgitated a slew of numbers related to the outbreak. "But we're not seeing a significant rate of rise in the rest of the state, and I think we can thank Haven for that."

"Thank Haven" had become a constant refrain around the CDC. There were several reasons this epidemic hadn't exploded into every city across the United States, and Haven was one of them. A cloud-based software program, it used proximity-based Bluetooth technology to track the spread of the disease. Public health workers worked with the sick person, using cell phone data—assuming the person consented—to trace their movements over the preceding few days. The Bluetooth coordinates of the sick person's movements were matched with a database of commercial establishments in the area, allowing the officials to notify the cell phones of anyone who'd been in the same area at the same time, while keeping the identities of both parties fully anonymous.

This related to the second reason—or reasons, really—we'd been able to slow the spread of CARS-ArV-02. Two characteristics inherent to the virus itself had aided us: the new variant of the virus, while much more contagious, also demonstrated a much shorter lag time between exposure and symptoms than did CARS-ArV-01, meaning contact tracers only had to deal with a few days' worth of potential exposures. This mutation also seemed to be most infectious *after* symptoms had started, reducing transmission by asymptomatic carriers. These two factors, plus a rigorous and early testing program combined with mandatory masking, had allowed the economy to remain at least semi-functional in the cities that weren't experiencing bad outbreaks.

Finally, in my opinion, the most salient reason we'd managed to contain the second-variant outbreaks in most places had just joined the meeting via videoconference: the president of the United States.

"Hello, people of the CDC," she said. She sat at the head of a long oval table filled with suits. Unlike the weary CDC participants, the president's people all demonstrated impeccable posture. No slouchers allowed in the presence of POTUS.

No slackers either. The day of the Tarifa ferry incident—the death that had awoken the world to the start of the pandemic—the president had convened a task force of public health experts, including academicians from major public and private research universities across the United States along with scientists from WHO and the NIH. Also present were representatives from USAMRIID, the Department of Defense's facility in Fort Detrick, Maryland. Finally, a group of economists and public policy people and community activists were seeded in, to prevent the eggheads on the science committees from going hog wild shutting things down if they didn't have to be shut down. A trained facilitator chaired every committee, in an attempt to prevent the kind of paralyzing interagency squabbling that ground these types of things to a halt. Success in this area had been mixed, certainly: no one was claiming things were good.

But they could have been much worse.

President Corbett had listened to our recommendations and had taken steps to ramp up the manufacture or purchase of essential items: reagents and specialized nasal swabs for testing, bioreactors for vaccine manufacture, sterile vials and syringes for hundreds of millions of people once a vaccine was ready, increased production of antiviral masks, a battalion of contact tracers, an increased supply of ventilators, an increased supply of PPE, an increased supply of anesthesia medications and antiseizure drugs, and various other necessities. Within a week, she'd browbeaten Congress into authorization for trillions of dollars of funding and delegated people to get the ball rolling on every available preventative measure. In the eyes of the medical community, the president of the United States had transcended mere mortality and become a kind of goddess. It was widely known that her interest in science and medicine long predated the artiovirus pandemic; she'd even named her daughter Mae, after the great Mae Jemison.

Now, though, I stifled a yawn as someone at the DOD spoke about infection within the armed forces. With a large, young population in close quarters, the military had been at extraordinary risk for the spread of disease, something to which they'd devoted an equally extraordinary amount of defensive and offensive planning. The planning had paid off: to date, no large-scale outbreaks had occurred among military personnel. The information from the military guy was interesting, but I found myself battling a sudden wave of exhaustion. Too disciplined to allow my mind to wander, I set an internal alarm to go off if anyone uttered any of my keywords and granted myself a short mental break. I'd learned this trick for enduring long meetings at the beginning of my fellowship, and it worked well. I focused on my breathing, allowing the words to wash over me but divorcing them from their meaning. After three minutes, feeling somewhat refreshed, I tuned back in.

Wally was up next. He presented data from the latest phylogenetic analysis of the virus, tracing back the two clinically relevant mutations to explore where they'd diverged. He also went through some material on animal reservoirs—now confirmed to be a specific breed of camel—and touched on the ongoing research into antivirals.

The president listened, her eyes locked on the screen. A woman of scrupulous integrity, she kept notes on every briefing she received, firing off questions to her aides later about anything she didn't fully comprehend. She churned out a few questions for Wally now, batting back his answers with more complicated questions until finally wrapping things up with a softball about total mortality counts in the United States. This was outside Wally's scope, but, like everyone else, he followed the news.

"I believe it is approaching one million, Madam President."

"One million. Kinda hard to fathom that number, yeah?" The president hailed from North Carolina and liked to deploy a friendly folksiness with all her *y'alls* and *yonders*, especially right before she flamed somebody to bits. Wally braced himself.

He wasn't her target, however. "Christiane," she called. On the screen at the tent hospital, Christiane jolted in her big suit, apparently not expecting the president of the United States to know her name or call her out. "Madam President?"

"Christiane, I'm sorry we missed your presentation earlier. Can you turn around for me?"

Christiane pivoted in a slow circle, keeping the tablet trained on her face.

"No, my apologies, Christiane, I mean, can you turn the camera around?"

Christiane complied. The rows and rows of cots came back into view.

"Walk forward for me, please."

We all watched as the camera drew closer to the nearest row of cots. At first, to preserve some semblance of decorum, the people in charge of the tent hospitals had tried segregating the rows by gender and age. For whatever reason—biology or behavior or some combination of the two—men tended to die at higher rates than women, so there were many more men languishing in these beds. They'd stopped assigning rows on the basis of gender and age once they realized the inherent cruelty in separating couples. As appalling as it was to witness your loved one circling the drain right next to you, it was more appalling to picture them dying all alone in the midst of hundreds of people. Now whenever someone new came in, they got placed next to their family or friends, if they had any present. This row, however, appeared to be all men.

"Thank you, you can stop there. Can this gentleman speak?"

The camera lurched forward a bit, revealing a young man in an oxygen mask with his eyes closed. The visible portion of his face reflected the dusky cyanotic hue I'd come to associate with imminent death. Sweat gleamed at his temples. His breathing, even over the oxygen mask, sounded in sonorous, irregular bursts.

"I think he's asleep, Madam President."

"Don't wake him up. Go on to the next one."

The next man appeared to be conscious, but barely. A reedy man in his thirties or forties, he lay unmoving save for his chest, which puffed in and out far too fast. He too had an oxygen mask clamped to his face, but his eyes fluttered open and closed. Christiane brought the camera closer to him.

"Hold it so he can see me," commanded the president.

"Sir," said Christiane to the man. "I have President Corbett here. She'd like to speak with you."

"Oh, sure . . ." said the man, managing, even in his weakened state, to roll his eyes a little. As Christiane lowered the tablet and he caught sight of the people on the screen, his eyes flew all the way open.

"I am sorry to disturb you, sir, but thank you for talking with me," said the president. "Are you able to speak comfortably?"

The man pulled down his oxygen mask. Immediately his work of breathing increased; he drew in a loud, labored breath but kept his eyes trained on the tablet. "I'm," he rasped. "Not. Going to make it."

The president did not attempt to argue with this assertion. Instead she studied the man for a moment, a bright fluidity shining in her brown eyes. She didn't blink. "What's your name? If you don't mind sharing it, that is."

"I'm . . . Nathaniel Amir, ma'am. Nate."

"Mr. Amir, Nate, I can see it's hard for you to breathe, so I won't keep you long."

An explosive cough escaped Mr. Amir, flinging a dark red glob of sputum onto the tablet. For a moment we might as well have been viewing him through a ruby. Christiane wiped the tablet with something and retrained it on Mr. Amir, who wore an expression of horror at having coughed up part of his lung onto the president of the United States.

"I'm sorry . . ."

"Do not," said the president, "be sorry. I'm sorry, Mr. Amir—Nate—for failing you. Tell me what you need. I'll do anything I can for you."

"Is there any," said Nate. He stopped, breathing heavily, and started again. "I need . . ."

"Go on," said the president. She sat, straight-backed and square-shouldered, her face free of makeup, her ears and neck unadorned with jewelry. She regarded Mr. Amir for a long time without blinking. "It's okay."

Nate struggled onto his forearms, rasping in a shuddery breath. Like the president, he'd mastered the knack of digital eye contact, never looking away from the camera, even as he worked to take in enough air to speak. "My wife," he said finally. "My girls. They're home. Can you . . ."

"Would you like us to check on them? I can have someone do that right now."

"Yes," said Nate. Another pause as he sucked in air, the sound magnified by the speakers in the room into a scuttling inhuman scrape. "Yes, please. Ayshana . . . Sasha, and Lynnie. Please." He stopped again. "I need to know . . . they're okay. Before . . . I die."

"We'll find out for you," said the president. Her posture remained rigid, but her tone had softened, so much so that several people jerked their gaze from the screen, startled. "We'll check on them for you, Mr. Amir, and we'll help them if they need anything. I promise you, I will see they get anything they need. You have my word."

Mr. Amir nodded, slumping back onto his pillow.

"I pray you'll find some peace," said the president, her tone so gentle she might have been whispering to a sleeping baby. A tear slid down her cheek and bumped across the edge of her mask. "All of us in this room are praying for your survival."

He nodded at her, acknowledging her statement even as he shook his head. "No peace," he said. "I'll worry about my girls . . . 'til . . . my dying breath." He pulled up his mask, took in a deep breath, and pulled it down again.

"Ma'am?"

"Yes?"

"Thank." He sucked in another breath and held on to it. "You. For everything. You've done."

CHASTENED BY THE president's demonstration, I lost the next few minutes of the meeting. It's one of the dangers of academic medicine: you focus on metrics and lose sight of the beautiful, messy, heart-stabbing reality of the human beings those numbers represent. Afterward, the president hadn't spelled out her message to us, but she hadn't needed to; the image of the breathless, gasping, dying Mr. Amir, whose only concern when offered the full assistance of the president of the United States had been the welfare of his family, would be burned into our brains forever. And her: I will never forget the absolute stillness of her face, the burning focus of her gaze as she'd trained it on Mr. Amir, narrowing the world to the two of them. In that moment, none of us had dared to breathe, transfixed by the shared pain of the most powerful person in the world and an ordinary man who would not live through the night. More than anything else, that tear sliding down the president's face defined the crisis for me.

Every facet of medicine dealt with this paradox: to be a good clinician or a good researcher or a good public health advocate, you had to care about the essential force of humanity behind your work. And yet, if you focused too hard on those you were trying to help, grief and dismay would defeat you and thereby hobble the very aims you sought to achieve. To cope with all the dying, you had to act like all the dying wasn't happening, or was happening only in some shadow-world form, the events separated from their impact. If you weren't a psychopath to begin with, you had to protect yourself by adopting something of the psychopath's talent for dissociation. If that applied to clinicians and researchers, it must apply even more to the woman running our nation, who bore on her small shoulders the weight of all her people.

Eventually, President Corbett disconnected from Mr. Amir and returned to the cold business of triaging an entire country. She made one painful decision after another, weighing the options with the full measure of her formidable intelligence before issuing a series of clear, carefully articulated plans. But underneath the steeliness etched into her face, I could still see the track of that solitary tear sliding down her cheek, more precious than any diamond.

14 The Archaic Clock

COMPTON

NEW YORK CITY
172 Days After Patient Zero

THE WAVE CRASHED THROUGH NEW YORK, FLATTENING buildings, toppling the Statue of Liberty, and sweeping away vast swathes of the city before receding and leaving the dazed survivors to totter out into the sunlight with their fists raised in silent defiance. Just as you'd expect in a good apocalyptic film, the monster had been vanquished by the resilience of the human spirit, and all was, or would be, well again.

Compton flipped her laptop shut. Disaster movies were having a moment, which was kind of ironic if you thought about it. She'd have thought people would desire escapism of a happier sort, like sappy romances and feel-good flicks about heroic dogs. But here she was, battered by insomnia, glued to every stupid, low-budget tornado/asteroid/sunspot movie she could dredge up from Netflix.

She rolled to her side and glanced at the clock: 4:39. Still too early to get up. Through her unshaded window poured the grayish-orange haze of the city. In pre-ART days, she'd slept in total blackness engineered by way of a pair of expensive motorized blackout curtains, a purchase any ER doctor would consider well worth the cost. When you had to shift your sleep cycles from night to day to midafternoon on a random, rotating basis, you became a devotee of every sleep aid imaginable. But now, for some reason, Compton couldn't stand the dark.

It being late November, there was a *lot* of dark.

With a brief whirring sound punctuated by a decisive click, the number on the clock changed to 4:40. Every minute of the day, this archaic clock made a scritchy, whirring, clicking sound as the numbers changed inside the burled fake-wood veneer of its exterior. A marvel of primitive engineering, the clock contained a Rolodex of stiff black cards with numbers printed on them—or half numbers, to be precise—and a 60-hertz, 120-volt power supply that caused little internal wheels to spin, which activated little gears, which flipped the top or bottom half of the little number cards. There was nothing digital about it.

The reason Compton knew so much about this clock, this noisy little relic from the 1970s, was that Ellis had loved it. He'd had a fascination with small machines, taking them apart and putting them back together whenever he was bored or agitated. He'd possessed a fleet of four or five disclike robotic vacuums, which he'd lovingly and devotedly disassembled and reassembled on a regular basis. He had liked to deploy them all at once, sending them around the not-overly-large apartment, cheering them on as they bumped around the rooms munching up dog hair and Cheerios and Rose's little elastic ponytail holders.

Compton had always hated this clock, although she'd long since become accustomed to its noise. Now, though, she couldn't bear to part with it, or the Roomba vacuums either. If Ellis had been buried, she'd have considered burying him with the oldest and frailest of the Roombas so he'd have something to tinker with in the afterlife, but, like most victims of the ART virus in the city, he'd been cremated without so much as a funeral. Instead, she'd boxed up all the Roombas except the newest one, and shoved them into their bay in the building's basement. The smallest one she'd bequeathed to Lawrence, who carried it around all day like a doll. He even slept with it.

Compton dreaded the day stretched before her, with its endless minute-by-minute clock flips. She didn't have anything to do until nine o'clock tonight, when her girlfriends had scheduled a Zoom. She didn't have to work today. In fact, since the numbers of infected in New York had begun to fall over the past few months, she now had one or two or even three days off every week.

During the months she'd been killing herself at work, she'd at least been able to block the specter of her grief. Inside the hospital, the urgency of saving as many other lives as she could provided the ultimate distraction, and at home, her exhaustion overwhelmed her. She'd never in her life slept as deeply and as dreamlessly as she had during those weeks.

Here, now, surrounded by all of Ellis's things, in their home, in his bed, with his children, there was no escape. She'd given Mildred three days off, exhausted by the effort of having to hide her grief. The late-fall weather, as if ordered up by a vengeful god, matched the mood of the city: bleak and gray and unseasonably frigid, enough so that being outdoors provided little respite. Her pain, massive and all-consuming, never left her alone for an instant. For the first time ever, she understood why sometimes people could not cry.

A tiny rustling sounded at her bedroom door. Inch by inch, the door swung open, so hesitatingly that at first she thought she must be imagining it. But no: after a minute or so the dim light from her bedroom window illuminated a rectangular patch of hallway floor.

A small, indistinct shadow stood outside the patch of light. With agonizing slowness, Lawrence inched into view. First one foot, then the curved grip of a hand on the doorframe, then a sliver of his cheek. Over the course of the next five minutes he tiptoed across the room and eased himself and the remaining Roomba onto the foot of the bed, then repeated the whole painstaking process of oozing his way up to the empty pillow beside Compton, where he placed the Roomba beside him, before gradually, ever-so-slowly lowering his head down. He then spent the next five minutes scooting backward in tiny increments until he'd nestled himself against her. Finally, after another few minutes, he let out a long sigh and his breathing again became regular.

Compton didn't tell him she was awake. His entire young life had been spent under the burden of not making excessive noise when his poor, sleep-deprived mother tried to catch a few hours in the middle of the day after being up all night. Her heart swelled at his consideration: he'd wanted to be with his mother, but even in the face of his fear or loneliness or sadness, his eight-year-old self had possessed the discipline to think of her needs first. He hadn't wanted to wake her when she too was tired and sad, perhaps understanding on some instinctual level that sleep was her only respite. So he'd crept in as quietly and slowly as he could, protecting her. She tucked an arm around him and pulled him closer, hot tears pricking her eyes at the warmth of his skinny little body.

And she went to sleep.

SOMEHOW, THE DAY passed. Compton helped Lawrence with his schoolwork, played Unicorn Princess with Rose, and chased after Baby Walter, who toddled around at warp speed trying to eat things. She read aloud from the children's favorite book, *Meet Wild Boars*, for the ten thousandth time. She fixed breakfast, lunch, and dinner, and then cleaned up after breakfast, lunch, and dinner. (Lawrence refused to allow her to run the surviving Roomba, terrified that with no competent fixer around, it would suck up something inappropriate and choke.)

Bedtime for the children approached. Compton put Rose and Walter into a bath together and watched from the doorway as they gleefully splashed each other's naked bodies. Having pronounced himself bath supervisor,

Lawrence perched with lordly grace upon the closed lid of the toilet and shouted orders at his siblings not to splash. They splashed more. Frustrated at being ignored, he hopped up and switched off the bathroom light.

Startled out of her slump against the doorframe, Compton reached to turn the light back on. As soon as the bathroom lit back up, Rose protested.

"Turn it back out, Mommy!"

"But then you'll be in the dark, sweetie."

"Mommy, listen. I heard the enviramen is hurting. By too much lights."

"Where did you hear that?"

"Wow in da World." *Wow in the World* was an NPR science podcast. The children were addicted, especially Rose, who suffered from a crippling crush on someone on the show named Guy Raz.

"So we should be doing everything in da dark," concluded Rose.

Okay. It was bedtime. This could work.

"Are nightlights okay?" Compton asked, plucking Baby Walter from the bath and drying all his many fat folds in the light of the hallway. She slapped a clean diaper on him and tickled his tummy, at which point, with an expression of intense concentration, he pooped. She removed the new diaper, cleaned him up, and replaced it. Chortling with delight, he reached up and twisted her nose.

She set him down and handed him his favorite thing in the world, the television remote. He immediately placed it to his ear and made little hooting sounds. This remote was actually a decoy that no longer worked on the television, but it served its purpose: distracting Baby Walter long enough for her to get Rose out of the bath. She rubbed Rose's golden ringlets dry and instructed her to go find her big girl underwear.

Now for Lawrence.

"I'll be staying up late tonight," he informed her, as she beckoned at him to exit the bathroom. "So I'll sit right here for now."

"Nope," she said, forcing a cheerful tone into her voice. She lifted Lawrence from the bathroom doorway. He went prone as soon as she picked him up, so she carried him down the hall facedown, arms out and behind him, like Superman.

"Make-a-U-turn-when-safe-to-do-so," squawked Lawrence in a robotic voice Compton recognized as belonging to the GPS lady from their car. "Make-a-U-turn."

They reached the door of the boys' room. Lawrence tried another tact. "This is bullying," he shouted. "You can't attack a minor."

"How about you read to Rose?" suggested Compton. "Maybe some *Ivy and Bean*?"

"Yes, okay," said Lawrence. "I'll get the book." He loved being the one to read the bedtime story. It took an agonizing amount of time for him to get through a chapter, though, partly because he had to sound out some of the words but mainly because he often stopped to offer commentary on the actions of the characters.

Compton hollered at Rose to go listen to the story while she went to retrieve Baby Walter from the hallway. She found him in the bathroom instead, one chubby arm raised to hurl the remote into the still-full tub. Her face burned as she realized she'd forgotten to drain the water. She snatched him up, startling him so that he let out an affronted howl. Jostling him up and down, she scurried to the kitchen to prepare his bottle.

Back in the boys' room, she and Baby Walter settled into the blue cushioned rocker. He didn't need her to hold his bottle anymore, of course, but the rocking and cuddling soothed them both, transforming him into a compact, drowsy, milk-scented lump in her arms. She shut her eyes and listened as Lawrence read to Rose, both of them curled together at the head of his single bed in their footy pajamas. Every now and then he paused to explain to Rose some motivation or perception of the characters, or to point out something interesting in the illustrations, or to offer his take on what the correct course of action would have been. Rose listened with rapt attention. For the first time all day, a little of the pinched feeling in Compton's chest dissipated.

"Rose," said Lawrence. He flipped a page. "Have you noticed my new reading style?"

"Yes," said Rose with great positivity.

"Good. Pay attention. From now on, I will be pronouncing the word 'what' as 'HWOT.' It sounds more professional."

"*Hwot*," said Rose.

"Very good. *'That's hwot you think,' said Ivy. 'I'm getting really good at escaping.'*"

Lawrence finished the chapter, and, for once, neither he nor Rose protested as Compton tucked them in and kissed them. Baby Walter had stone-cold passed out in Compton's arms and had not awoken during the perilous transfer to his crib, a small miracle. Trepidatiously, she patted him on his diapered, pajamaed bottom, which stuck up in the air. As the door shut behind her, she expected some delayed squall to erupt, but all was silent.

The kitchen glowed with the eerie LED under-counter lights Ellis had insisted upon installing. Rooting around in the cabinet, Compton extracted a bottle of Malbec—too good to drink alone, but what the hell—and uncorked it. She carried a glass to the study. Curling into the fat, cushioned reading chair, she wrapped herself in a worn chenille blanket, flipped open her laptop, and clicked on her news app. She had an hour to kill before the Zoom with all her girlfriends, and mindless wine-fueled web surfing seemed as appealing a way as any to spend it. You had to do something to keep your mind off things.

Work had a tendency to creep into her thoughts, regardless of what she did. Example A: her shift three days ago. Less than six months into the pandemic, the bread-and-butter cases of an emergency department once again dominated her shifts—chest pain, abdominal pain, fractures; not to mention the predictably unpredictable shit that showed up on every shift, like erections that would not resolve and little kids who'd eaten batteries and some dude who'd managed to lodge a fishhook in his eye. Who fooled around casting fishhooks in the middle of Manhattan?

There was always one case from every shift that stuck with her, depositing a tiny seed of anxiety in her mind. The anxiety seed would bide its time before sprouting into a full-fledged horticultural horror, coiling ugly tendrils of panic around the sulci and gyri of her brain, worming its way from her subconscious into her conscious mind until she could think of nothing else. She'd had a bit of a tendency to obsess over cases gone wrong before ART, but now—now she did it every day, even over cases where nothing had gone wrong. The what-ifs would not leave her alone.

This time it had been a young mother, a twenty-eight-year-old named Rosita Sosa. Rosita was a knockout; the perfect planes of her face drew the surreptitious eye of every man in the department; they'd glance at her, do a double take, and then look away as if they had pressing business on the other side of the ER. Helpless fools. Rosita Sosa didn't notice. Rosita Sosa had lost her mind.

Her distraught husband was no help. Gibbering uselessly, he couldn't focus enough to give a coherent history, leading Compton at first to consider the possibility that some environmental problem had affected both spouses. But no: the husband was mentally intact, just wracked with grief. She left the room and went to the doctor's lounge, where she got a cup of coffee from the machine and a little packet of crackers from the snack drawers. She took them back to Rosita's room and handed the items to her husband, guiding him gently to a chair. "Here," she said. "Sit. You must be exhausted."

Rosita's husband ate and drank as Compton threw him some softballs, easy stuff about where they lived and the ages of their kids and whether they'd traveled recently. He started to calm down, and she kept her voice reassuring, keeping him talking, before slipping in a few questions about his wife. This time, he'd settled enough to answer.

Rosita had seemed normal until about a week ago, when she began forgetting things. She'd space on the name of their baby or start a task and abandon it midway, without ever realizing she'd been involved in it. A gifted artist, she possessed a roomful of supplies but seemed bewildered one morning by what to do with a can of linseed oil. She placed her purse in the refrigerator and a can of Coke in the baby's crib. It wasn't until she'd yanked up her dress and peed in the hallway, however, that her husband became truly alarmed. He wanted to take her to a doctor, but his job didn't provide insurance, and they were barely eking out enough to pay their bills, so they decided to wait. Then this morning she'd woken up aphasic—no speech whatsoever. On exam, she demonstrated myoclonus—involuntary muscle jerks—and, when Compton tried to get her to walk, ataxia. She could bear weight, but her gait was lilting, wobbly, uncoordinated. There were no focal findings; no localization to one side of the body or the other. Compton suspected a stroke, but where in her brain would a stroke produce this constellation of symptoms? And why? Why would this happen to a twenty-eight-year-old?

The CT scan of the brain showed nothing unusual. Compton performed a lumbar puncture, drawing off spinal fluid for analysis, but the immediate results weren't consistent with a brain infection, like you might see with encephalitis from bacteria or a mosquito-borne illness, for example. Bloodwork was also normal. They got lucky while waiting for a bed upstairs; an MR scanner was open and could take her right then.

Afterward, waiting for the MRI results, the husband again became tearful and agitated, his head bowed over Rosita's chest as she stared into space. Compton checked on them when she could, but juggling half a dozen complex other patients made it difficult. She ran through Mrs. Sosa's labs again, tuning out the sounds of the department: people crying and yelling, the clatter of the printers, the swish of the big automatic doors behind her. Nothing.

Then she got a call from the neuroradiologist.

"Interesting scan, Dr. Compton," he said. She didn't know this guy, but his voice, both condescending and squeaky, set her teeth on edge. "We're looking at diffuse patchy T2 weighted and FLAIR signal abnormalities, seen throughout the cortex and subcortical white matter, the basal ganglia and the thalami, but there are some additional oddities."

"What the fuck," mouthed Compton. Did he think that sentence was comprehensible?

"I'll send the full report shortly," he said. "What's the clinical picture?"

"Rapidly progressive dementia in a healthy twenty-eight-year-old. Some difficulty walking."

He whistled through his teeth. "It fits. Hmm, let's see. The cerebellum looks robust, actually. Not sure what to make of that. On another note, you might consider FDG PET imaging to help differentiate limbic encephalitis, which can have FDG avidity in the mesial temporal lobes."

"Pretend," suggested Compton, "that I don't speak radiologist."

"I'm sorry," he squeaked, and suddenly she felt guilty for judging him. Perhaps he was a nerd, not a jerk. "I guess I geeked out a little. It's an unusual scan, especially in this age group. There's some diffuse inflammatory process going on here. I'd be very worried."

"I'll pass that on to the admitting doc, but what are you thinking? This isn't a stroke, then."

"Nope," he said. "It's odd, almost like what you'd see in certain kinds of autoimmune encephalitis." He hesitated. "But there are some unusual findings here. The gradient echo sequence shows extensive tiny punctate hemorrhages, which you don't usually find in an AE. The pattern doesn't fit perfectly with any described entity I can think of."

"Thank you," she told him. She hung up, baffled. What in the world could have caused her patient's brain to fail so quickly?

This was a once-in-a-lifetime case. But then, extraordinarily, the very next day she encountered it again, this time in a forty-one-year-old man, a lawyer at one of the big firms in Midtown. He'd been fine until a couple of weeks ago, at which point he too had started doing odd things: calling random people from his contacts list and asking them long, nonsensical questions; getting stuck on an elevator because he couldn't remember how to get to his floor; showing up at an old boyfriend's apartment in Brooklyn, convinced he still lived there. His husband, bewildered and distressed, had brought him to the ER when he too had lost the ability to speak. By the time he hit the emergency department, he'd been seizing nonstop. His scan, while not exactly the same as Rosita Sosa's, shared enough similarities that it provoked a tingle of fear. This could not be a coincidence.

Now, at home, Compton set a reminder to herself to follow up with the neurologists caring for these patients to see if any diagnosis had been made or any commonalities identified. In the meantime, she needed something to displace from her mind the image of the vacant faces of her patients.

As though she'd summoned him, Ellis drifted into her thoughts. They'd spoken for the last time while she was marooned in a hotel room in Spain, waiting out her mandatory isolation period so she could return home. In their conversations during those days, they fixated on how to respond to the emerging new reality: should they pull their money from the market? A few people had turned up with the mysterious new illness in New York; should they pull Lawrence and Rose from school? Stockpile supplies? Cancel meetings? Over the last few days, they'd discussed these matters with only a slight undertone of fear. By this point it was clear Compton was okay. Her friends had recovered or had not gotten sick. Even Vani, the only one to be hospitalized, gave every indication of a full recovery. Perhaps the man on the boat and the handful of others who'd died had been aberrations. Perhaps the illness would not spread widely. The world had only just embarked on its inexorable path to chaos, and neither of them yet appreciated how bad things would get.

Ellis—whose remaining life span at that point clocked in somewhere under that of the common mayfly—had called for the last time just as she'd been about to step in the shower. There had been no indication of the momentousness of the occasion. In fact, by now reassured of Compton's health, he sounded upbeat.

"California lo-ove!" Ellis was no rapper—this went without saying—but lack of ability had never dimmed his enthusiasm for any form of song. Compton had to hold the phone a couple of inches away from her ear. "Hey, El."

"City of Compton! Ba-da-da-dum-dum-dum . . ."

"What's up?"

He broke off. "Nothing. Just missing you."

"Can you put the kids on too?"

A sheepish tone crept in. "I'm at work. I've been going in to help wrap things up."

"Oh, Ellis." She hesitated, uncertain of what to say. They had agreed not to discuss the life-upheaval-move-to-the-country thing until they could do it in person, so for now they remained in a weird state of limbo. Ellis had given notice at his job. Meanwhile, she'd been detained in a foreign country, which was causing no small amount of consternation at her hospital. An ER doctor going AWOL for three weeks created hardship for the other doctors, who had to make up her shifts. Everything was a mess.

"I know, I know. I just wanted to hear your voice for a minute."

"I'm about to jump in the shower. Why don't you call me later when you're home with the kids?"

That was it. A few hours later, he'd seized, and a few hours after that, he'd died. Oh, the irony of it: she'd been smack-dab in the middle of Viral Ground Zero and yet here she sat, her brain whirring and her nerve endings fizzing, her lungs expanding and contracting, her heart ticking with metronomic regularity. Ellis had had one fifteen-minute meeting with a woman who'd recently returned from a work trip to Europe, and now the only things remaining of him were memories and a pile of ash.

By all accounts, his illness had clobbered him with the ferocity and rapidity of a meteor strike. His doctors had promised—perhaps a bit too ardently—that he had never fully regained consciousness. When she thought about it—when she could bear to think about it—she'd focused on this timeline as the only small blessing amid the tragedy of losing him. He had not known he'd died alone.

She couldn't remember: in that final call, had she said she loved him?

Surely she had.

She wrenched her attention to her laptop. Ignoring all the articles related to the virus, she scrolled down with one thumb, the wineglass gripped in her other hand. She glanced at a story about some celebrity's dislike of some other celebrity—really, who cared?—and skimmed one of those Twitter compilations of amusing social failures. Even in the midst of catastrophe, people were still drunk-texting the wrong hookup, creatively misspelling public signs, and succumbing to atrocious hairstyle mishaps. Reassuring in a life-goes-on sort of way, but even other people's funny fuckups failed to hold her interest for long. She scrolled farther down the feed before sitting up straight to transfer the Malbec to a side table.

She'd already passed the headline that had caught her eye, so she had to scroll back up. There. In bold font: *The Last Days of Dr. Aboubakar Seidou: The World's Patient Zero.* Compton scanned the introductory paragraph. The Moroccan authorities had identified the man who'd died on the Tarifa ferry a week or so before she and her friends had boarded the same ill-fated boat. He'd been a physician in Central Africa, but he'd had a journal on his person at the time of his death, and somehow the press had gotten hold of it.

The author of the piece, a freelance reporter in Spain, had written a serialized, semi-fictionalized account of the final weeks of Dr. Seidou's life, based on his journal writing and media reports. This last installment detailed his final hours in Tangier. Compton began reading it in a hungry gulp.

To put it mildly, she was not unacquainted with the effects of the ART virus. She'd survived a mild course of the illness herself. She'd read dozens if not hundreds of papers about it, and she'd treated dozens if not hundreds of patients with it, some of them moderately affected and some who had died. Some of her colleagues had died, heading into patient rooms time and time again, aware of the odds of dying themselves and forging ahead nonetheless in the time-honored tradition of healers.

And, of course: Ellis.

And yet. Throughout all this immersive exposure to the artiovirus and its effects, she'd never contemplated such an in-depth perspective of someone else's experience. The author of the article attempted to place himself in the mind of Dr. Seidou as he became ill, weaving together an omniscient point of view with the doctor's perspective, resulting in an oddly lyrical ode to a man who'd died without ever realizing his death would change the face of the planet.

She read for a period of ten or fifteen minutes, her feet curled under her, the wineglass gripped in one hand. The story engaged her, detailing the first leg of his trip, where he'd hitched a ride with an unsavory but rich acquaintance who'd driven south from Chad into the tip of Cameroon, skirting along the edge of the brownish waters of the Logone River, eventually cutting west toward Nigeria and then north toward the deserts of Niger and Algeria. This was not a route anyone would undertake lightly; at the very least, there were likely to be multiple stops to repair the vehicle, and at the very worst, an unfriendly encounter with the terrorist group Boko Haram. Ordinarily, on the unlikely chance that you had to travel between N'Djamena and anywhere far away, you would fly. Seidou, however, had been on a plane twice in his life—once to get to medical school in Cuba, and once to get home—and the experience had been marred by an extreme amount of turbulence.

The slightly safer driving route would have been to cut around the north side of Lake Chad and avoid Nigeria altogether, but Seidou's friend had business in Maiduguri and Yobe, so through Nigeria they went. From Yobe, he'd embarked on a four-thousand-kilometer slog along the Trans-Sahara Highway to one of the northernmost points of Africa. According to the authorities who later tried to piece together his route, this portion of the journey mostly took place on buses, although at least once—in Algeria—he hitched a ride with a caravan.

By the time Aboubakar Seidou reached the port terminal, the throbbing in his head had consolidated into an unendurable and unrelenting grip. Mild at first, it intensified rapidly, coiling around the curved planes of his skull, pressing inward on his brain until it was all he could do not to groan aloud. He was a strong man, well versed in ignoring discomfort, but this pain defied repression. It hurt so badly it blurred his vision.

He'd made it from Chad to Tangier without a major crisis, or so he'd thought, until this blinding headache struck. He arrived three days ahead of schedule, still feeling fine. On impulse, he purchased a ferry ticket to Spain. He'd heard of the Islamic architecture in the Andalusian region of Spain and wished to see it for himself, if only from the outside. He had hours to kill, so he got himself to the old section of town, with its whitewashed buildings, narrow alleys, and colorful doors, and eventually stumbled upon Café Cherifa, a small literary gathering place with a view of the sea. Seidou was too modest to fancy himself a writer, but he enjoyed transcribing his experiences into a battered old leather-covered journal, which he'd now almost filled. He settled himself at a table amid a few bookish types pecking away at their laptops. A warm, sea-scented breeze wafted in through the open window, brushing along the bare skin of his forearms.

After he finished writing, he went for a walk in the bustling medina, sampling fresh dates and nuts and a variety of small, brightly colored fruits; for his wife, Zara, he purchased a precious bag of saffron, ground by the vendor as he watched. For his two daughters, he selected small silver filigreed bracelets from an elegant shop, haggling pleasantly with the merchant until they reached a mutually satisfying price. Like most physicians in Chad, Seidou had very little money; these gifts and his sightseeing trip to Spain would cost him dearly.

Still: hope of a different life lay ahead.

Tangier was a wonder. He'd been here twice before, on layovers on his way to and from medical school in Cuba. He'd never gotten over his awe at the bustling city, but unlike some Chadians educated abroad, Seidou had been eager to return to his homeland to assist his people. Despite his incubation in Western medicine, he retained a fundamental connection with the place of his birth, not the least of which was the wife he loved.

So it was with mixed feelings that Seidou surveyed the intoxicating streets of Tangier. He was educated, trilingual, a gifted physician. It was not impossible that he could find work in a Francophone country such as Morocco. He had contacts with his classmates around the globe and was able to arrange an interview with a private hospital in Tangier. If things worked out, he'd return for Zara and the girls.

As he roamed the market, the headache was beginning to make itself known, pressing the sides of his skull with steely fingers. As would anyone hailing from Central Africa, Seidou assumed he was suffering a bout of malaria. He dug through his bag to find a dose of quinine.

By the time he reached the port terminal building, some two hours later, it was no longer possible to ignore the pain in his skull, which had been joined by a squeeze of putrid nausea. Stomach churning, he moved uneasily through the first checkpoint and baggage screening, shading his eyes against the white-hot brightness of the Moroccan sun. A breeze blew in off the Strait of Gibraltar, tempering the heat and providing some small mitigation to the constant urge to vomit. An involuntary cough rattled up from his throat, an attempt to clear the sensation of something heavy and inert lodged in his chest. For the first time in his life, he experienced the indescribable sensation of air hunger.

He fought not to panic.

Around him sounded a buzz of disparate languages; he recognized English, which he did not speak well, and French and Arabic and Spanish, which he did. Briefly, he considered appealing to one of the Arabic speakers for help finding a doctor, but then disregarded this idea almost as quickly as it had come. As a doctor himself, he knew there was nothing a physician could do to help him standing in a ferry line. If he'd been thinking clearly, he'd have left. Instead, he became fixated with getting aboard the ship so he could obtain a sip of water.

Compton looked up from her computer, thinking about this. Until the last moments, Dr. Seidou could not have realized his condition was lethal, given that he was the first person in the country known to die of it. No one had the luxury of disregarding the symptoms of even a minor cold any longer; if you suffered a cough or a headache, you also suffered a hefty dose of fear. Gone were the days when a sniffle was merely an annoyance. She stared back down at the description of Dr. Seidou's last moments until the words blurred, thinking how strange and random it was that her life had nearly intersected with this man's—had intersected, by one degree of separation, since he'd passed on the virus to the ferry worker who'd given it to her.

On board the ship, another line. Already he'd begun to garner annoyed looks from the other passengers at the sound of his ragged cough. He tried to suppress his need for air, but it created an immediate burning in his throat and chest. Another swell of panic gripped him; he was breathing harder and quicker but less successfully, every inhalation delivering less and less oxygen. A burning, insistent pain flared in his chest and he rubbed at it, still gasping and coughing. A few people edged away from him.

He staggered from the line, toward the stern of the ship. By now his thirst had turned savage, his throat raw and burning, its epithelial lining peeling away in sheets. He needed a drink.

People liked Dr. Aboubakar Seidou for the kindness in his gaze and his broad smile, but also because his deep-set brown eyes offered a window into the agile mind beyond. One glance at him and you knew his type: he was a listener. He possessed an extraordinary ability to tune out his surroundings and focus on whatever subject was at hand, making him a sought-after conversational partner. He seldom spoke of himself, preferring instead to take in both the words and inferences of his companions, and, as a consequence, his was a singular presence in a land where everyone spoke whatever was on their minds.

In his capacity as the only physician for hundreds of square miles in central Chad, Seidou worked at a clinic but he also made house calls, traveling from village to village, seeing all manner of illnesses and injuries, doing what he could with the scarce resources he possessed. Unusually for a physician, he attended to newly delivered babies out in the bush, in the small huts set aside for that purpose, trying to stave off the claws of the invisible reapers who drifted like smoke in the birth huts, biding their time. Being born was a perilous act in this part of the world.

Treating infants was, in fact, his favorite part of his job; he loved the miraculous promise in their small furled bodies, the precious grasp of their tiny fingers. He mourned the ones who died and celebrated the ones who lived.

In the adults and older children, he debrided skin lesions and ulcers, treated dehydration, and—constantly, always—sought antimalarial medications for the afflicted, battling as best he could all the other diseases caused by the microbial invaders that hungered for his people: typhoid, tuberculosis, meningococcal meningitis, schistosomiasis, even leprosy and cholera. The ubiquitous demons of the Western world, cardiopulmonary disease and cancer, were less a concern here unless people lived long enough to develop them. In the Lake Chad basin region, mothers still occasionally watched in helpless horror as their children died of polio or measles.

Her eyes glued to the page, Compton read of how much good Seidou had done for his patients with so little. Like her, he could never predict what conditions he'd encounter in an average day's work, and yet it seemed it was not an encounter at work that had killed him. No one knew at the time, least of all Aboubakar Seidou, the exact origin of his symptoms. His journal indicated he had stopped multiple times on his journey through Niger and Algeria, possibly in regions where he might have encountered camels. It was possible he'd come in contact with a camel at home too; he didn't own any, but several of his patients did.

However it happened, he, or someone he'd met, must have brushed against the specter of an enigmatic killer.

The particulars were never uncovered.

As she continued reading, Compton found her own breath quickening. Just when she'd thought she couldn't bear any more suffering, here came earnest, saintly Dr. Seidou, gripped with guilt at the thought of leaving his patients in Chad but exultant at the miraculous possibilities ahead. His poor wife; his children. What had happened to them, and how long had they waited before they had learned he would never come home?

An ominous sense of familiarity gripped her, as if she knew which words the author of the piece would employ a split second before she read them. Had she seen this article before? Read an excerpt, maybe? But no: that wasn't right. It wasn't a literary *déjà vu* accosting her; it was a personal one, the mental images conjured by the writer transforming in her mind's eye to her own experience aboard the same ship. It wasn't this man's face she saw, his white teeth set against the urge to rattle, but the clenched jaw of the woman she'd tried to save. And it wasn't only her; it was the same futile battle against death she'd waged on behalf of so many of her patients. She'd seen these symptoms too many times, understood them on a visceral level as if she'd experienced them herself. Coughing. Trying and failing to get air as your lungs filled with a sacrificial army of defenders, little cellular soldiers of your own immune system lining up to self-destruct in a valiant but doomed attempt to contain the onslaught. What would it be like to die this way, felled from within?

Compton flung her computer away, her own breath so short she had to lean forward with her face on her legs. It didn't work. She felt dizzy; the room began to spin in great swooping circles, accompanied by a rising tide of sound. Like the components of a pointillist painting, the sound tide seemed to be composed of a thousand tiny daubs of static, all swirling and coalescing into an escalating roar, blotting out the hush of the AC vents and the chitter of the ice maker and the tinny, distant sound of a siren from so far below. Compton's heart clanged, juddering inside her chest with the ferocity of an industrial drill. A few more seconds of this and her chest would burst open, shards of bone spraying out in a great blossoming fractal of red. She could no longer feel the rest of her body, her fingers and toes and limbs having violently detached from her core, leaving only the unbearable agony in her torso and the great throbbing noise in her brain. She felt herself panicking, and this panic begat more panic. Now her breath came in irregular hitches, huge shuddering intakes of air that somehow still failed to give her oxygen. It took everything she had not to start screaming, but she managed it; screaming would wake the children and they'd be frightened. That thought, forcing its way through the noise, provided a tiny shelf of stability amid the roiling winds of her terror. Some detached still-rational corner of her mind observed wryly that she'd managed to transform an imaginary experience of the virus into a very real somatization of it. This wasn't a virus. This was a panic attack.

The irony of this approximation, even in the midst of horror, was not lost on her. And neither was this: Ellis—alone, or at least without her or any of his family—could have experienced something like this in the moments before he'd seized. What if everyone had lied to her about his level of consciousness? What if he'd known? Had he felt terror? Grief? Agony? She'd never know, and she'd never be able to console him or reassure him or tell him goodbye. Losing a loved one was not the ultimate grief; she knew this now. The ultimate grief was realizing the suffering of one you loved and being helpless to do anything about it.

She lowered her head between her knees and forced herself to breathe.

15 Refrain from Embracing

HANNAH

SAN DIEGO
172 Days After Patient Zero

HANNAH SMOOTHED HER HANDS OVER HER STOMACH, thrilling at her new silhouette. At this, her eighteenth week of pregnancy, a smallish but discernible swelling was apparent. Finally—finally!—she'd felt her baby move, a series of quick, tenuous flutters, as if her belly contained a tiny elf tapping on cymbals.

Ten minutes remained before the video chat with her friends, but Hannah busied herself setting up her ring light, arranging the laptop on a stack of books to present a better angle, and fiddling with items in the background, all adjustments she'd perfected during the many virtual visits she'd had with her patients. A clench of anticipation in her gut joined the percussive elf's gentle thrashings; a lot was going on in there right now.

She couldn't wait to speak to her friends. She knew better than to gush about her happiness; when she thought of what Compton must be feeling, with the loss of her husband, and Georgia and Kira, whose fiancé and friend, respectively, were deathly ill in other countries—a bit of her own joy shriveled. It gutted Hannah not to be able to go to her friends and console them. She'd been raised with a belief in southern comfort—

the nonalcoholic kind—in which you showed up in person and took care of the bereaved person's needs. You cleaned their house, you cared for their children, you loved on them. You anticipated the things they'd be unable to do and you did them. And above all, you fed them. By force, if necessary, so no one pined away from a lack of nourishment.

The appointed hour arrived. By now, everyone in the country held a deep animosity toward the idea of videoconferencing. At first, most people had made an effort to look presentable—they might not be donning full-on business attire, but they wore tidy clothes and makeup and whatnot. Now, though, standards had relaxed. People were apt to sign in for these things resembling Kim Jong Un on a bad hair day, half of them probably naked from the waist down.

This videoconference was different, at least in anticipatory terms, if not in hygiene. Hannah had organized a weekly session months ago, which had endured through all the Zoom fatigue. It turned out to be a wonderful thing, sustaining them through all the upheaval. Why hadn't they done this in the pre-ART days?

The computer's speakers issued happy bloopy noises as, one by one, the women signed on. Bloop! Zadie appeared, her genial face lighting up as she caught sight of Hannah. Bloop! Georgia: wearing a pair of giant orange-framed glasses almost the exact shade of her hair, lying on her back on a stack of bright decorative pillows with the camera held above her. Bloop! Emma: a little too far away from the screen, her Nordic-blond hair swept back in a tight ponytail. Bloop! Vani: waving vigorously before turning to holler at someone off-screen.

Now only Kira and Compton were missing. Compton had been conspicuously absent from these meetings for months, but lately she'd joined them, sometimes only at the end, sometimes for the whole thing, although she mostly stayed silent and listened to everyone else chatter. Kira too, had missed many of the virtual get-togethers, too busy to devote any time to anything not a matter of literal life or death.

"So, Hannah," said Zadie, leaning toward the camera. Behind her, a wall of books filled the screen, their various spines creating a dizzying patchwork of color. Hannah could make out Zadie's row of cardiology texts and pediatrics books, their titles embossed in gold. "How are you feeling?"

"Tired," admitted Hannah. "But, you know, sort of floating." Even now, almost five months into the pregnancy, she still had moments where she'd forget and then when something reminded her—bumping her little belly into the table, feeling a flutter from her very active baby—her heart would cease beating for a moment, suspended in a formless state of wonder, and then resume a beat later in a crashing explosion of joy. Nothing was ever going to beat this feeling. Nothing.

"Are you still off work?"

"I am for now, yeah. I'm going back for one day next week to deliver one of my patients with twins." The mention of work—the thought of anything requiring her or Harry to leave the house—punctured the fragile bubble of her joy. How could she be happy when every facet of normal life threatened her baby?

They tried not to dwell on the pandemic during these calls, but every time, it worked its way into the conversation, so they'd taken to giving a brief rundown on their respective cities. Zadie and Emma, in Charlotte, were faring well. The first wave had hit them harder than the second, by which time the city had polished its contact tracing and its quarantining enough to spare its population the worst of it. Zadie's husband, Drew, and Emma's husband, Wyatt, had escaped unscathed; between them only one child, Zadie's son Finn, had been seriously ill, and he'd recovered.

Vani, in Kentucky, reported next: her family was fine, and her internal medicine clinic, in a small town, had also fared relatively well regarding the virus but had been battling a whole host of secondary miseries brought on by the turmoil. Georgia was about to speak when the computer blooped again—twice—and within the space of ten seconds, both Kira and Compton had joined.

In contrast to their appearance in Spain, both of them had visibly aged. Kira, who never wore makeup, usually rocked a fresh-faced, olive-skinned outdoorsy look, but now an unhealthy pallor infused her face. Her short hair had grown out to a length Hannah had never seen before. If someone shaped it into a bob, it might be halfway chic, but it had gone dormant in a split-ended free-for-all. She'd shoved the whole mass of it back with a bandana.

Compton, though. Hannah couldn't remember a time when Compton hadn't looked polished. Hers was the kind of beauty stemming from finesse: precisely shaped eyebrows, meticulously maintained skin, enhanced eyelashes, perfect posture. All of that was gone. Compton with slumped shoulders and twin caterpillars crawling across her forehead was shocking enough, but also the skin along the fine angle of her jaw sagged, and a new constellation of wrinkles latticed her forehead and the corners of her eyes. She looked . . . in a word . . . old.

Hannah sought a view of Georgia, worried as always about her pregnancy. She appeared much the same, at least in part because she'd never made any effort to hide imperfections. As usual when something big was going down, Georgia hadn't reached out when Mark, her fiancé, had been ill enough to be admitted to a hospital in Amsterdam, where he lived part of the year; instead she'd gone AWOL from the group Zooms and re-emerged a month later with a terse announcement that did not brook any discourse on the subject. No one knew any of the details or how she'd been coping, but apparently Mark was still in the process of recovering.

"Georgia," said Hannah, deciding to try again. "How is Mark?"

Georgia chewed her gum, an unreadable expression on her face. For a moment Hannah thought she wouldn't answer, but then she shifted and said, "He's still weak as shit. In rehab, trying to relearn his ADLs. He won't be coming home anytime soon."

Hannah sat, shocked into silence. ADL was doctor shorthand for *activities of daily living*, which meant Georgia's fiancé was struggling to perform basic self-care tasks such as showering and dressing himself. He must have suffered some neurologic event, or ventured so close to death he became debilitated.

Emma voiced the question Hannah couldn't bring herself to ask. "Will he recover?"

Georgia's expression did not alter. In anyone else this might have read as callous, but Hannah knew Georgia well enough to know that for whatever reason, despite her vivid personality, she seldom displayed her most serious thoughts. "He will recover," she said. "It's going to be a long road, but he doesn't have any cognitive decline. He's still him. Just moving a lot slower right now. This virus is a *bitch*."

"Amen," said Zadie with feeling. There was a lamp behind her, which threw her face into shadow, but Hannah could still discern the softness in her gaze, mingled with unmistakable curiosity. "I'm so sorry none of us have met him. What's he like?"

Georgia brightened a bit, apparently pondering how to summarize Mark to the group. "He's a thinker," she said finally. "An underappreciated quality in a man, I've found."

"How are *you* feeling?"

Georgia blew a bright-pink bubble with her gum, allowing it to pop on her face. "I feel heavy," she said, peeling the gum off her chin.

A new face, framed in sculpted black hair, appeared beside Georgia's on her nest of pillows. "I can vouch for that," said the face, which belonged to a fine-featured Asian man who, Hannah was nearly certain, was Georgia's closest friend, a family medicine doctor. "I strained my back trying to lift one of her legs the other day."

"Jonah!" said Zadie. She leaned back in her swivel chair, a big grin creasing her face. "What's happening? Are you taking care of our girl?"

Apparently Zadie knew him too, this Jonah. Hannah recognized the name: Jonah Tsukada, from Charleston, who'd moved to San Diego at the same time Georgia had.

"I am taking care of everything," Jonah announced, prompting Georgia to roll on her side and give him the eye.

"Jones, what are you talking about?" she said. "You don't clean up or anything. You don't even cook."

"I procure food," said Jonah.

"Jonah and I are sheltering in place together," said Georgia. "We didn't like being alone."

"What?" said Hannah. "What about your fiancé?"

"I just told you," said Georgia shortly. "He's still in the Netherlands; it's too long a trip until he's stronger. Even if he was fine, they aren't letting people in or out of the country."

"I'm sorry, I meant something else," said Hannah. She paused, considering how to phrase her question without giving offense. "He doesn't mind you living with another man?"

Georgia's entire face crinkled in merriment. "Nope. Mark likes Jonah."

Hannah risked a glance at the other faces on the monitor, most of whom seemed to be suppressing amusement with varying degrees of success. "What is it I don't get?" she asked, hating the embarrassment in her voice.

Jonah took pity on her. "I'm a friend, not a romantic rival to Mark," he said. He wrapped an arm around Georgia, devotion written all over his face. "Though I do love her."

Georgia swatted at Jonah's head with her unencumbered arm, an equal sappiness written on her face. "Too vague," she said to him; and then to Hannah: "He's extremely gay."

"Oh," said Hannah. Heat flooded her face. "I'm sorry."

"Sorry?" Jonah cocked his head.

"I mean, sorry I misunderstood, not sorry you're gay," said Hannah, and then dropped her head into her hands and moaned out loud at having said something so terrible. After a moment of startled silence, a symphony of laughter broke out; most of them—including Georgia and Jonah—howling so hard it was a wonder Hannah's computer didn't explode. When she calmed down enough to speak, Georgia directed her comment to Hannah. "This right here is why I love you."

"I'm so sorry. I worried you were breaking up with your baby's father. But it's wonderful you have someone there with you," said Hannah, directing a timid smile at Jonah, who returned it.

"Georgia, I wanted to ask you—" said Zadie. Behind her a redheaded child flew through the air, arms rotating in frantic circles, and crashed into something off-screen. Zadie darted away and returned a moment later. "Everything's fine," she said, a bit breathlessly. "Georgia, I wanted to tell you to holler at me once the baby comes if you need help figuring anything out. As you can see, I'm a spectacular parent."

"Sure," said Georgia.

Emma waved a hand to get attention. It was a bit tricky, the protocol for these videoconferences. Half the time everyone spoke at once, and the other half everyone waited to see whose turn it was to speak. "You have, what, two more months? Jonah, are you going with her to the prenatal visits?"

So Emma knew Jonah too.

". . . went to the one where they explained how elderly, how completely *ancient* she is, in terms of, you know, actually having the baby," Jonah was saying, "and that's when I knew I needed to move in for the duration."

"Jonah fainted," said Georgia.

"What?" yelped Jonah. "I did not *faint.* May I remind everyone, as a family physician, I have delivered babies." He thumped his narrow chest. "Not the least bit squeamish."

"In medical school, you said you fainted during a delivery," said Georgia. She chomped her gum. "Not since then, I would assume, but you didn't look too lively during my last ultrasound."

"It was really hot that night in med school, George. Anyway, I don't need to deliver babies now because I don't live in the wilderness where there are no ob-gyns. But it's like riding a bike, probably; you remember what to do. Not that I'd want to deliver *this* baby, but for the record, I'm stellar with the miracle of childbirth. I was just worried about you."

"You talk about having to do a Pap smear on a patient like it's a fate worse than death."

"I think I speak for the entire world," said Jonah, "when I say no one enjoys Pap smears. Performing them, or receiving them, or even hearing about them."

"Truth," said somebody, but at the same time, Kira spoke. "Public health people like Pap smears," she said. "Especially in impoverished countries. Less women dying of cervical cancer."

"I concede the point to Mother Teresa," said Jonah.

"Right on, Mama," said Georgia to Kira, and then she leaned in toward Jonah and ruffled his hair. "I'm teasing, babe. I can't believe you ditched Edwin to move in with me for the duration."

"If Edwin loves me, he will wait," said Jonah. "You needed *somebody* to rein you in. Besides"—he offered Georgia a glance of open adoration, which she returned—"I couldn't let the mother of my godchild waddle through the end of her pregnancy all alone."

"Aw," said Zadie, grinning, while at the same moment Emma said, "Ew."

"I'm so jealous of this lovefest," said Vani, who'd been divorced from her deceitful husband for some years now. "Georgia, you are the luckiest woman."

"I am," agreed Georgia.

"I don't know how in the world we got on the subject of Pap smears a minute ago," Vani said, starting to add something else, but she was drowned out by one of her kids, flying behind her on-screen with a shriek like a nosediving jetliner, followed a second later by another even louder one. Vani muted herself and yelled something at her kids. Everyone laughed.

Vani unmuted. "I think my kids must have coordinated with Zadie's," she said. "They're playing a game called Crash and Burn and it's getting kind of literal. Anyway. How's work going for everyone?"

"I'll take this one," said Emma. Her being a trauma surgeon in Charlotte, hers was the career Hannah found most intimidating. "At first I had a little respite. For the first time in recorded history, there was one minute where nobody was wrecking their cars while drunk or distracted. People shot each other a lot more, though, so there's that. And now trauma has exploded: last night we had a dozen assaults: fists, knives, gunshot wounds, and two people who got attacked with a machete. All the GSWs died."

Hannah blinked in horror.

"We slowed down in our low-acuity clinic visits," said Zadie, who also lived in Charlotte. "People weren't seeing their pediatricians and were getting diagnosed with murmurs, and other patients were missing follow-ups, so it's led to a few worsening conditions."

Kira cocked her head. "Have you seen any increase in cardiac defects compared to usual?" The question sent a shiver through Hannah; they were not yet seven months into the pandemic, so very few women who'd been infected in the first trimester had yet given birth. No one really knew, yet, how the virus might affect the unborn.

But Zadie's answer was reassuring. "Not at all."

Still, a pinch of consternation settled across Hannah's brow. She saw it when her own visage on the screen caught her eye, and resisted the urge to run her finger along her forehead to smooth it out. She started to say something to change the subject, but Vani beat her to the punch, saying something about how she was seeing far fewer patients than normal—her patients, in rural Kentucky, were suffering from the economic and psychological impact of the virus, if not the virus itself—but Compton interrupted her. They both apologized and waited for the other to speak.

Compton took the reins. "Kira," she said in a voice so creaky Hannah almost flinched. "I hate to ask this, but is there any kind of new virus circulating? One causing encephalitis or some other kind of brain impairment?"

Kira's eyes swung sideways, presumably to lock in on Compton's image on her screen. Her voice took on a sharp tinge. "Why do you ask?"

"I've seen a couple of weird cases. Young people, with dementia that comes on rapidly, some with seizures. Increased T2 signal intensity on MRI but no obvious cause."

"Do they have artiovirus?" asked Hannah timidly.

"PCR negative, although both had antibodies, so they must have had it at some point in the first wave. They aren't sick now, though."

"Can you get permission to send me their medical records?" Kira appeared to be writing something. She stopped and looked up. "Have there been any other cases like this at your hospital?"

"I don't know." Compton's face settled into a masklike rigidity, as if she were gritting her teeth. "I just . . . This was just this week. If it had only been one patient, I wouldn't have even mentioned it, but two patients . . . I don't know what to think. What are you thinking? Could this be related to artiovirus somehow?"

"We're tracking some clusters of similar cases, but there's nothing I can tell you yet," Kira said, adding, "I hope it's not related."

This reassured no one. A somber silence descended upon the group, broken by the cry of a baby. Compton jumped up and returned with her toddler in her arms, settling back into her chair with his downy head nestled in the crook of her elbow. She bent her head over him, making little shushing sounds.

"Should we wrap up?" Hannah asked, as quietly as she could.

Compton raised her head. "No. He's asleep. I'll put him back in a second." But she didn't move. "Hannah? Do you remember that first baby you delivered in medical school?"

"Of course!"

"Will you tell me that story?"

They'd heard most of each other's stories ten thousand times by now, but Hannah launched into this one again, puzzled but pleased that Compton would want to hear it again.

She'd been standing in the hall. This was back in the days before posh L&D suites and Press Ganey patient consumer surveys and aromatherapy and water births and all the rest of the stuff hospitals had been doing to market themselves less as deliverers of medical expertise and more as deliverers of resort-quality birth experiences. Back then they had separate labor, delivery, and recovery rooms, all sporting a certain utilitarian dreariness. Even for a teaching hospital, it was a bit on the grim side.

Hannah, dressed in her short white medical student coat, had completed her first clinical lesson in patient care—how to read a rhythm strip—and had found herself lounging against a greenish cement wall, staring at the sample printout she'd been given and fervently wishing for some labor to commence so she could put her newfound knowledge to use. The attending physicians and the residents, on the other hand, were all fervently wishing for a lull so they could score some breakfast before the chaos began, and seeing how there wasn't anyone in active labor at the moment, they'd all vanished as soon as the lecture ended.

". . . and the residents were getting coffee or something," Hannah said now. She waited as Compton held up a finger; she stood and moved out of view. She returned a moment later without her baby and nodded for Hannah to continue.

"Then this man poked his head out into the hall and said, 'Doctor, come quick!' I didn't answer, because of course I didn't think he was talking to me. But he was hollering and pointing, so I checked behind me and there was no actual doctor, so I ran in and looked at his wife's strip. It did not look like contractions, so I was calm and reassuring, just like they said to be. 'It's going to be a while, probably,' I said. 'Can I get anyone anything?' But the man was still yelling, and the woman was carrying on too, which made it hard to hear." Hannah paused and took a decorous sip of her water. It could be hard to gauge someone's interactivity on a videoconference, but Compton appeared to be listening intently, staring at the screen with her wineglass in her hand.

"I raised the sheet," Hannah continued, "and there was this baby's head, which at first I did not even recognize as a human head. I think I screamed. But there was no time to even think about it because the little body shot out at me. I caught it before it went over the edge of the bed, thankfully. I didn't even have gloves on. Everybody was dead silent for a second, staring at me, and then I said, 'Uhhh . . . it's a boy!' and then they were all cheering."

She looked up; everyone seemed engaged. Georgia said, politely, "Whoa."

"Yeah! The nurses rushed in and shoved me out of the way, but the dad came over and patted me—I might have been hyperventilating a little—and he said I did fantastic. Turns out the lady had six kids already. But before the nurses got in, while I was holding him, he opened his eyes and looked up at me, and I realized mine was the first face he'd ever seen."

It still shook her, all these years later, the memory of that tiny wizened gaze. For one moment, the baby's little eyes had fluttered open and the weight of his innocence had floored her. Here in her arms was an uncorrupted soul. He knew nothing of the world, understood nothing, and in these, the first moments of his life, he faced a future of infinite possibility. He possessed the power to master the quantum computer, to bring about world peace, to alter the trajectory of the universe. Or—he might be abused by the all-powerful adults who should be caring for him; unable to defend himself, he could die horribly, as legions of children have since time immemorial. Or he could be raised by scoundrels and become a scoundrel himself, one of the malignant hordes motivated only by their own gain, indifferent to suffering and truth. He knew none of this, knew nothing of good and evil and random chance. His eyes were full of fathomless wonder.

She'd never seen him again, but he'd changed the course of her life.

Something in her expression must have conveyed the depth of her emotion on the subject, because Compton set down her wineglass with an odd gentleness. "You're very lucky, you know," she said, her eyes fixed at some distant point beyond Hannah.

"Because I figured out what I wanted to do?"

Compton met her gaze. "Because you are doing what you love."

Total silence. The obvious question occurred to everyone, but no one, it seemed, had the balls to ask it. After an awkward thirty seconds or so, Vani spoke.

"Compton," she said. "We love you. Do you want to tell us how you are?"

Compton appeared to be trying to arrange her face into a smile but could manage only a wry wince. She sighed, a long, shaky exhalation. "I don't know. I'm getting by."

Now Zadie spoke, her earnest, round-eyed gaze directed straight at the camera. "What are you feeling about your job?"

Without any warning at all, Compton's hands flew to her face. A sound erupted from her, harsh and barking. It took Hannah a second to understand that Compton was sobbing—sobbing so violently her wineglass tipped and splintered as the little table beside her shook. She was saying something, but none of them could make it out.

"I don't want to go back."

Was that it? She didn't want to go back? Her heart thundering, Hannah focused as hard as she could on Compton's words. Yes: now it sounded clearer as she repeated the phrase over and over, gasping it like someone was beating it out of her. "I don't want to go back. I don't want to go back."

Hannah's longing to burst through the computer screen into Compton's New York apartment and wrap her arms around her friend was so intense it caused her actual physical discomfort. She doubled forward as her breath caught, lodged in the center of her chest as if it had been pinned by an ice pick through her sternum.

Compton's sobs abated. She lowered her hands, her expression a mixture of shame and hopelessness. After a few beats, her head tilted and her eyes shifted. She reached a hand toward the screen. "Hannah, no," she said.

Puzzled, Hannah regarded her own rectangular image box on the screen. Her reflection stared back, tears streaming down its face. She watched her own shoulders shaking as she reached a hand back toward the warm screen, as if she could lace her fingers through Compton's. They left their hands there for a moment, blocking their faces from view.

"Don't cry, Hannah," whispered Compton.

But now tears coursed from everyone's eyes, even Jonah's. The screen had filled with hands, the crinkled lines of their palms in extreme close-up, the closest they could get to holding one another until the world righted itself again. All these months of fear and suffering and responsibility; all this devastation, medical and economic and societal. Contrary to popular wisdom, it didn't feel good to cry. It felt exhausting and helpless, this pointless and biologically mysterious phenomenon of leaking clear fluid from your eyes in times of distress. Hannah had tried as much as possible to stay positive throughout it all, afraid a wash of negative emotion could somehow transform itself into a biochemical message and affect her child. But now, just like the rest of them, she let loose.

After an indeterminate period of time, they settled down, everyone emitting sighs and hiccups, wiping their faces on whatever was handy. A heavy calm descended. Perhaps that was the point of crying, Hannah thought: to numb you.

"Well, that was intense," said Georgia finally. "Everybody okay?"

"No," said Compton, and then her voice broke into a low-pitched hacking sound finally recognizable as a laugh. "But at least you guys are fucked-up right alongside me. It's comforting, in a weird way, watching you cry with me."

"A time to weep and a time to laugh," said Hannah. Her face went still as she remembered that laughter gave way to mourning in the next line of the biblical verse.

Zadie, however, picked up the thread and spun it in a positive direction. "Also," she said, "a time to heal."

Compton looked baffled. "That's an old song, yes? By the Byrds?"

"It's Ecclesiastes," said Vani and Hannah together. Politely, Hannah hushed so Vani could explain, but Vani motioned at her to continue. She spoke almost without thinking. "Chapter three, verses one through eight. It's one of the most beautiful passages in the Bible, but also one of the most unsettling because it doesn't shy away from the inevitability of sorrow. We are promised war and grief and weeping and death"—she couldn't look at Compton's image, now immobile on the screen—"but also there's a time for love. And peace."

"And," said Vani softly, "a time to embrace."

"If I recall correctly," Georgia said in a wry tone, "there's also a time to refrain from embracing. Pretty much sums up our circumstances this year, doesn't it?"

This broke the spell; even Compton broke into a genuine smile.

Georgia handed her phone to Jonah, who aimed it at her as she struggled up onto her elbows. "Listen. I've been giving some thought to something and I have a proposition to make. Y'all might think I'm crazy, though."

"Does that mean crazier than normal, or . . ." Zadie let her voice trail off, smiling.

"Yes, crazier than normal. Well, fuck; what even is normal now?" Georgia was talking fast. "But I've had this idea, and Jonah and I have been talking it over, and I want to do it."

Vani: "Please. The suspense is killing us."

Georgia sat all the way up. The bulk of her abdomen loomed in front of her, already enormous. She rested her hands atop it. "I want you guys to be there for the birth."

"How—"

"On a Zoom. Jonah can film it and you all can be with me when she's born. She's due the last week of January. Eight more weeks."

She gazed straight ahead, stroking her belly, and then spoke off-screen to Jonah, who still held the phone's camera. "You don't have to get all up in there with the camera or anything. Keep it tasteful."

"Tasteful, got it," said a disembodied Jonah. "Don't worry."

Georgia redirected her attention to the camera. "Hannah?"

"Yes?"

"Would you be okay with delivering my baby? I heard my OB is taking an early retirement and I don't like her partners. I could ask her about switching care. I mean, if you were okay with that."

"I would be okay," said Hannah. A soaring chorus rose in her chest, making it difficult to speak. "But I don't have privileges at your hospital."

"I'll go to yours."

"Yes," said Hannah. Impossibly, tears welled in her eyes again. "Yes. I would be so honored to deliver your baby, Georgia. I would love that."

16 | A Redneck with a Snowplow

KIRA

ATLANTA, GEORGIA
232 Days After Patient Zero

MY PHONE BUZZED IN THE GLOOM OF A STORMY JANUARY afternoon. During the weekends, I kept it set to night mode so it cast a sepia-toned light upward against the wall behind the desk until I reached to move it. I read the text—from Declan—and video called him back.

He answered on the first ring. Behind him, I recognized the flat white expanse of the headboard of his bed and the edge of a framed violet-hued painting we'd bought together last year from a street artist in Madrid. He was home.

"Surprise," he said. His hand traced a circular path in the air in front of him, encompassing his bedroom. "Guess who finally got discharged from rehab?"

Wordlessly, I studied him. Tissue and color had fled his face, leaving him wan and drawn, cheekbones too prominent, lips pale. The thready smattering of silver at his temples had increased. But his eyes burned, fully alight. There was no diminishment in the vitality of his gaze or in the emphasis in his movements. Over the last couple of months, he'd been texting me, first from the hospital and then from the rehab facility, but this was the first time I'd seen his face.

He'd survived a prolonged assault from the artiovirus, which, in his case, attacked his lungs and heart with a viciousness so severe he'd hovered on the brink of death for a near-impossible length of time. I'm not one to anthropomorphize critters—especially a nonliving entity like a virus—but you'd have to lack imagination altogether not to wonder if the artiovirus hadn't somehow perceived the threat he posed to it. It made for an arresting image: a swarm of viral soldiers targeting the human targeting them.

"I'm so relieved you're home, Dec," I said finally, and listened as he described the indignities of hospitalization and rehabilitation, glossing over the horrible bits until the experience sounded almost funny. Sponge baths of his groin from people in space suits, IV starts and blood draws from inept student doctors who'd survived the virus and been pressed into premature service, and, once he could eat, presentation of the world's most unappetizing meals.

"Canned peas," said Declan with feeling. He placed both hands against his head as if squeezing it. "Nuclear-colored Jell-O. It's almost like they *wanted* me to die."

"Dec," I said gently. "What happened with the lab?"

"My lab," said Declan, with no change whatsoever in his positive tone, "is closed. Luckily we didn't lose anyone, but most of us got sick."

"What about the clinical trials for the nanobody? Did you get samples to the university before you got sick?"

Silence, then: "No."

I waited, uncertain what to say.

He offered a gentle smile. "It's not all bad. We did lose all the remaining samples of the original drug, except, I guess, for the one you have, but the university took over everything while I was gone. They've resynthesized the ART-specific nanobody, and they don't have to go back through the ethics committee again for patient approval. AEMPS"—this was some sort of regulatory agency—"is expediting everything. Everyone is throwing resources at it. I'm not . . . actively involved, but the trials will finish soon, and that's the important thing. Hopefully this one will be the answer."

"Oh, Dec."

"It's okay," he said. "I'm alive, and we got far enough that they can replicate everything. I'll get better, and I'll get back to work."

"Are you . . . okay . . . with this?" I asked, puzzled by his upbeat attitude.

He took in a breath and regarded the screen silently. I thought at first he'd become mired in regret over his personal losses, but his eyes shifted as an unmistakable longing crossed his face. "Kiki," he said softly. "I wish—"

He broke off and the moment drew out. My senses sharpened, along with a little kick of anticipation. What was he going to say?

"Yes?" I urged him.

He regarded me for another beat but must not have found in my face whatever he sought, because he exhaled and leaned back against the headboard, shutting his eyes. When he spoke again, his voice rang with its usual easy jocularity. He fluttered a hand by his temple. "Nothing, sorry. I got seized by a useless thought."

I wanted to press him, but something struck me. "Dec," I said. "When you got sick, did you take it? Your drug, I mean?"

He laughed, a quick, short bark. "No, I did not. I might have risked it if I'd realized what was happening. But I don't remember anything from getting sick. The first thing I knew I was waking up eons later with some bossy-arse nurse digging her knuckles into my chest and yelling at me to breathe. The lab was long since shut down by then, so, yeah: no idea yet if Humpy will work in humans. For all we know, he'll kill them." He hesitated and met my eyes. "But no worries, Kiki. I'll get going again. I want to be a part of ending this thing."

WE SPOKE A few more minutes before signing off, and almost immediately my phone rang again. I knew who it was this time without even looking: Vani, who texted me each year on this date—January 28—at this hour to commemorate the most eventful day in the history of our friendship.

This year's text began with the usual happy birthday wishes to Beau and the usual pointed reminder to me of how instrumental she'd been in his birth. This never failed to make me simultaneously smile and grimace; after the passage of seven years, the memories of that awful, incredible night have been told and retold, distilled down as part of my family lore until what remains has achieved the glittery, polished status of a fable. I'm no longer certain what is real and what's been embellished, but it's a hell of a good story.

Beau had been born on a snowy night in January. It was a date that would become infamous in the city, and even the country; a winter storm paralyzed Atlanta, stranding people in their cars for upwards of eighteen hours. When the first late-morning flakes began to fall, panic swept the city as every business, school, and government office made the regrettable decision to let out at the same time. Within minutes, hundreds of ill-prepared commuters spun out and crashed. The interstates snarled to a dead stop, clogged with wrecked cars and trapped eighteen-wheelers. Some people staggered out of their cars, abandoning them in the middle of the roadways in search of refuge in grocery stores and gas stations; others hunkered down in their shrouded vehicles, peeing into soft-drink cans and calling in frantic updates to loved ones as their cell phone batteries dwindled. Children spent the night in their school gymnasiums, their little bodies pressed together, their inadequate lightweight coats rolled into pillows. The landscape across the city resembled something from the front lawn of the White Witch, studded with terrible, silent statues of flash-frozen southerners.

Okay, I'll admit it: that last description might involve a little bit of hyperbole. As far as I know, people had not instantly turned to ice, at least not on a Narnian scale. But the rest had been true, and it had been bad. The national media, especially in the upper latitudes of the country, swept into a fever of righteous schadenfreude as metro Atlanta shuddered to its knees. *Snowmageddeon. South Parked. The Ice Age Doomsday Zombie Snowpocalypse.* The citizens of Boston and Minneapolis and Buffalo watched the nightly news broadcasts with no small degree of glee as every announcer in the northern half of America reported that the snow-removal apparatus of the city of Atlanta apparently consisted of one intoxicated redneck with a plow duct-taped to his Ford F-150. You might, said the smirking announcers, reasonably wonder what calamitous amount of snowfall it took to create such an epic mess. One foot? Two? Could it be . . . three? The Yankee ridicule soared to the stratosphere as a CNN reporter—stranded at headquarters off Marietta Street—shamefacedly admitted the final snow accumulation: two inches.

Two inches. That was all it took to transform I-85 into a vast parking lot. And that was all it took to prevent me from reaching the hospital when the labor pains began.

The initial plan had been for me to call Vani, who was temporarily living with her parents, when my time was nigh. Vani would collect Rorie and deposit her with a colleague before driving me to Emory, where she'd stay with me and wipe my brow and whisper encouragement as my fatherless baby boy made his entrance into the world. But when I reached her, she sounded alarmed.

"Now?" she yelped. "Now? Kiki, have you looked outside?"

"It's snowing. I know," I said through gritted teeth. The pains had started hours ago, but I'd dismissed them as Braxton Hicks until their strength and regularity made them impossible to ignore. Now I'd timed them to be three minutes apart. I needed Vani to come.

"It's more than snowing. It's *icy*," said Vani, who considered anything below sixty degrees to be intolerably arctic. If I'd been capable of a normal degree of focus, I'd have appreciated a certain wildness in her tone that went beyond distaste of the cold. But another contraction started and it silenced me.

"Kiki? You okay?"

"Hahhhhhhh," I breathed, trying not to whimper.

"Oh God," said Vani. Her tone changed again. "Kira, I'm stuck on Lindbergh."

This was one of the main thoroughfares in Buckhead, a road that often fell victim to rush-hour traffic snarls. "Well, hurry," I said, once the contraction abated.

"I can't hurry. I can't do anything. We haven't moved in ages."

"What?"

"Turn on the TV."

I carried the phone to the living room, the only room with a television. Rorie and I had moved to Atlanta from Africa two months before my due date, residing in a two-bedroom apartment designed by the blandest person in the universe. I'd named it the Beige Box because of its beige walls, beige carpets, beige tile, and beige counters. Someone had gone rogue in the bathroom and installed a white toilet, which gleamed like a tooth amid all the beige.

I hated this place. If you started in the doorway and panned out and up, like a Hollywood camera at the end of a film, you'd see our apartment was one of twelve identical apartments in the beige building, which was one of thirty identical buildings in a beige complex, which was one of hundreds of identical boring, boxy, beige complexes in this part of town.

But this was what I could afford. I padded—lumbered—across the beige carpet to the beige couch and groped between the cushions for the remote. "Turn it to CNN," commanded Vani's tinny little voice from the phone. I complied and gaped at the image on the screen: a sixteen-lane section of I-85, bisected by a concrete median, dusted in white and strewn with cars. The cars sat immobile, some of them angled to the side, some turned backward, broken up by the occasional rectangle of a jackknifed semi.

"What happened?"

"It's snowing."

"Okay . . ."

"I'd classify this situation as hell freezing over," said Vani. "No one is going anywhere."

"Vani. I'm going to have the baby. Today, I think."

"Listen, don't do that," she said. "Hold off until tomorrow."

"Vani—" Another pain seized me.

"Oh, Kiki, I'm sorry." The music stopped; she must have switched off the car's sound system. "I'm going to call 911 for you."

"Okay, but," I said. My voice came out distorted by pain. "Rorie's here."

"I'll get there somehow, I promise. Can a neighbor take her until then?"

"I don't know any neighbors. I—" I gasped, leaning forward. A gushing warmth slid down my thigh, pooling onto the carpet.

"I'll figure out something. It will be okay, I promise."

While no one would relish the thought of a solitary home delivery, I wasn't as worried about the mechanics of the process as one might expect. I'd delivered dozens of babies in Chad, almost all of them without anesthesia of any kind. Delivering my own baby would occur from a different vantage point, to be sure, but if Vani or an ambulance couldn't reach me, I was confident I could do it.

What complicated everything was Rorie. She'd been playing in her room, but now, lured out by the siren call of television, she crept up beside me.

"Hi, Mommy."

From her father, Rorie had inherited beautiful brown skin and deep brown eyes. She had a tiny, rounded nose and pearly teeth and the careless, luminescent beauty of childhood. She cast a glance toward the television and a sly flicker lit her eyes. "How about Dora, Mommy?" she said.

When I didn't answer, she expounded, enunciating each word. "*Dora . . . the . . . Explorer.*"

"Mommy isn't feeling great," I managed.

"Oh! Okay!" To my surprise, Rorie didn't press her case. This was unusual; since we'd arrived in the States, Rorie had fallen under the sway of the television, lobbying for it with the single-minded fervor of a seven-year-old who could not understand why anyone wouldn't want to indulge in this throbbing, noisy miracle during their every waking second.

I eased myself onto the couch, panting. If no ambulance arrived, could I do this myself without terrifying my daughter? The walls of the Beige Box might as well have been constructed of cloth for all the good they did in blocking noise, so I'd have to figure out how to explain the sounds to Rorie. Having given birth once before, I doubted my ability to do it silently.

Rorie reappeared in the living room, dragging behind her an overstuffed red tote. She'd changed clothes; instead of the pink velour pants and garish Disney sweatshirt she'd been wearing, she was now clad in what appeared to be a pillowcase. I rallied up from the depths of my self-absorbed pain to do a double take. It was indeed a pillowcase; a fine blue cotton one from my bed, with three ragged holes cut out for a neck and arms.

"What—" I began.

"Shh!" Rorie puttered around, extracting a slew of items from the tote bag. "It's time for Spa!"

I peered at an odd array of items as she lined them up on the coffee table. A sleep mask from our last flight. A half-melted soy candle from the bathroom. A toy whisk. (A toy whisk?) Rorie's beloved copy of *The Big Book of Celestial Facts*. A fluid-filled globe.

Rorie picked up this last item and gave it a vigorous shake before handing it to me. Inside the plastic ball, a blue color swirled. "Breathe," she commanded.

A contraction began. I sucked in air and blew it out through pursed lips, trying to envision the pain receding away, carried out on a gust of wind over a peaceful sea. Instead, the pain glommed up at the horizon, forming a cartoonish tornado that headed back toward me with a vengeance. I blew harder.

"That's very good," said Rorie approvingly. She spoke in an affected voice, somehow managing to sound both lulling and bossy. After pulling a pink plastic bottle from her bag, she pecked at the lid until it popped up. "I'm now going to rub lotion into your head."

"Wait," I said, feebly. "No, wait . . ." but it was too late: Rorie had plopped a glob of Johnson's Baby Lotion onto my forehead at the hairline. She picked up the whisk and swirled the lotion into my hair, creating an enormous greasy tangle.

"Arghhhhhhhggt," I moaned.

"Now I will tell you soothing facts," said Rorie, "and then we will have classical music until you are calm."

The contraction ebbed. If I was going to escape from Spa, this was my chance. Instead, I sank back on the couch and allowed my eyelids to drift most of the way down, so only a sliver of beige was visible. Everything went fuzzy.

"Relax," boomed a voice directly into my ear, "and I will tell you about black holes."

My eyes flew open. Next to me, Rorie's hand rose, clasping a thin cylindrical object. Wincing, I understood what was going to happen a split second too late. Rorie tootled her recorder, loudly, right next to my ear.

She stopped and drew in a breath. "Soothing music." She blasted the recorder again, at several screechy pitches.

"Rorie," I said. "I have to tell you something."

"Did you know black holes can burp out star dust?"

"Yes. No. I don't know. Rorie, your baby brother is coming."

Pertly, she looked around. "Where?"

I patted my belly. "He's coming out."

Rorie nodded. "I know, Mom. He will be very small and helpless."

She placed the recorder at her lips, and I flinched, casting my eyes around for something to distract my determined little daughter. "How about some more soothing facts?"

The next contraction rose, tsunami-like. It started in the center of my abdomen and hardened, and hardened, and hardened until my organs flattened and my spine cracked. How did you bear the unbearable? Beneath me, the couch shattered and crumbled, the floor turned to dust. Later, when this was over, would I revel in the knowledge that I'd unleashed an ancient, inexorable power, one that no man would ever experience? Or would my mind file down the memory of relentless, ferocious pain, smoothing the edges to make it seem as if it had been tolerable? I couldn't remember experiencing this much pain the last time.

A strange guttural sound escaped me. Rorie fell away, the beige room fell away. The only sensation on earth came from the unfathomable force in my belly.

Gradually I became aware of a small scrabbling noise. "Mom. Mom." Rorie picked up my hand and stared soulfully into my eyes. I blanched at the thought that she must have been frightened by my pain.

"Mom?"

"Yes?"

"The Great Wall of China is made of sticky paste and rice."

"Thank you, darling," I rasped.

"It can be seen from space."

"Well. Sort of."

She picked up the candle. "Let's turn this on."

"Maybe later, sweetie."

"Mom, you are not being funnable."

The doorbell rang. Oh sweet mother of God, the cavalry was here. "Can you get that?"

Rorie had already charged for the door. There was no foyer in the Beige Box—the feng shui was terrible in here—so the front door opened right into the couch. Vani burst in, clad in some sort of winterized caftan, bringing with her a frigid gust of air. "Oi!" she yelled. "It's apocalyptic out there."

"Vani," I said. "Get me out of here."

"Of course! Do you still want to . . ." She looked at me and trailed off. "My God. What happened to your hair?"

I didn't waste time explaining my Spa Hair. "I need you to rescue me before another contraction hits. And"—I cast my eyes toward Rorie—"can you figure something out for her?"

Vani's face changed. She hugged me, hard, and then obliged with the request to occupy Rorie's attention, bribing her into her bedroom with an iPad and a bag of contraband gummies before returning to sit down on the couch. She lifted my hand and squeezed it. "How far apart are they, my friend?"

"I don't know. They were three minutes earlier." A stir rippled across my abdomen—not a contraction but a precursor signal, the feeling before the feeling. My heart quickened in dread. "Can you take a look before we get in the car?"

"Take a look? You know I'm an internist, right?"

"Please, Vee." I waved a hand in the direction of my bedroom. "There's a medical bag under the bed with sterile gloves. I don't want to get in the car if things are imminent. There's been no sign of EMS. They're probably dealing with all the crashes."

"Oh dear. OB was never my forte," said Vani, but she heaved herself off the couch and headed down the hall. She returned a moment later with the kit. "You know, I'm thinking we need to move you out of the living room. Just in case."

"Wait," I gasped. The contraction seized me, eclipsing everything. A roaring started in my ears, a great oceanic swell in concert with the pain. Underneath it, faintly, I heard myself whimpering.

"Oh dear. Oh dear," said Vani helplessly as the pain receded. Her face contorted, presumably mirroring whatever she saw on mine. "We need a doctor."

"We're both doctors. We're doing this. Help me get to the bedroom, okay?"

Getting me off the couch—a low-slung saggy affair—proved to be a comedy of errors. Once we conquered that, Vani helped me lower myself to the bedroom floor, and, with great ceremony, snapped on the sterile gloves. "You know I never really mastered the maneuver where you measure the cervix. It always feels like mush."

"Vani, shut up, please."

"I've encountered an obstacle to this birth. You still have your underwear on."

"Hurry!" I lifted my hips as best I could. Vani yanked off the underwear, flinging them behind her.

"Here goes," she said. Her brow scrunched as she navigated my nether regions. "Oh man. I don't know about cervical dilation, but this hard thing is a baby head. I don't think we have that long."

"Okay. You need to go in the kitchen and get string and hot water and scissors. There's rubbing alcohol under this counter to sterilize the scissors. Grab towels too."

I fought my way through another contraction, alone. It struck me suddenly, as the contraction faded, how startled I'd have been nine months earlier to be told I'd be giving birth on the floor of a featureless Atlanta apartment without the one other person on earth who'd longed for this baby. How many times had I willed myself to go on without Daniel, who'd died seven months ago of some unidentified febrile illness? How many times had I forced myself to regain composure in these last months? That Daniel's son would be born here, a world away from the place of his conception, bereft of the paternal love that should have been his; the thought slashed my heart with a burning ache. Normally I did not allow myself the indulgence of envisioning him, but for a moment—just a moment—I slipped, conjuring an image of Daniel as I panted on the floor. At baseline, his face had contained a glorious expressivity: mirth and kindness, calm and vitality. He'd won people over at first glance, reeling them in with the beacon of his smile and the force of his personality, so expansive, so generous. His voice: a hint of Africa from his mother, a hint of France from his father, warm and solid.

My baby's father; my husband. Daniel.

The longing for him overwhelmed me. For once, I welcomed the next contraction.

VANI RETURNED, SLOSHING a bowl of water. The next twenty minutes passed in a delirium, punctuated by pain and blood and effort. At the very end, just before the little soul I'd created with Daniel came into the world, I saw him again: smiling, his eyes warm and full of pride.

ALL THAT PAIN, all the bittersweet agony of labor, all the fumbling drama in the snowstorm: all of that had led to Beau. From the moment of his birth, he'd seized my heart in a way nothing ever had before or ever would again. I didn't love Rorie any less than Beau: surely a statement every mother in the world could understand. I'd die for both of them, willingly and instantly. But Beau, with his old soul and his repertoire of empathetic expressions, was his father incarnate. The universe had robbed me of the love of my life and then brought him back in the midst of a tempest, the swirly snowy winds somehow transferring my lover's soul into his boy. From the first time I held him, I knew what a gift he was.

Now, on Beau's seventh birthday, I slid out of my chair and Face-Timed Vani. "He's in the living room," I said in a whisper. "I'm going to surprise him."

Beau sat, his hunched back to the door, at a tiny red table. Even viewing the back of his head, I could sense the intensity of his concentration as he wrote in his notebook. Stepping lightly, I snuck up behind him and tapped his small shoulder. "Call for you," I said.

Beau turned, wearing an expression of anticipation, which upgraded into delight as he caught sight of the phone. "Auntie Vani," he said. "I am so happy to see you!"

"I'm happy to see you as well," said Vani. Her eyes, so large and dark, shone through the pixilation of the phone screen. Suddenly I remembered how she'd cried, holding Beau up to me in the moments after his birth. "The happiest of birthdays to you, beloved godchild."

"It has been *wonderful*," said Beau. Oh, this child! It had not been wonderful; it had been a remarkably crappy birthday, with no friends, no party, no big fuss other than a terrible collapsed cake I'd attempted to bake. Beau had eaten an entire piece of the dense, undersweetened wad of gunk and pronounced it delectable. *Delectable* was his new word for every bit of food he encountered.

"What's been wonderful, sweet boy?" asked Vani.

Beau offered a sunny smile. "My mom's been home," he said.

Ouch. I left Beau with the phone, prattling to Vani about a story he was writing, and slipped into a windowed nook off the kitchen I'd commandeered as my home office. We no longer lived in the Beige Box, fortunately. The new house, shingled and viney, sat in a wooded lot and possessed a lot of age-related quirks, but what it lacked in modern design it more than made up for in personality.

I fired up my laptop to read emails. Over the last few weeks, we'd established a clinical investigation team to build a database of every suspected case of what we now were calling—with apologies to Alex Rodriguez—AAROD.

AAROD stood for artiovirus-associated rapid-onset dementia. Joining Erika and Hai were a squad of other med epis who performed field surveillance, kept track of hundreds of biological samples, interfaced with hospitals, and crunched numbers from dawn to dusk.

What they'd discovered was chilling.

Based on the data from New York, one in every twenty survivors of the first variant of the virus went on to develop dementia. The percentage was lower for the second variant, but it didn't matter how sick you'd been initially; if you'd had the virus and recovered, your chance of losing your mind down the road seemed to be between one and five percent. The younger and healthier you were, the higher your chances were of suffering the complication. When it occurred, it occurred with catastrophic rapidity, and so far, nothing anyone had tried could completely reverse it. We didn't know why it happened either. Early histologic samples of the brains of the afflicted suggested an autoimmune-like condition. But we didn't have enough biopsy data to confirm the specifics because AAROD didn't kill you. It robbed you of your mind and left your body intact.

Since many of these patients were in the prime of their lives, brain biopsy samples were hard to come by. Most of the time, the team had to wait for the victims to die of other causes and then seek permission for a specialized autopsy to be performed in a hot-zone lab, which often meant a fraught transfer of the body. Nobody assumed AAROD was contagious, but then again, we didn't know for certain how it was happening either. What if CARS-ArV-01 increased your susceptibility to some other infectious agent?

Needless to say, when this discovery went public, it was almost certain to cause a panic. The stock market was showing signs of climbing out of the toilet after what had been one of the worst crashes in history, and nobody looked forward to seeing it plunge again. Already, neurologists and internists and ER docs in New York City, as well as a few other places, were beginning to sound an alarm. It was only a matter of time before the battered market imploded at the news. The national task force and the president had been briefed and were working on a planned announcement. I didn't envy them; how did you tell people about something like this when you had no reassurance to offer?

Beau wandered into the room, still holding the phone in front of him. I flipped my laptop shut; I didn't need Beau wondering aloud what a brain biopsy was.

"Aunt Vani wants to talk to you."

"Hey, Vee," I said, taking the phone from Beau. "Thanks for listening to him for so long."

"My pleasure. He's the perfect child."

"Ha," I said. I opened my computer again as soon as Beau left and clicked on another depressing email. "I don't think he'd ever bathe or change underwear if he weren't forced."

"That's a Y-chromosome thing," said Vani dismissively, flicking a wrist. "They outgrow it in the teenage years when it finally dawns on them there's a direct correlation between hygiene and hooking up."

"Speaking of teenage boys, that's the only beautiful thing about the collapse of civilization. Nobody's allowed to touch other people, which means my teenage daughter can't hook up with any of these hairy ogres." I felt a little mean after this pronouncement; Gnash or Hash, or whatever his name was, was probably a nice kid. After all: he was somebody's beloved child too.

"Right on," said Vani with real feeling. She also had a teenage daughter. "But they're all withering. Reggie cried for about five hours last night when he realized there isn't going to be Little League this spring."

I pumped the brakes before the conversation could devolve into a variant of the same sad lament repeated every day by every parent on the globe. You could talk for hours about the psychological impact on the poor little flowers in the attic, but to me these discussions only accentuated the heartbreak. I needed to get back to work, where my team at least stood a chance of impacting this newest disaster.

"I gotta go," I said. "Love you."

"Love you too," said Vani. "Oh wait: I didn't even tell you the big news."

"What big news?"

Vani paused, savoring the moment. "Georgia," she said, "is in labor."

GEORGIA'S LABOR COULDN'T have come at a better time: a Sunday, when I was home and stood a decent chance of being able to make the virtual delivery. Still, with a first child, this could drag on for days. Vani said Hannah would text us a link when Georgia was midway through the second stage so we could all cheer her on.

In the meantime, I'd better get as much done as possible. Before settling back into work, I checked on Beau, who assured me he had plenty of work to keep him busy, and then Rorie, who'd announced after lunch that she'd be reading in her room.

Rorie's room, when I entered it, contained only a hazy cloud of dust motes, floating in a yellow pool of light from the desktop lamp. A lump in the bed appeared promising but turned out to be a tangle of Rorie's tattered blue comforter and her battered stuffed duck, Mr. Quackers. Puzzled, I checked the rest of the rooms in the house, including, with mounting alarm, the attic. Rorie was not in the house.

I opened the front door and surveyed the yard.

Outside, the rain slanted down almost sideways. The tops of the pine trees danced in the winter storm, whipped back and forth by the gusting wind. A river of water, colored a lurid, opaque orange from the dirt of a nearby house under construction, surged past the house at the curb. There was no way Rorie would have gone out in this on foot. Where could she be?

I texted, to no avail. Rorie didn't reply to the first text, or the second, or the third. She didn't answer repeat calls either, which constituted a grievous violation of my parental phone policy. The deal we'd struck obligated Rorie to answer my calls unless she was dead. Anything nonessential could be covered in a text, so if I called my daughter, I expected an answer.

Still more irritated than alarmed, I went back inside. The likeliest explanation—that Rorie had fallen asleep somewhere and I'd overlooked her—meant I needed to check all the rooms again.

I did, finding nothing.

Now my irritation took on a tinge of worry. I returned to my desk and woke up the computer, opening the tracking program I'd installed on all our phones. A big market existed in the area of teenage surveillance software, promising worried parents they could not only track their recalcitrant offspring in real time, but also gauge the speed of the cars in which they traveled, and in the case of certain known associates, determine who was with them.

I had never before had occasion to use the program but figured it out in short order. And lo and behold, Rorie did indeed appear to be in a moving vehicle. Her blinking dot didn't follow any of the MARTA lines, so she must have been in a car.

Rorie's light stopped moving. According to the software, she was at or near the intersection of West Peachtree Street and Redwine Street, which meant not only was she still in Atlanta—probably at a red light—

she was still in the Norcross neighborhood. If I'd been in a better frame of mind, I might have revisited my frequent contemplation of how clichéd it was to live near one of the ten thousand Peachtree Streets in Atlanta. If you stopped a random person on the streets of Mogadishu or Guangzhou or Hyderabad—or anywhere—and asked them to tell you something, anything, about the city of Atlanta, most likely they'd blurt out "Peachtree Street" and amble away.

Rorie's dot blinked alongside another dot. I reverse-searched the phone number of the other dot, helpfully provided by the spy app. It came up registered to somebody named Paul Bettis.

Paul Bettis? The name meant nothing to me. I searched Rorie's high school directory and found a Bettis family, who had two children enrolled: a ninth-grade daughter named Rebecca and a son, a junior named Christopher. Christopher? I opened Rorie's contacts list, which I'd synced to my own computer, and searched "Bettis." Sure enough, there it was: Crash Bettis.

Trying to contain a near-homicidal rage, I grabbed my car keys and flung open the door to the garage, then spun around back into the house. "Beau," I called. "I have to run out for a minute. Can you take a break and come with me?"

"Okay," Beau called back agreeably. "I will change my clothes."

"You don't need to change," I answered, but it was too late; he'd already disappeared into his bedroom. A few minutes later he emerged, his little face peeking out from a puffy silver space robot costume. Two springy antennae adorned the hood, wobbling wildly with each step Beau took.

"Ready, Mom!"

I decided not to ask. Opening Herman's door, I ushered Beau into his booster, and we screeched backward out of the garage, hitting the river of orange water at the curb hard enough to send up a ten-foot spray. "Wow!" yelled Beau. "Cool." I adjusted the wipers to their highest setting, sending them swishing across the windshield with just enough force to achieve minimum visibility. I had to inch along the street. A toxic mixture of anger and fear commingled in my throat, threatening to choke me. If I could barely drive in this deluge, how was some teenage boy—named Crash, no less—likely to fare? If Rorie managed to survive her joyride, she'd still be risking death at the hands of her own mother.

I pulled over to check the GPS on the tracking app, which I'd opened on my phone. Pulling over made me uneasy—it would be difficult to avoid rear-ending a stalled car in this mess, even on the side of the road—but luckily Rorie's dot hovered only a few blocks away. Inching forward with the hazard lights blinking, I navigated to the spot where I expected to find my daughter.

A parking lot. Ordinarily this would make things tricky: I didn't know what kind of car Crash Bettis drove, and the GPS dot wasn't precise enough to distinguish between cars in a lot. But despite the low amount of circulating virus here, Atlanta remained buttoned-up; many people still avoided going out if they didn't have to. The lot contained only a handful of cars, and even in the lashing rain, I could rule out a few of them on sight. An Oldsmobile Cutlass; no. That was an old person's car. Crash could have borrowed his mom's SUV or his dad's sports car, but I was willing to bet a high school kid had his own car, and it probably wasn't a minivan or anything too pricey. There. Over in the far corner of the lot, a silver Mazda hatchback had stopped lengthwise under a cluster of oak trees, about as far away from the other cars as possible. That must be it.

I hazarded a glance in the rearview mirror. Beau, his antennae twanging, sat in the back seat placidly awaiting elucidation as to what we were doing circling around this random parking lot in the rain. Easing into a spot a few spaces down from the Mazda, I gripped the door handle hard enough to turn my knuckles white and forced myself into a fifteen-second pause as I adjusted my mask. "I'll be right back, honey," I said finally.

"Okay, Mom."

Gritting my teeth, I stepped out into the gale. Too late, I wished I'd donned a raincoat before leaving the house. I charged up to the Mazda, approaching the driver's side back seat first, and yanked on the door handle.

It opened. Without thinking, I threw myself into the car, relieved even in the grip of my fury to escape the rain. For one startled moment I entertained the idea that I'd entered the wrong car; why hadn't I tried to make out something through the fogged-up window first? It was hot and damp and noisy in here. The speakers boomed so loudly my hands flew, unbidden, to my ears.

My first confused impression: the front seat appeared to be inhabited by an abnormally broad-shouldered hulk of a human being. Then, a split second later, the hulk twitched and came apart and I found myself staring at Rorie and a boy.

Rorie, thank God, was fully dressed. So was the boy. Both their maskless faces had frozen in shock; wide-eyed, openmouthed, they stared back at me before Rorie's face unfroze and rearranged itself into an expression of pure horror.

"Mom! What are you *doing*?" she shrieked. "What are you doing?"

"Hello," I told the boy calmly. "I'm Dr. Marchand, Rorie's mother. And you are . . . ?"

With an expression of comical stupidity, the boy reached up and pushed on his chin to close his mouth. Ten awkward seconds passed. ". . . Crash," he said.

"Well, Crash," I said. "It's your lucky day. I'm not calling your parents to report you, even though, may I remind you, people are not supposed to be mingling. This, to me," I waved my hand at the front seat, "looks pretty mingly. Am I right, Crash? You are mingling with my very young daughter? Go home and tell your parents you've decided to ground yourself until you're twenty. Okay?"

"Okay," he mumbled, hitting the button to start the ignition. "I'm sorry, ma'am."

Rorie's expression of abject horror had not altered. "Mom!"

I jerked a thumb toward the door. "Out. Now."

With a last stricken glance at Crash, Rorie scooted away from him and opened the passenger door. She slammed it hard after exiting, leaving me alone with Crash.

"I'm so sorry," he said. Without the distraction of Rorie's fury, he and I had the opportunity to regard each other more closely: he had fair, wavy hair and a nice, dopey face, currently arranged in an expression of contrite shame.

"Look," I said, softening somewhat, "I know it seems like Atlanta's in decent shape right now, but in the last week there's been an uptick in the numbers of the virus. It's not gone, and you do not want to get it. Stick to phone calls."

"Yes, ma'am. I sure will."

"Okay, then," I said.

Back in my own vehicle, I encountered Rorie in the front seat. Every aspect of her body language screamed defiance: crossed arms, pursed lips, a resolute stare out the window. The interaction with Crash, brief though it had been, had drained away some of my rage; teenagers, I knew, were not hardwired to be excellent analysts of risk-benefit ratios. Still, I couldn't believe Rorie had so brazenly defied me.

"We will discuss this when we get home," I said, in as pleasant a tone as possible, not wishing to alarm Beau.

"No," said Rorie. "I hate you." In an anticlimactic afterthought, she added, "And I hate Herman! Why can't we have a normal SUV like everyone else?"

My rage returned, almost causing me to run off the road. At least Crash had been apologetic! It took every ounce of self-control I possessed to prevent myself from shouting at Rorie about how stupid, how willfully *dumb* she was being. Even in a non-plague era, a teenager caught sneaking around with the opposite sex against the explicit instructions of her parent didn't have a leg to stand on when it came to justification. But now? Now she risked not only her own health but the health of her mother and brother, and, by extension, all the people with whom I worked.

Back at the house, we divided ourselves into factions: a sulking, disdainful Rorie, her phone confiscated, in her bedroom; and me, shaking with anger, at my desk. Poor Beau, his antennae quivering both literally and metaphorically, stood in the living room trying to figure out what had happened to produce the palpable tension in the air on this, his seventh birthday.

Sweet Beau; caught in the middle again. I went to him and picked him up and kissed him, bobbling him on my hip to make his antennae twang, even though he was too big to be bobbled.

"Promise me you'll never become a mean teenager," I said. "A meanager. Promise me you'll never become a meanager."

Beau put his hand over his heart. "Mommy. I will never become a meanager. I promise."

I'D HAVE GIVEN anything, later, to have him take those words back.

17 The Omnipotence Paradox

HANNAH

SAN DIEGO
232 Days After Patient Zero

HOW MANY BABIES HAD SHE DELIVERED OVER THE YEARS? Hundreds? A thousand? Ten thousand? Hannah wished she'd kept track. For the most part they blurred together, a sped-up montage of life in all its messy glory; and also, occasionally, the most profound of sorrows. The sorrows, she tended to remember in excruciating detail. They came infrequently, but when they did, it was impossible to forget them. She was no stranger to providing gynecologic care for her friends and acquaintances. It was a given in this field; the women in your social circles sought you out. But all of them—all these people in San Diego—knew the fully formed adult Hannah. They didn't know the misplaced optimism with which she'd navigated medical school or the naive doormat she'd been in college or the timid, awkward Hannah of her high school days.

Georgia knew at least one of those versions, but any resurrected memory of their old lives appeared to be the furthest thing from her mind at the moment. As Hannah expected, she'd declined an epidural and now paced around the sun-drenched birthing room, periodically stopping with her hands on her knees to breathe through a contraction.

She radiated strength: hair bundled into a red knot atop her head, muscular limbs gleaming with sweat, a black mask with a see-through panel in the front. When the pains came, she gritted her teeth and hissed through them, which, in a form of unconscious solidarity, Jonah had begun doing as well. The two of them paced and gritted and hissed, and in any reasonable universe they would have looked ridiculous, but in this one, somehow, they were fierce and beautiful.

The first stage of labor drew to a close. Fittingly, the sun had begun to set, the light from the west-facing window dimming and growing rosier as the sky cycled through its most spectacular palettes: clear bright blue to molten orange to a soft, velvety indigo stretching above a silvery sliver of sea. Jonah busied himself setting up two iPads on tripods, as the nurse, Laura, helped Georgia into the bed. Hannah reached a hand to flick on the overhead lights, but Jonah, his black eyes glimmering, stopped her. "She doesn't want any bright lights," he said. "No overhead fluorescents, okay?"

Hannah switched on a retractable OR-type light hitched to the ceiling by a mechanical swing-arm, aiming it at Georgia's open legs. Georgia waited for her contraction to end—hiss, hiss, hiss—and aimed a barb back at Hannah.

"Dude. Do not light up my beav. I don't wanna blind the baby."

"Of course," murmured Hannah, who would sooner publish photos of her vagina on Facebook than refer to it as a "beav." She swung the light away from Georgia so it provided some ambient illumination without fixing her perineum in a blazing spotlight, trying to avoid what she assumed might be a smirk on Jonah's face. She didn't know what she'd expected from Jonah's presence. No one in her practice had ever brought in a gay man as a birth partner before. But here he was, and he'd been marvelous.

"Still think it's a girl?" she asked Georgia, but it was Jonah who answered.

"Don't even bother with that question or you risk getting swatted." He patted his hip. "I know from bitter experience."

He moved by the bedside, holding Georgia's hand and speaking to her in a low murmur Hannah couldn't quite make out. She fussed with the drape and the implements on the Mayo stand, leaning forward to try to distinguish Jonah's words. He'd linked up the tablets, one about ten feet away, capturing a view of Georgia's face and torso for the medical school friends to watch. The closer, more intimate video livestreamed to Georgia's fiancé, Mark.

Hannah'd ferreted out what information she could about Mark. He didn't have a Wikipedia page but was mentioned on the page of the famous man for whom he worked, which declared him to be instrumental in the finances of their complicated-sounding biotech venture capital firm. From this, Hannah had painted a portrait of a man who sounded like the last person on earth she'd have picked for her free-spirited friend. Georgia with some corporate suit in finance? From the tone of various other articles in which Mark had been mentioned, he must be loaded; another thing that didn't square with Georgia's lifestyle. She made good money as a urologist—even here in California, where the high cost of living and puny remuneration drove a lot of physicians elsewhere—but she lived like she was still in college, insisting on a minuscule house decorated with a plaid thrift-store futon and a lot of framed concert posters. But that was Georgia for you: things that bothered other people barely registered to her.

She knew this much: Mark, like Kira's friend Declan, had gotten sick midway through the first wave and had been in a tent hospital in Amsterdam much like the one here in San Diego before convalescing in a rehab facility. Hannah wasn't certain but thought Amsterdam's rate of infection had been similar to San Diego's; they'd had a small outbreak compared to other places, but that was because as soon as you got sick, you were isolated at home or in the tent if things got bad. In both cities, heathy visi-

tors were not allowed in these grim white structures, leading to a lot of conspiracy theories about death camps and culling the herd and illicit medication trials, but Hannah knew the truth: every single person who worked in those places was a living saint, their duties often ending in unbearable bedside vigils with the dying, listening to them cry out for the loved ones they'd never see again.

Whenever she could, she cast a surreptitious glance at the tablet linked to Mark, to whom she'd waved when Jonah first opened the connection. Not surprisingly, Mark's face was somewhat gaunt, the poor resolution of the video accentuating the hollows beneath his cheekbones and the long angle of his jaw. He had long, slender fingers and dark hair and silvery beard stubble that cast a glimmer whenever he moved his head. But mostly she noticed his eyes: an indeterminate greenish color, they conveyed the same mixture of intellectual curiosity and emphatic kindness she associated with Georgia. One look at his eyes and she'd understood what Georgia had meant when she'd described him as a thinker.

"Mark." As soon as her contraction ended, Georgia inclined her head toward his tablet, which Jonah obligingly scooted a few feet forward. A sheen of sweat coated her temples and her collarbones; in the soft light, the pupils of her eyes appeared enormous. "It won't be long. Our baby's coming."

Mark closed his eyes for a moment; when he opened them, they were glazed with tears. "I wish I was there with you, George."

"I wish I'd been with you when you were sick, babe," Georgia whispered. "I'm so sorry."

Behind her face shield, Hannah felt her eyes fill.

Mark leaned into the screen, gesturing toward Georgia. "I also wish I could take away all your pain."

"Fuck this pain," said Georgia, and now her voice came out strong through her mask. "I own this pain. It's bringing me our baby."

Another contraction gripped her.

Hannah could see the baby's head, poised at the threshold between born and unborn. In a few moments the world would gain a new citizen; who knew to what majestic heights this little soul might rise? In a burst of valor, Georgia bore down, pushing with such intensity the sternocleidomastoid muscles in her neck appeared to be on the verge of bursting though her skin.

As she coaxed her friend through the last moments of the delivery, a disagreeable sensation nudged Hannah, pushing gently and then more insistently at her. When Georgia had first asked her to deliver the baby, her imagination had guided her straightaway to a place of happiness: a babe sleeping in Georgia's arms, a room pulsing with joy. Throughout her career, though, she'd never quite lost the visceral fear that something could go wrong during a delivery—it was drilled into you in training: the eventuality that one day, no matter how careful or good you were, you'd lose a child and maybe even a mother. Even if there hadn't been a pandemic, she'd have worried about these things for her own pregnancy, but somehow, with Georgia, the risk of a bad delivery hadn't seemed real to her until now. This wasn't a high-risk delivery but, because of Georgia's age, neither was it low risk. Even without the ever-present threat of the pandemic, bad things could happen: an amniotic fluid embolus, meconium aspiration, uterine inversion, some unknown but catastrophic effect of having had the virus . . . Somewhere, some cosmic force could assert itself and rain ruin upon them before they saw it coming. Once this line of thought established itself, Hannah found it impossible to banish. The nudge at her back distilled into a tight little knot of fear. Until her own babe was born, this surely would be the most meaningful delivery of her life. What if things went wrong?

She regarded Jonah and Georgia again. Their heads were almost touching, Jonah's dark one bent toward Georgia's. In between contractions they watched the left-hand iPad, where Mark's tense face filled the screen; and the right-hand iPad, where images of Kira, Zadie, Emma,

Compton, and Vani flickered in their rectangular boxes, all of them muted like a small chorus of ghosts. Their silhouettes loomed against darker backgrounds; it was very late on the East Coast of the United States and very early on the western border of Europe.

"This will be the one, I think," she said to Georgia, who nodded and clenched Jonah's hand as her features contorted. Out of nowhere, Hannah's earlier unease massed and gathered strength, forming a terrible, unassailable certainty: something was wrong with this child. She knew it; knew it with the same conviction as she knew a new sun would rise in the east or that wantonly taking the life of another human being was wrong. Some things you knew without knowing why you knew them. It did not matter that Georgia's ultrasounds had been blessedly free of malformation or that her bloodwork had been stone-cold normal. Like all expectant mothers in this terrible year, she must have endured unceasing worry in light of this new pathogen ravaging the planet. Georgia'd suffered an infection in her first trimester, the most vulnerable time of a pregnancy. Until women like Georgia gave birth, no one knew what artiovirus in the womb might mean for children. Hannah had encountered no reports of birth defects yet, but now, as Georgia held her breath and pushed, the slamming, clanging alarm bells in Hannah's chest would not subside.

Her hands trembling, Hannah delivered the baby's head. With the next push, deftly, she rotated the little body and freed it, lifting the child away from the sheltering body of its mother.

Holding her own breath, she regarded it.

It was perfect. Like all newborns, it possessed scrunched features, tightly closed in defiance of its crashing new reality, until some primeval physiologic impulse compelled it to take in its first breath of air. As the baby's mewling cries filled the room, Hannah's throat contracted in a hard little rasp of joy. She'd been wrong. The baby was okay. Georgia was okay. She swiveled toward Jonah and motioned to the infant. He peered at it, eyes wide, and a tear slid down his face. Hannah held a finger near her lips and Jonah nodded, wordlessly agreeing not to call out the baby's sex.

The nurse placed the baby on Georgia's chest to be evaluated and dried off, and, after waiting the requisite minute, to have her cord clamped and cut. Georgia bowed her head at the baby nestled against her, sucking in air hard enough to indent her mask. After a moment, she whispered something into the baby's ear. When she raised her head, she was crying too.

"Mark," she said, raising her shoulder to elevate the baby's head toward the camera. "Meet our daughter."

FOUR DAYS AFTER the birth of Georgia's baby—a healthy girl whom she'd named Joanie Ruth—Hannah stood in her kitchen on a Saturday morning, one hand on her knees and the other rooting through the refrigerator in search of something cool to drink. Her throat felt dry and sandpapery and her eyes burned. She'd slept poorly last night, unable to find a comfortable position in this, the twenty-sixth week of her pregnancy. She'd abandoned in-person grocery shopping, terrified of unnecessary exposure, so it had fallen to Harry to keep them supplied with food and beverages during the lulls between grocery deliveries. He'd stocked the kitchen with an array of unpalatable man-food: processed sticks of sausage, energy drinks, unshelled but heavily salted pistachios. His one concession to her request for fresh fruit and vegetables, a pack of those slimy denuded baby carrots, rested all by itself in a corner of the veggie drawer. Hannah ripped a hole in the plastic and nudged out one of the carrots but abandoned it on the counter after a surge of nausea struck. It looked like a squat, oblong orange thumb.

She straightened up, her hands on her hips. Her back ached, a dull ribbon of pain running down the length of her spine. Keeping her hands on her hips, she inched down the interior hallway bisecting the house.

Their home, a small red-roofed Spanish Colonial, typified the architectural style in this neighborhood. On one side, the public rooms: the kitchen, the living room, a light-filled den leading to a tiny enclosed backyard; on the other, the main bedroom, a guest room, and a smaller third bedroom that, until now, had been the designated home workspace.

Harry puttered in the office-turned-nursery, whistling a plaintive earworm that sounded like the theme to *Jaws*. She took him in as she reached the doorway, stopping to rest a hand on the doorframe to catch her breath. His hair had grown out a bit from its usual buzz cut, allowing a few rogue tendrils at the base of his neck to flip up in the beginning of a curl. He wore his favorite ancient T-shirt tucked into his favorite faded jeans, a combination emphasizing his trim, stocky form; he was all biceps and delts and hard, angled jaw. He'd finished assembling the crib—a monstrously expensive splurge from Restoration Hardware—and now fussed with the strands of the mobile he'd selected, trying to disentangle them. The room's decor reflected the uncertainty of the baby's sex, which they'd elected not to discover early. Soft neutrals dominated the color scheme, everything gray and beige and cream except for the mobile, a garish primary-color representation of the solar system. Touched by Harry's delight when he'd presented it, she hadn't been able to bring herself to point out that it didn't mesh with all the soothing, tasteful neutrals. If Harry wanted their baby to stare up at an azure Earth and a ruby Mars and a giant, swirly orange Jupiter, then that's what their baby would do. Maybe she—or he—would become an astrophysicist.

"It's beautiful, honey," she said. She was looking at the gleaming golden slats of the crib as she spoke, and so she missed most of whatever expression Harry'd been initially wearing as he contemplated her. She swung her glance toward him in time to watch his smile melt. From there, his face slackened into free fall, bottoming out in a dull, frozen dread.

"Harry, what is it?" Her fingers gripped the doorframe harder. Suddenly, it was difficult to stand.

Harry crossed the room in two strides, reaching her as her legs gave way. He eased her over to the little daybed where she'd planned to breastfeed the baby, setting her up against a mound of ivory pillows. Her entire back had transformed into a rigid sheet of pain, screaming in protest as she tried to lean against the bed. "My back hurts," she said. Her voice came out faint.

"Let me see your hands," said Harry. If her voice had weakened, his had grown coarse and loud with fear. She lifted her hands, puzzled, and Harry snatched them up, covering them with his own hands so she couldn't see them.

"No, no, no," said Harry, letting her hands drop. He stood up and sat back down and stood up again, both hands pressed to the sides of his head. Slowly, Hannah looked down.

It took a moment to register. The tips of her fingers had turned a faint but sickening blue, the ugly marker of cyanosis, which was itself the ugly marker of a disease characterized by a lack of sufficient oxygen. Along with everyone else in her medical school, Hannah had learned the term *cyanosis* in the first year of classes, a time they spent largely parked in lecture hall seats, but she'd never before considered the etymological underpinnings of the word. In retrospect, *cyan* was obvious; it referred to the color blue, in this case the unnatural bluish hue of skin deprived of its core fuel. *Osis*, a suffix derived from Latin, denoted a pathological state.

Blue. Pathology.

Blue pathology.

A whimper escaped her. The sight of her hands seemed to have punctured her core, dismantling some protective inner shield and unleashing a host of physical pain. A symphony of symptoms cascaded into her awareness: the large muscles of her calves and thighs and butt ached; her lungs and throat burned; her skull contracted, squeezing her brain and draping over it an opaque blanket of confusion. She shivered and then tried to stop shivering because it inflamed all the pain. Every square inch of her throbbed as if she'd transformed into a sickening rotten bruise.

If her body had opted to go all in on the experience of the virus, her mind took the opposite tack. She allowed a gray fuzzy wash to settle over her, blurring her thoughts. She knew she didn't want to think, but still, somehow, she wondered: what had Harry seen in her face to frighten him from across the room?

"Show me a mirror, Harry," she whispered. He didn't answer, just turned and looked at her, a dull glaze in his eyes. With enormous effort she heaved herself to her feet and dragged herself over to the far wall, where Harry had hung a small mirror in the shape of a beaming sun. The gold of its rays complemented the slats of the crib and the spiky, branching arms of the pendant above her head and a hammered metal frieze of decorative butterflies Hannah had placed on the wall opposite the crib. Everything in here was peaceful and beautiful, so beautiful the sight of it dislodged another ache. Her baby, her baby . . .

She looked in the mirror. It framed the circle of her face, the corona of the sun hiding her hair and granting her a kind of leonine elegance. As soon as she allowed herself to focus on the details contained within the mirror, though, she knew why Harry had reacted as he had. Her eyes, bloodshot and sunken, and her skin, too pale, were bad enough. But her lips! Cracked and tinged with purple, they belonged on a corpse.

She tottered back to the bed, the aching continuing to intensify. Her skin froze and burned as the air from the vent overhead blew against it. The littlest whisper of touch from the sheets hurt. Allowing her body weight to settle onto her back and buttocks hurt. Air whistling down her scorched windpipe hurt. But nothing hurt as much as her heart, her soul, at the thought of what oxygen deprivation or the virus could do to her unborn baby.

"Hannah," said Harry, sounding frantic. "What do we do? You can't go to one of those tents."

"No," she murmured. "You're supposed to stay home if you can."

"But what if you can't? Can you go to the regular hospital?" He touched her forehead and recoiled. "You're burning, Hannah."

"I'm cold."

"What will we do?"

"Listen," she said. She had to stay calm and comfort Harry, and she had to think this through, but trying to focus sent a spear of pain through her head. "Call Natalie." Once Hannah's pregnancy was well established, Nia had transferred care back to Natalie Cheema, another of her partners.

Dimly, she heard Harry on the phone, his voice shredded into an urgent splinter-edged bark. She'd been on the receiving end of this call several times before; they had a checklist of questions for the patient or her family to answer, and, based on those answers, they either sent the pregnant patient to the hospital, to a negative-pressure maternity room, or they performed a video evaluation and directed a supply kit to her home. Even with cyanosis, most expectant mothers did well on home oxygen and electrolyte-containing fluids and video evaluations. This method of treatment limited the exposure of the L&D staff and kept enough beds open for the sickest of the sick or for women with complicated pregnancies. Most—but not all—pregnant patients survived.

Most—but not all—babies survived.

"Hannah," Harry said, setting down the phone. His shoulders shook. "Oh, Hannah."

"Our baby," she said.

"Not the baby. You." He faced her. Tears streaked down his face, disappearing into the bristly thicket of his morning stubble. "I can't—I can't live without you. Please, Hannah."

"You don't have to live without me," she said gently. She had to pause for breath between the words, but a sense of urgency gripped her: she had to comfort Harry. "You'll take care of me and the baby, and we will be okay. Go now"—she motioned toward the door—"go on, do whatever Natalie said."

Harry stumbled out. She focused on breathing, feeling every molecule of air razoring against her trachea on its way down to the swamp of her lungs. She intended to use the pain as a distraction from her fear, but it didn't work; the pain only amplified her terror, reminding her of what she stood to lose. She'd done better with Harry in the room.

Like a welcome mirage, Harry reappeared, wearing latex gloves and a new mask. A large basket with a wicker handle looped over one of his arms; in the other, he carried a water bottle. From the basket he pulled Hannah's plushest throw blanket, her foam pillow from their bed, a book from her nightstand, her phone, and an array of smaller items from the bathroom. Kneeling, he placed a straw in her water bottle and held it for her. When she finished drinking, he twisted the top from a little tube of Vaseline and rubbed it gently across her lips. He tucked the blanket around her and eased the pillow under her head and carefully, delicately, brushed her hair off her face. He set up a stool as a nightstand and arranged on it all the toiletry and comfort items, lining them up in a regimented circle along the perimeter: Harry's little army of bedside sentries.

She waited as he performed these ministrations. When he'd run out of items to distribute, he slumped back on his heels. "I spoke with Dr. Cheema."

"What did she say?"

"She's coming herself—"

"No!"

"No, honey, it's okay," he said. "She's only a minute away, closer than an ambulance. She's bringing a pulse ox and electrolytes and an oxygen tank and medicine and a—one of those belts or wands that monitors the baby's heartbeat, or contractions, or whatever. She said you'd know what to do with it. She's going to leave the stuff on the porch. If your oxygen level is low after the face mask or the baby looks bad or you get worse, then we call 911 and they'll take you to the hospital—not the tent; she said because you're pregnant, they can't take you there—and she'll make sure nothing bad happens to you or the baby."

Hannah digested this. It was unlikely Natalie had assured her husband nothing bad would happen; even now, both doctors and the general public remained overly reliant on anecdotal tales to try to gauge the outcome of a pregnancy when the mother suffered a severe infection. She reminded herself that Joanie Ruth had so far proven to be healthy. But studies were starting to trickle out about miscarriages—spontaneous abortions—and late pregnancy loss, even if little was yet understood about long-term effects on the fetuses who survived a mother's severe infection. Complicating matters, the fetal side effects of the antiviral drugs in play could not be studied for ethical reasons. They might help an unborn child or they might harm it. No one knew.

In addition, doctors generally took some care in choosing their words when discussing outcomes, offering hope when there was hope to offer and trying to temper expectations when things looked grim. As Harry's wife, Hannah would say anything she could to ease his anxiety. Natalie would have a different perspective: as Hannah's doctor, the stupidest thing she could do was promise nothing bad would happen. But Hannah knew as well as anyone: patients and their families heard what they wanted to hear.

"I feel better after drinking the water," she told Harry. This, combined with whatever Natalie had said, seemed to boost his spirits; he rocked back and forth, his eyes brighter.

"Hannah."

She looked at him.

"Will you pray? For you and me and the baby?"

Unlike Hannah, Harry did not ascribe to a specific religious doctrine. He attended church with her happily enough, but she suspected this stemmed from his enjoyment of the social aspects of gathering with five hundred other people and not from any deep-seated theological hunger. He didn't pray, and as far as Hannah could tell, he didn't extend any thought to the week's biblical sermon outside of the one hour he spent in church on Sundays. They'd danced around the question of faith in the beginning of their relationship, until one day, after a few weeks of dating, she'd decided to be blunt.

"What do you believe?" she asked. They'd sat, surrounded by strangers, in the middle of one of those steak houses where the chefs juggle knives and catch eggs in their hats. To his credit, Harry didn't feign ignorance at her question. In front of them, their chef's hands blurred as he made vegetables sizzle and dance. Smoke rose; flames shot up. The diners roared their approval.

"I don't know what I believe," he said. "I've never been able to extricate my thoughts from the central paradox of it all."

"What do you mean? The omnipotence paradox?"

He leaned toward her, his eyes alight. "No," he said. "It seems I've already been betrayed by my theological ignorance. What's the omnipotence paradox?"

"It's an age-old dilemma: if God is able to accomplish anything, how does that explain something unobtainable?"

"What, like defying the laws of physics?"

"Yes," she said, "but no. There are debates about logical absurdities, of course, but this concept is more of a riddle. The classic question—reduced to very human terms—is this: could God create a stone too heavy for Him to lift? Either way, the argument goes, there is something He could not accomplish, and therefore there is no such thing as omnipotence."

"Were you, by any chance," Harry said, "a philosophy major in college?"

Hannah smiled, nodding her thanks to the chef as he deposited a steaming mound of rice onto her plate. "I was a theology major."

"Well. I am way out of my depth in this conversation. I majored in political science. Which, let me be the first to tell you, is a useless major if your goal is gainful employment."

Hannah wanted to hear more about Harry's past—she knew he'd

been in the military—but even more than that, she wanted to return to the subject at hand. She couldn't see herself dating any man who wasn't a committed Christian. "So what paradox did you mean?"

"Ah," he said. He took a long swig of his beer and set it on the counter. "I suppose it's the same question that bothers every person, religious or not, at one time or another. Some variation of the age-old lament: *Why does an all-powerful God allow suffering?* And I've heard"—he held up his beer glass, trying to ward off any protestation—"I've heard all the arguments about suffering as a counterpoint to joy and the limit of human knowledge and the gift of free will and just about every other theory there is, but I cannot square any of those with the scale of the agony that exists in our world. On our earth there is devastation and pain and suffering. I've seen it, Hannah. And yet, we are supposed to pray to God for the things we need—not simply the things we want, but the things ensuring our survival and our humanity and our decency? And if we obtain what we need—the cancer is cured, the kidnapped child is found unharmed, the famine ends—then it is evidence of God's benevolence, but if children are murdered and tortured and starved while liars and brutes are rewarded, it's an example of us not understanding what we needed?" His eyes did not leave hers once. "I want to believe in God, Hannah; I do."

After that conversation, the first of many, they'd never come around to each other's way of thinking, and ultimately they'd stopped discussing it, but by then she loved him. Hannah knew Harry had lost both his mother and his brother as a child, and he'd witnessed atrocities in the Middle East during his deployments. She didn't know—he wouldn't say—which of these things had affected him the most, because he wouldn't talk about any of them. Or perhaps something else had happened that he'd never told her. Still, he never said anything disparaging about her faith. She'd long ago made her peace with their differences, but she'd always harbored hope that one day Harry would come to share her belief. She'd pictured this event occurring in a blast of cinematic glory; a dramatic declaration, a literal come-to-Jesus moment in which faith would explode like a bomb into Harry's soul and instead of devastation he would experience the peace and grace and thankfulness she felt at the touch of God.

"Why do you ask me to pray?" she whispered now, hopeful.

He met her eyes and she saw his love for her.

"Because," he said, "it will comfort you."

This wasn't what she'd longed for, but she took his hand and began to pray.

18 Fragile and Exquisite

KIRA

ATLANTA, GEORGIA
236 Days After Patient Zero

FOUR DAYS AFTER BEAU'S BIRTHDAY, I'D FINISHED PUTTING him to bed—ignoring Rorie, who'd gone to her room, still refusing to speak to me—when Wally called. For months, Atlanta had dodged the metaphorical bullet, and now in the waning days of the last wave, I'd almost—but not quite—been ready to heave a sigh of relief. Other cities had gone down; New York first, certainly, with its population density and its mass transit, but other less comprehensible places too: Laredo in Texas, and Spokane in Washington, and a slew of random small towns in Nebraska. Some places seemed to escape almost unscathed. It was an unfathomably weird virus, but, in the end, it appeared we had it in the grip of a slow strangulation, forcing the R_0 ever downward. Not only that, but approval of the first vaccine could be days away. I expected Wally to comment on the vaccine news, but when he spoke, his voice was anything but exultant.

"We've got a surge," he said. "A big one."

"What? Where?"

"Here. Here, Kiki. I got a call a few minutes ago from the county public health director, who's been monitoring the situation at Emory. You saw the local admission numbers yesterday."

"Yes, but—"

He didn't give me time to finish. "We've had dozens of artiovirus admissions in the last few hours."

I sat on the side of the bed, one hand drifting to my mouth before I yanked it back down again. Why was it so damn hard not to touch your face?

"Dozens? In a few hours? Where?"

"They're all being directed to the tent hospital." Most cities had begun doing this, both for safety and to maintain enough resources in the actual hospital for normal emergencies.

"How are supplies?"

"I'm told they're good," Wally said, adding, "I also heard we're supposed to receive a large compassionate-use shipment of Artenivir."

Artenivir was an experimental antiviral treatment not yet approved by the FDA. The initial data trended toward limited success in adults, but it had been discontinued for children after it had been discovered it caused a massive inflammatory reaction in children with fevers. In any case, Artenivir was a stopgap, useful if you were already quite sick; the country had pinned most of its hope on a vaccine.

"Do I need to come in tonight?"

"Wait until tomorrow, Kira. The team will work tonight, and we'll have better data by then."

Hanging up, I crossed the room to the kitchen and helped myself to a tiny pour of Blanton's. Standing at the darkened window, I sipped the bourbon and attempted to will my mind into blankness. If only I could erase from my thoughts, for even a short while, the sheer overwhelming impact of the events of this year. All the deaths, all the suffering; all the disruption and loss.

For a moment my efforts to smooth out my worries seemed successful; I dissociated, a shadow-person standing in a shadow-room, the whiskey burning its way down my throat the only proof of life. I drank and I floated and I didn't think.

The buzzing of my phone brought me back. I didn't intend to answer; whatever it was could wait until tomorrow. Unless, of course, it couldn't wait until tomorrow. That was the problem with being a subject matter expert at the CDC during a plague involving your personal virus. Almost nothing could wait.

This call didn't involve work, though: Georgia's picture lit up the screen. I might have let it go to voicemail but for two things: first, Georgia never called anyone; and second, she'd just had a baby. Curiosity flooded me as to how my freewheeling friend was handling motherhood. Perhaps she wanted parenting advice.

I answered a split second too late. I'd just lifted a thumb to jab at redial when the phone rang again. I answered it reflexively, assuming it was Georgia calling back. "Hey, how's it going? Are your breasts about to fall off?"

A brief silence, then from a voice that wasn't Georgia's: "No worse than usual, and not any more than usual, I guess. They looked a lot better before I had kids."

I held the phone out and peered at it. It was not Georgia; it was Zadie.

"Oh, sorry," I said. "I was expecting Georgia—she just called."

"Oh," said Zadie. "So you already know." Her voice, usually so lilting and animated, held a curious flatness.

"Know what?"

"I thought you just spoke with Georgia."

"No; I missed her. I thought you were her, calling back. What's wrong?"

"Hannah's sick," said Zadie. A choked keening filled the phone; she'd given up the effort to hold off tears. "It's bad, they think."

"Oh no," I breathed. I backpedaled through the room until I bumped the arm of a chair and fell into it. "What— Tell me what you know."

"Georgia texted her a few times to ask something and she didn't answer, even after a day. That's nothing like Hannah; she'd never ignore a message from one of her regular patients for that long, let alone from Georgia. She didn't know Harry's number, so she sent Jonah over to leave a note on their door and Harry texted her. She'd been sick but was doing okay at home at first."

"Is she—is she in the tent hospital?"

"No, she's in the regular hospital because of the late-term pregnancy. They can't deliver a baby in the tent."

"She's what—twenty-seven weeks? She's not in labor, is she? Is she on a ventilator?"

"I don't know." Zadie's voice broke again. "I don't know. Georgia said she'd text us all as soon as she speaks to Harry."

I sat, unmoving, after the call ended. Every few minutes the headlights of a passing car sent a strobe of white light juddering across the wall; from somewhere outside came the sound of a dog barking in short, agitated bursts. Otherwise darkness and stillness pervaded the room. A heaviness fell over me, binding me to this chair. I couldn't imagine moving.

The phone buzzed again, this time with a text sent from Georgia to all of us: Kira, Compton, Vani, Zadie, and Emma. All of us except Hannah.

From Harry: H on vent

A short period of nothing, everyone frozen in the act of digesting this news. Zadie followed with a question.

What about the baby?

For an unbearable length of time: nothing. Then, finally, three blinking dots indicated Georgia was typing something. Given how much time elapsed, I expected a lengthy message, but when the reply came through, only three words appeared on the screen:

Waiting to see

GEORGIA CONVEYED THE rest of the details, at least as much as Harry could convey them to her: Hannah had been treating herself at home and improving on oxygen when she had hemorrhaged and lost consciousness. The medical team taking care of her had transfused her and placed her on the ventilator. Her pulmonary function wasn't good enough to allow them to try to wean her off it, so for now she remained sedated.

So. Was this it? Was this how Hannah's lifelong dream of motherhood would end? Was this how her own life would end? A boiling anger, sudden and startling, suffused me. Had there ever been a crueler case of infertility than of a woman who spent her days and nights surrounded by pregnant women?

I didn't have to try to imagine Hannah's reaction when she'd learned she was carrying a child; she had called us all the first chance she'd had. She hadn't sobbed or shrieked or even smiled. Her voice had been low and reverent, so suffused with joy she could hardly speak. Even Emma, the most stoic of us, had teared up on that call.

What I could not imagine was Hannah's reaction if she were to awaken and discover she'd lost her baby. Or worse: Harry's reaction if she were to die.

A DAY LATER, the Atlanta tent hospital was full.

I sat in my nook, working from home today. I'd just closed another email update on Hannah—no significant change—in preparation to sign in to yet another virtual task force meeting. This one held more promise than most; we'd be getting updates on various clinical trials: the convalescent serum trials, the Artenivir trials, the monoclonal antibody trials, and most important, the excellent data from the near-complete vaccine trials. President Corbett had announced a plan to transform the tent hospitals—where possible—to vaccine administration centers to implement a quick rollout. In addition, I was hoping to hear whether human trials were underway at the European university that had taken over Declan's nanobody. I'd authenticated myself and was waiting for the meeting leader to sign in when I sensed a presence behind me.

"Mommy."

I swiveled, expecting to see Beau, but it was Rorie who hovered a few steps away, still in her pink shortie pajamas. At five-seven, she now eclipsed my height by a couple of inches, although I outweighed her by a good twenty pounds. Still, I found it disconcerting to look up to my child, especially when we argued. Nothing in the preceding days had thawed the stalemate between us: Rorie still bristled with hostility every time she came in contact with me, while meanwhile I alternated between fury at Rorie's actions and a peculiar ache I came to accept as guilt. I'd been absent for months while my little girl had been fending for herself.

I started to say something about how unusual it was that Rorie had risen before she had to—a first throughout the pandemic, since, like most teenagers, Rorie would sleep until noon if given the opportunity—but the words died in my mouth as Rorie spoke.

"I don't feel good."

Someone in the meeting began speaking, his voice chiming out from the computer speakers as he ran through an introduction of all the people on the call. Even though it breached virtual meeting etiquette, I disabled my video, replacing my own live image with the static professional photograph the CDC insisted on using in all my public media interfaces even though the photographer had snapped the picture with my mouth open and my eyes half-shut. I'd tried pointing out that the public wasn't likely to be reassured by an image of a stoned-looking public health official, to no avail. Once the photo made it into the system, it'd been impossible to get rid of it.

I felt myself blanch as I swung back around. Rorie's dark hair floated across her face, covering one eye; the other, unfocused and glassy, stared past me at nothing. Her breath, fetid even from this distance, came too quickly.

For a beat: absolute nothingness. I felt nothing, acknowledged nothing, thought nothing. If I could have extended this silent, pulsing hole in time, I would have done so, but my respite ended with a crash. Fear struck with all the subtlety of a nuclear explosion, sending my pulse skyrocketing.

Springing from the chair, I placed a hand to Rorie's forehead. Blazing. I led her to the couch and darted to my bedroom, where I kept the medical travel bag. This bag had seen better days; battered and dirty, one of its seams had unraveled and its faux-leather surfacing had flaked off in places, giving it the mottled appearance of a small diseased animal. No matter; it did its job. I yanked out a stethoscope and pulse ox, affixing the oximeter to Rorie's finger while I listened to her lungs.

The examination did not prove to be terrible, but neither was it good. Rorie's oxygen saturation was ninety-four percent—worse than it should have been but okay; survivable. Her lungs sounded junky, but she moved air well. Her temperature—elevated at 102.0—was concerning but not appalling. She wasn't cyanotic, and while she appeared a bit dehydrated, she drank the water I gave her and kept it down.

"Mommy," said Rorie. She shut her eyes and rested her head back against the sofa cushion, her breath still coming heavily. "Do I have the virus?"

I stroked her forehead, smoothing Rorie's hair back. "I don't know, darling." She shivered and I tucked a furry blanket around her, unable to keep myself from running my hands along her delicate shoulders. My mind raced, posing and rejecting and analyzing a thousand thoughts at once.

"My skin hurts when you touch it."

"I'm sorry, Roar," I said, yanking my hands away. "I'm going to call your doctor, okay? They have these kits we can get so I can take care of you here."

Rorie's eyes fluttered. Lately, some of puberty's physical cruelty had afflicted her; to her dismay, her chin broke out, and her nose, once so dainty, seemed to have lengthened and widened a bit, even as the angle of her jaw had flattened. It did not matter. I suppose every parent feels the same conviction when they regard their child: no matter their physical imperfections, nothing on earth could ever be as precious, as wholesome and fragile and exquisite, as your child in repose. The flushed stillness of those sweet features; the utter and absolute dearness of that little face.

I made Rorie drink some chicken broth—the medicine of the ages—and a sports drink, and then sat with her until she grew drowsy, clenching my fists to keep myself from stroking her hair. Once she seemed deeply asleep, I made a flurry of phone calls and texts, planning my strategy should Rorie get worse. In only a day or two, the artiovirus had gone exponential. The closest tent hospital, with room for hundreds of patients, could no longer accept more, and wouldn't accept a minor alone, in any case. Many of the hospitals prioritized children, but they too neared capacity for caring for the critically ill. I needed to keep Rorie well enough to stay home.

After a moment's hesitation, I called Wally to apologize for bailing on the meeting.

"Kiki, it's fine, I'll fill you in," he said. In the background, I could hear the muted chatter of voices; he'd gone in to work, then. "The epi teams are churning, as you might expect. The news that the plague has reached our figurative house may be freaking out the press, but it's bringing out the best in our people."

"The plague has reached my literal house," I told him. "Rorie is sick."

Silence.

"Wally?"

"I'm coming over," he shouted. "I'll be there in twenty minutes. What do you need?"

"Wally, no. You haven't been sick; I have. Unless she gets worse, I'm taking care of her here. We have a home kit coming; she'll have oxygen and I'll be able to monitor her. I can even give her IV fluids if I need to."

"Kira, I—"

"I promise I'll call you the instant anything changes. You have my word."

His voice took on the raspy tinge it always did when he got overwrought. "How is Beau?"

I froze. Unlike Rorie, Beau tended to be an early riser, bouncing awake all full of seven-year-old vigor, eager to see what fresh excitement the day held. He seldom slept past seven; eight at the absolute latest.

I pulled out my phone. It was 8:42.

"I have to go," I said hoarsely, hanging up over Wally's squawking protests.

I tore down the hall to Beau's room, my feet scrabbling on the loose runner, my hands grasping the doorframe to arrest my slide. The instant I entered, I breathed in the acidic, unmistakable tang of vomit. Placing a hand over my mouth to prevent my own rising bile from surfacing, I launched myself over to the window and yanked up the shade.

The dim room flooded with a blaze of sunlight, illuminating Beau's things: his orange bookcase, where he'd arranged his favorite books by the color of their spines; his curated shelf of Legos; the small red table and chair where he wrote and did art.

Beau didn't stir.

I flung down his comforter and outer sheet, both printed with *Star Wars* characters. Underneath, Beau lay on his side, curled like a shrimp.

At some point in the night he'd both vomited and urinated, caking the fitted sheet with a damp crust of foul-smelling fluid. His forehead shone, drenched in sweat. The skinny concavity of his chest wall rose and fell in sickening, unnatural hitches, every intake of breath punctuated by an audible rasp.

I moaned as I lifted him out of the mess. As if from some great remove, I heard myself sobbing as I carried him down the hall to the bathroom, where I tore off his pajama bottoms and his tiny little boxers. His skin burned to the touch as I sponged him off. Gently, I laid him on his side on the bath mat and flew down the hall to the living room, retrieving the pulse oximeter and the medical bag and my phone. As promised, Rorie's pediatrician had messengered over a green army-type bag containing a professional version of the ART Care Kit for doctors, which I snatched from the front porch before running back to the bathroom.

His oxygen level: eighty-eight percent. Hurriedly, my hands shaking, I snapped together an oxygen mask and a length of clear tubing, connected it to the tank, and slipped the green straps over Beau's head. Thinking better of this, I removed the mask and checked Beau's mouth and throat for any retained chunks of vomit he could choke on. Finding none, I replaced the mask.

Next I checked his blood pressure and temperature. While the cuff inflated, I voice-dialed Wally but didn't wait for him to say hello once the connection went through. "I can't talk right now," I shouted, "but find out what the pediatric bed situation is at the hospitals, and call an ambulance for me if there's anywhere they can take the kids. Tell them it's emergent and text me back."

I hung up before Wally could yelp out more than a word. Beau's temperature, nearly 105, was too high, and his blood pressure, 68/48, was too low. I ran a beach towel under cold water and placed it over him, pulling one of his spindly arms clear. From the medical bag I removed an IV kit and a bag of saline. It had been a long time since I'd started an IV on anyone, let alone a critically ill child, but I'd punctured enough veins in Africa to be able to do it in my sleep. I scanned his limbs, settling on the bluish smudge of cephalic vein in the crook of his arm.

I missed on the first stick. Biting my lip to keep from releasing whatever god-awful sound was building up inside me, I tried again, and this time got a flash of blood, but the vein collapsed before I could thread the cannula. I forced myself to breathe slowly and deeply for a count of five, sitting on my hands to arrest their rattling, trying to calm the frantic hammering of my heart enough to do what I needed to do. On the third try I got it. I attached the IV tubing and hung the bag from one of the pulls to the bathroom cabinets.

Okay, now what? I'd tackled the ABCs of resuscitation—airway, breathing, and circulation—so I proceeded to examine the rest of him as best I could, trying to think like a doctor instead of a mother. From a neurological perspective, results were mixed: Beau was unconscious but responsive to pain, given that he'd tried to draw back his arm when I'd started his IV. His pupils constricted when exposed to light, and he didn't display any of the positioning associated with severe brain damage. I couldn't remember the precise criteria of the Glasgow Coma Scale, but I guessed he was somewhere around an eight or nine—not reassuring but not indicative of the worst possibility either.

As I listened to his lungs, I heard a dull, crunchy rattle, but he didn't bring up any sputum as he breathed. A recheck of his oxygen saturation showed improvement after the face mask; now he registered at ninety-three percent. His skin still felt fiery to the touch, but I didn't see any evidence of bleeding—no petechiae or bruising, no blood in the mucous membranes of his mouth or nose or eyes—and no rash.

Forcing myself to focus on assessing Beau had calmed my panic, but now that I'd run out of interventions, a wild, brittle terror rose within me. He needed a hospital; what if there were no ventilators left in the hospitals? Only one thing in my past compared to this. When Daniel had become ill and died in our village in Chad—ironically with an unidentified febrile illness much like this one—I'd been flooded with grief. I felt now as I had then—worse, even—incapacitated, my heart galloping with dread and terror. Every beat sent another gush of despair into my system until I thought I'd burst from my skin.

My phone rang: Wally. I snatched it up. "What did they say?"

"They can take them both," said Wally. He was breathing hard. "An ambulance will be there any moment."

"Thank you," I cried.

"Mike Zhou is on call and he'll see them." I searched my mental database: Zhou was a pediatric intensivist, a short, jokey tube of a man. "Also Gretchen Crosthwaite." This name I knew professionally: Gretchen was one of the top pediatric infectious disease specialists in the region. "They've got one pediatric negative pressure room waiting, and if no one arrives in the meantime, it's theirs. Kira, listen." He paused. "They aren't letting parents in the rooms."

"No!"

"Hold on. They're making an exception for any parent who has already survived infection, plus they know you understand infection control measures. You're not going to tear around like a dumbass and expose the staff. But"—his voice dropped—"if they let you in, you go in there to comfort your kids. You're not the one who should manage this. Mike and Gretchen know what they're doing, and they'll take care of your children as well as anyone in the country could. They know every single option available at this point. You have to let them take on the burden of whatever happens."

"I will. I promise."

"Kira, damn, I wish I—"

"They're here!" I leapt up. "I have to go. Wally—thank you—"

Before I hung up, I heard his last words. "Tell them I love them."

19 | The Grace of a Breathing Machine

KIRA | **ATLANTA, GEORGIA**
237 Days After Patient Zero

THE ROOM IN WHICH THE CHILDREN HAD BEEN PLACED—white-walled, with cheerful framed cartoon drawings of various animals—had been intended for one patient, not two, but the nurses had crammed in a second bed and turned the space into its own mini-ICU. Rorie, awake and hysterical at first, had been sedated, and now, at nearly four o'clock in the morning, dozed again, pawing fitfully at her oxygen mask in her sleep.

Beau had been intubated in the ambulance by a woman in a full biohazard suit and placed on a ventilator on arrival to a segregated section of the emergency department. After a blitz of central lines and imaging and medications, he'd been wheeled up to join Rorie. Since there wasn't room between the beds for a chair, I slumped between them on a wheeled stool, my head resting on Beau's bed atop my crossed arms. The ventilator shooshed and shushed and puffed into the dim room, the green numbers from its electronic display casting little beads of light into the semidarkness. A band of fluorescence flickered out from the gray control board behind the beds, and a ridge of white light seeped from the cracks underneath the doors leading to the hall and to the bathroom. Finally, the window shade remained open, ushering in the dusky orange sky of the medical complex at night.

From outside the room came a dull but rapid thudding sound. I raised my head, listening. The sound intensified as its source drew nearer: the unmistakable noise of at least several people running. Barring some remarkable occurrence—a fire, or a threat—only one event produced a crowd of people hauling ass down a hospital corridor.

A code.

You never wanted a code to occur in any part of the hospital, of course, but someone coding on a pediatric floor produced an urgency all its own. The footfalls moved past our room to a room three or four doors down. Even from that distance and through the closed door, I could hear the urgent dinging of the monitor alarms and the muffled sound of people shouting through their masks.

This kept up for thirty minutes or so before an abrupt silence descended. The silence stretched and stretched, and I drifted into an uneasy, uncomfortable half consciousness, my body's desperate attempt at sleep sabotaged by a jumbled mental horror show of sights and sounds from earlier in the day. My brain would not shut down. Every time I neared sleep, I'd replay the frantic beeping of a monitor or the clipped staticky bursts of an EMS radio or the sound of Rorie's cries when she'd realized the extent of her brother's illness. I sat up, grinding my knuckles against my closed eyelids.

The ventilator continued to shush. On the wall behind me, a clock ticked.

The door to the hall nudged open, revealing a human form silhouetted against the bright hall. At first I thought the figure was another figment from the depths of my overtaxed subconscious, but then the person tiptoed into the room, heading toward me. In any other era—in any normal hospital stay—it would be routine to have interruptions all through the night. People checking vital signs, people adjusting medication drips, people drawing morning labs at infernally early hours. But now the hospital took what precautions it could to protect its workers, limiting intrusions and requiring extensive disinfecting protocols for those entering and leaving the room. From the station in the middle of the hall, the staff could monitor the children, sending in respiratory therapists or nurses only if necessary. Blood draws were as limited as possible.

The figure making its way into the room was wearing a regular mask with a clear panel. As it neared me in the half-light, it took on the specific features of a man: shaggy dark hair, straight eyebrows, a broad face dominated by cheekbones elevated in a permanent smile.

Mike Zhou.

Warily, I regarded him. "No filter-cartridge mask?"

"No." He slashed a hand into the air for emphasis. "I usually wear it to reassure people, but, you know, the virus—it did its best against me and failed. They tell me I have the most robust antibody response the lab has seen."

I nodded. "I had a good antibody response too."

"We are lucky," he said. "It makes me very popular around here. I do many of the nursing tasks."

"From what I understand, you weren't hurting for popularity before this."

"Yes, very true. I am the most popular man." His default grin grew larger. I could see why he enjoyed a reputation as both a child and parent charmer.

I gestured toward the hall. "You're on call tonight?"

"I am not," he said, "on call. I sleep here now, while things are so bad. My ICU colleagues, Drs. Joshi, Marsh, and Crosthwaite, they do not have immunity, so for now I hold down the fort as much as possible. We all work," he added, trying to stave off any protest, "but I do not have a wife or children and I do have the antibodies, so . . ." Another room-lighting grin. "This floor is my temporary home."

"Mike," I said. "That must be brutal."

"Pffft," he said. "For the families, yes; very brutal. The little patients, they make the heart ache. But it is the nature of the job. You fight the good fight."

"Yes," I agreed, but at the same time I shook my head. Was Mike Zhou the most resilient man on earth, or had his experience loosened some fundamental screw?

"Ah, now," he said. "I come to talk to you about the children. Beau and Rorie. I happened to be awake, and, forgive me, I thought you might be too."

This reference to the code, oblique though it was, quelled my curiosity. I found I didn't want to know if the child had lived. By contrast, I did want to know—desperately—what Zhou thought of my children's chances.

"Tell me," I said.

He didn't have a stool, and the typical patient-room hard plasticized sofa had been removed to make space for the extra bed, so I stood, feeling awkward about sitting while he was standing.

"Nope," he said. "No standing. You look like you're about to keel over, and then I'd have to resuscitate you, and I'm not so good with adults. Better you sit."

I returned to the stool. He was correct; standing for even a brief moment had made me woozy.

"Okay, now," he said. "With most parents I try to gauge how likely they are to understand the technicalities of what we do and then how likely they are to want to *hear* the technicalities of what we do, and I temper that with how likely they are to lose their shit completely when and if they hear, and then I make a plan of how and what to tell them. But you?

All that goes out the window. You understand what's in the chart, even if I don't tell you."

"I haven't seen their charts," I said. "I only know what you and Gretchen told me earlier."

"Okay, good. Good. We'll go over everything now."

Zhou spoke for the next ten minutes, running though the latest lab and imaging results, the children's response to treatment thus far, and the remaining tools in the medical arsenal. In regard to possible treatments, the country had advanced from the beginning of the pandemic, most of the details of which I could recite in my sleep. Did recite in my sleep, in fact; more than once, I'd woken up muttering about protocols or numbers.

"The bottom line," said Zhou, "with Rorie, we have concern that her inflammatory markers are rising, and her pulmonary function showed some decline throughout the day as her oxygen requirements increased. We'll get another film in a couple hours and see where we are, okay? I am concerned about a secondary bacterial pneumonia. But I think you need to brace yourself for the possibility of a breathing tube."

I jerked my chin in acknowledgment, my mouth too dry to speak.

"And Beau. Dear sweet boy, he is fighting so hard. We're seeing some vent resistance despite the new settings. The serum, we think has not been a success thus far, but it's early. This you know. So now what?" He rubbed his hands together. "We are going to try everything, Kira. No stone unturned for your boy. Conventional therapies first, okay, and we'll try the off-label medications I discussed with you. Today, I think, will be critical. But I am here all day. I will not leave you."

"Thank you," I managed. Tears flooded my throat; some great primitive wash of terror rose from my gut, strangling any other words.

Zhou might not have children of his own, but he was no stranger to the sight of a parent dissolving in grief. He retrieved a thin, cheap tissue from its box on the nightstand and swiped it, gently, beneath my eyes. "Here, now," he said. "The tears, they make you tired. Kira, you cannot sleep in here, there is no room. You should go home, just for a little while, and gather your strength for the children."

"No," I said. The thought of Rorie waking alone to the sight of her brother tethered to life only by the grace of a breathing machine; no. No, I'd stay right here.

Zhou sighed. "Of course," he said. "Of course. I will have them send in some extra blankets. Perhaps you can make a nest on the floor."

20 The Wilds of Connecticut

COMPTON

NEW YORK CITY
237 Days After Patient Zero

IN CONTRAST TO THE HEIGHT OF THE PANDEMIC, NEW YORK hummed with activity on this, an ordinary Saturday afternoon. Life here had settled; despite a last-ditch effort by the virus to conquer Atlanta and a few other scattered places, in most areas of the United States the infection seemed to have diminished, if not outright burned itself out. Here in the hospital, the halls thronged with all the usual denizens of a medical center, hustling by with seeming normality on their way to the cafeteria or to visit their sick grandmother or to extract someone's problematic gallbladder. *Seeming normality*, of course, being a relative term, because if you looked closely, quite a bit had changed.

First, masks. They covered all the faces here in the emergency department, but that wasn't out of place in a structure designed to battle illness; even in the pre-plague days of eight months ago, nobody would have glanced twice at a bunch of people parading down a hospital corridor in surgical masks. Unlike, say, the subway or the grocery store, where even now Compton could not help envisioning a time traveler from the recent past staring in bewilderment at all the covered faces, wondering if the apocalypse was nigh or what. There were still some mask holdouts scattered here and there who bellowed in outrage at the idea of sissified government weaklings trying to tell them what to wear, as if the government weren't already insisting they wear things like seat belts and, for that matter, clothes. But for the most part, those people lived in areas where they hadn't been cremating their relatives day in and day out. In New York, if you encountered a maskless person, it often meant they had survived the illness and tested positive for antibodies, which, so far, correlated well with immunity to reinfection.

Masks—or the lack of them—weren't the only clue, however. For obvious reasons, few people wanted to shake hands anymore. Some people elbow-bumped or put their hands together as if in prayer, but most people seemed to be employing a sort of combo head-nod-half-bow thing. Compton liked the head-nod-half-bow; it felt dignified and respectful.

Another clue to the new world: the government had begun distributing colored pins to the population to indicate immunity. They planned to ramp this up once the various vaccines had been distributed, so people would have instant visual reassurance about the lack of infectivity of a stranger in their orbit. The pins contained some kind of glowing biometric sensor activated by your fingerprint to make them harder to fake. Immune people's pins glowed green.

Between the masks and the big glowing pins and the head bowing, it was all very *Star Wars.* You almost expected a two-headed person with their eyeballs on stalks to come slithering around the corner of the ER, complaining the pain medicine their primary care doctor had prescribed for their hangnail was not getting the job done and could they *please* have a script for hydrocodone, like, *right now*?

Yep. Mostly back to normal.

The opiate-requesting hangnail patient had been a real one—a human version, not a two-headed version—and after a respectful and earnest presentation on Compton's part about it not being good medical practice to prescribe addictive opioids for minor conditions, the hangnail stormed out, hollering at top volume that she was going to trash Compton on the Press Ganey survey for being such an evil bitch and also on every doctor-rating website on the whole freaking internet. The fact that she referenced the Press Ganey survey by name probably meant Hangnail had received a great deal of them in the past, which in turn probably meant she'd spent an inordinate amount of time in hospital emergency departments.

You were not supposed to reference patients in terms of their diagnoses, on the theory that it dehumanized them. In the privacy of her mind, Compton did so anyway, particularly if the patients in question were ornery. Names were irrelevant in the emergency department, but a diagnosis was not, or so she told herself.

This self-serving rationalization was tested by the rest of the day's patients, almost all of whom turned out to be heartbreakers. Some days were like that; the intensity never let up. It began after Hangnail—whom Compton had now christened Vengeful Hangnail—with a sixty-four-year-old woman presenting with headache. Rapid testing for ART in the screening area outside had been negative, and her story didn't sound infectious anyway, an assumption that was even likelier to be true when she coded in the CT scanner with a massive aneurysmal bleed. At the precise moment Compton was trying to revive her, three gunshot wounds to the abdomen arrived, all of them curly-haired teenaged girls and all of them near death, and, as it turned out, all of whom had been shot by their father. Apparently, according to EMS, he reported he'd also tried to shoot himself but "missed."

Next to the ravaged teenaged sisters was a room with a middle-aged diabetic man on the verge of death from overwhelming sepsis, whom Compton knew and liked because she'd seen him perform his stand-up comedy routine at a bar near her neighborhood. Another ambulance rolled up with a pedestrian-versus-car suffering a Le Fort III fracture—a hideous injury that basically split the face in two—and bilateral femur fractures; yet another ambulance delivered a postpartum college student who appeared to be having an eclamptic seizure. And that was just the ambulances; the waiting room, stuffed with the walking wounded, was also a seething hell.

At first, Compton kept her cool, focused on doing the things that had to be done. But her own breathing grew irregular as the carnage piled up. She tried—she tried so hard—not to make the obvious comparison. This was all normal ER stuff, even if it was happening in an unfortunate spate. It wasn't a return to those endless days and nights of pandemic patients. It wasn't a return to seeing nurses work themselves to a literal death. It wasn't a return to futility, helplessness, confusion, and inadequacy. It wasn't a return to blue-lipped people begging her to contact their husbands, their wives, their parents, their children, relying on her to remember to convey their last mortal message to their loved ones in case they died. She wasn't weeping, holding the hand of a twenty-year-old Asian man drawing his last breath eight thousand miles away from his mother, her tears pooling behind her face shield where she could not wipe them away. It wasn't an eternal wave of grief.

It was just a normal bad day in the ER.

BY THE TIME she reached the apartment that night, she still hadn't made a decision about what to do regarding her job. She'd sweated through two sets of scrubs today. She'd had to hide in the bathroom for a good ten minutes at one point to breathe through an overwhelming sense of panic. The panic reinforced itself because she knew if she couldn't control it, she wouldn't be able to go back out there, and if she couldn't go back out there, people were going to suffer as the system ground to a halt. You couldn't just magic up a fresh ER doc because one of the current ones was freaking out in a toilet stall. Her colleagues, just as swamped as she was, couldn't pick up her slack.

But what could she do? How would she support her children if she didn't work? Ellis's death had left them in an uncomfortable financial situation. Their life insurance policy had collected a fortune in premiums over the years, but after a series of milder pandemics in the past, the insurance companies had carved out an exclusionary act-of-God-type rider for future pandemics. They hadn't paid a dime when Ellis died, although they'd sent a gushing "heartfelt" letter of condolence. Compton set fire to it, reflecting that in the entire history of the universe, no one had ever been consoled by a bullshit form letter from an insurance company. The only payout associated with this letter would be if she suffered a fury-induced stroke, thereby precipitating a reimbursable cause of death from which her orphaned children would benefit.

Sarcasm aside, Compton's situation paled in comparison to the plight of thousands of her fellow New Yorkers who hadn't had the privilege of wealth to begin with. Everywhere you looked: someone who'd lost all income, someone declaring bankruptcy because they couldn't pay hundreds of thousands of dollars in medical bills, penniless children who'd lost both parents, or broken parents who'd lost both children. A virus might not discriminate, but people sure did. If you were rich, you fled the city for your second home or bought yourself a top-notch BSL-3 mask from a biocontainment lab or told your white-collar employer you wouldn't be working until you felt safe. You barricaded yourself and ordered what you needed, and people who had no choice about working brought it to you.

And when it was over, you did what Compton did and looted your mutual funds to replace the income of your lost spouse. Or at least that's what you did if you were medium rich and you'd lost your husband. You paid some other person to care for your children and clean your home so you could go to your job. And you tried to tell yourself you would keep doing your job, because your investments were dwindling and your children needed a provider and it was weak to think of quitting just because you sweated and hyperventilated every time you went to work.

The children slept, having been put to bed hours ago by Mildred. A heavy dread settled over Compton; this time of evening sucked beyond all measure. Earlier, she'd tried to call Kira but hadn't been able to reach her. How many years had it been since Kira's husband had died? Six? Seven? Now, looking back, a deep sense of shame assailed Compton that she'd been so ignorant of what Kira must have gone through, especially that first year after Daniel's death when she'd endured a pregnancy, a transcontinental move, a grueling fellowship, and the birth of her son. At least Vani had been there for her.

Compton had always seen herself as the odd man out. Perhaps she alienated other people in some way of which she herself was not quite aware. Within their complicated seven-way friendship, certain factions and allies had developed, which Compton supposed was normal. Zadie and Emma had always been insular within the group, even moving to the same city after residency. Vani and Kira, who'd been united during school, had stayed in close touch, always seeming to herald the big events in each other's lives, both good and bad, with unconditional support. Georgia, the dissident of the group, had never seemed to need or desire a female confidant, but she nonetheless moved comfortably within the friendship, darting in and out of their endeavors at the behest of whatever mysterious whims activated her. Plus, she had Jonah, and it was a good thing she did, because Compton found herself at a loss to envision how Georgia was dealing with the onset of motherhood without Mark, her partner. You couldn't reach out to Georgia, though, even if you were trying to help; you had to wait for her to reach out to you.

Finally, Hannah. While not aligned with any one person more than any other, Hannah served as the glue bonding all of them. Everyone loved her.

The thought of her triggered fresh grief. They'd found themselves rudderless in her absence; in the past, when anything had happened to one of them, Hannah had directed the efforts at celebration or consolation, relentlessly and sweetly hectoring everyone else until they rearranged their schedules to be able to do whatever was needed. Now they needed a Hannah to keep them informed about Hannah. Zadie had been trying to fill in, even though with four kids, a busy cardiology practice, and a congenital tendency toward dysfunction, she wasn't an ideal successor as the group organizer. Georgia, who'd met Harry in San Diego several times now, kept them apprised of Hannah's condition whenever Harry passed along information. She'd survived the worst of her illness, it seemed. Off the ventilator now for a few hours, she had to be awake enough to have asked about her baby. But neither Georgia nor Zadie had been able to reach Harry, and so no one knew Hannah's current mental or physical state. The last they'd heard, the baby had not died.

Compton switched on a solitary lamp in the living room and tried to watch TV. She landed on a show about a bunch of flawlessly made-up women hurling insults at one another. Their giant glossy pink lips moved and moved, but they might as well have been hissing in that snake language from *Harry Potter* for all Compton could understand them. She stared blearily at the TV, too tired to lift her arm to turn it off.

Ellis had rarely watched TV, but having grown up in Toronto, he'd been an avid hockey fan. When the Maple Leafs played the Rangers, you couldn't get him away from the television. He always made an occasion of it, doling out popcorn and juice to the kids, donning a Leafs jersey so ancient it had turned translucent. He'd sat right where Compton sat now, yelling urgent instructions to the players with his clean Canadian diction. Once he'd spilled an entire beer in his lap and hadn't noticed.

She rubbed the nubby plaid arm of the chair, tears leaking from her eyes. Why was this fucking thing still here? It was, as her Kentucky grandmother would have said, ugly as sin. The rest of their furniture adhered to a minimalist Swedish-modern aesthetic imposed on them by a haughty design consultant at the furniture place, but this chair was a holdover from Ellis's bachelor days. He'd fought to save it. Compton almost laughed, thinking of it now: having an argument over a young husband's college man-chair was so clichéd it was practically an American marriage license requirement. But that's what they'd done, and Ellis had emerged the victor. Compton had bitched about this chair almost every day of their marriage.

Now Ellis was gone and the chair remained. Like roaches and Styrofoam, it would probably survive a nuclear blast and be unearthed at some unimaginable point in the future by post-historic aliens, who would marvel at the blinding hideousness of its green and orange design. They'd never know of the absolute dearness of its most frequent occupant, with his intermittent blond beards and his irritating inability to gain weight and his weirdly endearing tendency to correct other people's grammar. They wouldn't know about his insane plan to abandon financial security and traipse off to the wilds of Connecticut to grow organic vegetables and make birdhouses.

Bawling openly now, Compton let her tears fall on the chair, as if christening it with her pain. In her current state of dysfunction, this seemed reasonable. Maybe the chair would cry too, if it could. Surely it missed Ellis. For fuck's sake, she was losing her mind, anthropomorphizing a piece of insensate furniture. Was this a normal part of grief?

Without giving herself time to consider her actions, Compton jumped to her feet and set off down the hall. She passed the door to her bedroom and slowed as she reached the door to the boys' room. Moving with exquisite care, she twisted the handle and crept into the room. Lawrence slept flat on his back, legs crossed, his hands behind his head, as if he were a ruminative sunbather. He always slept in weird positions, like a living art installation. *Boy in Contemplation of the Heavens.*

Baby Walter slept like a baby, complete with a thumb in his mouth and his fat diapered bottom up in the air. Cautiously, Compton scooped him up, rotating him so his head rested in the crook of her arm. He stirred and ejected his thumb but didn't awaken. She carried him back down the hall to Ellis's chair and eased into it. The solid little tank of the family, Baby Walter had failed to inherit the leanness of either of his parents. Now that he was eighteen months old, he had the heft of a small hippo. The mass of his toddler head on Compton's inner elbow produced a sizzling pain along the distribution of her ulnar nerve, but she squeezed the compact warm mass of him as if he were a lifeline. When you thought about it, he *was* a lifeline, a literal flesh-and-blood link to his father.

"I miss your daddy," she told him. "You don't know how pissed he would be to miss seeing you turn into a person. You're fashioning your own ideas and beliefs and accomplishments; you learn something new every day. You are remarkable." Compton kissed his head and paused, honesty compelling her to reflect that Baby Walter's main opinion that week had revolved around a firm conviction that potty training was not for him. Still.

"They tell me I need counseling. It's normal to feel traumatized at the site of a trauma, they say, especially when you have to return to it over and over," she said, mumbling into Baby Walter's hair. "All true. In my case I find it more than a little ironic I work in a place that's literally called the trauma bay."

Baby Walter sighed in his sleep and squirmed in her arms. She shushed him, rocking back and forth.

"I guess pretty soon we're going to have to start calling you something else," she murmured. "You can't be Baby Walter forever. It was never the most original nickname, anyway. Toddler Walter doesn't roll off the tongue, though, does it? I wonder what your daddy would say."

Baby Walter's lower lip drooped open, revealing four of his ten teeth. Like Rose, he was fair, with a silky cap of hair curling at his temples and rosy, cherubic cheeks. Compton's arm was about to fall off, but she couldn't bear to shift him. She nuzzled Baby Walter's head and breathed him in. He smelled like warm sweet milk.

"Ellis," she whispered. "Ellis, I miss you."

Ellis, predictably, did not answer. Something else grabbed Compton's attention, however; she leaned forward and stretched her hand as far as it would go to retrieve the remote so she could turn up the volume on the television. The bitchy frenemy show had paused for commercials. The current image on the screen—a white farmhouse set in a meadow and backed by a hillside of spectacular fall foliage—dissolved into an aerial view of a row of redbrick buildings along a river, all of them nestled between two lovely, low mountains. Big letters appeared on-screen, hovering above the buildings.

KENT, CONNECTICUT

Compton knew she was seeing a series of curated photographs from a tourism ad, not a posthumous message from Ellis. Still, she couldn't tear her eyes away. The river view gave way to a pedestrian's-eye glimpse of charming main-street storefronts, complete with dormers and front porches and sidewalk cafés. Then a lane leading up to an old-time covered bridge. A New England clapboard church topped with a steeple. A horse barn with a detached silo.

A woman and a little child in a field, chasing a golden retriever.

"Ellis," she whispered again. "You're being really fucking unsubtle." This time the tears clung to her eyes but didn't fall. Gently, she placed Baby Walter into a corner of the sofa and sat beside him, clutching her iPad.

Google came up, offering all the information in the world.

Hospitals near Kent, Connecticut, she typed.

21 | Triage

KIRA

ATLANTA, GEORGIA
240 Days After Patient Zero

THREE DAYS. THREE DAYS IN; COULD THAT BE RIGHT? I FOUND I could not remember the day on which my children had arrived at the hospital. It had been a rainy day, or maybe it had been blustery and sunny, or maybe it had been a frosty night. I couldn't remember. Had we arrived in the daytime or in the nighttime? A vague memory surfaced of crystalline stars glittering against a black sky, but that couldn't be right, because you couldn't really see the stars in the middle of metro Atlanta; not like that. This must be some other memory, perhaps from my time with Daniel in Africa. From the stars of the African sky, you gleaned some sense of the depth and vastness of infinity. From the Atlantan sky, you often gleaned only smog.

"Kira," someone said. Wearily, I raised my head and then sprang to the side. To my astonishment I realized I must have dozed off while standing. How could I have fallen asleep? Around me bustled a pod of puffy-suited people: a respiratory therapist, two nurses. And Dr. Zhou.

"My dear," he said. He motioned toward the wall with the window, where I spied perhaps a cubic foot of unoccupied space. We wedged ourselves against opposing walls at the corner, this being the most privacy the room afforded.

"I'll give Rorie another half an hour," said Dr. Zhou. "Okay? We will buy her a few minutes with these adjustments"—he motioned toward the respiratory therapist, who was messing with Rorie's BiPAP machine—"so you can talk with her, and then we must intubate her. It's remarkable she's held out this long, but the strain is becoming too much, I fear."

Rorie's lungs had held steady but her other organs were failing, first her kidneys and now her heart, overtaxing her system with fluid despite all the interventions. As a mother, I could not allow myself to process what Rorie's labs indicated. As a physician, I knew.

I could not think of anything to say.

"And Beau," said Dr. Zhou. For once his face lost its perpetual smile. "In a few minutes we will all step aside so you might have some time with him as well."

"Thank you," I said, and then my mind made some kind of fatal adjustment and I understood. "Now?" I asked. "You think it's going to be now?"

"I think very soon," said Dr. Zhou in a voice so laden with tenderness I would have wept if I hadn't been weeping already. "You will be right here with him, yes? That is what he will know; his mother was with him the entire time. You will be holding his hand and kissing his cheek and he will know."

The doctors had tried everything, for both children. All the antiviral drugs, approved and off-label and compassionate-use; all the different respiratory interventions; steroids and serum and semi-experimental treatments. My eyes shifted to Beau's monitor; his heart rate, which had been racing along at a rate far too fast, had now started its final, inexorable slide down. He didn't have long.

I nodded dully. One of the nurses, the one with the kindest eyes, dragged over the wheeled stool to the bedside and guided me to it. Obediently, I sat, but then swiveled my head, searching for my bag.

"What do you need, honey?" said the nurse, her gloved hand on my shoulder.

"My phone."

The nurse exchanged a puzzled glance with Mike Zhou, but she handed me my bag and waited while I rooted through it. Once I held the phone in my hand, I checked the battery, and though it had entered the red zone, enough juice remained to make a call. Good.

"Can I be alone?" I asked.

"Of course, Dr. Marchand. We'll be right outside if you need us, and we'll be back to see to Rorie in a little bit." With a final, awkward squeeze of my shoulder, the nurse and the RT and Mike Zhou left.

An update from Vani showed on the phone's screen. She'd jumped in her car the instant I'd called her but was still hours away, somewhere in the midst of the Tennessee mountains. Next: Wally. I'd called him earlier and asked him to be here, directing him to first stop by my office. I'd thought there would be more time.

"Wally," I said, dialing him again. "Wally, Wally, pick up the phone."

I let it ring through to voicemail and then called again, hoping against hope he'd answer, but he didn't. This was it, then. No more hope. Until now I had not believed it.

As Dr. Zhou had instructed, I picked up Beau's hand. Despite the warmth of the room, his small fingers were cold. I rubbed them between my hands, then gently set down one hand to pick up the other one to rub it too. Trying to ignore the alien tubes protruding from his mouth and nose, I kissed his face; first his little stub of a nose, then the delicate skin of each of his eyelids and the precise fine slash of each of his eyebrows and the smooth curve of his forehead. I stroked his curls and watched them spring back, remembering my surprise upon seeing his hair after his birth; who would have predicted a blondish-brown Afro?

Beau: it meant *beautiful* in French. An apt name. Never had there been a more beautiful child, not in spirit or in flesh. His sunny nature, his kindness. His bright, sparkly interest in the world. His singular devotion to the downtrodden.

He wasn't perfect; no child was. A fierce stubborn streak ran through him, surfacing at odd moments. On occasion he would be instructed to do something and he'd refuse—rare, but it happened—and when it did, no force on earth could persuade him. He could be distractible, struggling to complete tasks because of a tendency to daydream. From time to time I'd caught him in a lie, although I had to admit his lies usually sprang from some nobler purpose, sparing someone's feelings or taking the fall.

But his heart! His essential goodness. I laid my head on the foam of his hospital mattress and gave in to my grief. The entire world flickered and dimmed, swooping in on itself until only a pinhole remained. I felt myself drift, my mind detached from its moorings. The muted sound of my own sobbing filtered in as if I were hearing it from a very great distance.

Sometime later—minutes, maybe—a tentative hand at my back brought me crashing back to reality. I raised my head to see Wally, gowned and gloved and masked. The CDC had made him shave the Molestache for a better seal on the mask, I remembered, which he'd complained about for weeks. It had been like losing a thumb, he'd said. His skin—the visible portion of it—was haggard. He looked much older.

He didn't speak, but he handed me a small insulated container. I unzipped it and stared at the contents. Declan's nanobody drug.

"Don't ask me what it is," I said. "It's better if you leave before they figure out you snuck in here."

Wally locked eyes with me. "I'm going nowhere."

"I want to make this clear: you don't know what's in the bag and you don't know what I'm about to do." Having absolved Wally from complicity in my action, I returned my attention to the vial, and all at once my spine turned to ash. I slumped forward, almost dropping the bag.

"I have to pick which one of them gets it," I whispered.

Behind his face shield, Wally's eyes widened. He looked from Rorie to Beau and back to Rorie.

"It's not likely to work," I said. My voice came out full of such raw desperation that Wally flinched. "This version has never been tested against ART. As far as I know, it's never been given to a human at all. And even if it stops all the viral replication cold, they're already so sick . . ."

The monitors beeped and Wally flinched again. I knew the course his mind would chart: he'd realize—or he'd guess—where I had gotten this drug and why I hadn't used it before. An untested drug: even with treatment, anaphylactic shock could kill the recipient. It could cause any number of other unforeseen problems. On the other hand, if it worked, it would save the life of my child based on a privilege other dying patients did not have. It was profoundly, elementally unethical to do what I was about to do. I waited for Wally's reaction, knowing I would administer the drug no matter what he said.

"Can you split it?" he asked finally.

"No," I said. "It's dosed by kilogram and there's not enough here to fully dose either of them. I can't dilute it any further if I want one of them to have a chance. I have to choose."

Wally didn't ask the obvious question. He'd know who I picked in a moment anyway, when I administered the drug. I busied myself removing the outer foil from the lid of the tiny glass vial, revealing an aluminum ring with a spongy center. I swiped an alcohol wipe across it and plunged the tip of an 18-gauge needle into the vial, sucking the precious fluid inside into a syringe. When it had filled, I removed the needle, turned the syringe upside down, and tapped it.

"I'm going to give it to Rorie."

DECLAN HAD GIVEN me the drug during those final, fraught moments in Spain last June, right before I'd stepped into the taxi that would take me to the airport in Seville. From there, the kids and I would catch a plane to Madrid and then home to Atlanta. We were tired and afraid; I'd endured a three-week separation from Declan and the children until I was released from isolation and could return to Seville. Both of us knew, with the illness in its infancy, it might be months or years before we saw one another again if the local epidemic went global. But at the same time, on some level, I hadn't allowed myself to process the very real possibility that something could happen to him, or to any of us. The human brain isn't equipped to deal with worst-case scenarios. Some mysterious psychological quirk protects us from believing in the validity of our nightmares, allowing us to dismiss bad things even as we acknowledge their existence. When this protective mechanism fails, we become paranoid and phobic, and when it works too well, we dismiss rational risk assessment in favor of sunshine and roses. Rarely do we strike the perfect balance.

I knew this and I knew these particular risks; it was, after all, my entire *raison d'être* to assess them. Still. I had survived my bout with the virus and my long isolation. Very few viruses cause global pandemics or even human pathology of any kind. Most likely, this would burn out.

"Here," Declan had said, thrusting a small insulated bag at me. "Keep it in the dry ice until you're home."

"What? What is this?"

"Right now it has the catchy name of DM-07945843-01. It's the viral vector containing the nanobody. It didn't work against the previous strains of artiovirus we tried, but what if it works against ART?"

I didn't touch the bag. "Why would you give it to me?"

Declan met my gaze. "Insurance policy. If it gets bad here and something happens to me, I don't want every sample of the drug in the entire world to be in one place. We have five extra doses right now and I'm giving you half of one of them, based on what we think the ED50 will be for a seventy-kilogram man."

"Why give me a partial dose?"

"I don't want you to be tempted to use it. I don't know if it's safe."

"So send it to some big biopharma lab to safeguard it."

"I'll have to, probably soon, if we want to speed up. Listen, Kiki." He grasped my hands. "I trust you. This drug represents most of my career. If you decide you're pissed at me for some reason, you could ruin my life."

"I would never do anything to harm you. But you don't need to give me this."

"I know. I want to. Just keep it in case something happens to me."

I took him in. One last close-up: his black hair, threaded in front with a hint of silver, the intensity of those blue eyes. The vitality in his trim body. "You know what? I'm going to miss you."

"Not as much as I'm going to miss you."

Those were the last words I heard from Declan's lips for quite some time. The drug sat in its little bag in an industrial-grade freezer, untouched, through the first wave of the pandemic. If Declan's weight-based calculations were correct, I had enough drug to treat one person, weighing about eighty pounds. Rorie weighed more than this, and I'd have to hope it would still work for her; there was no way I could count on having enough to treat them both.

Wally did not ask me to explain my choice. He probably figured it to be triage: when forced to choose among the dying, we were taught to first save those with the best chance of survival. In this room, you didn't have to be a doctor to make the call. Beau was so close to death you could almost hear the snapping of the tethers between his soul and his body. I'd been too afraid to give it to him when he first became ill. What if it killed him?

I couldn't put it off for another moment: I had to give the medicine now.

I don't know why I chose Rorie. Maybe it was triage—it was drilled into me, after all—but also maybe atonement for the favoritism she'd always seen in me when it came to her brother.

I loved them equally; I did.

I had to hurry. Setting Wally to guard over Beau, I turned to Rorie. I was afraid to inject the drug into Rorie's central line, where it would zoom straight to her heart. Unless the clinical trials in Spain had progressed further than I thought, she'd be the first human being to receive it. It could cause a massive allergic reaction and kill her outright. It could turn out to have an unforeseen effect, killing T cells or targeting some essential cytokine or frying the liver. Who knew?

But what other choice did I have? Putting Rorie on a ventilator would improve her oxygenation and ventilation, but it wouldn't stop the domino chain of her failing organs. She could be too far gone for any medication to work at this point, but her chances were better than Beau's. I uncapped the syringe, tapped it, and adjusted Rorie's arm, aware of the seconds melting past us. I felt Wally's presence behind me, heard the rustle of his gown as he hovered, undoubtedly anxious for me to depress the plunger and inject the drug.

A hand gripped my wrist.

Rorie's eyes opened. Her mouth moved behind her mask, but I couldn't make out the words. I leaned in, my head inches from Rorie, and still, I could not understand. With effort, Rorie pointed to her mask. I loosened the lower strap and lifted it a fraction.

"No, Mommy," said Rorie. Her eyes drifted shut, then fluttered open. "Please."

"Honey, it's a medicine from Declan. He gave it to me, before. It might help."

"No."

"Rorie," I said, at a loss. I couldn't administer an untested drug to someone if the someone in question refused it, even if it was my child. I had to make her understand. "Baby, it might save your life. I— We don't know exactly what it might do. It could be dangerous. But Declan said they thought it was going to work."

"Beau."

"He's—he's okay, darling." I'd be damned if I'd tell Rorie Beau was dying. If Rorie didn't make it, she'd go out as peacefully as I could ensure, and that meant without blaming herself for having contributed to her brother's death.

But Rorie knew; I could read it in her eyes. She shook her head.

"Honey, I have to try this. I can't—I don't want to lose you. Please, my love." Rorie's face blurred behind my tears. I fought to keep my hands steady.

Rorie reached across to block the port of her IV. "Beau," she said.

In a flash, I understood. Rorie wanted me to give the drug to Beau. She must have overheard the conversation with Wally. I wracked my brain; what, exactly, had I said? What should I say now?

"Beau is very sick," I told Rorie finally. "I don't think it will help him."

I had replaced Rorie's mask strap, but there was still no mistaking the word Rorie mouthed. "Try."

Rorie kept her hand over her IV port. I swung my head toward Wally, who stared back, wild-eyed. Rorie removed her hand from the port and fumbled around for my hand, trying to say something else. I lifted the mask again.

"My life," said Rorie. "My choice."

My tears blinded me, but I heard Rorie's next words.

"This is what I want, Mommy. Please, give it to Beau."

PART FOUR

AFTER ARTIOVIRUS

22 | I Feel Guilty for Not Feeling Guilty If You Feel Guilty

KIRA

ATLANTA, GEORGIA
Eighteen Months After Patient Zero

THEY SURROUND ME IN THE GARDEN OF THIS BUCKHEAD home, the three of them: Vani, Hannah, and Compton. Vani leans into me, one of my hands clasped in hers; Hannah and Compton stand behind the iron bench, their arms encircling us both. The night is not cold enough to see the vapory condensation of their breaths, but I can hear each of their soft exhalations, mingling and swirling together in the night air around me, creating some invisible protective bubble. I'm not a hugger by nature, but the embrace works the way they intend; for a moment, gratitude for the decades-long friendship I've had with these women supersedes my other thoughts. It doesn't quite drive from my mind the images that plague me—that moment in the hospital room, making the fateful choice between my children—but it soothes me enough that I can function again.

"Vani," I say, still immobile, "you've made my fingers go numb."

"Shit! Sorry!" she yelps, letting go of my hand. Everyone moves and the bubble bursts; Compton is laughing, straightening her hair; Hannah dabs at her eyes and flutters her hands. I stand, shifting my torso from side to side, stretching as if I am about to run onto a football field instead of what I am actually about to do, which is enter a gigantic holiday party in Buckhead and deliver a speech about our national experience during the pandemic, hoping to inspire a few of the bazillionaires present to kick in a hefty donation to the research I champion. I still do not have a clue what I will say.

Employing the telepathy for which she's famous, Vani comments on this. "We know you can't talk about the kids. But are you going to personalize the talk at all? Or keep it factual?"

"I know from personal experience not to try to convince anyone with facts," I say.

My friends laugh, but it's true. It is a peculiarity of human nature that we care more about smaller things than we do bigger ones, and we care more about anecdotes than we do evidence. If you stop a random guy on the street and tell him millions of people died horribly from an unknown virus, he'll express polite horror. Still, though, his concern will almost certainly be filtered through a veil of protective denial; vast numbers of people dying—especially elsewhere—is too abstract a concept. But if you show him a photo of a grieving mother, forced to doom one of her children so another might have the chance to live, that's different. This time the horror will be unfeigned. Our inability to process a widespread catastrophe explains why we express genuine dismay when a developer hacks down a magnificent eighty-year-old oak tree, but we cannot muster up similar outrage in response to the devastation of the rain forest in Brazil or the effect of trillions of tons of carbon dioxide emissions on our environment. It's too overwhelming.

"I could share a few stories from the ER with you," Compton offers. "God knows I've seen plenty of them."

I consider this. Compton has never told us much about those harrowing days in the emergency department during the first wave, a time that coincided with the loss of her husband. For the longest time afterward, she dimmed, contracting into a shell version of herself, answering our questions with rote precision while managing to avoid saying anything that meant anything. She still does this from time to time; I'm not saying she's recovered. But since her move from the city, some of her natural snarkiness has returned. I've never been so relieved to hear a bunch of piercing, inappropriate complaints.

"It's a good idea, but you know I can't tell your stories the way you'd tell them," I say. "But I am curious: how are you liking the new house and the new job?"

To our collective shock, at some point after Ellis died, Compton sold her apartment in the city and bought an honest-to-God farmhouse outside a small town in Litchfield County, Connecticut. I could no more picture Compton living in a farmhouse than I could picture the Duchess of Cambridge living in a rusty-roofed shack with a potbellied stove affixed to its sagging front porch. Perhaps to ward off any suspicion she might be delusional, Compton had sent us tons of photographs of her new place, revealing a battered white clapboard two-story house with a pitched roof and a latticed porch, plopped in the middle of a ridiculously bucolic field. Behind the house, the field stretched all the way to the gentle swell of the Taconic Mountains, visible this time of year as a brownish-blue smudge against the horizon.

The house wasn't the only change. Instead of applying for a job in the emergency department of the closest medical center, Compton had accepted a position with an insurance company, working from home to analyze charts. This, she'd explained, would allow her more time to be with the children and engage in a variety of wholesome non-Comptonish domesticities, such as baking and vegetable tending and sewing.

"Sewing?" Emma had exploded on one of our weekly Zooms after hearing this news. "Com, you don't know how to sew."

"I sew people," Compton pointed out, a little archly. "I don't see how hard it could be to sew inanimate fabric. At least a piece of cloth isn't going to try to bite me while I'm fixing it up."

"I tried to sew an outfit for Delaney once," said Zadie. "There was quite a bit of math involved."

"I'm good at math."

"Are you going to *wear* whatever you sew?" Vani herself wore an expression of alarm, clearly unable to picture Compton in anything other than scrubs or a tailored Max Mara frock.

Compton narrowed her eyes. "You guys. I'm not going to sew my own wardrobe. I was thinking a tablecloth or something."

"Still . . ."

Now, in Atlanta, a pensive look crosses Compton's face at the query about her new circumstances. "The kids have adapted. I worried Lawrence would kick up a fuss—he's a city kid. He likes museums and shows, and he had a best friend, Hamid, he wouldn't want to leave, and a school he loved. But he didn't react at all like I thought he would. He was very subdued."

"Was he depressed?" Hannah asks quietly.

"I don't know. Probably. It's not like him to accept change without a mighty battle, but right before we moved he got almost docile about everything he was instructed to do. He'd been spending a huge amount of time with this little round vacuum of Ellis's, even taking it to school with him when the kids all went back. I had to buy him a bigger backpack, and even then, the vacuum plus his folders and his lunch made him walk all hunched over, like a little old man."

I have a sudden mental image of Lawrence as a baby duck imprinting on some piece of machinery, toddling after it in the blind hope that it will care for him, and this vision affects me so deeply I almost have to swipe away tears. Wasn't there a children's book about that, a duck or a bird or some little bereaved creature seeking a missing parent in a junkyard, hoping every moving object would love him back?

Compton stops and stares into the distance, flinching at whatever she sees. When she speaks again, her voice is rusty. "One day I get a call from

Lawrence's teacher. She says some fifth graders got into Lawrence's bag and found the vacuum and they tore a piece off it, and now he's in the principal's office because he hit one of them. His teacher couldn't get him to stop shaking. He'd been doing pretty well before that, but afterward he quit speaking altogether. Well, that's not right—he didn't quit speaking altogether; he'd answer me if I asked him anything, but he wouldn't initiate conversation. When I told him we were moving, he didn't say anything, and finally I asked him how he felt about it, and he said, 'I want to do what you want, Mommy.' So I questioned myself a thousand times about whether it was the right thing."

"Oh, Compton," says Hannah, her big eyes shining in the dim light.

"It's okay, Hannah. It is. For a while after the move, he stayed quiet and un-Lawrence-y, but we got another dog, a Lab mix from the shelter, and now the two of them run around the yard like they're on fire. He likes his new school and he made a friend, the little girl who lives in the next house up the road. They play by the creek and build forts and go camping with her dad. I can't believe it, but I think my little city slicker is becoming a country kid."

"What about the little ones?" Hannah asks.

"They're managing too. Rose is her same dreamy self anywhere, happy as long as she can dress up. She remembers New York and Ellis, but I can see her memories getting fuzzier by the day; I think she's forgetting him. Walter, of course, is clueless."

Vani: "And you? How's it going with the vegetables?"

Compton laughs, the same tinkly ironic titter I thought was an affectation when we first met. "The vegetables all died, and I can't bake worth shit," she says. "Turns out I hate all that kitschy country crap."

"So," I say, "no sewing?"

"Fuck no. Everything I sewed looks like it was produced by a four-year-old. Which it was, because Rose took over all my projects when I abandoned them."

"What about the insurance job?"

"I hate it," she says. "It's boring and un-doctor-y and I miss people. Even the drug seekers and the drunks and the frequent fliers and the hypochondriacs and the brawlers. It's become clear to me I connect to them on some fundamental level that I'm never going to achieve with homeschool mommies and people who quilt and can their own vegetables. That was Ellis's dream, not mine. The fuckups are my people."

"So . . ."

"So," she says, with a foxy grin, "I'm going back to the ER. Over in Danbury. I hired a country wench to come resuscitate the garden when it warms up, and she's going to teach Rose and Lawrence and Walter to bake bread. I've got a standing date with Lawrence for a weekend in the city once a month, and when Rose and Walter are bigger, they'll go too. So I think we're all going to blend our natural state of being with our new state of being. We are still us, except we live in the boonies now."

"Will you move back to the city?"

Compton loses the grin. "No," she says. "No, never. I'm not gonna lie: I miss the culture. The food, the shops, the diversity. The pulse of the city. But even taking Lawrence back for a weekend feels like trying to revive the past in a city full of ghosts. I don't want to move again either. Every other city seems like a feeble imitation of the original to me, and I'm not a second-best kind of gal. There's something fulfilling and rewarding in challenging myself to accept a new way of life instead of seeking to re-create what I had before. That life is gone. I haven't got the balance of our new life right yet, but I will."

Hannah is dissolving at this speech, her makeup sliding in gray streaks down her face as she bats at her eyes. "Why did you tell us all this now, Compton?" she wails. "We still have to go back inside. Kira has to give her talk."

"Kira's not bawling," points out Compton, although in truth I feel like bawling right alongside Hannah.

"Here, babe," said Vani, handing Hannah a tissue.

"Oh, sweet little Lawrence," burbles Hannah, her hand to her heart. She blows her nose, a great honking sound that startles some garden creature into flying from a nearby bush.

I think maybe Compton is trying to stifle a smile, but she guides Hannah back to the bench and rustles a small mirror out of her handbag. "How are *your* little ones?" she asks.

Hannah blows her nose again. "Ah," she says, and as if a switch has flicked, her tearfulness is replaced by the delighted sappiness she displays whenever anyone mentions the girls. The mooniness of her expression is so endearing and so characteristic, it's the face I see whenever Hannah comes to mind. "They're indescribable," she says. "I feel guilty for leaving them."

"Hannah, don't," says Vani. "Because I feel fabulous leaving mine, but then I feel guilty for not feeling guilty if you feel guilty."

"I gotta admit," says Hannah, "it's heaven to sleep through the night in a bed by myself." She smiles, her arms wrapped around her torso, hugging herself. "But yeah: I haven't quite gotten to the point where I don't think about them. They're always there in the margins of my mind somewhere, hovering like angels. Or cherubs, really, with their big eyes and their smooth little faces and fat little bodies." She laughs, partly I think in self-conscious embarrassment at the indulgence of her description and partly with genuine pleasure at the thought of the babies. It's an indescribable relief to see the bliss on her face when she talks about the children—it's bliss to see her face at all when for so long we thought we might not ever see her again. Days on a ventilator, a week in intensive care, a month in the hospital—she might never have recovered. But recover she did, and she gave birth to Gianna, who by all accounts seems to be a sweet-natured, cognitively normal, physically robust little girl. She's the spitting image of Hannah, just as Joanie Ruth is a tiny personification of Georgia.

A low-level buzzing fills my head, intensifying until everything else recedes into the background. I sit back and allow it to amplify, thoughts and words swirling until at last they coalesce into one coherent thought. "Hannah," I say, interrupting them. "I know what I'm going to say in my talk."

She looks up from the mirror, her cheeks pink from her efforts at wiping away the streaky mascara. "Oh, that's great, Kiki. What?"

"I'm going to tell them what happened to Georgia," I say. "If it's okay with you, I mean."

23 The Magic Bullet

KIRA

ATLANTA, GEORGIA
Eighteen Months After Patient Zero

BACK IN THE HOUSE, I'M LESS AFFECTED BY THE HEAT AND the babble and the crush of people than I was earlier. Making the decision to talk about Georgia has unhitched some coil of reserve within me, and I feel a surprising unconcern about not only the speech but also my own circumstances. If I can tell this room of strangers about what happened to my friend, then surely someday I can tell my friends the details of what happened to me, or, more specifically, how I've reacted to what happened. I've never been one to believe in the cathartic power of spilling your guts. It works for some people, obviously; I don't deny the efficacy of psychotherapy or close friendships or journaling. I'd experienced it a bit in my own writing, the sense of release that accompanies letting go. If you stop guarding your secrets, you relinquish the need to maintain all those mental walls. You're free.

In theory, anyway. But in my own experience, trying to talk about my guilt regarding the decision to administer an unregulated, untested drug—and the subsequent decision of which child to try to save—left me wracked and useless after the only therapy session I'd attended. It exhausted me, dredging up those feelings. After leaving, I felt so much worse than I had when I entered, I vowed never to go back. Probably that was the wrong approach; I'm certain the therapist would have urged me to slog through the worst of it to emerge on the other side, stronger and freer. But I couldn't face it. I never returned.

Now, though—now, suddenly, I feel differently. Maybe it's the passage of time; maybe it's hearing Compton speak so openly. But this crowd needs to hear something focused and personal. If I cannot talk about my own experience, maybe Georgia can—anonymously—be my proxy.

Before long, I'm back in the big room, where I see Josh, the guy who assisted me in Operation Urn Rescue, at the margin of the crowd. He grins and gives me two thumbs up as I make my way to the far end of the room. Someone has assembled a makeshift stage area in front of the colossal fireplace, which is a dreadful idea: the fireplace is in the process of consuming what appears to be a full-sized redwood, causing the air in front of it to undulate in shimmery waves from the heat. Dolly or Delilah or whatever her name is—the hostess—ascends the one step to the platform and with both hands dabs at the invisible sweat at her temples, the flames behind her casting a sinister Dantean glow onto the twenty-foot wall of stacked stone as they roar and leap. This, I think, is going to be like giving a speech in hell.

"Welcome, everyone," says the hostess.

No one responds; it's too noisy. The clatter of dozens of conversations bounces off the walls and mingles with the woodsmoke, everyone gesturing, raising their voices, laughing with the kind of full-throated exaggeration you see only at parties and when your boss tells a lame joke. I battle a wave of nausea.

"Settle down, y'all," she tries, waving her hands back and forth in a wimpy arc in front of her chest. Still, nothing. For a moment I hold on to the hope that I'm off the hook, but then the hostess raises two fingers to her lips and releases a wolf whistle that could compete with a lumberjack.

This does the trick; conversation ceases and a few people clap, impressed that tiny Dahlia—that's her name, Dahlia—knows how to whistle like that. Against my will, I'm impressed too.

"Ah," says Dahlia, "that's more like it." She launches into a little speech about scientists and the CDC and Giving for the Greater Good, which comes across as sincere but a little too slick. I scan the faces in the room—a group of polished, bejeweled, attractive women and polished, hearty, healthy men—and wonder: how many of them lost someone?

Dahlia hands over the reins, and the attention of the crowd shifts to me. My friends hover near the front: Compton expressionless, brandishing a martini like a shield; Vani attentive and sparkly-eyed; Hannah, her fingers fidgeting with the pearly top button of her dress, wearing a look of nervous encouragement that paradoxically drains my confidence. I focus instead on a florid-faced older gentleman in a green blazer; his bloated air of disengagement somehow bolsters my ability to refocus.

Dahlia, the hostess, has already inflicted my résumé upon the crowd, so I don't bother with my credentials. I also don't bother to mention that I'd left the CDC in disgrace. It's still an organization I value.

"I'm here to speak to you tonight about the language of disease," I say. "Hearing this, you might be suspicious I'm going to inflict upon you a painful mess of Latin suffixes and incomprehensible, ten-syllable microbial classifications—and your suspicion is not misplaced. There's some science in the stuff we do, of course. I happen to dig that shit, but that makes sense, given what I do for a living."

From those who are listening, a bit of confusion, followed by uneasy laughter at my cursing. People are still chatting and drinking and checking their phones in corners of the room, although many of the people nearest to me appear intent on my words. I address the next comments to them.

"For you guys, though, I am reserving the non-boring aspects of my profession. Battling infectious diseases is a bad-ass job. Look at the militaristic language we employ against the enemy: *Big-gun antibiotics. Magic-bullet therapy.* A *shotgun approach.* With this last mechanism, I have to admit, the onslaught of friendly fire often takes out our more beneficial bugs too, but . . . desperate times call for desperate measures. Right?"

I get some nods but also some bewilderment: no one is sure where I'm going with this.

"Desperate measures," I repeat. "It sounds like the name of a bad thriller, doesn't it? I picture some steroid-bloated blockhead with an ammo belt slung over one shoulder, the bullets in his bandolier lined up like a row of gold-and-black dinosaur teeth. He prevails against ridiculous odds, surviving twelve-story falls through plate-glass windows and all manner of high-speed automobile crashes, all while dodging a hail of gunfire from lesser dudes. If a woman is involved in this nonsense, she's always slim and underdressed and has apparently undergone a personality resection."

More laughter. The people in the corners are filtering toward the center, replacing their phones in their bags and their pockets, directing their attention toward me. I can see the absorption on their faces; this is not what they'd expected.

A rustle in the back of the room catches my eye. Someone—a man—edges his way through the crowd, nodding in apology to the people he displaces. He reaches the front and offers me a broad wink.

Wally.

Instantly, I'm sucked into a slipstream of time. It's been eighteen months since the death of the first human being known to be infected with ART; it's been ten months since my own children contracted the virus; and it has been nine months since the release of the vaccines that ultimately brought the pandemic under control. In the time since the fateful moment when I asked Wally to go to the office, retrieve a package from the freezer, and bring it to me at the hospital, I've seen very little of him.

He never blamed me for what I did, even though administering a drug still in its trial phase constitutes a grievous breach of the ethics of our profession. Afterward, I reported my action to the CDC so he wouldn't have to do it. I didn't wait for them to investigate me. Instead, I offered my resignation, which they accepted.

In the months that followed, Wally did attempt to stay in touch, calling and texting and emailing when he could. He stayed busy at work, often working one-hundred-hour weeks, but despite his insane hours and my self-imposed seclusion, he never stopped offering to visit.

Now, at the sight of his face, with its deep furrows and crazy eyebrows, I'm flooded with affection. Even the reconstituted Molestache is a welcome sight. I've missed him so much. He's watching me attentively, smiling at my mention of dimwitted but hot female sidekicks. I owe it to him to make this speech a good one.

"Here's where the superhero trope breaks down," I say. "When mass destruction did actually threaten the world, it wasn't some muscle-bound dipshit who saved us, but our scientists and doctors. Chief among them plenty of women." Lots of nodding: plenty of people in this crowd are familiar with the female-led group of immunologists at the Vaccine Research Center at the NIH who partnered with a pharmaceutical company to develop and mass-produce the first vaccine.

"There are too many people to thank by name. Our vaccine developers. The scientists in Spain and Morocco—the index countries—who worked together to share the first genetic sequencing with the world, kicking off an unparalleled degree of international collaboration. The developers and producers of billions of rapid tests. President Corbett, for her brilliant, capable early response. And most of all, always, the physicians and nurses who battled around the clock to save our lives at great personal risk to themselves. This last group tends to wear scrubs, not skintight camo pants, and I'd guess most aren't built like Hollywood action stars. But they are the true heroes."

Light applause. They're digging it now. Before I lose them, I speak again.

Time to make it personal.

"Before ART became global," I say, "I went on a trip to southern Europe, where I was one of the first people from North America to contract CARS-ArV-01. A bit ironic, because, as our hostess informed you, I've spent the majority of my professional life at the CDC studying this family of viruses, waiting, I suppose, for something like this pandemic to occur. I had a mild case and recovered without incident. My traveling companions and I isolated or quarantined ourselves for the requisite amount of time, concerned about the disruption to our health and our jobs and our families but innocent at the time of the massive upheaval our society would be facing in a matter of weeks. Personally, we felt we'd dodged the bullet, assuming that surviving an infection would confer some degree of immunity to reinfection—which we now know is largely correct. Although this is not the case for all viruses, infection with both variants of CARS-ArV does protect you from getting the same illness again."

I hazard a glance at Green Blazer and see an avid stare replacing his detachment; there's no doubt he's interested. I don't look at Hannah.

"What we didn't know then, of course," I continue, "was the nasty secret embedded within the genetic code of the virus. Within months of the initial outbreak, physicians all over the world were reporting strange neurological symptoms in otherwise healthy survivors. They were seeing people presenting with signs and symptoms of a debilitating and premature form of dementia."

No need to elucidate: everyone here is all too familiar with the catastrophic reach of AAROD. It, almost as much as the virus itself, upended our society, causing a form of panic all its own.

"Eight people traveled in my group that day," I say. "Two were my children and one a former boyfriend; they didn't contract the virus then, and neither did my friend Hannah. The other four of us got sick after exposure to a dying person on a boat. All of us recovered." I stop and take a sip from the water glass I'm clutching. "Or so we thought."

A hush encompasses the room, the buzzing transformed to a frozen tableau of people clutching wineglasses and small square plates of canapés, their eyes round and their lips parted as they wait to see where I'm going with this story, although by now it must be clear. The silence contrasts so greatly with the previous babble that I can make out the sound of a toilet flushing in another room, the unlucky occupant of that bathroom apparently unaware his activity is audible to all of us.

"My friend began to show signs of AAROD not quite one year after we returned to the States," I say. I focus on modulating my voice, keeping it steady, so I don't allow an inadvertent change in pitch to reveal what I'm feeling. Oh, Georgia: a blackbird flutters in my chest, its eyes shining with horror, all beak and horned nails and sharp, angled wings. It takes all my resolve not to press my hands against my chest to still it.

"She didn't know what had happened to her at first," I say. "One day she heard her new baby crying and couldn't remember who the child was or how she'd gotten there. The first symptoms of neuronal loss are often subtle: forgetting things, mild short-term memory deficits, the kind of thing we all experience at one time or another. Easy enough to dismiss, right?

"But then the seizures started."

In the beginning, Georgia's seizures weren't dramatic. But they escalated quickly: by the time Jonah called 911, they came so closely together she couldn't recover from one before the next one started. After a series of unsuccessful attempts to stop the seizures, her doctors induced a coma to protect her brain. Even with the increasing awareness of AAROD, it took a long time to confirm her diagnosis.

"Her doctors tried everything: high-dose steroids, IVIG." No one in the crowd moves or speaks, although I see several faces streaked with tears; they're thinking, no doubt, of their own loved ones. "She did improve: after several days, she was weaned off the phenobarbital—the medicine keeping her in a coma—and her EEG looked better. They prescribed anti-seizure medication and let her go home."

I've tried, many times, to envision what this period of relatively lucid time must have been like for Georgia. She knew what was coming and could do nothing to stop it. While ordinarily she keeps her own counsel—except for her friend Jonah, with whom she shares everything—this time, she talked to all of us. Well, *talked* is not the correct verb. She did speak during one unforgettable group Zoom, and she met with Hannah multiple times in person, but mainly she wrote. She wrote us all emails and texts, but also each an individual letter. The letter she sent me seared itself into my brain after one reading, and I have been unable to open it since.

Once you begin showing symptoms of AAROD, time is not your friend. People vary in the severity and presentation of the disease, but if stricken with the very worst version of the condition, at most you have a couple of weeks before your mind disappears into a hazy slush of confusion and incomprehension. You're robbed of your cognition but also your rote memory: you might forget how to do the most basic things, such as showering or brushing your teeth. As with Georgia, you could suffer seizures, sometimes subtle but sometimes full-blown, requiring your doctors to dose you with barbiturates to induce a coma. If you escape that, your ability to walk could be compromised; you might wobble uncontrollably. You also lose the capacity for entertainment: you cannot read or watch television or converse or draw or play games, meaning your days drift by in an endless vista of staticky nothingness, as far as anyone can tell. Perhaps, the neurologists tell us, the right temporal lobe is less affected, because music is one thing to which most AAROD patients seem to respond; many of them will listen, awake but with their eyes closed, for hours.

Faced with this future, Georgia did not fall apart. If it had been me, all I can think is I'd have disintegrated, wasting the precious hours left to me in an agony of mourning. The temptation to grieve must have been overwhelming, but whatever private moments of anguish she experienced, Georgia kept them exactly that: private. To us, she displayed only an uncompromising resolve to control what she could, and therefore she launched herself into the first effort any mother would take: making plans for her child. I don't know the particulars of how her conversation with Mark went down, but I can imagine it: recovering but trapped in Amsterdam, he'd yet to hold his child, and now, faced with the news that he might never again see his lover in any kind of meaningful way, he had to help decide what to do for their baby.

"We made a decision," announced Georgia to us all, one blustery evening in May, a few weeks after her first symptoms. She sat, straight-backed and fierce, on a wooden porch swing, its thick ropes creaking in the breeze coming up from the sea. Her favorite huge orange-framed glasses covered her eyes, blurring them behind semi-opaque reflections of light. She wore a purple sequined T-shirt unapologetically hugging the contours of her still-inflated belly. The sky, glowing orange from the setting sun, set her hair aglow, creating a towering corona of fire atop her head.

Next to her, Jonah sat with his arms encircling his knees, his face resting sideways on his crossed arms. He wore an expression of such terrible emptiness I couldn't stand to look at him. Georgia, her voice strong, said, "We don't know when Mark will be able to return. He's better, but he can't get a commercial flight, so he's going to borrow his boss's jet or charter one, or, I don't know, fucking steal one if he has to, but he has to get approval from authorities in both countries before they can file the flight plan. So in the meantime, my first thought was for Jonah and Edwin to keep Joanie Ruth if I can't"—she hesitated for a moment and then resumed, her voice steady—"*when* I can't care for her anymore."

A small sound, barely audible, from Jonah. On-screen, almost in unison, everyone averted their eyes.

"But then I didn't want to impose on Edwin," Georgia said. She scooted closer to Jonah and stroked his hair, shushing him when he started to object to her statement. "He's already given me his husband all this time."

Almost violently, Jonah swung his head to the side, brushing tears away with his knuckles. Whatever the reason, no one could fault Georgia for questioning his ability to take on a newborn; his black hair, normally so sculpted, shot out from his head in all directions, and grayish stubble peppered his face. Wrinkles creased the front of his shirt, which, if I recalled correctly, was quite a departure from his usual tidy appearance. I couldn't help wondering, though: if not Jonah to care for Joanie Ruth, then who? Georgia's father died when she was in college, and, under circumstances Georgia had never explained, her mother had been absent from her life since she'd been a tiny child. As far as I knew, she had no other close relatives.

"So, starting next week," Georgia continued, "until Mark gets here and can take her, Joanie Ruth and I will live with Hannah and Harry and little Gianna. After that, she'll live with Mark, but she'll be with Hannah's family whenever Mark travels, and, since he travels constantly, she'll wind up with two families to love her. Three, counting Uncle Jonah. Hannah is her godmother and Jonah is her godfather, but she's going to call them Auntie Hannah and Uncle Jonah and she'll grow up seeing Gianna as her sister. Hannah will teach her grace and kindness and Jonah will teach her bad jokes and not to take any bullshit from the man, and she'll be happy and smart and thoughtful and loved."

Neither Hannah nor Jonah appeared capable of teaching anyone anything. Jonah's silhouette, backlit by the sun, had transformed to a quavering hulk; his neck was bent so I could no longer see his expression. Hannah's face, red and streaked with tears, had gone slack.

"Wait," said Vani, leaning toward the screen. "Wait, wait. What do you mean 'after you are gone'?"

"My body is not me," said Georgia. "My mind is me."

"You are not going to kill yourself," said Compton bluntly.

"I thought about it, sure," said Georgia. "If it weren't for Mark and Jonah and Joanie Ruth, sure, I'd have done it."

Jonah spoke for the first time, leaning forward. His voice sounded different than I remembered; older. "Her doctors are doing everything they can to halt the progression. Immunosuppression. Maintenance IVIG. Plasma exchange. Some experimental stuff." His eyes roved the screen, presumably searching for me, because when he spoke again it was me he addressed. "Are they—is anyone close to finding—"

I knew, of course, what he wanted. "I'm hearing some things about reversal of demyelination and neuronal repopulation. Stem cell infusions, some other things. But it's early, I'm not sure . . ."

An absent expression drifted across Georgia's face, and for the millionth time I remembered, with a horrible jolt, she must have periods of confusion now. It was possible they'd get longer and closer together until they blended into one seamless vacuum, sucking up any remaining lucidity, erasing her essential Georgianess. We all waited as the silence stretched.

"What," said Georgia eventually, not seeming to realize minutes had passed. She edged a thumb into Jonah's hunched torso. "Wake up, sleepyhead. You're falling over."

"You were telling them you aren't going to hurt yourself," said Jonah in a strangled voice.

"No," agreed Georgia, switching gears with ease. She still appeared composed. "I'm going to hibernate until some scientist fixes this thing." Her eyes roved, searching the screen until they settled on me. "Kira, you're on this, right? It's happening. Someone will cure it."

"We'll figure it out," I promised her, although I held no such certainty. We'd never been able to reverse the damage caused by prion diseases like Creutzfeldt-Jakob, for instance, which wreak cerebral havoc in the brains of their sufferers, or certain kinds of demyelinating conditions like fulminant multiple sclerosis. But in the case of some similar kinds of encephalitis—brain inflammation—there had been more progress. Even now, doctors were advancing in the treatment of brain inflammation caused by the body's own immune system. The research scientists arriving at work day in and day out, daunted but unbowed by all the failure so far, would never stop trying.

"Well, light a fire under their asses," said Georgia. "I gotta see my baby girl grow up." She pushed the ground with her feet, sending the swing rocking backward and forward, and drew her knees up to her chest, matching Jonah.

"Georgia," said Zadie tentatively, her soft southern voice blurred. "I'm sure she must be sleeping, but . . . would it be okay for us to see Joanie Ruth?"

"Oh shit, y'all," said Georgia, leaping forward off the swing; she stumbled a little, and Jonah caught her by the waist before she fell. "I forgot you guys haven't seen her much." She leaned forward, Jonah's arms still encircling her abdomen, and tapped her head. "That's just normal forgetting. On top of everything, I have new-mom brain, or whatever they call it. I'll go fetch her."

"Let me do it," said Jonah gently. In contrast to a moment ago, he radiated steadiness as he eased Georgia back onto the swing, tucking a quilt around her hips. "You stay and chat with your friends."

"Mind her little fontanel," yelled Georgia to Jonah's disappearing form. I recognized the quote from her favorite movie, *Raising Arizona*. She leaned back against the swing, smiling. "She's a good baby."

"I'm sure she is," said Zadie, the perfect oval of her face glazed in a sheen of tears. "Feisty like her mom?"

"She's spirited," agreed Georgia. Her eyes drifted past the camera as if she were intent on some vision only she could see. "She's too little to talk, but when she makes noises, she looks like she's trying to say something specific. She has a way of looking right into your eyes as she makes these emphatic sounds. I think she's trying to tell me something."

Jonah returned, cradling Joanie Ruth in the crook of his arm. Retrieving the baby had calmed him; he moved with purpose, his back straight. He kept his head bent toward her, murmuring in a lilting tone too soft for me to make out the words. The baby rustled appreciatively, one pearly-toed foot and one dimpled fist working their way free of her blanket.

"She was still awake," Jonah said. He eased down on the swing next to Georgia and settled the baby in her arms, minding, as instructed, the soft spot on her skull. Georgia bent her head to Joanie Ruth and cooed something in a low tone; I couldn't see the baby's face, but from the energy and alertness in her little body you could make out her interest in her mother. Georgia shifted, rotating Joanie Ruth upright and toward the camera so we could all see her.

My first impression: she resembled Georgia. She had a beautifully shaped head, round and fine-boned, but even through the adorable curve of her baby cheeks you could make out the planes of the cheekbones that would one day emerge. Her eyes were huge and clear, a greeny hazel rimmed by a line of dark blue, and the fine wisps of hair curling around her tiny ears glimmered red-gold, a shade or two lighter than her mother's.

It was her expression, though, that most displayed her genes: alert for such a young baby, quick, a little saucy. She regarded the screen in front of her as though she were studying all the faces on it, trying to memorize us. She cocked her head, and I half expected her pink lips to part and release a torrent of curse-laden humor. Instead she sighed in a series of truncated little gasps—she sounded like a minuscule train chugging—and extended a curvy, tiny arm toward us.

"Hi," we breathed, almost collectively. I heard my own voice, mixed with the others: "Hi, Joanie Ruth." "Hello, sweet girl."

"Weh," said Joanie Ruth. As Georgia had said, her babble seemed to reflect a sincere desire to communicate; she watched us, intent and tolerant, for a long time, as if waiting for us to respond with the correct answer. Eventually her head drooped back against her mother and her eyes drifted shut as Georgia cuddled her against her chest. Our last image on that call was of Georgia and Jonah and Joanie Ruth—Jonah's dark head and Georgia's red one both bent toward her drowsy baby girl, the three of them locked in a tight little circle against the darkening sky.

"THAT'S THE LAST time I heard her speak," I tell the crowd in the Buckhead home. "A week later she began to forget names, and a few days after that, she could only manage answers to yes-or-no questions. By the end of the next week, she could say almost nothing. The woman we love was gone."

The crowd watches me. A blond woman in the front is sobbing silently, her pretty features contorted into a gargoyle of pain. The man next to her, a silver fox old enough to be her father—perhaps he is her father; they look a bit alike—rubs her shoulders, murmuring something into her ear until the two of them slip from the room. They're not the only ones to take this personally. Plenty of the people standing in front of me wear wretched looks. I'm the ultimate buzzkill.

"How is she now?" someone asks, quietly, from the middle of the crowd.

"She's alive. She's started an intensive regimen of physical and cognitive therapy."

There's a rustle of interest, but I move on, deciding to limit how much I tell them about her current condition. I don't want this speech to evolve into a Q&A about AAROD. "Most of you here tonight know someone—or know of someone—who's been affected," I say. "We've learned a lot. We know AAROD is an autoimmune condition. It's not direct viral toxicity to the brain; instead, in some unlucky people, the virus triggers the creation of antibodies that react to proteins on nerve cells. It can cause your gray-matter neurons to go haywire or your white-matter neurons to lose their protective covering, or both, and this can cause seizures and dementia. We don't know what the future holds; could there be a later cohort of dementia patients we've yet to identify? Could there be another complication manifesting itself years down the road? Our scientists and physicians killed themselves—literally, in some cases—caring for patients, developing a vaccine, and seeking a cure, both for the virus itself and for the sequelae it causes."

Murmurs of appreciation from the crowd. The vast majority of humanity reacted to the artiovirus vaccine with the kind of full-blown joy that greeted the development of the polio vaccine in the 1950s. Even people inherently suspicious of vaccines tended to get on board once they saw AAROD threatening their children.

"Until ART, we'd forgotten how lucky we were not to be at the mercy of killer contagions to the same degree as our predecessors," I say. "We took vaccines for granted, or we refused them. Want to know the name of the human being who is often credited with saving more lives from disease than anyone else in recorded history? It's Edward Jenner, the eighteenth-century physician whose work led to the development of the vaccine that ended smallpox. But even before Jenner, people in Turkey and China and Africa were utilizing inoculation against viral threats. The artiovirus isn't the last time humanity will face such a threat; it will happen again. And again. And each time, thanks to people like you, we will be a little more prepared."

Time to bring this home. "We need your help tonight," I tell the crowd. "Right now, as we speak, there are groups of scientists working around the clock to find a cure for AAROD. Immunomodulators, capsid stabilizers, monoclonal antibodies, gene silencing, infusion of stem cells—all of these are in trials now, and we need your help. All of us in this room are fortunate in more ways than one—we are alive, with our cognition intact—and we have financial resources."

I wait a beat, locking eyes with Hannah in the front row. A film of tears coats her eyes and her hair has unraveled from its knot and the skin on her neck is a patchwork of mottled red and white, but she's beautiful. I think of her with a baby on each hip, and then I think of Georgia.

Her ferocious intellect. Her perverse sense of humor. Her notorious disregard for current fashion. She exhibits—exhibited—a disregard for several other things as well, most notably the opinions of others. Opinions, being inherently subjective, didn't interest her. She considered spending unnecessary money to be stupid, politics to be dominated by vile halfwits, and most social niceties to be an impediment to progress. She did appreciate culture, though: she would laugh uncontrollably at old reruns of *Saturday Night Live*, her head thrown back and all her fillings showing, until you'd find yourself laughing uncontrollably too. Georgia's laugh, more than anything else, defined her.

"We have to help bring back the ones we love," I say, and I step off the stage.

24 There's Always Another Crash Waiting in the Wings

KIRA

ATLANTA, GEORGIA
Eighteen Months After Patient Zero

IT'S LATE BY THE TIME I GET HOME. HERMAN'S ENGINE PUTters for a few beats after I switch off his ignition, sort of like a final, pleased burp after a meal, reminding me he's due for the car equivalent of a colonoscopy. I sit for a moment in the stillness of the garage, running my hand over a rip in the gray vinyl of the driver's seat. I've taken to patching these with Dermabond, one of the rejiggered forms of superglue emergency departments use in place of stitches, and it looks like Herman could use another batch of the stuff.

I need this moment of stillness. Tonight required an obscene amount of adrenaline: for me, there could be no more draining trifecta of events than navigating the ordeal of public speaking, an overwhelming social scene, and the emotionally charged memories I'd resurrected. My battery is spent: I slump against the seat back, feeling the sluggish thrum of blood through my carotids. My mind congeals in a paste of flickering images and twisted fragments of conversation. This happens to me every time I have to interact with a considerable number of people at once; afterward, my brain replays the highlights and the lowlights, torturing me with grotesque, misshapen representations of how I must have looked and sounded, until finally my mind winds its way through some sort of filtering process and allows me to rest.

I'm weird; I know.

When I rouse myself enough to trudge into the house, I'm expecting to bump my way through the darkness of the tiny mudroom, but to my surprise as the door swings open I'm greeted with a rectangle of cheery yellow light spilling from the kitchen. The pendant above the island must be switched on.

In the kitchen, Rorie sprawls across three stools, her butt on the nearest one and her long slender legs stretched across the others. She's sipping something steamy from a brown mug she made at a kiln in Africa when she was small; it's hideous, but naturally I've never been able to part with it. She sets down the drink as I drop my handbag onto the counter.

"*Madre*," she says easily, arching her back and stretching. She's wearing teeny lacy shorts and a giant sweatshirt with the word *KALE* emblazoned across the front in blocky collegiate lettering. Her hair is frizzy and gloriously unkempt.

"Hey, you," I say. "What are you doing up? And what are you drinking?"

She nods toward the lumpy cup. "I couldn't sleep, so I made tea."

"Hmm," I say. The only tea on the shelf is Zest Black, which I bought last year during a stretch of all-nighters because it advertises itself as having extra caffeine. I glance in Rorie's cup, and sure enough, she's already downed half of it. "You know what would help more? Warm milk."

"Ewww," she says, but she doesn't protest when I pour out the acrid contents of her cup. I heat a quantity of whole milk in a saucepan, adding a little vanilla and cinnamon when it starts to froth, and present it to her with a flourish. She wrinkles her nose appreciatively. "This actually smells kinda delicious."

"It is delicious," I say. "My mom used to make it for me when I was little if I was bummed out. I thought it had magic powers."

"Nanna's the nurturing sort," she says and then grins wickedly. "Not that you're not, Mom. I didn't mean it like that."

I gesture toward the milk. "I'm nurturey. Exhibit A right there."

"Well," she says and giggles. Even though she's mocking me, hearing anything resembling a sweet peal of laughter out of this girl is cheering. I pour myself a cup of milk too and clunk it against hers.

"Happy Christmas break."

"Oh, man," she says. "I'm gonna sleep 'til noon. Every day."

A scalding film adheres to the surface of the milk, but in identical motions we blow on it, sip, and grimace at the heat, prompting Rorie to laugh again. She has the same rollicking, musical laugh as her father, and for a moment I'm adrift, caught in another of these recurring interludes of disbelief that Daniel has missed his daughter as she passes through the rest of her childhood phases on the way to adulthood. Gap-toothed, glitter-obsessed elementary student; gawky, giggly middle schooler; hostile, occasionally sappy teen; thoughtful, earnest almost woman—if only he could see her now, for even a moment. What will our daughter be in a year, in ten years, in twenty? What are her motivations, her beliefs, her attributes, her goals? What kind of mark will she leave on the world?

"When I was little," the current Rorie says, breaking into my reverie, "I never wanted to be anything like you."

I snort. "I'm not sure how to respond to that."

"I don't mean it as an insult," she says. "Well—I did mean it as an insult at the time, because let's face it, you are deeply uncool and you are always on my case. But now I can see it's beyond cool that you do all this stuff to save people's lives. That's, like, a really important thing, Mom."

"It's *like* an important thing or it *is* an important thing?" I ask in my most pedantic voice, and then Rorie and I both burst out laughing at my caricature of myself. If she's become more thoughtful, then I've become more self-aware. Having a child who points out your flaws will do that for you.

She takes a slurp of her milk and turns to me, unaware there's a foamy white mustache above her lip. "Mommy," she says.

I start to point out the milk mustache, but something in her tone arrests me mid-syllable. She huddles in her sweatshirt, gripping her mug with both hands, appearing suddenly much younger. For an instant, fear pierces my heart: she's going to tell me something terrible—she's pregnant or she's in some kind of trouble. Crash—the illicit boyfriend who wound up infecting her and, subsequently, her brother with the virus—is long gone, banished from Rorie's life with the finality of a despot ordering an execution. He's okay—he barely got sick—but as far as I know, Rorie never spoke to him again after she recovered from her illness, too stricken with horror at the consequences of her little rebellion to bring herself to see the boy whose face personified her worst failure. For a long time she didn't date at all, but for a lively girl like Rorie, there's always another Crash waiting in the wings. She'd cycled through a few of them, but I'd thought none of them had stuck.

"What is it, Roar?" I ask.

She's staring at the ground as if it holds some immense magnetic appeal, but after a visible effort, she brings her eyes up to meet mine. The expression on her face burns me; it's the same look she gave me when she told me to give the drug to Beau, the expression I thought would be the last one I'd ever see from her. It's a reflection of such intensity and shame I know immediately what she's trying to do.

"I'm sorry." Her voice slows and thickens, becoming almost unrecognizable. "I'm sorry I went out. I'm sorry for what I did to Beau."

In a flash I'm on her, gathering her into my arms, rocking her head against my chest. "You do not have to apologize," I tell her. "You were young and frustrated and lonely, and you made one bad decision. Everybody does dumb stuff at that age. I know you're sorry; I've always known. You don't have to say it."

"I want to say it." Her face is contorted. "I'm sorry. I'm so sorry."

It's true; I have known of the depth of Rorie's remorse from the instant the EMTs arrived to place Beau in the ambulance. I saw it flash through her, confusion giving way to terrible, irrevocable knowledge, itself followed by the realization that her remorse for such a sin was too weighty to put into words and was therefore a useless, damning emotion. How do you apologize for breaking a rule when the result of your action is catastrophic?

I knew what she felt because I felt it myself. How quickly I'd accepted Rorie's plea to treat Beau! She'd given me permission to do the thing I longed to do in the panic of that tumultuous moment: to try to save my baby boy. Beau, the living reminder of the husband I'd loved so much, a child who never gave me a moment's trouble, the child Rorie had always accused me of favoring: in the end, I'd had to make a choice, and I'd chosen him. I administered the medicine to Beau, even though I believed it futile, even though Rorie had a better chance. Nothing I did from that moment on could ever allay my guilt. How could I have betrayed my daughter to try to save my son?

I should have refused her request. It made no sense medically; he was too far gone and she was potentially savable, and the instant the golden-hued liquid had glided its way up Beau's IV and into his vein, I'd begun feeling the first icy shiver of regret, but of course by then it was too late. I've spent the last ten months in an agony of useless, stupid self-condemnation. Just as Rorie had.

But Rorie, despite the odds, had lived. Her recovery had been slow and marred by setbacks, including an inflammation of her blood vessels that ultimately left her with reduced kidney function. But you cannot tell, looking at her now, that once she'd spent so many weeks in the hospital.

I pull her a little bit away from me so she can see my face. "You do not ever need to apologize to me," I say, the words coming out so low and stilted that Rorie stops crying and looks at me in confusion. "It's me who needs your forgiveness."

Yes, she asked me to do it. That's no defense. I can almost feel the air around me quiver with the sickening, unbearable thud of rejection as she pulls away from me, but then, suddenly, she's plastered to my chest, hugging me with such ferocity I can't breathe. "Mommy," she says. "You wanted us both to live." She reaches up and touches my cheek tenderly, the way I'd stroke hers when she was tiny and couldn't fall asleep. "You were never better to Beau than me. I know that. It just seemed like everyone loved Beau more because he's more . . . lovable."

"Oh, Rorie." I grasp her sweet face; it's blurred behind my tears. "You are every bit as lovable as Beau." I think, suddenly, of Rorie as a toddler, fierce and bright and funny, and as a little schoolchild, infinitely curious and infinitely energetic. Observing her as she observed the world turned everything new and wondrous for me too; she's always had the power to transform the people around her, to tug them into her own universe, where everything burns hotter and brighter. I love her so much I cannot put it into words.

But I try. I murmur to her all the things I should have said long ago. I'm not good at this, conveying emotion, acknowledging feelings, but I talk to her about her early childhood and about losing her father and my decision to study infectious diseases after that. If it hadn't been for her, I tell her, I could not have gotten through it, that dark and awful period when Daniel died. I've never spoken with her about the pain of losing Daniel, and she listens silently, occasionally reaching up to swipe away my tears. She doesn't ask me any questions, and I think it will still be a long time before we smooth out this new phase in our lives, but the difference I feel in myself from a few moments ago is massive, startling; I finally understand why people use the analogy of a weight being lifted when they've confessed to someone else a thought they've long kept to themselves.

When I finish, we sit, locked together, and ponder our separate transgressions. She's so heavy and solid in my lap that my legs have gone numb;

I can feel her heartbeat through my own chest wall, thumping along steadily and reassuringly. It's no wonder babies are soothed by rhythmic shushing; their mother's heartbeat is the first sound they ever hear and it's all-encompassing, dominating their world until they are born and it vanishes. Like a heartbeat, this comfort with Rorie won't last—tomorrow she'll freeze me out or I'll yell at her or one or both of us will piss off the other, but for now I luxuriate in the warmth of her skin against mine and this strange new peace I'm finding with my almost-adult child.

"Whew," I say. "I wasn't expecting that. I thought you were going to tell me about some boy drama."

She gives me an arch look. "I'm not the one with boy drama."

"Yes, well." I wave a hand around, attempting nonchalance, and then smile in spite of myself. "I think all is . . . going pretty well in that department."

Rorie grins back, delighted. "Is he coming back to help with the move?"

"He" is Declan, who showed up on our doorstep a month ago with a small jewelry box and an uncharacteristically anxious demeanor. Fully recovered, he'd flown uninvited across the ocean with the intention of carrying out some kind of grand proposal—a pop-up choir, skywriting across the Atlanta horizon, a banner draped across the entrance to the neighborhood; who knows?—but chickened out. He spent a miserable night in a generic, boxy hotel near the airport, booked a return flight to Spain, canceled it, booked a rideshare to my neighborhood, canceled it, booked another one to my doorstep, walked around the block four times, returned to my house, rang the doorbell, and promptly crumpled to his knees, his head hidden in the crook of his elbow. When I answered the door, I thought it was a ding-dong-ditch until a small squeak sounded and I looked down. Without removing his head from his elbow, Declan proffered the little velvet box in my direction, balanced on the tip of his other, outstretched arm.

"Pleasedon'tsayno," he mumbled into his arm.

"*Dec*lan?"

He looked up with an expression of such comical agony I took a step backward. "I can go," he said.

"Are you . . . are you asking me to marry you?"

His face retreated back to his elbow. "Yes."

I sank to my knees, facing him. I inspected the contents of the little box but left it in his hand before reaching my hands to his shoulders. Inch by inch, he raised his head, and we regarded each other's face; mine no doubt wide-eyed and openmouthed, his now riddled with a few new lines and a bit of a sagging chin but still dominated by those burning, brilliant blue eyes. His face haunted my sleep, nearly as much as Daniel's.

I remembered the way all the air had left my chest when his sister called and I thought he'd died.

"Yes," I said. "Yes."

"Yes?"

"I would love to marry you, Declan."

He whooped, a long, loud cry of joy and relief, and in his excitement flung the jewelry box into the air. We had to spend a half hour combing through the dirt at the base of my neglected boxwoods before we finally found the ring.

We're still ironing out the logistics: Where will we live? What will happen with my job?

To my surprise, Rorie favored moving, explaining without a trace of irony that she was done with Atlanta, and anyway, staying too long in one place led to "mental stagnation." She'd always liked the sound of living in Spain, really, she said.

I brush her hair back from her face, still smiling at the memory. "It's late, but . . . do you want to go peek in Beau's room?"

She leaps off my lap. "Yes!"

She's smiling again, the tears gone. She's not an adult, not yet. I forget how malleable this age is, monstrous feelings arising out of the blue to consume you before they disappear in a puff of smoke, replaced by some other equally compelling but contradictory emotion. She grabs my hand and we inch down the hall in an exaggerated tiptoe, avoiding the creaky floorboard by the bathroom door, stepping over a pile of towels Rorie's dumped in a mildewy heap outside her bedroom door for the laundry fairy to scoop up and resuscitate. We reach Beau's room and crack the door—it creaks too, unless you open it an infinitesimal bit at a time—and once it's fully open, Rorie precedes me into the room to gaze upon Beau's twin bed.

In another universe, this room would be a shrine, Beau's bed a time capsule from the night he got sick, all his toys and books scattered as he'd left them that last day. In this universe, though, he's asleep in the bed, curled on his side the way he always is when he sleeps, his slight figure barely a rise under his puffy down comforter. His curls have been cut, sadly; he insisted on it in the middle of second grade, wanting to look like some British footballer or other, but we can see the still-childish curve of his cheek and the curl of his lashes and the bottom half of his top two teeth. He breathes deeply, contentedly, dreaming of some Beau-ish thing: exploring the ruins of a castle with a pack of friends, maybe, or rescuing a changeling baby from a river, or who knows what.

"He's pretty cute," whispers Rorie, gazing on her sleeping brother. Something in me cracks open, its hard edges softening and dissolving and spreading through my bloodstream to every corner of my being. It takes me a moment to recognize what I'm feeling, but then I get it: It's relief. It's gratitude.

It's joy.

"He is," I whisper back, reaching for her hand. "He is."

Epilogue | Familiar Behavior Patterns

KIRA

TANGIER, MOROCCO
September of the Following Year

UNDER A BRILLIANT, SHIMMERY SUN, OUR SHIP CRUISES through small breakers in the strait, churning up a white spray of wake as the coastline of Spain recedes into the distance behind us. It's a glorious day: all blue and white and crisp, the air tangy and sweet, vibrating with the squawk of seagulls above the rumble of the ship's engines. I offer the man at the refreshment counter my credit card and collect an armful of sparkling waters, threading my way back past the line until I reach my friends. We've set up around a small cocktail table as far in the room as it's possible to be from the spot where the young ship employee died the first time we made this voyage, three years ago; I don't know if it was an intentional choice on Compton's part when she put her bag down or a case of snagging the first open table she saw, but I'm glad not to linger on that side of the ship.

Today started early. I woke with the sun, watching as the first reaches of eastern light turned the wall in our hotel room from charcoal to cool blue to a bright, blinding white. Declan, back in our home in Seville, texted me early to say he and Beau are planning to spend the day in the lab, Beau working on the illustrations for the book he's writing and Declan analyzing data on his latest project: an inhaled nanohybrid that can cross the blood-brain barrier. The two of them spend a lot of time together. When Declan and I married—the service marred by a scowling but magnificently re-mustachioed Wally—he'd promised me two things: first, he'd adopt my children, and second, I wouldn't be obligated to work in his lab. I've gone back to fieldwork, my first love, and I travel a great deal.

Rorie's having a lazy day: she spent last night with her girlfriends. They're off work today and will undoubtedly sleep late before heading to their favorite street café for coffee, where they'll sit and sip and giggle and try to envision the vast changes in their lives when they scatter for college next year. Rorie, who is applying early decision to Vanderbilt—my alma mater—says she's planning to pursue a premed course of study. I've tried not to overreact to this news; of course, she might change her mind. Seventeen is a fickle age.

But still. I believe Rorie will become a doctor.

Whatever Beau will choose to do with his life is an open question. Depending on the day, he vacillates between psychology and professional soccer, or social work and writing bestsellers. Why not? I know enough not to burst his bubble on the issue of professional soccer or writing bestsellers, but he'd be excellent at the other two.

Every day, I wake and experience it again: an overwhelming rush of gratitude for his life. He should have died, but he lived, the combination of Declan's drug and Dr. Zhou's last-ditch heroics coming through in the end. Children are remarkably resilient, emerging intact from medical scenarios an adult would never survive, but still, it stunned the team taking care of him when he made it through that worst night.

After it became clear Beau would live, I confessed to Mike Zhou what I'd done and informed him I would be reporting myself to the CDC. Like Wally, he must have felt enough pity not to chastise me, but the next day he did order a blood test to quantify the viral load in Beau's bloodstream. When the results came back—nearly undetectable—it was the first and only time I ever saw him cry.

We pieced it together later, the synergistic effect of the experimental drug with the therapies Dr. Zhou employed, and while it didn't turn out to be a game changer for every ill patient, Beau's experience led to several other patients receiving the drug under compassionate-use criteria even as the formal trials progressed. It pains me to say this—I never wanted this—but Declan insisted on naming the medication Kiravimab. In a beautiful twist of irony, the single-domain antibody in Kiravimab is obtained by immunization of camelids with the desired antigen, which then employs a vector—part of a virus, basically—to deliver the isolated mRNA to human cells. If that sounds confusing, then picture this: camels and a virus brought us down, and camels and a virus helped save us. Few people realize it, but the history of science is crammed with poetic justice.

Ultimately, the human trials demonstrated a forty percent reduction in mortality. It helped save Beau, and many others, until the vaccines were ready.

Or maybe, as Hannah believes, it was not merely the science and the medicine that saved Beau but the hand of God, reaching down to grant my son—and my daughter—a reprieve. They stayed in the hospital for weeks, recovering, but recover they did. In any case, I was spared the agony of so many other mothers throughout the world in this pandemic. I thought he would die, and he lived.

I do not deserve forgiveness for choosing to give the drug to Beau. Just because he lived doesn't mean my choice was the ethical one; no one could have predicted this outcome. For the entirety of my life I will suffer shame for prioritizing him over my daughter—and every other dying child on the floor that day—but I'm learning that shame can coexist with acceptance. I do feel pity and sympathy for the me that existed that night;

exhausted, terrified, so battered by grief I could barely assess whether it was day or night. I made a terrible decision that saved both my children. What am I to make of that?

NEXT TO ME, Vani hogs the double bed, curled on her side almost diagonally, her full lower lip fluttering in a delicate snore. The six of us spent the day yesterday in Cádiz, a charming coastal city in Andalusia, exploring the ancient, windy alleys and the lush parks, eating and drinking so much last evening I'd had to unbutton my pants at the restaurant. The day before that had been equally decadent from a waist-circumference standpoint: my friends had stayed with me and Declan and the kids in Seville, and we'd parked ourselves around the wrought-iron table on the rooftop balcony until four in the morning, chomping on an array of tapas and guzzling Cava until none of us could see straight. No one wanted to end the evening; the temperature hovered in that sweet spot you only seem to find on vacation—not too warm, not too cool—all velvety night air and starry sky and soft, caressing breezes wafting off the river a few blocks away. I sat next to Vani on one backless bench, her calves draped over mine; on the opposite bench, Zadie and Emma had propped their backs against each other in a failing effort to keep Zadie upright. Periodically she'd lurch to the side, spinning her arms, and Emma would grab her before she fell over. Compton and Hannah flanked us in chairs at each end of the table, Hannah dozy and pink-cheeked with her feet curled under her, Compton's tiny figure still straight-backed despite her ability to down twice the amount of sparkling wine as the rest of us. At one point, Dec came out brandishing a couple of Cavas in one hand, their glistening green bottles clinking against one another as he walked.

"Bottle service," he said, grazing the top of my head with a kiss before sliding onto the bench next to Zadie. "Whoa! Maybe we should cut you off."

"Dec . . ." said Zadie. "Dec, Dec, Dec. I'm so glad Kiki married you after all." Ignoring my kick under the table, she swatted a thick sheath of honey-colored hair from her face and reached for his chin, which she turned from side to side to inspect. She'd been laughing at something Compton was saying and her breath was still coming in snorty gulps, making it hard to understand her. "Dec, have I ever told you . . . that you look a lot like Rolfe from our med school?" and then she let him go and fell into a near-hysterical recounting of a few of our most memorable escapades from those days: the time she paged the head of the neurosurgery department and read him a dirty limerick, thinking he was our friend Rolfe; the time Emma won a contest she didn't realize she'd entered for the worst dancer at a gay bar she didn't realize was a gay bar; the time one of the attendings on our psych rotation challenged Hannah to undergo analysis and she agreed, only to discover after two weeks the "attending" was actually one of the psychiatric patients; these could have been any one of a hundred other such stories. Have you ever seen a grown person suddenly morph into a teenager when they're around their parents? It's a universal phenomenon: human beings slip into familiar behavior patterns when they come in contact with certain people, regressing to the personality and mannerisms and responses they associate with that relationship. That's how it is for us when we get together on these trips, except instead of transforming into surly hormone-ridden adolescents, we become twenty-six-year-olds again: animated, loquacious, aflame with verve. Everything revs up and everything's funny.

Well: not everything.

It's been more than a year since Georgia was admitted to a facility in San Diego, a squat, sprawling, red-roofed affair perched on the edge of a cliff overlooking the Pacific. Unlike most such places in the past, this one opened as a hybrid hospital/long-term care facility, a place dedicated to improving the neurologic functioning of AAROD patients. There's a patient care wing and a research wing, and it's federally funded with a lottery for patients so it's not weighted toward the affluent. It's got million-dollar views, according to Hannah, who visits regularly along with another local friend of Georgia's, an orthopedic surgeon named Camille who is married to Mark's boss. Georgia may or may not appreciate the vista from the big windows in her room, but she does seem to enjoy walking the sandy paths in back of the building, turning her face toward the sun, and holding up her arms to catch the wind. Hannah and Jonah and Mark take turns bringing Joanie Ruth, who toddles between the adults on the steep path down to the beach, where they sit and sift the sand between their fingers, venturing every now and again to the shore break to feel the surf splattering against their feet. Both Joanie Ruth and Georgia shriek with joy at the cool kiss of the ocean, Hannah says, their glimmering coppery heads cocked back at the same angle, their teeth all showing in an identical gorgeous grin.

I love this: Georgia still smiles at the beach.

Thinking of Georgia at the shore, I smile too, but mine is a wistful half smile, laced through with the same sharp zip of pain I get every time she crosses my mind. She's made great strides—literally—with her physical and occupational therapists, but the thought of her caged alone in her mind is unbearable.

I wish the girls could have brought her on this trip, especially on this ferry, but the logistics were a nightmare. I'm comforted—as we all are—by the thought of Jonah, who visits her every evening, and Mark, who visits every day if he's in California. The two men, along with Jonah's husband, Edwin, have become close friends as they've taken turns reading to her and selecting music playlists and participating in the intense cognitive therapy her doctors have prescribed to try to retrain her brain while we wait for a cure. Since she began a new experimental treatment regimen, there have been glimmers of hope: a few weeks ago, according to Jonah, she spoke.

Silence when he told us, then the same question from everyone simultaneously. "What did she say?"

"She said 'Jonah,'" said Jonah, and then he had the grace to blush. "Or more likely, she was trying to say 'Joanie Ruth.'"

I could have kissed him. Since then she's added a few more words, mostly names: *Mark. Hannah.* And me: she asked for me. I'm flying to see her the week after we return.

I distribute the drinks, passing one each to Zadie, Emma, Compton, Hannah, and Vani. None of us has the stomach for alcohol so early in the day, especially after the debauchery of the last several days, but we're all thirsty. We got up early and walked out without our bag of water bottles, but as I'm about to start chugging mine, Hannah waves her sparkling water and says, "Wait."

We look at her. Even after being so sick, she never quite lost her baby weight, and the extra pounds suit her; her shape is as smooth and healthy and lush as a perfectly drawn charcoal figure. She's gone nautical and retro in her dress theme: long white pants, a flowy blue-and-white striped shirt, big round sunglasses, a scarf in her fair hair. "A toast." She raises her bottle. "To our annual trip!"

"Our trip," we echo. I down my fizzy water so fast there's a decent chance it's going to spray out of my nose and douse everyone in a ten-foot radius. The thought makes me giggle, which makes everyone giggle, I suppose because I am not by nature a giggly person, and on this particular occasion I don't even have the excuse of alcohol. I'm punchy and hungover, but there's no denying how good this feels, having the six of us together again.

After our ship docks in Morocco, we disembark, clear customs, and pass through the glass-walled terminal building into the sunlit brightness of the streets of Tangier. At the curb stands a trim man in a blue baseball cap, his gaze fixed on the flood of passengers as they exit. He catches

Hannah's eye and straightens, heaving both arms above his head, waving them from side to side in giant enthusiastic arcs.

"Dr. Geier!"

Hannah raises a hand in return, which turns into a prolonged mutual bow—the world's new handshake equivalent—as she reaches him. "Hi. Hannah Geier," she says, beaming.

He beams back, removing his ball cap—emblazoned with the letters USA in red embroidery—and doffs it in our direction, revealing a head of closely trimmed black hair. "It is my very great honor to meet you, Dr. Geier, Dr. Marchand, Dr. Anson, Dr. Colley, Dr. Compton, and"—he bows to Vani, bringing up the rear—"Dr. Darshana."

I am impressed with this guy's memory, particularly since he would have had to study copies of our god-awful passport photos to know who is who. "Likewise," I say cautiously when it's my turn for a bow, unable to remember his name from the travel itinerary Hannah has emailed us.

"I am Hassan Kacemi. This," he says, gesturing to a man standing behind him, "is Nasire Radi. He will be our driver."

We begin with a drive through the city, which is divided into two sections: the old town and the modern town. These sections are chiseled into their respective large hills and divided by a valley, providing sublime views in every direction. It's September and hot, but the climate is more temperate than you'd expect, cooled by the strong breeze wafting in from the sea.

We pass through a neighborhood dotted with expensive homes, which Hassan says is called the "California" section, and then along a road winding through lushly landscaped mansions clustered on a hillside with views of the sea below; these, Hassan tells us, belong to various Moroccan and Middle Eastern dignitaries, who favor the city for their vacation homes. This includes the summer palace of the king of Morocco and the renowned seventy-four-acre summer estate of the king of Saudi Arabia. Nasire turns out to be a famous Moroccan author who owns a small literary café, and he and I talk about our projects: his latest book and my now-completed memoir, which is making the rounds of literary agents. Hassan pauses us for a brief photo op at the spot where the Atlantic Ocean and the Mediterranean Sea meet in the Strait of Gibraltar. This, as they say, is where Europe and Africa kiss.

We line up for the photo, and, as always on our trips, Hannah's brought a blown-up representation of our missing friend. She's cut out a giant photograph of Georgia's head and torso and affixed it to a stick; in it, Georgia is grinning, holding up her hands with both middle fingers extended, her red hair whipping in the wind. It's our last photograph taken of her before she contracted the virus, snapped on the bow of our previous ill-fated ferry ride to Morocco.

"Wonderful, wonderful," says Mr. Kacemi, motioning to us to scoot to the right. "Little bit more. Ah yes. This is perfection." He holds up Hannah's cell phone, squinting as he adjusts the image. "Who is the head?"

"Our friend Georgia," says Vani. "It's our tradition to include any of our friends who can't make it on our trips."

"Ah," says Mr. Kacemi, peering at the screen with a thoughtful expression. He snaps the photo and returns the phone to Hannah. "Perhaps she will come back with you the next time."

"Perhaps she will," I say, my hand curling around the cell phone in my pocket. I haven't said anything to my friends, and I probably won't until later—much later—but I cannot help thinking of the review board that just granted approval for a clinical trial involving a new technology aimed at the neurons affected by AAROD. Given the success of Kiravimab against the artiovirus itself, Declan's company has enjoyed spectacular funding for their latest project. Around the world, other research continues, the brightest minds of humanity engaged in the never-ending quest to end suffering.

It's early, far too early, to hope.

But this I believe: someday, Georgia will join us again.

AUTHOR'S NOTE

Dear Reader,

As you might imagine, I've been fielding some questions about the origin and content of *Doctors and Friends*. I'm happy to address the most burning issue on everyone's mind: namely, whether or not Wally's Molestache is listed in the official beard categories recognized by the CDC.

The CDC does in fact publish a facial hair infographic with delightful names like French Fork, Chin Curtain, and the Zappa. Sadly, the Molestache is not depicted, but I think we can all agree it should be.

Now that that's settled, let's turn to the issue of this novel's origins.

It is not based on COVID.

I've been mired in my own personal pandemic since 2018, when I had an idea inspired by my father. My dad wasn't a doctor, but he was a brilliant, MacGyver-ish guy (much like the protagonist of *The Martian*, if you ever read Andy Weir's fantastic sci-fi novel). He could invent anything, build anything, and understand anything . . . with the notable exception of fashion, which baffled him. There's a scene in *Doctors and Friends* where Kira intervenes just as a colossal water tank is about to burst at a party. This actually occurred at my wedding. My dad happened to have duct tape and a siphon on him (because who doesn't take duct tape and a siphon to a wedding?), and he saved the fancy club from flooding. Like my father, infectious disease docs are innovative and scientifically minded.

Since I write medical fiction, I decided I'd make my new protagonist a fashion-challenged, globe-trotting ID doc . . . in the midst of a brand-new worldwide viral pandemic.

To the irritation of everyone around me, I became obsessed with virology. These days it is not unusual to wander into a grocery and overhear a conversation about the latest mutation in a protein spike, but back then people could only listen to me babbling about nanobodies and nucleocapsids for so long before their polite smiles would fade and they'd begin desperately edging away. In my defense, real events inspired my obsession. The inspiration in this case, however—and I cannot stress this enough—did not include COVID-19. At the time I fired up the first draft of *Doctors and Friends,* we were all still running around with naked faces, blissfully ignorant of what would befall us in 2020.

Instead, media accounts of other epidemics prompted my interest, especially the 1918 influenza pandemic and the 2014 Ebola outbreak in Western Africa. At first, work on the novel advanced slowly as I was consumed by research.

Then, sometime in mid-2019, I read Richard Preston's *Crisis in the Red Zone,* a fascinating work of nonfiction detailing an aid camp in Liberia where two medical workers contracted a highly lethal strain of Ebola. At the same time, a dose of an experimental medication—one of only a few doses in the world—became available to the medical director of the camp. (If you're wondering how *that* happened, you're gonna have to read the book.) He faced a brutal decision: which of his two dying colleagues to treat—or whether to try the antibody drug at all, since at that point it had never been administered to a single human being. If he did nothing, both people almost certainly would die. If he administered the drug, he'd have to choose between them—and the drug itself might kill the recipient.

Upon reading this account, I immediately thought *My gosh, what if those two people had been his children?* Lest you worry I'm a psychopath, the mantra of all fiction writers is to create the worst plausible moral dilemma for our characters. Think about it: have you ever read a novel where nothing bad happens? This idea maximized Kira's ethical quandary, but writing the ICU scenes with her children turned out to be such a wrenching process, I almost quit.

Shortly thereafter, in a bizarre coincidence, I learned of a real-life scenario not unlike Kira's. I'd been corresponding with two physicians who practice in Chad and was astonished to learn they'd endured an agonizing saga after their children were exposed to rabies—two of them badly—and there wasn't enough vaccine and immunoglobulin in the entire country to treat more than one child. (I won't relay their outcome here, but the impact of these doctors is so remarkable, I hope they'll one day publish an account of their experiences.)

In addition to the physicians in Chad, I corresponded with more than four dozen infectious disease doctors, virologists, epidemiologists, ob-gyns, neurologists, and ER doctors, who helped guide me through their specialties. (Also, I'm happy to report that I was able to travel to Spain and Morocco with my own girlfriend gang from med school, where we met several pleasant and presumably disease-free camels.)

Even with all this forewarning, I certainly didn't anticipate COVID. For one thing, I never could have imagined how politicized the response to medical science would become in 2020. During edits, I made a conscious decision not to address our real-world pandemic response, even though anyone reading *Doctors and Friends* now is likely to apply the filter of their own experience to the fictional events in the book. Allow me to stress: the government in the novel portrays an idealized scenario I envisioned back in the good old pre-COVID days. The virus in the book is equally imaginary. It possesses different transmissibility and clinical characteristics and lethality than any existing virus. With some exceptions (such as the Zoom videoconferencing I added later), the political and societal and virological depictions in this book are not reflective of the

COVID pandemic. I made up that stuff, much of it long before I had a clue we were barreling toward an actual pandemic.

However, I did make some structural changes in response to COVID. My editor had a request: could I shift the story line so its focus included more of the other physicians in the book? Thus Compton and Hannah became point-of-view characters. Originally, so was Vani, but I loved her so much I decided to save her for a book of her own. Compton's was the easiest perspective because of my own background as an emergency medicine doctor; her scenes, initially told in conversation, became much more compelling when shown from her mindset. In light of everything nonfictional ER doctors experienced during our real pandemic, I'm glad I included these scenes—but again, they are imaginary.

Finally, what's not imaginary is that I contracted COVID myself in mid-2020. To be clear, millions of people around the globe suffered the loss of loved ones as well as medical and economic devastation during COVID. I was comparatively fortunate, but I did develop multiple long-term symptoms, the most impactful of which has been parosmia. (If you're not familiar with parosmia, it's disgusting. Look it up.) In a freaky coincidence, this occurred long after I'd written the AAROD scenes in the book. Not surprisingly, I've given a lot of thought to the irony of writing a novel focused on a bizarre side effect during a new pandemic, only to promptly develop a bizarre side effect during a new pandemic myself.

For my next novel, I think I will write about world peace.

BIBLIOGRAPHY

Appel, Jacob M., M.D. *Who Says You're Dead? Medical and Ethical Dilemmas for the Curious and Concerned.* New York, NY: Algonquin Books, 2019.

Barry, John M. *The Great Influenza: The Story of the Deadliest Pandemic in History.* New York, NY: Viking Press, 2004.

Foege, William H., M.D., M.P.H. *The Fears of the Rich, the Needs of the Poor: My Years at the CDC.* Baltimore, MD: Johns Hopkins University Press, 2018.

Kang, Lydia, M.D., and Nate Pedersen. *Quackery: A Brief History of the Worst Ways to Cure Everything.* New York, NY: Workman Publishing, 2017.

Kolata, Gina. *Flu: The Story of the Great Influenza Pandemic of 1918 and the Search for the Virus That Caused It.* New York, NY: Farrar, Straus and Giroux, 1999.

Levitt, Alexandra M., Ph.D. *Deadly Outbreaks: How Medical Detectives Save Lives Threatened by Killer Pandemics, Exotic Viruses, and Drug-Resistant Parasites.* New York, NY: Skyhorse Publishing, 2013.

McCormick, Joseph B., M.D., and Susan Fisher-Hoch, M.D. *Level 4: Virus Hunters of the CDC.* New York, NY: Barnes & Noble, Inc., 1996.

McKenna, Maryn. *Beating Back the Devil: On the Front Lines with the Disease Detectives of the Epidemic Intelligence Service.* New York, NY: Free Press, 2004.

Moalem, Sharon, Ph.D., with Jonathan Prince. *Survival of the Sickest: A Medical Maverick Discovers Why We Need Disease.* New York, NY: William Morrow, 2007.

Oldstone, Michael B. A. *Viruses, Plagues, and History: Past, Present, and Future*. New York, NY: Oxford University Press, 2010.

Osterholm, Michael T., Ph.D., M.P.H., and Mark Olshaker. *Deadliest Enemy: Our War Against Killer Germs*. New York, NY: Little, Brown & Company, 2017.

Pendergrast, Mark. *Inside the Outbreaks: The Elite Medical Detectives of the Epidemic Intelligence Service*. Boston, MA: Houghton Mifflin Harcourt, 2010.

Preston, Richard. *Crisis in the Red Zone: The Story of the Deadliest Ebola Outbreak in History, and of the Outbreaks to Come*. New York, NY: Random House Publishing Group, 2019.

Rasmussen, M.D., M.S., Sonja A. and Richard A. Goodman, M.D., J.D., M.P.H. (Eds.) *The CDC Field Epidemiology Manual*. New York, NY: Oxford University Press, 2004.

Wright, Jennifer. *Get Well Soon: History's Worst Plagues and the Heroes Who Fought Them*. New York, NY: Henry Holt and Company, 2017.

ACKNOWLEDGMENTS

I owe an enormous debt to the physicians and scientists who advised me during the writing of this novel. Needless to say, they have more important things to do than attempt to resuscitate imaginary people. I'm humbled by both their intelligence and their generosity in granting me access to their fields.

Please know that any implausibilities or biases are solely attributable to me and do not reflect the perspective of these experts. Some of them answered questions or allowed me to interview them; some read background scenes or passages specific to their circumstances; a few read the entire manuscript. Any errors stem from my failure to heed their advice.

One conflict I had to resolve: scientists wish to qualify their statements for maximum accuracy, whereas novelists wish to avoid the boredom-induced death of their readers. This means I had to abandon many passages reflective of the complicated realities of epidemiology or virology or biotechnology in favor of more simple but less precise language. Also, in certain scenes I deliberately took a bit of creative license, partly to improve the drama and partly due to my editor's gentle observation that perhaps the story didn't really flow when the characters insisted on hammering home the distinction between esoteric concepts such as, say, basic and effective reproductive numbers. Consider the following example of excised dialogue:

"Why not share the basic reproductive number?"

"Because the effective reproduction number is more useful," said Kira. "It's the product of the R_0 *and the susceptible host population (*x*). Therefore* $R=R_0x$ *estimates the potential for spread while taking into account the implementation of control measures, such as isolation and quarantining."*

Even in nonmedical writing, I tend to overuse big words, which many tormented readers of my previous novels have pointed out. Thanks, guys. Believe it or not, it could have been even worse. Every character in the book might sound like a meganerd (i.e., me) if it wasn't for my long-suffering editor. I do not know how she makes it through my intolerable word snarls. Thank you, Kerry!

Spoiler alert: on a related note, I'd like to address the miraculous recoveries of some of the characters. My editor talked me out of an original, grimmer ending, even though it was medically more plausible, and she was right. That's the beauty of fiction: sometimes it delivers unexpected grace and a joyous ending when we need it most.

Speaking of unexpected grace, I owe my deepest gratitude to the following groups and individuals:

My people! The emergency medicine doctors:

Heather M. Clark, M.D.; Kari Dechenne, M.D.; Danielle Dire, M.D.; Sarah Edwards, M.D.; Susan Geiger, M.D.; Gerri Goertzen, M.D.; Emily Hyatt, D.O.; Angela K. Johnson, M.D.; Sara Kirby, M.D.; Dorothy Konomos, D.O.; Tony Locrotondo, D.O.; Olen Netteburg, M.D.; Erin Noste, M.D.; Olga Otter, M.D.; Anuj A. Parikh, M.D.; Matthew S. Partrick, M.D.; Kimberly Pringle, M.D.; Audrey Stanton, D.O., M.P.H.; Cristi Vaughn, M.D.; Michelle Walther, M.D.; Svetlana Zakharchenko, D.O.; and all the others who aided me.

In what other field can one so perfectly combine a love of science with an immediate ability to ease suffering? To all the BAFERDs out there, I admire your brilliance and compassion and unceasing devotion to a career where someone's always trying to die on your watch. It takes a toll, working a job where skill is paramount, sleep is scarce, circumstances are unpredictable, and any moment can be life-altering—or life-ending—for everyone involved. But you carry on, usually without thanks. We all owe you.

All hail the infectious disease doctors, immunologists, biologists, and EIS-trained docs:

If the world didn't properly appreciate you before, we do now. Thank you for turning your formidable intelligence and ineffable spirit toward conquering our microscopic foes.

Gretchen Arnoczy, M.D.; Marylou Cullinan, M.D.; Catherine J. F. Derber, M.D.; Jennifer Espiritu, MD.; Jessie Glasser, M.D.; Freshta Jaghori, M.D.; Sheena Kandiah, M.D., M.P.H.; Sara Oliver, M.D., M.S.P.H.; Catherine Passaretti, M.D.; Kimberly Pringle, M.D.; Elizabeth P. Schlaudecker, M.D., M.P.H.; Rebekah Sensenig, D.O.; Kara M. Jacobs Slifka, M.D., M.P.H.; Julia Sung, M.D.; Cynthia Turcotte, Ph.D.; Philip Vernon, Ph.D.; and everyone else in the fields of virology, infectious disease, and epidemiology who was kind enough to help me.

The neurologists:

Sandra A. Block, M.D.; Mausumi Lidogoster, M.D.; Sheela S. Myers, M.D., M.S.; and Waimei Tai, M.D. Literal brainiacs! You guys impress me to no end.

The obstetrician-gynecologists:

Hina Cheema, M.D.; Natalie Crawford, M.D.; Jennie Hauschka, M.D.; Kelli Miller, M.D.; Danae Netteburg, M.D.; and Lora Shahine, M.D. You are lovely. Thank you for answering my questions and/or your support of my new career.

The radiologists:

Heather Frimmer, M.D., and Karen Rampton, M.D. So grateful for your sharp eyes.

And the pediatrician: Kristen Borchetta, D.O. Thank you!

To my groups:

I'm so grateful for the Charlotte Mecklenburg Library, the Charlotte Writers Club, the Charlotte Readers Podcast, Authors 18, and the WFWA. Special shout-out to the admins and members of the Physician Mom Book Club, especially Nicole Brammer Hubbard, for her support (and all the intriguing pathology posts), and to the admins and members of the most excellent Women Physician Writers group. Huge, heartfelt thank-you to the amazing sisterhood of the Charlotte Area PMG & Female Physicians. Also, to all the other PMG subgroups I'm in: y'all are so much fun and so informative and just so cool.

To my fellow physician fiction authors Dr. Sandra Block, Dr. Saumya Dave, Dr. Jennifer Driscoll, Dr. Heather Frimmer, Dr. Bradeigh Godfrey, Dr. Nadia Hashimi, Dr. Lydia Kang, Dr. Judy Melinek, Dr. Sheryl Recinos, Dr. Kristine Scruggs, Dr. Meghan Maclean Weir, and Dr. Ismée Williams (and so many more!): I am honored to be among your ranks. It requires truly singular brain chemistry to churn out imaginary drama in the midst of all the real-life mayhem.

Special thanks to Dr. Bradeigh Godfrey, for her treasured friendship, her support, and her always insightful developmental edits. And also her mad bookstagram skills.

To Drs. Danae and Olen Netteburg, you are an inspiration. I could not admire you more.

To the fiercely brilliant Dr. Kizzy Corbett, thank you for letting me borrow your last name for President Corbett. I'm in awe of all you have done for our country, for the advancement of science, and especially for women in STEM.

To my friend and fellow author Youssef Chebaa Hadri, thank you for such a gracious welcome to the dazzling city of Tangier. I look forward to a return visit and a long literary discussion.

To Abdennour Mezzine, fellow doctor and author, it has been such an honor to correspond with you. Thank you for your service on the front lines in Morocco and for your kindness to a fellow writer.

To my beta readers: Heather Burkhart, Bess Kercher, Lisa Kline, Lara Lillibridge, and Betsy Thorpe, my apologies for the wretched early drafts. Your suffering makes me a better writer.

To the Ink Tank: I love each and every one of you.

To my San Diego author friends: Liz Fenton, Michelle Gable, Kristina McMorris, Sue Meissner, Lisa Steinke, and Kate Quinn, I am so lucky y'all treat me as an honorary Californian. And I'm so fortunate to bask in the glow of all your massive success. #writergoals

To my writer buds Anne Bogel, Julie Clark, Molly Grantham, Jennifer Klepper, and Colleen Oakley: You are the people I turn to when I need a laugh, a boost, or an idea. Thank you.

To P. J. Vernon: One night I read all the texts we've ever sent each other about our books and I laughed so hard I hurt myself. You are witty and lovable and brilliant and an absolutely terrifying thriller writer. Now that I think about it, that's such a weird combo. Makes me love you even more. #BathHaus

To Hitha Palepu and Ashley Spivey: I adore our little triumvirate. Thank you so much for the literary support and the friendship.

To the Berkley team—Fareeda Bullert; Craig Burke; Lauren Burnstein; Kerry Donovan; the Marys, both Baker and Geren; Colleen Reinhart; Natalie Sellars; Lindsey Tulloch; Christine Legon; and Claire Zion—so many beautiful books exist because of you. I am honored that mine are among them. Thank you.

To Kathleen Carter, publicist extraordinaire: You are outstanding at what you do. Thank you.

To the world's best agent, Jane Dystel: I'm so fortunate you champion my work. You are a dear friend.

To Pamela Klinger-Horn: Thank you for your early support for *Doctors and Friends*. You make people want books, which is the coolest thing ever.

To all the bookstores, libraries, and bookstagrammers: The world would be a bleak place without your literary evangelism. I wish I could list you all!

To Writing Group, INK (aka Tracy Curtis, Bess Kercher, and Trish Rohr): I'm not sure what we did to bring down the wrath of the universe upon us last year, but I am certain we could not have made it through without each other. You are such a blessing and so talented.

To my med school babes: Jill Howell Berg, Whitney Arnette Jamie, Kelli Miller, Kristin Rager, Christina Terrell, and Casey Dutton-Triplett: If your patients ask, none of the individual characters in *Doctors and Friends* are us, but our decades of devoted friendship definitely provided the inspiration for this novel. I'll never stop being grateful that we found each other that first week of medical school.

To my beloveds: my sister, Shannan Rome; my best friend, Heather Burkhart; and my extraordinary mother, Judy Martin, I don't think I could bear life without you, let alone get these dang books written. There is no one on earth I look up to more than the three of you.

To Jim, Katie, Alex, and Annie: Never has a wife or mother been blessed with a more glorious family. You are all funny, feisty, and dear beyond words. I love you.

And finally, to COVID: Fuck you.

DOCTORS and FRIENDS

Kimmery Martin

DISCUSSION QUESTIONS

1. If you could take a vacation anywhere with your closest friends, where would you want to travel together?

2. The novel explores the concept of friendship as a fundamental human relationship, portraying a group of women who've been close for most of their adult lives. Have you experienced this kind of long-term friendship in your own life? In what ways did the characters lean on one another as they were fighting to survive this pandemic?

3. *Doctors and Friends* immerses the reader in some of the day-to-day responsibilities of physician specialists in emergency medicine, obstetrics-gynecology, and infectious disease. Which of the medical specialties was most fascinating to read about?

4. Kimmery Martin has stated that the scenes from Compton's perspective felt the most natural to write because of her own background as an ER doctor. Have you ever read a novel in which one of the main characters shared your career or field of study?

5. The main characters in the book are all female. Did you enjoy the portrayal of the supporting male characters? If you were able to select between Wally, Jonah, Declan, and Dr. Mike Zhou as a real-life friend, which one would you pick and why?

6. Each of Kimmery Martin's novels has been a spin-off of the previous one, focusing on different protagonists but set in the same fictional universe. Dr. Georgia Brown was a minor character in *The Queen of Hearts* and the protagonist of *The Antidote for Everything*, but she is also a pivotal character in *Doctors and Friends*. If you read *Antidote*, did prior knowledge of her character change your reaction to her fate in this book? If you haven't read the previous novels, are you curious about her backstory?

7. Hannah—an ob-gyn who is described as the most nurturing of the group of friends—struggles with infertility. Toward the end of the pandemic, she is finally pregnant but leaves the safety of her home to go into the hospital to take care of Georgia—a decision that costs her dearly. Meanwhile, Compton and her colleagues risk death on a daily basis in the emergency department. If you were a doctor in this scenario, would you put your own life at risk to care for others?

8. The characters face many difficult losses over the course of the book. Which hit you the hardest?

9. Did you have a favorite character? What about their story resonated most with you?

10. Kira's choice—the most difficult one a mother could face—defines the pandemic for her. What would you have done in her situation?

11. According to the author, in the original, "more medically plausible," draft of *Doctors and Friends*, Kira's choice resulted in a fatal outcome. What's your opinion of the outcome for Kira's children and career in the novel? Would different consequences have negatively or positively affected your experience of the book?

Author photograph by Stephen B. Dey, master photographer, CPP

Kimmery Martin is a former emergency medicine doctor, born and raised in the mountains of eastern Kentucky. A lifelong literary nerd, she teaches writing seminars and narrative medicine courses, speaking frequently at conferences, medical schools, and bookstores around the United States. She lives with her husband and three children in Charlotte, North Carolina, where she serves on the Board of Trustees of the Charlotte Mecklenburg Library.

CONNECT ONLINE

KimmeryMartin.com
Kimmery.Books
KimmeryM
KimmeryMartin

Ready to find
your next great read?

Let us help.

Visit prh.com/nextread

Penguin
Random
House